"My *quarrel was* [...] *rence* Temple-combe alone, and it shall [...] ver be permitted to harm you," Dominic said quietly. "Our ways must part here."

"Forget Dominic Fane," Verity murmured. "Is that indeed what you would have me do?"

He tried to say that it was, but his courage failed him at the last. Must he renounce, with all the rest, even a place in her memory?

"No, by God!" he said in a shaken voice. "Remember me!" And, catching her in his arms, crushed her lips beneath his own.

"So shall I be avenged indeed," he added, and let her go. . . .

Sword of Vengeance

SYLVIA THORPE

A FAWCETT CREST BOOK

Fawcett Publications, Inc., Greenwich, Connecticut

SWORD OF VENGEANCE

THIS BOOK CONTAINS THE COMPLETE TEXT OF
THE ORIGINAL HARDCOVER EDITION.

A Fawcett Crest Book reprinted by arrangement with Hutchinson Publishing Group

Copyright © 1957 by Sylvia Thorpe

ISBN 0-449-23136-4

Printed in the United States of America

10   9   8   7   6   5   4   3   2   1

Sword of Vengeance

I

Conspiracy in Alsatia

DARKNESS had come early that night, a sultry, moonless darkness, breathless and stifling, which lay like a pall over the reeking streets and brought little relief from the oppressive heat of the day. Torpor possessed the city, and laid its heavy hand even upon the old district of Whitefriars, whose inhabitants were people of the night rather than of the day. The place was notorious. Fleet Street bordered it upon the north; the river lapped its southern boundary, casting unhealthy mists over narrow streets and labyrinthine courts, and into crumbling mansions which once had housed the nobility but now teemed with beggars and criminals. Such was Alsatia, a city within the city, a stronghold of evil into which no constable or creditor dared venture.

In a garret chamber of one of the vast, mouldering old houses, Dominic Fane lay upon his wretched pallet, with his hands clasped beneath his head, and stared grimly at the sword which was propped against the wall close by. The feeble glimmer of the rushlight which was the room's only illumination gleamed on a hilt of wrought silver, and the worn scabbard encased a blade of the finest Toledo steel. It was his one remaining possession of any value, and now the time had come when he must choose between parting with it, or degrading it to the trade of robbery and murder by which so many of his present neighbours lived. The only other alternative was starvation, for to a fugitive debtor such as he, the ways of honest employment were closed, and Alsatia was the only refuge.

Even there, such a blade would fetch a good price, enough to provide him with food and shelter for a time at least, and yet he could not bring himself to sell it. His reasons for this went deeper than the mere reluctance of a soldier to leave himself unarmed, deeper even than fondness for a possession which had been his since boyhood, for to Dominic Fane that sword was a weapon dedicated, sworn to the fulfilment of a

7

vow made long ago, and the hatred which had obsessed him for fourteen years. To that end he had cherished it through all the vicissitudes of a roving life, keeping the slim blade keen and bright, and perfecting his mastery of it until now, when he fought, his weapon seemed like an extension of himself.

He shut his eyes for a moment, and a loathed name quivered in letters of fire behind his closed lids. Templecombe! Even now, it still had the power to sicken him with the memory of old betrayal, and with bitter contempt for a coward who shrank from paying the price of his sins. The score had stood high between them at the outset, and every ensuing year of failure and frustration had added to it. He thought of the shifts to which he had been put to live, of the soldiering he hated and the weary wanderings in foreign lands, and resolution hardened within him. He would not sell the sword. Now that he was in England again after ten years' absence, within reach of the enemy who must by this time have forgotten him, he would not be cheated of his vengeance. If robbery and murder were the only means by which to achieve it, then rob and murder he would, until at last he held Sir Lawrence Templecombe at the mercy of his sword.

As though to confirm that grim decision, heavy footsteps sounded on the creaking stair which led to his door, and the door itself was thrust open. Fane raised his head, but after a cursory inspection of his visitor, dropped it again upon his hands, vouchsafing no remark. Undeterred by this reception, the newcomer advanced into the room, shutting the door behind him.

Fane continued to regard him without enthusiasm. Nat Trumper, or Red Nat, as he was more commonly known to the denizens of Alsatia, lodged in the room below, and was a rogue of the first water. By trade a footpad, he was only too ready to turn his hand to any other sort of villainy if the price were high enough, and since he possessed great physical strength and a certain rough courage, was something of a local hero. Soon after Fane's arrival in the district, Red Nat had sought to enlist him in one of his ventures, but Dominic, learning that he would be required to cut throats as well as purses, had curtly refused. He neither liked nor trusted Nat Trumper, and his situation then was not as desperate as it was later to become.

Since that time they had exchanged barely a dozen words, so it was the more remarkable that Trumper should seek him out. Fane had no wish to ally himself with Red Nat, but he was curious to know the reason for this visit. He said nothing, but lay still, watching the man from beneath drooping lids.

The effect of that steady regard began to make itself felt. Red Nat had dragged forward a stool and seated himself close beside the pallet, but now he hunched his great shoulders and said, in a tone of forced geniality: "Ye're not over-friendly, and me bringing you the chance to mend your fortunes."

"Are you?" Fane's voice was cold. "I thought I had made it plain to you that I am no murderer?"

"Who said aught o' murder? 'Tis a small matter of abduction only." He chuckled, and digging finger and thumb into his pocket, produced a coin and spun it into the air. Fane saw the gleam of gold, and his eyes widened a fraction. "There's fifty o' them bright beauties for you, my lad, if you join with me."

"Fifty guineas?" Dominic repeated incredulously. "Who the devil would pay you such a sum as that?"

"Never mind who's paying me," Trumper retorted. "There's fifty for you, and the same for me and Giles. Well, Fane, what d'ye say?"

Dominic propped himself on one elbow and took the coin from Trumper's fingers. It was undoubtedly a golden guinea, and his mystification increased. He was still at a loss to understand his own inclusion in the project. Giles was Red Nat's confederate and boon-companion, and that he should share such good fortune was natural enough, but if a third were required, Nat could take his pick of the needy ruffians about him without approaching a man who had already shown himself to be possessed of inconvenient scruples.

"You are generous," he said at length, with that faintly sardonic intonation which so often sounded in his voice, "but why come to me? You will scarcely expect me to believe 'tis done out of kindness."

"'Tis done because you're the only man to serve my purpose," Nat replied frankly. "This venture takes us out of England, and Giles and me speak no tongue but our own. You've fought in foreign wars, and you'll know something of foreign speech."

Fane's frown deepened. "Whither do you go, then?"

"To France. There's a wench as someone wants to be rid of, but hasn't the stomach to have killed. We're to carry her as far as Paris and leave her there, in some quarter o' the town like to this. Without money, o' course, so as she can't win back to England."

"A noble plan, by my faith!" Dominic's lip curled. "It would be more merciful to slip a knife between her ribs and have done with it. Or do they hate her so much?"

Trumper shrugged.

"What matter, so that we are well paid? She's naught to us."

"Who is she?"

"Oh, a pox on your questions! All I know is that tomorrow night she'll pass through a certain street in a sedan chair, wi' servants in blue and grey livery. There'll be the chair-men and a link-boy, but three of us can deal wi' them easy enough."

"If she travels so she must be a person of some consequence. Have a care you do not stir up a hornets' nest."

"We shall be safe away before they start to sting. No one will look to see her taken out of England." Nat hitched his stool nearer and strove to mask anxiety with impatience. "Will you have done wi' talk, and answer aye or nay?"

Fane did not reply at once, and for a minute or two there was silence in the dingy room. The two men, one hunched on the inadequate stool, and the other stretched upon the pallet, staring down at the coin in his hand, formed a curious contrast. Red Nat's appearance fully justified his name, for that portion of his face visible between the tangle of flaming hair and fiery beard was of a florid complexion, and even his small, cunning eyes were bloodshot. His powerful frame was clad in clothes which, though worn and grimy beyond belief, had a certain ostentation which accorded well with their wearer's swagger and general air of consequence, and his bulk and startling colouring took the eye.

Dominic Fane was a man of very different aspect. His clothes had been chosen for service rather than for show, and, though as threadbare as his companion's, were kept in a manner which indicated some fastidiousness, while his face was smoothly shaven. He was tall, lacking only an inch or so of Trumper's height, and wide in the shoulder, but lean where the other was massive, giving an impression of sinewy strength. He was very dark, black of hair and brow, and with a skin as swarthy as a gipsy. His features were harsh and bold, and a long scar across his left cheek lent him a slighty sinister appearance, twisting his mouth into faint, perpetual mockery, while beneath thick, straight brows his eyes were the clear golden-brown of a topaz, startling in that dark face.

"Well?" Trumper prompted impatiently, and the strange eyes lifted at last to meet his.

"It is an odd affair by any reckoning," Dominic said slowly. "I would need to know more before I set my hand to it."

"Ye're damned cautious, considering the price," Nat grumbled. "I know little enough myself. I was in the Ram's Head in Fleet Street, and the host, an old crony o' mine, said as there was a gentleman wishful to hire a few bold fellows, and willing to pay 'em well. That was enough for me, so he took me into another room, and there was my fine gentleman wi' a silk mask over his face. We came to terms easy enough, and he gave me thirty guineas as an earnest. The rest we're to have when the bird's safe caged, and we take him the ring she wears on her left hand as a token. Fifty guineas apiece, and another fifty to pay what's needful on the journey. What's left o' that we'll share between us when all's done."

"What was he like, this mysterious stranger?"

Nat shrugged. "Young, as I judged it," he replied indifferently, "and tricked out very fine in lace and velvet, wi' a great golden periwig. What does it matter, if so be he's free wi' his gold?"

What, indeed? Dominic looked down at the coin gleaming on his palm, and thought of all that the possession of fifty like it would mean to him. The proposal was an ugly one, but in that shining circle of gold lay freedom to pursue his quest for vengeance, so why hesitate because the victim was a woman? Had he not just resolved to use any means, however vile, to achieve his deadly purpose?

So Dominic Fane stifled the promptings of conscience, accepted from Trumper nine more pieces of gold to complete his share of the thirty already paid, and went forth with his new associates to seal the bargain at a nearby tavern. At first his unexpected good fortune filled his thoughts, and he entered with zest into planning the details of the ambush, but by the following evening, when he stood with Nat and Giles in the gloom of a dark alley, waiting for the victim to walk into the trap, his qualms had revived with renewed vigour.

In vain he reminded himself that the woman was a stranger who meant nothing to him, that if the young sprig of fashion who had hired Red Nat was driven to such desperate lengths, she was probably some greedy strumpet who would soon find a new protector in France. His misgivings would

not be stifled a second time. Over the past ten years he had
played a part in many desperate deeds, and seen the sack of
more than one captured town, but some innate chivalry had
restrained him from ever doing violence to a woman. His distaste for the present task increased with each passing minute,
and he had come near to regretting his part in it when a
whisper from Trumper jerked his wandering attention back to
the immediate present.

No moon rode the sky that night, and the street was only
faintly illuminated by lanterns hung here and there from the
house fronts. The entry where the three men lurked was mid-
way between two of these, and the street before them
wrapped in the densest shadow. A thunder-shower had fallen
earlier in the evening, and there were few people abroad, so
that the tramp of several pairs of approaching feet came
clearly to their ears. Then a light bobbed into view, its glimmer shining faintly on the sedan chair swaying between its
plodding bearers: a moment later, and the gleam of one of the
lanterns revealed a livery of grey and blue. Steadily the group
advanced, unaware of the peril so close at hand.

As the link-boy drew level with the entry, Dominic moved
swiftly, his drawn sword in his hand, and the flat of the blade
swept the torch to the ground. As he crushed the flame to extinction beneath his heel, his free hand shot out to grasp the
front of the bearer's coat. The slim blade flashed up, and the
hilt drove violently and accurately against the link-boy's chin.
When Fane released him he dropped in an inanimate heap
amid the filth of the roadway.

Red Nat and Giles had wasted no time, but it was Dominic
who wrenched open the door of the chair. A choking gasp
came from it cowering occupant, and he said in a savage
whisper:

"One sound, madam, and it will be your last. Out with
you!"

Red Nat shouldered him aside, thrust one great paw into
the chair and dragged the woman out. As she stumbled on
the wet cobbles he clapped his other hand over her mouth,
and Giles cast a length of cord about her body, pinioning her
arms to her sides. Half fainting with terror, she was powerless
to resist as he thrust a gag into her mouth, and, dragging off
her tall cap of stiffened lace, pulled her hood forward about
her face. Dominic, standing tense and watchful over the
fallen servants, caught the sound of a distant footstep, and at
his warning whisper Trumper swept the captive up into his

arms and all three of them plunged down the narrow passage in which they had hidden.

For several minutes they doubled to and fro through a maze of courts and alleys, and then Nat paused beneath a swinging lantern and set his prisoner on her feet. The hood concealed the fact that she was gagged, and the cord binding her arms was hidden beneath the cloak which Giles had cast about her. Trumper nodded his satisfaction, and thrust her roughly into Dominic's arms. "Giles and me will go ahead," he informed him. "Follow us close."

Without waiting for a reply he turned away, and swaggered off along the street with a hand on his henchman's shoulder. Dominic looked after him for a moment with narrowed eyes, and then urged the woman forward in the same direction, keeping a few yards in the rear. She was trembling violently, and her feet stumbled so that the arm he had set about her was needful more as a support than to prevent a bid for freedom, and his dislike of the whole brutal business, forgotten for a while in action, swept over him again.

They came without incident into Alsatia, and to the house where they lodged. In Red Nat's room, Giles kindled a light and Dominic led their prisoner to a stool by the wall, while Red Nat himself took his stand in the centre of the room, feet wide-planted and his thumbs hooked in his belt. As Dominic turned away from the woman, he said impatiently:

"A' God's name, let's have yon hood off, and see what manner o' prize we've taken!"

Fane ignored the command, but Giles scurried forward to obey. For a moment or two he bent over the captive, and then both gag and hood fell away. Red Nat drew a sharp breath, and then let it out very slowly, whistling softly between his teeth.

Almost against his will, Dominic turned, and then stood very still, staring in astonishment and growing dismay, for here was no painted courtesan such as he had expected. Instead, burnished curls the colour of a ripe chestnut were tumbled about the face of a frightened child; grey eyes, wide and terrified, glanced desperately about her; exquisite lips trembled pitifully. For a moment, shock possessed his mind, and then, hard upon the heels of consternation, came suspicion. This was a mystery deeper than he had supposed. Why should this young girl, so obviously innocent and of gentle birth, be condemned to the fate which Red Nat had described yesterday, and by whom?

For a space, silence possessed the room. The prisoner's frightened, bewildered gaze went from Trumper's towering bulk to the wiry, sharp-featured Giles, who stood with mouth agape and the kerchief which had gagged her still dangling from his hand, and thence to the dark, scarred face of Dominic Fane. It lingered there for a moment, and then returned, as though fascinated, to the red-faced, red-bearded giant in the middle of the room. She moistened her lips, and with a palpable effort found her voice.

"Who are you?" she said faintly. "Why have you brought me here?"

Nat Trumper recovered slowly from his first, blank stupor of surprise. Like Fane, he had expected a captive of a very different sort, but discovery of his mistake aroused in him neither dismay nor curiosity. If luck and a masked stranger chose to drop so rare a prize into his arms, Red Nat was not the man to complain. He swaggered forward to stand over the girl, viewing with indulgence her instinctive shrinking from him.

"That's my business, my pretty," he replied with a grin, "but you'll not find me hard to please, so long as you speak me fair."

He set a coarse hand beneath her chin and held her face turned towards the light while he studied it appreciatively, and then his fingers dropped to the jewel in the hollow of her throat and thence to the rich silk of her gown. She shuddered beneath his touch and closed her eyes, a little moan of terror breaking from her lips.

"Keep your mind on the matter in hand, my friend," said a sardonic voice at Trumper's shoulder. "There was some talk of a ring, as I remember it."

Red Nat, who was accustomed to his confederates waiting respectfully upon his pleasure, turned to stare incredulously at the speaker, to find, in the gold-brown eyes looking so coolly into his, only contempt and a kind of derisive challenge. It disconcerted him, and before he could make a recovery, Dominic had thrust him aside and was loosening the cords which bound the girl's arms.

She had opened her eyes again at the sound of a fresh voice, and was now staring apprehensively up at him, but he was wrestling with a stubborn knot and did not look at her. When the cords fell away, he took her left hand in his and lifted it; the slight fingers lay resistless in his hold, and on the third gleamed a gold ring, curiously wrought into the semblance of a minute pair of hands which supported a splendid diamond.

"By the Powers!" Trumper's wrath was momentarily diverted by the sight of so costly a gem. " 'Twould pay us better to sell that, and to the devil wi' the fine gentleman."

"Would it?" Fane's voice was more sardonic than ever. "By tomorrow, that ring will be a swift passport to Tyburn. I have never seen another such."

He slid the jewel from the girl's finger as he spoke. There was no violence in the action, yet she flinched as though he had hurt her.

"Do not take it, I beg of you!" she whispered. "It is my troth-ring."

A swift look of surprise answered her, and then he was frowning again at the ring. After a moment, he moved away to the far side of the room, signing to his companions to follow him. They did so, albeit with some reluctance on Trumper's part.

"I begin to think that we are playing with fire," Dominic said in a low voice. "The man who seals his troth with such a jewel as this is likely to be powerful—too powerful for us, should our part in the affair become known."

Their dismayed silence acknowledged the truth of his words. Giles scratched his head, and presently offered a suggestion.

"Belike 'tis him as hired us."

Nat snorted contemptuously, and glanced over his shoulder at the fair captive, drooping now on the stool with her face hidden in her hands.

"Damn you for a fool, Giles!" he growled. "What man in his senses would want to be rid of a dainty piece like that?"

"True enough!" Fane agreed with a frown. "If the buck had hired us to bring her to him, it would be the easier to understand. As it is . . ." he shrugged, and held the ring out to Trumper. "Best take it to him without delay. It grows more dangerous every minute, and the sooner we change it for honest gold. the better for us."

Nat stretched out his hand for the ring, and then appeared suddenly to change his mind. A look of cunning flashed into his eyes, and he shook his head.

"You take it," he grunted. "He'll be at the Ram's Head by now. Belike you can learn more from him than I did."

Dominic looked at him, and then at the girl. His faintly twisted lips took on a deeper, more ironic curve.

"As you wish," he said, "but she must be locked in my room above, and the key goes with me."

At that Trumper's fury, which sight of the ring had turned aside, blazed up again more fiercely than ever. His face took on a deeper tinge and his eyes grew suddenly evil, but he restrained anger for a moment in favour of sarcasm.

"By the Powers!" he sneered. " 'Tis a cursed Puritan! I should ha' guessed it when he turned coward at the thought of a little blood-letting." Then, with a sudden, overmastering rush of fury: "Look'ee, ye damned, snivelling rat, I didn't pick you out o' the gutter to be my conscience. Nat Trumper's the man as gives the orders, and don't ye forget it. I'll not warn ye again."

"I gave you warning a few minutes since," Dominic retorted coldly, "and I will repeat it now. Keep your mind on the matter in hand. This is a lady of quality we have abducted, not a servant-girl, and as soon as her family learns of it they will turn London upside down in search of her. It will be no easy thing to win free of the city. That much should be apparent even to such poor wits as yours."

The charge of dull-wittedness, and the scornful tone in which it was uttered, lashed Red Nat's rage to white heat. After one moment of stupefied silence he plunged again into speech, in which threats against his confederate, and his own intentions towards the prisoner, jostled each other in a jumble of obscenity. The girl, roused by the loud voice, stared at him in white-faced horror; Giles's wizened, old-young face was puckered with anxiety; Fane listened indifferently to the torrent of words until Nat seized the front of his coat in one huge, freckled paw. Then his tawny eyes blazed with an anger so fierce and so sudden that it checked even the red giant's fury for an instant. He dashed the hand aside, and spoke in a cold, level voice which seemed the quieter by contrast with Trumper's bellowing.

"You'll curb your filthy lust, you animal, until we are safe out of the country, or, by heaven! you will find your way across France without my help."

Giles plucked anxiously at Nat's sleeve. "Maybe he's right, Nat," he said hurriedly. "It won't do to risk all for want o' patience." He was half turned from Fane as he spoke, and he winked meaningly at his leader. "Let him be! The wench can't run away."

Trumper stared at him for a moment. Then he jerked himself free and flung himself down on the pallet-bed in the corner of the room, his wrath apparently subsiding as quickly as it had arisen.

"Do as ye please," he said sullenly. "Damme! I'm dry. Give me summat to drink, lad."

Giles made haste to do his bidding, and Dominic, pocketing the ring, went across to the girl. In silence he took her arm and drew her to her feet, in silence he led her up the stairs to the room above. As he kindled a light, he said abruptly, without looking at her: "The door is stout, and the key goes with me. You will be safe enough."

She stood in the middle of the room, clutching her wrap of grey silk closely about her over her lavender-coloured gown. Her rich attire was oddly at variance with her surroundings, as though a butterfly had strayed by chance into that gloomy place.

"You spoke of—of France," she said in a faltering voice. "What do you intend by me? Tell me, in the name of pity!"

He shot a swift glance at her beneath frowning brows, and stifled an impulse of compassion, and of unwilling admiration for the composure she was trying so hard to assume. Self-contempt made his voice harsh as he replied.

"You will learn soon enough," he said, turning towards the door. "We shall not keep you here for long."

He went out, locking the door behind him, and descended the ramshackle stairs. Outside Red Nat's door he paused; the key was still in the lock, where Trumper had left it, and the murmur of voices came from within. After a moment's deliberation he turned the key. He placed as little reliance upon his confederate's sudden acquiescence as upon his self-restraint.

II

The Black Mask

THE Ram's Head in Fleet Street was a small, furtive-looking tavern huddled between two larger buildings. The doorway was beetle-browed, and the tap-room lay below the level of the street. Dominic, stepping down into it, and stooping to avoid the low lintel, saw at once that its patrons were of little better quality than the denizens of Alsatia. There were, in fact, several familiar faces visible through the haze of smoke which filled the room, and he nodded curtly in response to more than one guarded greeting.

He could see no one even remotely resembling the man he sought, but when he approached the host and told him that he came from Red Nat, understanding gleamed at once in the fellow's eyes. He signed to Fane to follow him, and, leading the way to the rear of the building, jerked his thumb in the direction of a closed door.

Dominic watched his guide return to the tap-room, and then thrust open the door and entered. A candle burned on the table in the middle of the room, and beside the table a man was standing. He was of medium height and slender build, with a broad-brimmed hat set atop a golden periwig, and between the masses of gleaming curls, the blankness of a black silk mask concealed his face from forehead to chin.

Fane's glance swept over him in one swift, comprehensive survey. Here, at least, his expectations were fulfilled, for the silk-lined cloak, the richly-laced coat of blue velvet, the dainty sword, and the lace-trimmed handkerchief in one elegantly gloved hand, all bespoke the Court gallant. For perhaps five seconds the glittering eyes behind the slits of the mask remained fixed upon him, and then the exquisite gentleman said impatiently: "Well?"

The single syllable, spoken in a low, husky voice, fell upon Fane's ears with a sharp sense of shock. He had expected the man to be young, but this was a mere stripling, a lad who could surely be no older than the victim of his plot. His voice, and the youthful slenderness of his figure, were not those of a grown man, and it seemed scarcely possible that he could be the author of the monstrous scheme against the captured girl.

With that thought echoing in his mind, Dominic stepped forward and laid the diamond ring on the table. With a gasp of satisfaction the other snatched it up, holding it between finger and thumb so that the candle-light struck coloured fire from the jewel.

"So you have her safe!" There was no mistaking the gratification in his voice. "You have done well!" Then the blank, black mask and glittering eyes were raised again to the silent figure before him, and this time he spoke with a hint of suspicion. "The other man—Trumper! Why did he not bring this himself?"

"He is keeping close watch over the prisoner," Dominic spoke with grim meaning, his eyes on that unbetraying silken face. "That was a duty he would delegate to no one—once he had seen her."

A soft laugh came from behind the mask, a laugh with no pity in it, but a good deal of malice.

"I understand you, I think! I wish him joy of her." He drew off his right glove as he spoke, and slid the ring on to his finger. Dominic noticed that his hands were small and very white, the tapering fingers smothered in a mass of lace. "It is nothing to me, so that he does not neglect my orders. She is to vanish, you understand? There must be no possibility of a return."

Dominic shrugged.

"There is but one place, sir, from which none return."

"No, no!" The Black Mask looked up quickly; there was alarm in his voice. "I will have no killing, no bloodshed! Her death shall not lie upon my conscience."

Fane stared at him for a moment without speaking, for there was no doubt that the words had been uttered in all seriousness, and the fantastic hypocrisy of this dainty, perfumed youth filled him with disgust. At last he said, with a contempt which he made no attempt to hide:

"Her damnation must surely lie there! Is that a burden easier to bear?"

"Insolent!" The boy took a pace forward, hand upraised, then, perhaps realizing the folly of giving way to anger in such a place, checked the movement. He leaned back against the table, resting his hands on its edge, studying Fane narrowly, as though really observing him for the first time. "How came you into this business?"

"Because of the price you offered," Dominic replied dryly, and added, "the balance of which, I must remind you, has yet to be paid."

"Be easy! I have it here." The ungloved hand, with the diamond flashing upon it, disappeared into a pocket, and emerged holding a bulky purse. For a space the Black Mask weighed it thoughtfully in his hand, still staring at Fane. "I asked not 'why,' but 'how.' What is your name?"

"Does that matter?"

"I am curious."

"My name is Dominic Fane."

"Dominic Fane!" the other repeated slowly. "That is no

common name. I thought you were of different stuff to that rogue Trumper. You keep strange company, Mr. Fane."

The scarred, swarthy face with its piercing, tawny eyes and faintly twisted lips told him nothing. Fane replied briefly:

"My history, sir, concerns you not at all, my choice of company only in so far as it affects your own plans. Red Nat came to me because I have soldiered it in many lands, including France, and he knows no language but his own. I accepted his offer for the sake of the gold."

"Then take your payment!" He tossed the purse into Dominic's hands. "So you have travelled in France? Do you know Paris?"

"Well enough."

"Excellent! Now listen to me, Mr. Fane. You will choose some poor quarter of the town, where English travellers do not go, some quarter like to London's Alsatia, and you will leave the woman there. Without money, you understand, or trinkets which she might sell." He drew on his glove, and the fire of the stolen diamond was quenched; his voice was musing now, as though they were debating some trivial matter. "Since she speaks no word of French, I believe that her disappearance will be complete. Do you not agree?"

Dominic thought for a moment of the girl whom he had helped to abduct, and then of the degraded women in the streets of Alsatia, and knew an instant's temptation to fling the purse into the youth's masked face. The weight of it reminded him of the folly of such an act; he had been paid to perform a certain task, and paid well; the reasons behind it were no concern of his.

"I agree that if you are determined against taking her life, your plan is as good as any other," he replied curtly. "Fate plays strange tricks at times, but that is your risk, not mine." He bestowed the purse carefully in his pocket, and looked once more at the slender, foppish figure. "Is there aught else you wish to say to me? The sooner we are away, the easier our task will be."

"Nothing," the other answered emphatically. "My part is played. It now remains for you to play out yours. I wish you good fortune on your journey."

The words were very clearly a dismissal. Dominic bowed ironically, and, turning, went out of the room. His brisk footsteps died away along the passage, and after waiting a few minutes, the Black Mask followed. Avoiding the tap-room, he slipped out of the tavern by way of a door which opened on to a malodorous alley at the rear of the building. A moment later he had vanished into the shadows out of which he had come.

Dominic returned to the house in Whitefriars to find his two confederates still drinking in Trumper's room. They greeted him with questions concerning the success of his errand, and since no mention was made of the locked door, he concluded that neither had attempted to leave during his absence.

"Yes, I have the gold," he assured them, putting down a bundle he was carrying and pulling the purse from his pocket. "I learned naught, however, save that our fine gentleman is a very youthful, dainty buck, whose tender conscience revolts at the thought of bloodshed."

"Then ye found ye'd a deal in common, devil a doubt!" sneered Trumper. "To hell wi' him, and you, too. Let's see the colour of his gold."

Dominic emptied the purse on the table, and the others gathered round, watching with greedy eyes as he counted the heap of gold pieces into four separate piles, three of forty and one of fifty. One of the three he pushed towards Red Nat, another to Giles, and swept the third into his own pocket. The fourth he returned to the purse, and was pocketing that also when Trumper's heavy hand closed on his arm. "Not so fast, my lad," he growled. "Not so fast! I'll take the purse."

Fane's level glance met his. "It was agreed, was it not, that I should have the ordering of our journey? Then I will hold the purse-strings also. I've no mind to let you drink or gamble those fifty guineas away before we are out of England."

Nat continued to eye him suspiciously. It was true that the details of the journey were to be left to the one experienced traveller among them, but he relished neither Fane's suggestion nor the manner in which it had been made. Then he caught Giles's anxious, warning glance and decided to let the matter drop.

"Aye, that's so," he agreed in a grumbling tone, and nodded towards the bundle Dominic had brought in with him. "What's yonder?"

"Clothes for the girl," Fane replied shortly. "Did you suppose that we could hale her out of London in those silks and laces without arousing suspicion?"

Obviously this point had occurred to neither of them, and

Dominic began to wonder how they would have fared had matters been left entirely in their hands. At present, for instance, Red **Nat** seemed more concerned with the discovery that his supply **of** liquor had run out than with the success of the enterprise, and declared his intention of repairing to the nearest tavern. Giles assented eagerly, but Dominic frowned and shook his head.

"We leave at daybreak," he reminded them. "Best take a few hours' sleep while you can, for there will be no time to linger on the road."

This excellent advice fell upon deaf ears, for they had gold in their pockets, and no intention of allowing it to remain there. With set face Dominic listened to them clattering noisily down the stairs, and then he took up the bundle of clothes and climbed the remaining flight to his own room.

The girl rose from the stool as the door opened, and stood to face him, the candle at her side showing her to be still very pale, but seemingly more composed. Seeing her thus, he realized that for all its childlike delicacy of feature, there was a great deal more character in her face than he had at first supposed. The fine grey eyes met his with only a glimmer of fear far down in them, and in the lines of mouth and chin there was both courage and determination. He felt again that uneasy stirring of remorse, and looked away, and tossed the bundle on to the pallet-bed.

"These are clothes more suitable for travelling," he said curtly. "Be pleased to put them on. We shall leave in a few hours, and we shall travel fast. Take what rest you can meanwhile."

He was turning to go when at last she spoke, her voice low and urgent, scarcely more than a whisper.

"Wait!" She came swiftly and softly to his side, and laid hold of his threadbare sleeve. "Those other men—are they still below?"

He looked down at her, his eyes narrowing.

"No, they have gone," he replied, "but if you think to escape therefore, I fear you will be disappointed."

"They were talking of you while you were away," she said, ignoring the latter part of his remark. "Did you know that every word spoken in the room below can clearly be heard here?"

He did know it, and had wondered more than once what freak of structure or decay in the huge old house brought it about. A suspicion of what she had overheard was already taking shape in his mind as she continued hurriedly:

"The one you call Nat was angry because you would not let him have his way with me, and bitter because, so he said, they could not do without your help. The other laughed, and said something about the shares being larger between two than between three, and why waste money on a journey to France when the river kept so many secrets? Nat did not understand him at first, but in the end they planned to kill you and take your share and cast your body into the river. It was the second man's idea to go out to a tavern, and come back later to take you unawares while you slept."

"And you?" he prompted as she paused. "What did they intend there?"

"I was to share your fate," she replied, and a small, uncontrollable tremor shook her, "but—not tonight."

Fane was silent for a space, considering what she had said. It did not surprise him. He had realized from the moment of his dispute with Trumper that he must be on the watch for treachery, though he had scarcely expected it to come so soon. He realized now that he had been over-confident. In Alsatia, Red Nat was upon his own ground, but once he ventured out of it, he would be at a disadvantage; then, too, the sooner Fane was disposed of, the greater the profit would be.

"Why do you tell me this?" he asked at length. "Why warn me of their scheming?"

"I think you know why," she said quietly. "To win your gratitude, and perhaps your help, I heard them say that your share of the price paid to carry me off was fifty guineas. Restore me to safety, and you shall have ten times that amount."

"Or a cell in Newgate," he added cynically.

Her chin lifted. "I do not break my word."

"Perhaps not, but your family might not consider themselves bound by such a promise."

"I have no family, and those who have charge of my inheritance will do as I wish." She paused, looking at his patched and ragged clothes and worn boots. Only the twisting together of her hands betrayed her anxiety. "If necessity drove you to this, I bear you no grudge, for you would not let that brute below harm me. Take me home now, before they return, and any help that it is in my power to give you shall be given freely."

He looked down at her, considering the proposal, turning

its possibilities over in his mind. The risk attached to restoring her to her home was slight enough, for gratitude at her safe return should stifle any desire for vengeance on the part of her friends. The reward she promised might well place his own vengeance within his grasp, and he knew that his conscience would be easier if he saved her from further harm.

"Very well," he said at last, "I will take you home," and the girl let her breath go in a sob of relief which betrayed the measure of her anxiety. "We had best go without loss of time. There is a cloak here which will be sufficient disguise for you."

He picked up the bundle and was unfastening it when another thought occurred to him. He completed the small task slowly, and turned to face her.

"There is one thing you have forgotten," he said. "What of the enemy who is so eager to be rid of you?"

Bewilderment showed plainly in her face.

"What do you mean?" she replied. "I have no enemies."

"No?" he said sardonically. "Was it a friend, then, who hired Red Nat and Giles and me to abduct you and carry you across to France, and abandon you in some low quarter of Paris?"

Her eyes widened as bewilderment gave way to horror.

"Merciful God!" she whispered. "Is that what you meant to do?"

"It is what we were hired to do," he corrected her harshly. "That is why I took your ring, that he might have proof that we had you safe, and so pay the balance of the promised price."

"But who was he? What was he like?"

"He was a very dainty, foppish youth, but so closely masked that I saw nothing of his face, nor do I know whence he came. One thing, however, is almost certain. The failure of this attempt against you does not mean that no more will be made."

She had dropped on to the stool again and covered her eyes with her hand, but at that she looked up.

"That in no way concerns you."

"This stranger has seen my face and knows my name," Dominic retorted briefly, "nor do I think he is a man who will take kindly to betrayal. If I am to make enemies, I prefer to know who they are."

"But I cannot tell you! I have never given anyone cause to hate me so."

There was a break in her voice, and a note of growing despair, and he hesitated for a moment before putting into words the suggestion made earlier by Giles.

"What of the man you are to marry? Are you certain he is to be trusted?"

A flash of anger overcame her fears for an instant.

"That is to insult me. I trust him utterly!" Then, defiantly, she added, "Besides, he has not been in London this month past, and you spoke just now of this stranger's youth."

"Aye, he was, as I judged it, a lad not out of his teens."

"Then the absurdity of your suspicion is proved. Sir Lawrence Templecombe is nearly twenty years older than I."

Templecombe! The quietly spoken name rang in Dominic's ears like some hellish fanfare, and for a second the room seemed to reel about him. He raised his head to look at the girl, and she had the odd impression that those strange, golden eyes did not really see her, but looked through her and beyond to some dark prospect of which she was unaware. He said hoarsely:

"You are betrothed to Sir Lawrence Templecombe?"

"Yes!" She was puzzled, and a little frightened. "What is that to you?"

He continued to stare at her, seeing her no longer as a delicate and defenceless woman, but as his enemy's chosen bride. Gone in an instant was every instinct of remorse or compassion, swept away by the overwhelming force of his hatred, and by a savage exultation that his vengeance was within reach at last. Templecombe's bride! In the bitter triumph of that moment he could have laughed aloud.

Then, with a swift return of caution, he realized that he must do nothing to arouse her suspicions. She must be persuaded to trust him, to believe him her friend, if, through her, Sir Lawrence was to be drawn to his doom.

"I have heard the name," he replied, as indifferently as he could. "A West Country family, is it not?"

"Yes, of Shere, in Somerset. Sir Lawrence is there now." A sob quivered in her voice. "So far away—and I have no one else to help or advise me."

"Then you must place yourself under his protection without delay." Fane's words came glibly now, without conscious effort. "It is plain that whoever it was who instigated the attack upon you chose to do so at a time when he knew you to be unprotected. It follows, therefore, that only with Sir Lawrence can you be certain of safety."

"Yes, you are right," she said after a moment. "So now, if you will take me home——"

"I will take you to Sir Lawrence Templecombe," he interrupted.

"To Somerset?" She was startled, and a little suspicious. "That is not necessary. I have servants whom I can trust, and I will set forward in the morning——"

Again he interrupted her.

"Be not so sure of that. This masked stranger knew enough of your affairs to tell us in what manner you would travel tonight, the number of your attendants, even the hour at which you would pass along the street where we captured you. If he knows so much, he will know also of your intention to journey to Somerset, and an ambush on a lonely road would be no more difficult to arrange than an attack in a London street, but if you will permit me to escort you to your betrothed, your enemy will suppose you to be safely on your way to Paris. Believe me, it is the better way."

She hesitated, her eyes searching his face as though seeking confirmation of his honesty. Dare she trust him, this gaunt, dark wolf of a man who had the manner of her own class, and yet consorted with thieves and cut-throats? It was a frightening decision to have forced upon her in such a way, and after such an ordeal as she had undergone, this choice between braving the menace of an unkown enemy, or placing herself wholly in the power of this sinister stranger. Yet, was it a choice at all? Was she not already completely at his mercy?

Fane guessed the nature of the fears which gripped her, and sought about in his mind for some way of winning her confidence. Only one course suggested itself to him. He took from his pocket the purse containing the fifty guineas, and dropped it in her lap.

"Keep that, if you doubt me," he said curtly. "There is enough gold there for you to hire horses and servants once we are clear of London, and so make yourself independent of my escort. It is the money your enemy gave me for the journey to Paris. Use it instead to place yourself beyond his reach."

She made no reply, but took up the purse and sat staring down at its crimson silk and intricate embroidery. After what seemed a very long time she raised her head, and he thought that her face was even more pale and haggard than before.

"Yes, it is the better way," she said in a low voice. "There is no safety for me here in London. I will accept your escort, and that most gratefully. As for this," she held the purse out to him as she spoke; her voice was weary. "Come, sir, take it! That you offered it is surety enough."

He took it and restored it to his pocket, turning away so that he need not meet her eyes. Over his shoulder he said:

"Put on the clothes I brought. I will keep watch on the stairs lest Trumper and Giles return."

He went out without waiting for an answer, and took his stand at the turn of the stairs, reflecting on the strange chance which had placed that long-delayed vengeance within his grasp, and turning a deaf ear to the inward voice which already whispered that perhaps vengeance could be too dearly bought. In a very few minutes she crept out to join him, transformed now from butterfly to moth by the drab stuff gown and hooded cloak. He delayed only long enough to lock the door above, and, as he returned to where she stood waiting, he realized that in spite of all that had passed, he still did not know who she was.

"My name is Dominic Fane, madam," he informed her briefly. "May I know yours?"

"It is Halland," she replied, readily enough. "Verity Halland."

"Verity!" he repeated, with a trace of mockery in his voice. "That means 'truth,' does it not? A somewhat exacting title, no doubt."

He did not wait for a reply, but led her down the dark stairs and out of the house. It had been his original plan to go by water as far as Rotherhithe, and, landing on the southern bank, strike south-eastwards towards Dover. The river still seemed to him a safer way than the dark and dangerous streets, but now they must go upstream instead of down, if Somerset was their goal. Therefore he led his companion in the direction of Whitefriars Stairs, where a few seedy watermen were to be found at any hour, and, arriving there without incident, bribed one of the men to set out at once.

It was close upon dawn, and the sky was already lightening in the east, when at last Red Nat and his henchman returned to the house, for the tavern had furnished entertainment from which they found it hard to break away. Trumper's room was empty, and when their suspicions thoroughly aroused, they at length succeeded in forcing the door of the chamber above, no trace of the prisoner remained but her discarded finery in a shimmering heap upon the floor. There was nothing for them to do but curse their erstwhile comrade and revile each other, and while they were indulging in this profitless pastime, Dominic Fane and Verity Halland were riding through the glory of a summer sunrise towards whatever the future held of tragedy or of triumph.

III

Journey Towards Vengeance

IT was almost noon when Dominic realized that his companion could go no further. They had rested for a while at the inn where he had hired the horses, but they had taken the road at daybreak, and spared neither themselves nor their mounts. London was but an evil memory, and they rode now through a fair countryside dotted with farms and sleepy villages under a cloudless sky. While the freshness of early morning lasted it had been pleasant enough, but as the sun climbed higher the increasing heat grew irksome, and the horses' hoofs stirred up clouds of dust from the rutted surface of the road. To Fane, long inured to hardship, this was a small matter, but it was plain that whatever emotion had sustained the girl until now, whether fear of pursuit or eagerness to reach her betrothed, was failing her at last. She drooped in the saddle with her face hidden in her hood, her hands grasping the pommel before her, and the reins lying slack on her horse's neck.

To the left of the road, beyond a stretch of meadowland, a stream rippled along the edge of a small wood. Dominic cast a searching glance at his companion, leaned forward to grasp her horse's bridle, and turned both animals towards it. Miss Halland seemed unaware that they had left the road, and only when they splashed through the water into the welcome shade of the trees, and he brought their mounts to a halt, did she raise her head and look dazedly about her. He swung out of the saddle and went to her side.

"We will rest here awhile," he said briefly. "You are near spent."

She dismounted obediently, too exhausted to question his decision and thankful only that for a space the need for effort was past. The last hour had passed in a mist of unreality, with the sun-drenched road and green fields, and the horizon veiled in a haze of heat, whirling before her dazzled eyes; her head throbbed intolerably, and every bone in her body ached. Giddiness seized her as soon as her feet touched the ground, and she reeled against Fane's supporting arm. He assisted her to a grassy bank at the foot of an oak tree and spread his cloak upon the ground, and she dropped down upon it as though all the strength had gone out of her.

Dominic stood for a moment, looking down with some misgiving at her white, exhausted face. Then he went to fetch a flask of wine from the store of food and drink with which he had provided himself before setting out, and with some difficulty persuaded her to swallow a little. When she had done so, he folded the cloak she had discarded and placed it beneath her head and so left her, realizing that sleep was the only remedy for her weakness.

He tended the horses, then, leaving them to graze, went to kneel by the stream and splash the cool water over his face. The ample provender he had brought appeased his hunger, and, when his meal was done, he lingered by the stream, his thoughts drifting back over the events of the past two days, and forward to the time when the old score against Templecombe would be paid in full.

Beyond that he would not look, for what could lie beyond? His bargain with the girl he did not intend to keep, and so there would be no reward forthcoming from her grateful friends; more likely, he thought cynically, that the road he was treading now would lead him in the end to an ignominious death, but he would at least pay his debts before he died. It would be sufficient compensation to know that he had sent Lawrence Templecombe before him across the solitary threshold, that the years of patient, pitiless pursuit had not been vain.

The sunlight glowed on the meadow beyond the stream and thrust long, golden fingers into the stream itself; a dragonfly flashed across the surface of the water, rested for a moment like some monstrous jewel upon the grass, and was gone with a glimmer of iridescent green and blue; the deep boom of a bumblebee rose for a few seconds out of the drowsy hush of the summer afternoon, and the two horses stood close together where the shade was deepest, motionless save for the lazy flicking of their tails. It seemed that the nightmare

stench and squalor of Alsatia could not be part of the same
world as this peaceful place, but the man lounging by the
stream was deaf and blind to the pleasant scene about him.
His dark face was grim, and the golden eyes had that
curiously blank expression which had startled the girl the
previous night. They were eyes which saw nothing of their
surroundings, but looked instead upon some dark memory
compounded of hate and anger and bitter disillusion.

He roused himself at last, and made his way back to the
oak tree. The girl was still asleep, and he stood for a minute
or two looking down at her and speculating idly upon the circumstances of her betrothal. It was, he supposed, the usual
marriage by arrangement—the wedding of two fortunes, two
estates, rather than two individuals. Templecombe must be
forty now, while she was scarcely out of her teens, and
though she was fair enough, he would undoubtedly demand
more than mere beauty in the woman he chose to honour
with his hand. Fane remembered her proud defence of her
betrothed: 'I trust him utterly,' and laughed softly in bitterness and contempt. So had he trusted him once, and found
himself betrayed.

As though the sound of his laughter roused her, she stirred
and opened her eyes. For a second or two their glances held,
and then she sat up, brushing the tangled hair from her brow
and looking about her in bewilderment and some alarm.
She said breathlessly:

"What is it? What is wrong?"

"There's naught amiss," he replied brusquely. " 'Tis time
we were on our way, that is all."

"Oh!" Her voice was unsteady; a faint frown wrinkled her
brow. "I thought—but no, I was dreaming! An evil dream!"
She shivered, and pressed her fingers against her closed eyes.

"You are but half awake," he reassured her, "and sorely
in need of food. Come, break your fast, and then we must ride
on."

While he set the provisions before her she sat silent, leaning wearily against the massive tree-trunk behind her. The
memory of her dream still weighed upon her, and ugly suspicions were stirring in her mind, suspicions which had been
born the previous night, when he dropped the heavy purse
into her hands and she had looked upon it and found it
familiar.

From the implications of that discovery she had recoiled in

horror, and with the recklessness of despair cast herself upon the mercy of Dominic Fane. He had convinced her then that he offered the only chance of escape, but now Somerset seemed very far away, and fear possessed her once again. The chill courtesy of his manner should have reassured her, but she could not forget the panic which had swept over her when she awoke and, looking up into the bold, dark face and tawny eyes, realized how completely she was at the mercy of this forbidding stranger.

He had seated himself a short way off and was examining one of the pistols from the holsters on his saddle, but now he raised his head and directed a piercing glance towards her.

"You do not eat," he said curtly.

Verity started, and hurriedly took up some of the food, saying timidly as she did so: "What of yourself?"

"I ate while you were sleeping."

He turned his attention once more to the pistol. After a little, observing the care he bestowed upon the weapon, she ventured to ask: "Do you think we need fear pursuit?"

"Nat Trumper is not the only footpad in England," he replied, without looking up. "It is as well to be prepared."

"Oh!" she said uncertainly. "I had not thought of that."

Even to her own ears her voice sounded hollow. Dominic looked up, and for the first time a gleam of humour showed in his eyes.

"That does not mean you need fear a robber behind every bush," he added, "and should we encounter any such, it is likely they will pass us by in favor of more prosperous-looking travellers."

She regarded him doubtfully, but then the truth of his words dawned upon her. In the bright light of day his shabbiness was even more apparent than it had been by candlelight; from his broad hat with its bedraggled feather to the rusty spurs at his heels there was nothing to suggest a full pocket, and if there was a certain distinction in his appearance, it was in spite of his attire rather than because of it.

From her companion's appearance she passed, for the first time that day, to consideration of her own. The clothes he had given her matched his own for poverty, and all that remained of her former elegance were her little embroidered shoes. She stared at them, peeping incongruously from beneath the hem of her rough gown, and as Fane's glance turned in the same direction, a frown creased his brow.

"Those must be replaced as soon as we reach a town," he said. "To continue to wear them is to invite suspicion."

She did not reply to this, but instead, emboldened by the slight relenting of his expression, asked anxiously how long it would take them to reach their destination.

"A few days only," he replied, and now the mordant note was back in his voice. "Are you so impatient to reach your betrothed?"

Her heart was pounding unpleasantly and her mouth felt dry, but she forced herself to meet his eyes boldly.

"Yes, I am impatient," she retorted. "Do you think I can forget what has been plotted against me, or that it is a thought easy to face alone? Do not suppose me ungrateful, Mr. Fane! I know how great is my debt to you, and if we come safely to Shere it shall be—not repaid, for that it can never be, but at least acknowledged, in whichever way may best please you. But until we do come there, I must bear my burden alone, since only Sir Lawrence may share it with me."

Dominic sat silent, looking down at the pistol in his hand. The words, and the gentle dignity with which they were uttered, seemed to reproach the treachery he intended. Angrily he reminded himself that this was Templecombe's bride, that through her alone could he achieve his vengeance. Dishonour should be repaid with dishonour, betrayal with betrayal, and it would not be the first time that the innocent had been made to suffer with the guilty. Yet at the same time a curiosity he could not stifle prompted him to ask:

"Have you no one else with whom to share your troubles? No parents, no kinsfolk?"

"No," she said simply. "My mother died when I was six years old, my father before I was born. I had a half-brother, many years older than myself, but he, too, is dead. I was brought up by my grandfather, my mother's father. She was his only child and he loved her dearly. When she died, he took me to live in his own home, in Herefordshire, and I stayed with him until his death a year ago."

"And the inheritance of which you spoke last night," he prompted as she paused. "Did that come from him?"

She nodded. "Yes, he had no other heir. After his death I went to London, to stay with my brother's widow until my period of mourning was over and I could be married."

"Your grandfather knew of your betrothal, then?"

"Yes, it was his wish. Sir Lawrence's father had been his friend, and Sir Lawrence himself often visited us. I well remember the first time I saw him. It was that same summer when I first went to my grandfather's house—fourteen years ago—and his visit lasted for a long time. After that he came every year, and when I was twelve we were betrothed."

Fourteen years ago! The words rang mockingly in Dominic's ears to strengthen his dark purpose once again as he thought of that summer, that black and bitter summer when every hope and ambition of his youth had been laid in ruins. So that was where Templecombe had hidden himself, in the house of an old man who knew so little of him that he would promise him a loved grandchild for his bride.

"We were to have been married four years ago," Verity was saying, "but Grandfather was ailing then and I would not leave him. We knew that he had not long to live, and Sir Lawrence agreed that we should wait."

With an effort Dominic transferred his thoughts from the past to the present, for it had occurred to him that in this simple story lay a clue to last night's attempt against Miss Halland, and the identity of her enemy. He said slowly:

"Was your grandfather a rich man?"

"His estate was considerable, and carefully husbanded," she replied. "Yes, Mr. Fane, you might call him a rich man."

"And all his wealth is now yours?"

She nodded, watching him doubtfully.

"Who would inherit it, should you die unwed?"

"My nephew, James, the son of the half-brother of whom I told you. Why do you ask?"

"Because covetousness, madam, soon breeds hatred. I think you need not look far for your mysterious, youthful enemy."

There was a moment's silence, and then she shook her head.

"More youthful than you suppose, sir, if 'tis my nephew you suspect. Jamie is but five years old."

She got up as she spoke, and went lightly down to the water's edge, and knelt to rinse her hands. When she came back to him, shaking the drops of water from her fingers, it seemed that she had put the matter out of her mind, for she only said:

"Shall we ride on now? It must be growing late."

He did not attempt to pursue the subject, but with a curt word of assent went to saddle the horses. By the time this was done she had gathered up the remains of the food and resumed her cloak, pushing her tangled russet curls out of sight beneath the hood.

That night they spent at a modest inn in a little market town, where at Fane's suggestion they described themselves as brother and sister. Miss Halland retired early, and if her rest was broken by uneasy dreams, or during the slow hours of darkness her fears and suspicions returned to plague her, no one knew of it but herself.

They set off betimes next morning, and rode, as yesterday, through the warm, scented countryside of high summer. Verity was insensibly soothed by the peacefulness of her surroundings, and disposed to make light of her earlier alarm, and now curiosity concerning her companion awoke within her. She studied him covertly as they rode, and wondered what misfortune had brought him to such a pass that he was obliged to join forces with such ruffians as Red Nat and Giles, for that he was of the same order as those two rogues she could not believe. Finding no answer to the riddle in that dark, impassive face, she at length summoned up enough courage to question him.

She half expected a curt rebuff, but to her surprise it did not come. He told her briefly that he had returned to his native land after ten years spent fighting in foreign wars, for now, in this year of 1698, an uneasy peace had settled over Europe and there was little hope of employment for the hired soldier. In England, where at the demand of Parliament the army had been drastically reduced, he had fared no better, and eventually, having fallen into debt, was obliged to seek refuge in Alsatia.

Encouraged by her initial success, she asked other questions, and so persuaded him to tell her something of his travels. He was willing enough to talk of the places he had seen, and, though he touched but lightly on his own adventures, showed her more of himself than he either realized or intended, for through all that he said there ran a thread of loneliness and deep nostalgia. She had perception and sympathy enough to realize that here was a man who had known little of happiness or contentment, and she sensed, too, his distaste for the trade he followed. After a time she said curiously: "Why did you choose to be a soldier? 'Tis plain you have no fondness for it."

She regretted the question as soon as it was asked, for it wrought an abrupt change in his manner. A mask seemed to descend upon his face, as though some barrier which had been lowered for a space was raised again between them.

"When a man who is trained to nothing save the use of

arms finds himself obliged to earn his bread, there is but one profession open to him," he replied curtly. "I had to fight or starve. I chose to fight."

He urged the horses to a quicker pace as he spoke, and it was plain that he meant to say no more. From this taciturnity no remark could lure him, and so presently she desisted, and for a time they rode on in silence. She had already observed that he paused occasionally to look back along the road, and had supposed this to be a mere habit of caution natural to a trained soldier, but after a while she realized that these back-ward glances were becoming more and more frequent. Fi-nally he drew rein near the crest of a rise, and sat gazing back the way they had come with one hand shading his eyes.

"Is aught amiss, sir?" she asked anxiously after a moment.

"I am not sure. Look yonder!" He pointed, and she saw, far back along the road, two riders moving steadily in the midst of a small cloud of dust. "They have been in sight for an hour or more, gaining on us slowly, but none the less surely."

She shot him a startled glance. "They are pursuing us?"

He shrugged. "I cannot tell, and I think we will not linger to inquire yet awhile. The road is lonely hereabouts."

The horses moved forward again, and the other riders were lost to view as they passed over the crest of the hill and be-gan to descend its further side. Though out of sight, however, they were not out of mind, and it was perhaps because Ver-ity's thoughts were occupied with the disquieting possibilities conjured up by their advent that she did not give due atten-tion to the road. Whatever the reason, they had not gone an-other half-mile when her horse stumbled in a rut and came down, flinging her from the saddle.

She had scrambled up, shaken but unhurt, before Dominic could reach her, but though she was merely bruised, her mount had been less fortunate. The most cursory inspection showed it to be badly lamed. Verity looked from it to her companion, and tears of dismay and self-reproach gathered in her eyes.

"It was my fault, all my fault," she said in a low voice. "I was not attending. Oh, how could I be so careless?"

"Tears will not mend matters," said Dominic grimly. "The harm is done. I will take you up with me, and we must make what speed we can." He stooped to run a gentle hand down the horse's injured leg. "We must lead this poor brute. It can-not be abandoned here."

Verity made no reply. She stood with head bent, brushing the dust from her clothes with shaking hands and doing her utmost not to cry. Dominic repented a little of his harshness.

"Come," he said, more kindly, "it could be worse. We can hire fresh horses at the next village."

She looked up. "But those men behind us?"

"We must hope that they are honest travellers, as indeed they may well be," he replied, and lifted her on to his own horse. Mounting behind her, he added as they moved forward again: "You faced the substance bravely enough; do not let shadows alarm you now."

She managed to summon up a smile in answer to this, but it soon became apparent that her fears had a more solid foundation than a mere shadow. At their present slackened pace it was not long before the other riders came into view once more. As soon as they caught sight of those ahead they spurred forward at a gallop, and it scarcely needed a glimpse of the flame-red hair and beard of the larger of the twain to assure Fane that these were the hunters, and he and his companion the quarry.

He cursed softly, and, abandoning the lame horse, urged his own mount to its greatest speed. He had chosen both horses carefully, and now his care was rewarded by the gallant response of the fine animal beneath him. The distance between them and their pursuers began to lengthen, but Dominic knew that, doubly burdened as it was, his mount could not for long maintain the lead. No house or village was in sight; the road wound its way up a long hillside, bordered here by open pasture-land, but plunging a short way ahead into the depths of a beech-wood.

The horse was labouring now, but he forced it on without mercy until they were deep amid the trees, and out of sight of their pursuers. Then he reined in and slipped to the ground and turned to look up into Verity's white face and startled, questioning eyes.

"You must go on alone," he said curtly, and thrust the reins into her hands. "I will delay them here as long as I can. Do not draw rein until you reach the next village—it is not far ahead. Go to the inn and wait for me there." He dragged the purse of crimson silk from his pocket and pushed that, too, into her unwilling grasp. "Wait for an hour. If I have not come by then, hire an escort and make all speed to Shere."

"I cannot! I will not!" she exclaimed breathlessly. "What can you do, alone and on foot, against two mounted men?"

He dragged the pistols from their holsters, thrusting one into his pocket. "Do as I bid you," he said savagely, and struck the horse a stinging blow across the flank which sent it plunging forward.

Miss Halland, awkward in the unaccustomed saddle, and further hampered by the heavy purse in her hand, found that she had much ado to control her startled mount. Relieved of the man's weight, it bounded on with renewed energy, and she was quite unable to turn back, or even to draw rein. Next moment she had rounded a bend and was alone in the whispering woods.

Dominic took up his position behind the sturdy bole of a tree whence he could command a view of the road. He could hear the pursuit drawing nearer somewhere below, and before long the first rider came in sight. It was Giles, mounted on a strong grey gelding and grinning with exultation at the capture so soon to be made. Quite deliberately, Dominic took aim and fired, and Giles flung up his arms and pitched from the saddle. The grey reared in sudden panic, and then wheeled and bolted back the way it had come, dragging its hapless rider by one foot entangled in the stirrup.

Red Nat was close upon his henchman's heels, closer than Dominic expected. He fired his second pistol, and missed, and Nat flung himself out of the saddle, keeping the plunging, terrified horse between himself and the spot whence the shot had come.

Dominic cursed again, more vehemently than before. It was his sword now against whatever weapons Trumper was carrying, for somehow the fellow must be dealt with before he realized how he had been tricked. If he guessed that, and rode on after the girl who was now alone and unprotected— Dominic's heart chilled at the thought, and he drew the Toledo blade from its sheath.

He began to go cautiously down the hill towards Red Nat, taking advantage of every scrap of cover. Had it been anything but a beech-wood he might have succeeded in taking the red giant unawares, but the lack of undergrowth was against him. A pistol cracked, and he stumbled and fell flat as a sharp agony seared his side, though his fingers retained their grip on the hilt of the sword. He lay motionless, fearing a second shot, and then he heard Trumper's heavy breathing and heavier tread approaching him. So there was still a

chance! He tensed himself for one supreme effort, and as
Trumper reached him came swiftly to his feet, the sword
bright and menacing in his grasp.

Red Nat swore in anger and surprise, and started back,
taking that first deadly thrust on his own, clumsier blade,
which he bore naked in his hand. Dizziness seized Fane and
the bright world spun about him, and he parried the return
thrust by so narrow a margin that Nat's point ripped painfully across his arm.

So began for Dominic Fane the most nightmare fight of his
adventurous career, there in the sunlit beech-wood under the
summer sky. Red Nat's swordplay was clumsy in the extreme,
though his tremendous reach must at all times have made
him a formidable opponent, but the pistol wound was already
taking its toll. Dominic could feel the blood running down his
side and his strength ebbing with it; his sword hilt was wet
and slippery in his grasp from the gash in his arm, and his
usually strong and supple wrist responded but slowly to the
dictates of his mind. The grey boles of the trees, the sunlight
on the leaves, Trumper's red, sweating face and evil eyes
swam before him in a dazzle of colour that confused and
blinded him. There was a roaring sound in his ears which
drowned even the clash of steel upon steel, and each instinctive parry was slower than the last. Once he felt his point bite
flesh, and heard Trumper's gasp of pain and rage, but his attack continued with unabated fury, and Dominic realized that
the hit had been a trifling one. The sun must have gone
down, for there was no longer any brightness, but only a
dimness through which Red Nat's heated face and heavy blade
loomed monstrously. He thought he heard a shout, and then
his knees gave way beneath him, and he knew no more.

IV

Curiosity of a Young Gentleman

VERITY heard the pistol shots shattering the silence behind her, and the fluttering and twittering of frightened birds, and a sound between a gasp and a sob broke from her lips. She had control of her mount now, but in spite of an almost overmastering urge to turn back, she held on her way and did not even slacken speed. Whatever slight chance Dominic Fane had of winning out of the trap could only be imperilled by disobedience.

She had reached the summit of the hill and was racing over more level ground between the thinning trees. Next moment she was out again into the bright glare of the sunshine, and before her the road stretched in gentle curves across an undulating common, and a quarter of a mile away along its white ribbon two coaches with attendant outriders had come to a halt. As Verity burst from the shade of the trees, three figures detached themselves from the group and came galloping back towards her. She spurred to meet them, hasty words tumbling from her lips as soon as they came within earshot.

"Sirs, I crave your help for one who is sore beset! Two robbers attacked us, and he is alone and on foot. Oh, hasten, I pray you! Hasten!"

One of the three gave a sharp command, and his companions swept past with scarcely a check towards the beechwood. He who had spoken drew rein for a moment. He was very splendid, very handsome and very young. "Ride on, madam," he said hastily. "My sister is yonder, with her woman. You have naught to fear."

He was gone again in a swirling cloud of dust. Verity paused, looked over her shoulder, started slowly towards the distant coaches, halted again, and then wheeled her mount and rode back the way she had come.

It was very quiet in the beech-wood. The birds had settled again, the breeze whispered among the leaves, the road lay

deserted, dappled with sunlight and shadow. The sound of
swiftly retreating hoofbeats served to deepen the silence
rather than to break it. She checked her mount to a walk and
went slowly down the hill, and so came in sight of two horses
by the roadside, and a little group away to her left among the
trees. The young man who had spoken to her stood with his
back towards her, and at his feet another man knelt beside a
figure motionless upon the tawny carpet of rotting leaves, and
a shaft of sunlight fell directly upon them and showed the
scene in merciless detail. With a curious feeling of unreality,
Verity slid out of the saddle and walked towards them.

The gentleman turned as she came up, but she looked past
him to where Dominic Fane lay so quiet and still, with the
cruel sunlight playing across the grey pallor of his face. The
grizzled serving-man was staunching the wound in his side,
and the man's hands were red and the leaf-carpet patched
with a darker stain. She said in a whisper between white lips:

"Is he—is he dead?"

"No," the young gentleman replied hastily, "I think we
came in time. His assailant made off as soon as he heard my
men approaching." He took her arm and drew her gently
away, so that she could no longer watch the servant at his
task. "Rest easy, madam. Old Thomas has seen much soldiering, and knows well how to deal with wounds."

Verity leaned against the trunk of a tree and closed her
eyes, and the young man studied her curiously. Her hood had
fallen back, and the delicate face with its crown of red-brown
curls contrasted strangely with her poor attire. He said, rather
diffidently:

"Is he your husband?"

"Oh, no!" Her eyes flew open again as she uttered the swift
denial, and then she remembered her supposed relationship to
Fane. "He is my brother." She saw a flicker of surprise in her
companion's eyes, and added hurriedly: "We are on our way
to visit relatives in Somerset."

He inclined his head courteously, but she had the uncomfortable feeling that he did not believe her. Young as he
was—and he could not, she thought, be more than a year or
two older than herself—he had the air of a man well versed
in the ways of the world. That he was a person of consequence was obvious, not merely from the costly splendour of
his attire and the number of his servants, but also from his
manner, which had all the ease of one placed by birth and
position above the need of standing upon his dignity. She saw

his glance rest thoughtfully upon her hands, as though re-marking their soft whiteness, and had to fight against an im-pulse to hide them beneath her cloak.

To avoid that too perceptive gaze she turned away, and went to kneel beside Fane, taking his head in her lap and wiping his forehead with the corner of her cloak. The young man followed slowly, and stood looking reflectively from the gaunt, ashen face with its scarred cheek and faintly twisted lips to the fair countenance bent above it; the perplexity deepened in his eyes, but he merely said: "Well, Thomas?"

The serving-man looked up. "He'll do, my lord, he'll do," he replied cheerfully, and transferred his glance to Miss Hal-land. "Don't you fret, my dear! I've seen many a worse wound than this, and so has he, by the looks of him. 'Tis the bleeding was draining his life away, and now I've staunched that he'll do well enough."

Verity looked dubiously from him to his patient. To her inexperienced eyes, Fane seemed at the point of death, so still did he lie, with no sign of returning consciousness, and she was seized by sharp remorse. She had brought him to this. Had not her carelessness resulted in the laming of her horse they might have fled together until they came up with the young lord and his companions and so found safety, for Red Nat and Giles would never have dared to attack so numerous a company.

She became aware that his lordship was addressing her, and looked up blankly. He repeated his question, asking civ-illy how the misfortune had occurred, and she hesitated for a moment before she replied, wondering how much she might safely reveal. He noticed the hesitation, and it did nothing to allay a curiosity which was becoming greater with each suc-ceeding minute.

"Two men pursued us," Verity said at length, "and because my horse had gone lame we could not outdistance them. My—my brother made me take his horse and go on ahead while he tried to deal with them." Her voice quivered on a sob. "If only we had known, sir, that your party was so short a distance before us."

"Indeed, madam," he responded gallantly, "I regret most profoundly that ignorance of your plight prevented us from coming sooner to your aid, but it may not yet be too late to lay these villains by the heels. Did you see either of them clearly enough to describe him?"

Miss Halland seized eagerly upon this chance of ridding

herself and Fane of the menace of Nat Trumper. If he could be captured and imprisoned their danger would be past.

"One of them was a very big man with red hair and a beard," she replied promptly, "but the other I did not see clearly, though I think he was a smaller man."

" 'Twas the red-headed rogue we saw, my lord," Thomas put in. "He was alone, from what we could see of it."

Before his master could reply they heard the sound of horses coming slowly up the hill, and presently a rider came into view. He was leading a horse which, going very lame, bore a lady's saddle, and across the withers of his own mount the body of a man was slung. When he caught sight of the group among the trees he dismounted and, tethering the horses, came towards them on foot. Like Thomas, he was clad in livery of green and gold.

"I fear I lost the fellow, my lord," he reported shame-facedly, "but I came upon the body of another man at the foot of the hill. He'd been shot, and his horse must have bolted and dragged him with it." He glanced doubtfully at Miss Halland, and added: "He's not a very pretty sight, my lord."

My lord dismissed the corpse with an airy wave of his hand.

"The second robber, no doubt. I have no wish to see him. William, be good enough to transfer the lady's saddle to the black horse yonder, and then you and Thomas will remain here with this wounded man until I can send you the means to convey him to shelter."

Verity spoke without looking up.

"I thank you, my lord, but I will remain with my brother."

"Madam, it is not necessary. You may safely leave him in Thomas's charge while I escort you to my sister. He will be excellently well cared for."

"I do not doubt it, sir. Nevertheless, I will remain."

He regarded her with astonishment not unmixed with indignation, and she guessed that he was not accustomed to having his wishes set aside. Her gratitude towards him was profound and she had no wish to offend him, but a sense of obligation, sharpened by remorse, prompted her to stay with Fane. Her calm grey eyes met my lord's affronted blue ones, and even in the midst of indignation it occurred to him that this quiet dignity was strangely at odds with her appearance.

"As you will, madam!" he said shortly. "Assistance shall be

sent to you as speedily as may be. I will leave you now. My sister will be growing anxious."

He went towards his waiting horse, and Miss Halland watched with some disquiet as he mounted and rode away. The servant, Thomas, a middle-aged man with twinkling eyes in a seamed and leathery face, had listened tolerantly to the exchange, and now said reassuringly: "Don't you take no heed of his high-and-mighty ways, lass. He's a good-hearted lad, but he never could abide having his will crossed."

"Who is he?" Verity asked anxiously.

"The Marquis of Urmiston," he replied. "He and his sister, Lady Sarah, are on their way to Wiltshire for the wedding of one of their cousins." He paused, watching her shrewdly, and then added: "You've no cause to mistrust his lordship, my dear. He'll help you willingly enough, and want nothing in return."

Verity bent once more over Dominic, feeling the hot colour stain her cheeks. It was clear that the servants had accepted her for what she appeared to be, and she could not explain that her fear of the Marquis sprang from a very different source than Thomas supposed. That his suspicions had been aroused was very plain, and she could only hope that the rebuff she had dealt him would make him reluctant to risk another.

Presently, to her relief, Fane began to show signs of returning consciousness. His eyes opened and he looked up at her in bewilderment for a moment or two until memory returned to him. Then he tried to struggle up, but Thomas, on the other side of him, laid a restraining hand on his shoulder.

"Lie still, lad! The danger's past," he told him cheerfully, "but there's a wound in your side that'll break out bleeding again if you don't have a care. Bide still, and we'll carry you to shelter as soon as may be."

Dominic looked at the speaker, and then back at the girl, perplexity in his eyes. Verity made haste to explain.

"All is well," she said quietly. "By the mercy of God there were other travellers a short way ahead of us who came to your aid, and drove off the robber who was attacking you." She put as much meaning as she could into the latter words, and was relieved to see comprehension in his eyes. "The other man you killed, and the Marquis of Urmiston, whose servants these are, has hopes that the one who escaped may yet be taken."

The explanation seemed to satisfy him, for he nodded, and

relaxed again upon the coat which Thomas had folded beneath his head. Verity remained seated by his side, but in the presence of the servant there was little more that could be said, and they waited in silence for the coming of the promised conveyance. At last it appeared, a heavy coach lumbering awkwardly down the hill behind its four powerful horses, and she realized that his lordship must have divided his own party into two in order to waste no time.

With some difficulty the clumsy vehicle was turned about, and then Thomas and William came to help the wounded man down to the road. Supported on either side, he stumbled down the slope, and Verity was about to follow when she caught sight of the silver-hilted sword lying, forgotten, where it had fallen from his hand. She picked it up, shuddering a little at sight of the red stain dimming its brightness at the point, and bore it carefully after him, placing it, when she entered the coach, upon the opposite seat.

The two servants mounted and the little cavalcade began to climb the hill again, Thomas and William leading the spare horses. Within the coach, Dominic asked in a low voice:

"What tale did you tell them?"

She explained briefly, and he nodded.

"It was well done," he commended her, "and I trust they believe it. The servants do, I know, but what of their master? A Marquis, you said. Did he speak with you?"

"The Marquis of Urmiston," she replied. "Yes, he came himself, with the two servants, to your aid. He inquired how the misfortune befell, and asked me to tell him anything I could of the men who attacked us. I described Trumper, hoping that he might be captured."

"It would ease my mind if he were, but he is a wily rogue and well used to evading pursuit." Dominic shifted his position, and cursed softly with mingled pain and exasperation. "Damnation! I am as weak as a rat. Whither do they take us?"

"The man Thomas told me to the inn at the next village." She paused, watching him distressfully. "I cannot forgive myself for bringing this upon you."

He brushed this aside with some impatience.

"I shall do well enough. 'Tis not the first blood-letting I have suffered, nor yet the worst. Now heed what I say. When we come to the inn, stay close withindoors if you value your safety. It is easy to talk of capturing Red Nat, but if he can evade his pursuers, we may look to see more of him. Since he has followed us so far, he is not likely to abandon at the first setback."

She remembered the stain she had seen on his sword.

"But you wounded him, did you not?"

"A scratch, no more. Enough to enrage him, not enough to check his lust for vengeance." He leaned back wearily, but continued to watch her from under frowning brows. "You have not answered my question. Did this Marquis believe your story?"

She would not trouble him now with her misgivings, founded as they were upon so slight a cause. Lord Urmiston might be curious, he might even be suspicious of the strangers he had rescued, but as long as she adhered to the tale she had told, he could do nothing to verify his suspicions.

"Why should he not?" she countered calmly. "We are nothing to him, nor is it likely that he will trouble himself over us once we reach the inn. He believed what I told him."

Fane nodded, and closed his eyes, accepting her assurance more readily than he would have done had he been in full possession of his strength. To the girl he had made light of his wounds, but he was in considerable pain, and tormented by the prospect of further delay in the accomplishment of his vengeance. Had he not been patient long enough?

For a space they journeyed on in silence, the coach bumping over ruts inches deep and baked hard as stone by the summer sun. Every movement pained him, but he forced himself to make no sign until an exceptionally violent jolt wrenched an involuntary groan from his lips. Verity had been watching him anxiously, and at that she moved closer and set an arm about his shoulders, trying to steady him against the lurching of the coach.

He was too exhausted to make any protest, and for a time leaned heavily against her, while she wondered anxiously how much farther they had to go, and whether he was more seriously hurt than they had supposed. Suddenly he roused again, and tried to drag himself upright. "My sword!" he said hoarsely. "I dropped it in that accursed wood . . ."

"The sword is safe," she assured him quietly. "I brought it from the beech-wood, and will keep it safely until you can bear it again. Now be still, I implore you! You do yourself no good by this exertion."

He relaxed again, but looked at her intently.

"And when we come to the inn you will stay close, as I

bade you?" he insisted. "Give me your word that you will do as I say."

"I promise it," she replied tranquilly. "I will not venture out of doors alone."

He nodded, satisfied by the assurance. His head was whirling, and he closed his eyes again while disjointed thoughts born of pain and weakness drifted through his mind. She had brought the sword from the beech-wood. Few women would have thought of that, or retained sufficient presence of mind to keep the truth from their rescuers. She had wit and courage, this girl who blamed herself so bitterly for his present plight, against whose slight breast his weary head now rested. Templecombe's bride, who all unwittingly had saved the sword dedicated to taking Templecombe's life; a trusting child who cherished the man who meant, for his own selfish purposes, to betray her. He moved restlessly in her arms, beset by conflicting forces of hatred and remorse.

At last, after a journey which to Verity had seemed unending, the coach rumbled into a village street and halted at the door of an inn. By this time Fane was barely conscious, for Thomas's rough surgery had not withstood the jolting of the coach, and he was again losing blood from the wound in his side. Verity was frightened now as she followed the servants who, between them, supported Dominic into the inn, and was aware more of relief than dismay when they encountered the young Marquis in the narrow passage which traversed the house from front to back.

He seemed to have forgotten his ill-humour, and at once took command of the situation, directing the harassed landlord who hovered at his elbow to see the injured man comfortably bestowed, and himself coming forward to greet Miss Halland, taking from her the sword which she was clutching in both hands. She relinquished it without protest, but looked anxiously after her supposed brother.

"Pray do not distress yourself, madam," his lordship said earnestly. "I have sent one of my people to fetch a surgeon, and meanwhile I beg you to put your trust in Thomas. He is greatly skilled in such matters as this. Come, let me take you to my sister."

He led her towards a fashionably-dressed young lady who was standing in a nearby doorway. Lady Sarah, a fair-haired, blue-eyed beauty of seventeen, had been watching with lively interest the slow progress of Dominic Fane and his supporters towards the stairs, but she greeted Miss Halland with great

kindness, and if curiosity fairly sparkled in her eyes it did not
detract from the sincerity of her welcome. ·

"My brother has told me of your misfortune," she said
sympathetically. "Come into the parlour and rest. Our people
will look after your brother—I do not think I have been told
his name."

"It is Dominic Fane." Verity was too perturbed to think of
evasion. She allowed herself to be pressed into a chair in the
parlour, and a glass of wine was put into her hand. She did
not really want it, but forced herself to sip it while she tried
to collect her thoughts. After a little she looked up at her
benefactors.

"Forgive me," she said quietly. "As yet I have said no
word of thanks for all your kindness. You put us under an
obligation which we can never repay."

"I would, madam, that we might do more," Urmiston responded gallantly, and Sarah added:

"It would be a poor thing indeed, Miss Fane, if we could
not do all in our power to help a fellow traveller in distress.
My regret is that our men did not succeed in making prisoner
the villain who attacked your brother."

Verity murmured some civil reply, but kept her eyes downcast. It was confusing to be addressed by the name of Fane,
though it was undoubtedly prudent to keep her identity
secret; it would have been more prudent still, she thought
ruefully, to have concealed her companion's identity also, and
given him a false name, but it was too late now for anything
but regret on that score.

There was a pause, during which she sat sipping her wine
while anxious questions jostled each other in her mind. What
if Dominic Fane were to die? What if Trumper returned to
the attack? Why did this noble brother and sister treat her
with such friendliness? On the face of it, she and Fane were
humble folk who in the ordinary course of events would have
been left to the care of the servants. That they were not
seemed to suggest that the Marquis had guessed that she was
not what she pretended to be. The real truth he could not
possibly suspect, but that his suspicions had been aroused was
painfully clear.

This was indeed so. Her disguise did not deceive his lordship; it merely prompted him to wonder who she was and
why she had assumed it, and though he had earlier yielded to
a flash of ill-humour when she refused to leave her companion and go with him, he had not ridden far from her before

he regretted his hastiness. Both the hastiness and the regret were characteristic; the besetting sin of Robert Deverell, Marquis of Urmiston, was impetuosity.

He had confided his suspicions to his sister, but though they had discussed the matter and arrived at several possible solutions to the mystery, none of these satisfied him. He was convinced that the fair stranger's companion was not her brother; she had denied that he was her husband, and it seemed unlikely that he was her lover. Only one possibility remained, and that, had he but known it, came nearest to the truth. Sarah had suggested that some pressing danger had obliged the young lady to flee in disguise, and that the man was no more than a hired escort. The attack in the beech-wood supported this theory, and, if it were correct, Miss Fane, as she chose to call herself, was still in peril, since one of the attackers had escaped and her only protector was wounded.

Having arrived at this conclusion, his lordship decided that it was incumbent upon him to offer assistance. This decision was not entirely free from self-interest, for while his curiosity was piqued by the mystery surrounding her, his admiration had been aroused by her fair face, and he could not help reflecting that it would be pleasant to have so enchanting a creature regarding him as her saviour. "Tell me, Miss Fane," he said suddenly, "had you ever seen that red-headed fellow before?"

"No! Oh, no!" The denial came quickly, too quickly, he thought, observing her sudden pallor and the way in which her fingers tightened on the stem of her glass. "Not—not until he and his companion tried to rob us."

"To rob you?" My lord's brows lifted in polite surprise. "You mean they sought to hold you up?"

"Why, yes!" she faltered. "We evaded them and they pursued us, as I told you."

"They were, in fact, lying in wait for you?"

"For any chance traveller, I suppose." She remembered suddenly that Urmiston's party had been only a short way ahead, and stumbled into further explanations. "No doubt your lordship's company was too numerous for them to attempt, and so they fell the more violently upon us."

He inclined his head without speaking, and directed a quelling glance towards his sister, who seemed about to make some remark. She caught his eye and relapsed into puzzled silence. Verity recklessly swallowed the rest of her wine and then

sat staring down at the empty glass. She was making
wretched work of this deception, but what else could she
have said? To admit that Trumper and Giles had pursued
them from London would mean disclosing the whole truth, or
plunging into a maze of lies so complicated that she would be
bound to lose her way. So for a space she remained lost in
unhappy speculation, until Urmiston's next remark came to
startle her out of it.

He had walked across and poured himself a glass of wine,
and now turned to face her, leaning against the table behind
him. For a moment or two he studied her in silence, his
handsome face very serious, and then he said abruptly:

"Can you not bring yourself to trust us?"

"To trust you?" Her startled glance flew up to meet his.
"My lord, I do not know what you mean."

"No?" he retorted quietly, and lifted the glass to his lips,
watching her over its rim as he sipped the wine. "My dear
lady, I am not, I think, either blind or a fool, and a mere
ragged gown is not sufficient disguise for a lady of quality.
Moreover, those were no ordinary robbers who attacked you.
I had ridden ahead of my sister, with only one attendant, all
the way through those beech-woods, and for some distance
before that. Had robbery alone been their motive, they could
have waylaid me and been safely away long before the
coaches came up. I believe they had been in pursuit of you
for some time, or, if they were indeed lying in wait, it was
for you, and none other."

He paused, regarding her questioningly, while on the other
side of the room Lady Sarah leaned forward in her chair,
waiting with breathless eagerness to learn what would follow.
Verity looked from one to the other, distractedly twisting the
empty glass round and round between her hands.

"It would seem, therefore," the Marquis continued after a
moment, "that you are in danger of some kind, danger from
which Fane is no longer able to protect you. Oh, he is a gallant fighter, I grant you, but what if that red-headed
rogue evades capture and makes another attempt against you while
he lies wounded? Where will you look for protection then? I
say again, can you not bring yourself to trust us? You may
rely upon our discretion, and that of our servants."

"To doubt that, my lord, would ill become me, since we
stand so deeply in your debt." Verity spoke slowly, choosing
her words with care. "You are generous beyond what I
deserve."

"That I do not believe," he said earnestly, "but I confess that to leave you unprotected would sorely irk my conscience. It is unfortunate that we are expected, and so cannot delay here longer, but, if you wish it, a coach and an escort shall be placed at your disposal tomorrow morning."

"Tomorrow?" she repeated, and a tiny frown creased her brow. "So you suggest, sir, that I should desert my brother?"

He shook his head, smiling a little.

"I should not, if I believed him to be your brother. Oh, provision will, of course, be made for him, that he may be cared for here until his wounds are healed, but there can be no necessity for you to delay. Set forth tomorrow, and complete your journey to—Somerset, is it not?—in safety and comfort."

Verity got up, setting aside the glass, and walked across to the window, while they waited in silence for her reply. She was sorely tempted. Safety and comfort were things she had taken for granted all her life until these last two nightmare days. It would be so easy to accept, to drive away in his lordship's coach, protected by his servants. Fane was well supplied with money; the people of the inn would look after him, and once safe in Sir Lawrence's care she could send him the promised reward.

It would be so easy! The road which had seemed beset by so many difficulties and dangers had suddenly been made smooth for her; all she had to do was confide in these new-found friends and accept the help so generously offered. Then a thought flashed into her mind to check the first rush of overwhelming relief. It would be necessary to disclose Fane's part in her abduction, and Urmiston might not agree to let that go unpunished. Then on the heels of that first doubt, others came crowding. She was tempted by safety and comfort, but had Dominic Fane considered either when he stayed behind in the beech-wood to cover her retreat? She could not abandon him again. The innkeeper might be dishonest and rob him, or Trumper discover him and seek to finish his murderous work. With a sigh she turned again to face the room.

"I thank you, my lord, and her ladyship also, for your very great kindness," she said in a low voice, "but I cannot accept your offer."

Sarah's eyes widened with surprise and disappointment; the Marquis looked frankly incredulous. "Surely, madam—" he began, but she interrupted him with quiet dignity.

"My lord, pray say no more. I am more grateful than I

can tell for the generosity you have shown me, but what you suggest is impossible. I must stay with"—she hesitated for an instant, and then continued firmly—"with my brother. When his wounds are healed we shall go on our way together."

For a few moments longer his lordship continued to stare at her, while resentment kindled slowly behind the astonishment in his eyes. So the lady would have none of his help; she preferred the out-at-elbows adventurer lying wounded above-stairs. Lord Urmiston was not accustomed to defeat, and for the second time that day was betrayed into a show of ill-humour. He made a slight, disdainful gesture of acceptance and dismissal, and said haughtily:

"In that event, madam, nothing remains to be said. I am happy to have had the privilege of serving you, and trust that you may complete you journey with no further misfortunes."

Words and tone alike made it clear that she had been relegated to the status she had chosen. Her cheeks burned, but she stifled her mortification, curtsied gravely to them both, and withdrew from the room. In a very short while she heard my lord's imposing cavalcade resume its interrupted journey, and though she did not regret her decision, was obliged to summon all her resolution to conquer an illogical feeling of loneliness.

It was quite late when at last she sought the refuge of her own room, exhausted in mind and body, for there had been many arrangements to attend to and she was wholly unused to fending for herself. She had not seen Dominic since their arrival at the inn, but the surgeon who tended him had assured her that his life was in no danger, that he was hardy enough to make light of his wounds and would be on his feet again within a week.

Her most pressing anxiety was thus removed, but the dangers and difficulties of the day, together with the long, unaccustomed hours in the saddle, had brought her to the brink of collapse. She was about to tumble into bed when she remembered the purse of gold, which she had put into the pocket of her cloak as she rode back towards the beech-wood, and she decided that for greater safety she would sleep with it beneath her pillow. Five minutes later, with a feeling of sick dismay, and all thought of sleep abandoned, she forced herself to face the appalling truth. Somewhere, somehow, the precious purse had been lost.

V

Rogues and Vagabonds

FOR three days Dominic kept to his bed, forcing his body to rest though his mind chafed at the delay, and saw danger to his plans in every moment of enforced inactivity. He was consumed by a strange impatience to reach the moment when he would confront Lawrence Templecombe once more, and demand the reckoning so long delayed. He pictured the scene in a dozen different ways, and brooded darkly over past wrongs, deliberately goading his hatred to white heat, though that he needed to do so should have warned him how empty was the vengeance he now pursued. If any such doubt ever entered his mind he cast it forth again, or trampled it ruthlessly underfoot, telling himself impatiently that the scruples which occasionally prompted him to spare the girl were but sickly fancies resulting from his present weakness. She was Templecombe's bride, the predestined instrument of his vengeance, and that was how he must think of her, never as a person in her own right.

On the afternoon of the third day he rose and dressed himself. Years of hardship had given his body the toughness of steel and leather, and though he was still weak, and obliged to move with caution, he had no doubt that within another day or two he would be capable of travelling again. For this he was thankful. Uneasiness had been growing steadily within him, for despite her pose as his sister, Verity had not once approached him since their arrival, and it seemed to him that there was a constraint in the manner of those who tended him when he questioned them concerning her.

As he left his room and slowly descended the stairs, it seemed that there was a bustle of unusual activity about the inn, and before he was halfway down he heard Miss Halland's voice in the passage below. She was beyond his range of vision and what she said he could not catch, but there was a note of indignation and protest in her voice. With his thoughts flying immediately to Red Nat, he quickened his steps, and a moment later an astonishing picture was presenting itself to his affronted gaze.

Verity was standing in the middle of the passage, obviously arrested in the act of passing from one room to another, and in each hand she bore a large tankard of ale. For this reason she was unable to resist with anything but words the advances of a slim, shabbily-dressed young man who, with an arm about her trim waist, was endeavouring to bestow upon her a kiss which she was trying with equal determination to avoid.

For an instant amazement held Dominic motionless, and then he strode forward to grip the stranger's shoulder, just as Verity, catching sight of him, uttered a little cry. The young man wrenched himself free, and in one lithe, cat-like movement had sprung round and away, and was facing Fane with a bright, slim-bladed dagger in his grasp. Dominic's hand flashed instinctively to his hip, but he had left his sword in his bed-chamber and now stood defenceless. Next moment Verity had set her burden down anyhow on a bench by the wall and was between them, facing the glittering blade.

"Sir," she said imperiously, "put up that knife. My brother is unarmed, and moreover, has but just risen from a sick-bed."

For a few seconds the young man hesitated, his quick glance going from one to the other. He had bright, dark eyes in a humorous, expressive face, and an air of assurance which outweighed his shabby attire. Then he replaced the dagger in its sheath beneath his coat, and made her a magnificent bow.

"I crave pardon," he said airily. "It seems that I have blundered. I meant your sister no harm, sir, no discourtesy, even! I beheld beauty, and I saluted it—appropriately, as I thought. A pardonable error, I think! Few serving-maids, however well-favoured, are so jealously guarded."

"Serving-maids!" Dominic repeated, between wrath and bewilderment. "What the devil——"

"Dominic, I beg of you!" Verity's voice was urgent; her fingers gripped his arm with painful intensity. "Let be! No harm was done. I have forgotten it."

"Have you so?" He looked suspiciously at her, and then at the tankards on the bench. "What game are you playing now, I wonder?"

"I will explain it all, but have patience a moment," she replied in a low voice. "Wait here! I will be back directly."

She picked up the tankards again and bore them into a

room whence sounded a loud clamour of voices. The stranger looked after her and then glanced again at Fane.

"My presence is unwelcome," he remarked whimsically. "I will remove it, but first, sir, allow me to present myself. Barnabas Pike, actor, mountebank and vagabond, entirely at your service."

He bowed again, hand on heart, and then, as the other man made no reply, but merely stared at him beneath frowning brows, he shrugged slightly and walked away, humming a tune under his breath. After a minute or two Verity returned, and Dominic turned his frowning glance upon her. "Now," he said grimly, "perhaps you will explain the meaning of this mummery."

"Yes," she replied, "but we cannot talk here. Let us go into the garden."

He followed her out of the house and between neat rows of vegetables to a patch of grass where fruit trees grew. A gnarled and moss-grown trunk offered welcome support and he leaned gratefully against it, while the girl eyed him with some anxiety.

"You are not yet recovered," she said reproachfully. "You should not have left your room so soon."

"It seems rather that I tarried there too long," he said sardonically, and then, with a sudden spurt of irrational annoyance: "Hell and the devil! What has been going on here while I lay abed?"

Her eyes fell away from his, and she twisted a corner of her apron in nervous hands, very pale and striving desperately for composure. He watched her with impatience and growing uneasiness.

"Well?" he prompted harshly at length.

"I do not know how to tell you," she faltered. "You will be so angry, and rightly, for such carelessness is unforgivable." She broke off, drew a deep breath, and said with a rush: "I lost the purse you gave me."

Anger blazed into his eyes, and she thought for an instant that he would strike her. His hand did indeed lift, and she braced herself for a blow, white-faced but unflinching. Then his anger died as swiftly as it had arisen and he leaned back against the tree, his hand dropping listlessly to his side.

"You lost the purse?" he repeated in an expressionless voice.

He looked defeated, she thought, defeated and ill and tired

to death, and her ready compassion was stirred once more. She hurried into speech again.

"It shall be repaid, of course, every penny of it, as soon as we reach Sir Lawrence's house. I did not learn of the loss until late that same night, but as soon as it was light I tried to recover the purse——"

"You went back to that beech-wood?" he broke in.

"No, how could I, when I had given you my word not to leave the inn? I told the people here of my misfortune. They are kindly folk, and they sent their eldest son to look for the purse, but though he searched for close upon two hours, he could not find it."

"And then?"

"I did not know what to do, so I offered to work in the inn if they would let us stay. One of their serving-maids is sick and they were glad to accept my offer."

He stared at her, half inclined to doubt the truth of her words.

"You have worked like a common servant-girl?"

"What else could I do? In any event, 'twas better to be occupied than to sit idly brooding throughout the day. You are surprised, perhaps, that I am capable of such work? I assure you, Mr. Fane, my education included a practical study of all the duties of a housewife, and this was not so very different."

With a swift, unexpected movement he grasped her wrist and lifted one hand to look at it. Already its soft whiteness was spoiled, the slender fingers red and roughened. Miss Halland said defensively:

"Well, a little different, perhaps, but I deserve no better. I should be whipped for my wicked carelessness."

He let her go, and said with transient, sardonic humour:

"I doubt my arm is yet strong enough, madam, or I might be tempted to take you at your word." Then his voice hardened again. "Well, what now? We are but at the beginning of our journey, and I have only a shilling or two in my pockets."

"I have thought of that." Verity drew from her bosom a jewelled ornament on a golden chain, and held it out to him. "I was wearing that on the night you captured me, and pearl earrings also, and when we fled from London I hid them about me. The earrings went to the surgeon who tended you, but that should fetch a good enough price to pay for the rest of our journey."

Dominic took the trinket with a curious reluctance. It was

a pretty thing of gold and turquoise and pearls, and he had no doubt that she was right about its value, and equally certain that it grieved her to part with it. He should have been grateful that his intervention had prevented Red Nat from stealing it, as he had no doubt intended to do, but he was aware only of unwillingness to obtain money for their journey by the means she proposed. What the cause of this reluctance might be he did not pause to wonder, but its effect was uncomfortable enough to irritate him, and to prompt the sneer with which he replied.

"With this bauble in your possession, madam, I marvel that you did not continue your journey alone. I could have done nothing to prevent you."

Greatly though she had blamed herself for the loss of the purse, Verity felt that she had since done all in her power to make amends, and now the manner in which he had received the sacrifice of her trinkets stung her to a sharp retort.

"Had I desired that, sir, I would have had no need to sell my jewels. The Marquis of Urmiston was kind enough to place a coach and escort at my disposal had I chosen to accept them. By now I could have been with my betrothed."

The sneer in Dominic's face and voice became more pronounced.

"Or in some pretty love-nest of his lordship's choosing!"

"Oh, you are intolerable!" Tears of anger sprang into Verity's eyes, and quivered in her voice. "He made the offer in the presence of his sister, Lady Sarah, and he would not have done that had his motive been as base as you suggest. Have you lived so long amid evil that you can see no good, no selflessness, in anyone? Would to heaven I had gone then!"

"Why did you not? What held you back, if not suspicion of his lordship's honesty?"

"Why?" She spoke fiercely, a flush of anger in her cheeks, and met his mocking, challenging glance squarely. "I stayed because you saved me in London, and again that day in the beech-wood, and because you were wounded and might have need of a friend. I pay my debts, Mr. Fane!"

Watching him, she saw his expression change. The cynical mockery faded from his face, giving way to a look which seemed to suggest that he saw again some hideous picture which could never be quite banished from his memory, and she wondered, with pity and a tinge of fear, what phantom from the past had this power so to blind those golden eyes to the world about them. There was a long silence, broken only by the small prosaic sounds of the summer afternoon. "And so do I, madam," he said at last in a stifled voice. "And so do I!"

He turned away as he spoke, and went slowly through the neat garden towards the inn, but Verity stood still under the apple trees, her anger forgotten, watching him with wondering, compassionate eyes.

From a window of the inn, Barnabas Pike had been watching the couple in the garden. He bore the man no grudge for the rebuff dealt him a short while since, for there was no malice in his nature, but he possessed an insatiable curiosity concerning the vagaries of his fellow-men. Presently he left the window, and was soon questioning one of the other servants about this odd pair. The story came readily, and intrigued him more than ever, for lords and ladies, he knew, did not customarily concern themselves with such humble folk as the brother and sister appeared to be. He strolled back to the tap-room, and discovered Fane sitting alone by the window, morosely watching the girl whenever her duties brought her into the room.

Pike greeted him without embarrassment, and, sitting down beside him, endeavoured to draw him into conversation. He told him of the troupe of players of which he was the leader, and of the entertainment which they would present that evening in the courtyard of the inn, but these friendly overtures brought no response. Dominic's thoughts were fully occupied with his disastrous loss and with uneasy forebodings concerning the immediate future.

He could not rid himself of the conviction that Nat Trumper was still a factor to be reckoned with; wounded he might have been, and driven off by the armed servants of the Marquis, but it was not likely that he would so easily relinquish his prey. While Fane and Miss Halland stayed close within the inn he could do nothing, but Dominic felt that it would be strange indeed if the red giant were not hoping to make a second and more successful attack when they took to the road again.

Such an attack he was in no case to meet. His pistols had been lost in the beech-wood, and though Verity had retrieved the silver-hilted sword, he knew that he would be a fool to risk another bout with Trumper until his strength was more fully restored. Yet, impoverished as they now found themselves, they could not remain indefinitely at the inn.

The half-healed wound in his side had begun to pain him

again. He moved restlessly in his seat, and wished irritably that the loquacious Mr. Pike would take himself off. What devil possessed the fellow that he must needs pour his wearisome chatter into a stranger's unwilling ear? "... and from there," Barnabas was saying cheerfully, "we shall make our way into Somerset. We must not fail to be in Cloverton in time for Goosefeather Fair."

Dominic stiffened to sudden, attentive interest, for the player's idle words had recalled to his mind a hundred boyhood memories. Cloverton, the little market town whose streets had once been so familiar to him; the fair itself, held each year at the crown of the summer, three days of revelry which woke the small, sleepy place from its customary quiet; and Cloverton lay but a scant five miles from Shere.

He began to study Barnabas Pike with greater interest, while a tentative plan took shape in his mind. After a little he asked a few casual questions, and learned that the troupe of players was composed of a dozen persons of both sexes and various ages, chief among whom was Pike's mother. His father, it seemed, was dead, and Barnabas had inherited from him the leadership of this little company of vagabonds.

For a little while longer Dominic considered the possibilities thus laid before him, but since it was his nature to make all decisions swiftly, he did not delay for long. There was something oddly likeable about Pike, in spite of his self-assurance, and the chance was too good to miss.

"We, too, are bound for Somerset," he said abruptly at length. "In fact, our destination lies within a few miles of Cloverton, and we should have been there ere this but for an accident which befell us a short way back."

"I have heard talk of that," Pike replied candidly. "You were attacked and robbed, were you not?"

"We were," Dominic agreed grimly, "but, though I would not have it generally known, those who waylaid us were no ordinary highwaymen."

"No?" Pike's dark eyes were bright with interest. "What, then?"

"The leader, Nat Trumper—a curst rogue if ever there was one—I knew in London. He plagued my sister with his vile attentions, until I was forced to send him off with his tail 'twixt his legs, but, knowing his kind, I resolved to remove her from his reach, lest he attempt to take by force what had been denied him." Dominic paused, and glanced briefly at his companion's intent face. "I was not always what you see now, my friend, and if I have sunk low in the world, at least I have never dragged her down with me. There is a farm in Somerset, and a cousin who will gladly take her to wife."

He paused again, waiting to see what effect this improvization would have upon his hearer. Barnabas Pike, still watching him shrewdly, said: "He followed you?"

"He did. He and his companion came up with us in the beech-woods, and but for the Marquis of Urmiston's servants, it would have gone ill with us. Trumper was driven off, but, if I know him at all, for a time only, and I am at present in no case to protect my sister unaided. You tell me you are bound for Cloverton. Would it be possible for us to travel with you?"

Pike's brows lifted. "We take a roundabout road, with many halts, but if you are in no haste . . ."

"I am concerned more with safety than with speed." Dominic looked up; his tone was sardonic. "Do not think I am seeking charity. We are not entirely without resources, whatever you may have heard. All I desire from you is the protection of travelling with a numerous company."

For a little while Barnabas continued to ponder him with an expression hard to read. Then suddenly he smiled, his teeth very white against the brown of his face.

"To that you are welcome, sir, for as long as you have need of it. Our ways are rough and our life not always easy, but you may rest assured that among us your sister will come to no harm. They call us rogues and vagabonds, but we are honest enough—in our fashion!"

There was something reassuring in that quick, merry smile, and on a sudden impulse Dominic extended his hand.

"Had I thought otherwise," he said quietly, "I should not have sought to go with you. I am very grateful to you, Mr. Pike."

Later he told Verity of the provision he had made for the rest of the journey, and warned her to be ready to leave next morning. She heard him in silence, her grave, grey eyes on his face, and at the end said merely: "Is it wise, do you think, to set forth again so soon?"

"Such a chance will not offer again. If Trumper picks up our trail, you will need more protection than I can give you. What objection have you to travelling with these people?"

A faint smile quivered on her lips. "I have none, for they seem kindly folk, but would it matter to you if I had? I am concerned only lest your strength is not equal to the journey."

"Permit me, madam, to be the judge of that!" He spoke brusquely, but she thought to detect a note of weariness in his voice that belied the words. "A common soldier soon learns to make light of his hurts."

She was not convinced, and studied his face anxiously. For all his swarthiness of complexion, its pallor was unmistakable, and the bold jut of nose and brow and jaw more pronounced than ever. She could not rid herself of the feeling that she was largely to blame for their misfortunes, and though she had done her best to make amends, and even given way to a flash of temper when he seemed to belittle her efforts, there was no denying that but for the loss of the gold he would have had no need to drag himself out of a sick-bed on to the road, in the company of a troupe of strolling players who, however good-hearted, could have neither the time nor the means to care for a sick man.

"There will be other travellers passing this way," she said, laying a hand on his arm, "and I do not think you are yet strong enough to resume the journey. Let us wait a while. I have brought you near to death once by my heedlessness, but I will not let you risk your life so wantonly again."

"God's death, woman, have done!" he exclaimed, and struck her hand violently aside. "Save your tenderness for your husband, or for your dainty Marquis if you should meet him again. 'Tis wasted upon me! We leave tomorrow with Barnabas Pike and his company, so let us have no more argument on that score."

She shrank back, pale and trembling before that unwarranted blast of anger, looking at him with stricken eyes. Then with no further protest, without another word, she turned and left him alone; he stared after her, hating the quiet dignity which his hard words had failed to shatter, but hating himself more for having uttered them.

She did not refer to the matter again, and the following morning, obedient to his orders, was ready to leave when their new travelling-companions went on their way. The players travelled slowly, their carts jolting over the dusty roads behind plodding horses, while they themselves tramped alongside or rode in the lurching vehicles. They covered only a few miles a day, and at night, if no other shelter offered, pitched their camp on some stretch of common land, and practised their various arts by the light of moon and fire.

There was a thin, dark, intense youth who played a guitar and sang love-songs in a clear tenor voice, and his sister, a child of sixteen, thin and vital as her brother, with huge, lustrous eyes and a mane of wild black hair. She danced with the fierce ecstasy of a flame, but at other times was sullen and resentful, clinging close to Barnabas Pike and watching Verity with jealous eyes. There was a plump, good-natured girl with a fat baby on her hip, and a thin man who juggled and performed marvels of sleight-of-hand, and seemed in a perpetual state of melancholy surprise at his own skill. The rest of the company played their parts in the simple, bawdy plays which formed the main part of the troupe's repertoire, and all worked together in the easy comradeship of the road.

The composition of the troupe was constantly changing, and no surprise was occasioned by the addition of two more to its number, even though those two were not players. The man was sick, and the girl, though she took no part in their performances, soon made herself useful in another way, by mending and altering the tinsel finery they wore upon the stage. Her exquisite needlework soon aroused the admiration of the entire company, and she would sit sewing for hours in some quiet corner of an inn kitchen or one of the jolting carts, glad that she had found a way of repaying the rough kindness of these wandering folk.

For kind to her they undoubtedly were. They had realized, before the first day was out, that she was not as they were, sturdy and accustomed to hardship and fatigue, but the very sweetness of her nature aroused their sympathy rather than their resentment. She did not complain, though at the end of that first day's march she was almost dropping with exhaustion, and if the coarse fare they set before her was such as she had never eaten before, she accepted it as gratefully as though it were the finest of dishes. In that single day she had won them completely, even Maria, the little dancer, abating something of her hostility when she saw that the newcomer made no attempt to usurp her own place in the affections of Barnabas Pike.

But if the sister won their hearts, not so the brother. Fane had never learned the secret of popularity, and there was little in his looks or manner to inspire their liking. With Barnabas alone he achieved a degree of intimacy, for the younger man's friendliness would not be denied. He had been born to the life of the road, but he had contrived, heaven alone knew how or where, to acquire a smattering of education, and a speech and manner above his station. His accomplishments were varied, learned from past and present members of the troupe, for let a trick but catch his fancy and he would not rest until he had mastered it. He was a juggler, an acrobat, a fencer of some skill, and he could throw a knife with uncanny precision. In his hands the slim, bright daggers, one at least of which was never far from his reach, seemed imbued with life and weirdly obedient to his will, and a display of this particular accomplishment formed a spectacular part of every performance.

With the exception of their leader, the players held aloof from Fane, and though civil to him, left him severly alone. Dominic cared little for this. He was in no mood for conviviality. His wounds still irked him more than he would admit, and his state of mind did nothing to ease his bodily discomfort.

The loss of the gold had been a bitter blow, for without it he had little hope of making his escape, whatever the outcome of his encounter with Templecombe might be. He had sold the gold and turquoise ornament at the first town of any size which they visited, but the goldsmith who purchased it was suspicious of this shabby stranger and paid less than Dominic had hoped. By the time they reached their journey's end there would be little money left, but though he was now almost certain that it would cost him his life, he clung stubbornly to his plan of revenge.

Their first week with the players was uneventful, save in the novelty which this strange life held for them both, but on the ninth day after their departure from the inn, the danger which Dominic had foreseen manifested itself in no uncertain fashion.

They had arrived that afternoon at a fair-sized town, which Barnabas hoped would be more than usually profitable. Since none of the inns possessed a courtyard suitable for their purpose, the rough stage was set up in the market-house, the troupe taking up their quarters at an inn on the opposite side of the street, and there, as the sun was setting, Verity found herself alone. The inn servants had slipped out to swell the crowd about the market-house, but though Miss Halland had watched her friends' performances eagerly enough at first, this diversion was already beginning to pall. She was very tired, and had, in fact, been about to retire, when Meg, the plump girl, had begged her breathlessly to mend a large rent in the gown she would be wearing upon the stage.

This Verity had willingly done, for though Meg was heedless and foolish, her unbounded good-nature disarmed criticism. She repaired the gown neatly and swiftly, and then, carrying it over her arm, went out of the inn and across the street to the market-house.

The rectangular, pillared hall was open upon all sides, and at one end, beside the staircase leading to the rooms above, the stage had been erected. The larger of the two wagons was drawn up close behind it, and canvas slung between to afford a degree of privacy. Verity was obliged to skirt the crowd in order to reach it, and as she did so her glance fell upon a man standing close to one of the pillars and half hidden by it. His face was turned away from her as he looked towards the stage, but there was no mistaking his size, or the colour of the hair straggling from beneath the broad hat pulled low upon his head. It was Nat Trumper.

Her heart seemed to miss a beat, and then started to pound furiously as she slipped behind a burly onlooker and from the shelter of his broad back ventured another peep, which served merely to confirm her suspicions. For a moment she paused, uncertain, and then hastened on her way.

Meg was waiting for her with mingled impatience and anxiety, for it was almost time for her to take her place upon the stage. Verity helped her to struggle into the dress, but said anxiously as she did so: "Meg, do you know where my brother is?"

Meg, fumbling with the laces of the gown, shook her head.

"He was helping Barnabas a while since, in the barn beyond the inn. There was something amiss with the other wagon, and they were trying to set it to rights. Maybe he's still there, for I've not seen him since."

"And Barnabas?"

"Yonder!" Meg jerked her head in the direction of the stage, adding, as Verity gave an exclamation of dismay: "Why, what ails you, child?"

"I have just seen the man Trumper, he who wounded Dominic, in the crowd outside," Verity confessed. "He must have come seeking us."

"Mercy on us!" Meg stared at her, open-mouthed. "Best bide here, then, and not venture out again alone." She glanced over her shoulder towards the stage. "I must haste. Stay you here."

She moved away. Verity hesitated for a moment, and then lifted the canvas screen and stepped out; a few paces brought her within sight of the pillar where Trumper had been standing, but he was no longer there.

With fear clutching coldly at her heart, she looked rapidly about her, but Red Nat was nowhere to be seen. She went a little further, her glance ranging hurriedly over the crowd, but in vain, though it was impossible that so conspicuous a figure could be overlooked.

She was now only a short distance from the inn, and, remembering what Meg had said of Dominic's possible whereabouts, hastened on along the street and through the empty building. As she stepped out into the yard at the rear she saw that the doors of the barn were open, and a light of some kind burning within the shadowy interior.

She ran forward and peered into the building. It was not large, quite half its space being occupied by the wagon, and the rest cluttered with rubbish of all sorts, while a lantern, swinging from a hook in the low roof, cast a sickly light over the centre of the floor, leaving the corners in darkness. Fane was on the far side of the wagon, where the light was brightest, and she spoke his name as she hurried forward.

He had been kneeling beside one of the wheels, but at the sound of her voice he rose, brushing a hand across his brow in an unconsciously weary gesture. Verity gasped out her news, and saw his face harden to sudden grimness.

"Back to the inn!" he said tersely. "This place would be the veriest trap, and I am unarmed."

He turned to snatch up his coat, which he had cast across the side of the wagon, but a choking gasp from the girl brought him swinging round again. On the edge of the circle of lantern light, like some monstrous apparition conjured up by his words, Red Nat was standing, his great sword naked and gleaming in his hand.

VI

The House in the Wood

FOR the space of perhaps ten seconds not one of the three moved or spoke, and then Trumper shifted his position a trifle, resting the point of his sword on the ground and regarding the couple before him with evil satisfaction. He grinned, displaying broken and discoloured teeth amid the fiery tangle of beard.

"A trap it is, cully," he agreed amiably, "and one as you'll not come out of alive. As for you, my pretty, you can screech as loud as you like—there's none to hear. They're all too busy watching your friends in the market-house yonder."

As though to confirm his words, a distant burst of laughter and applause came faintly to their ears. Dominic moved forward a little, so that he stood between Red Nat and the girl, but the action was purely instinctive and he had little hope of saving her or himself. Trumper would not be restrained by any notions of fair play; he would have no hesitation in running his sword through an unarmed enemy, and since his great bulk was blocking the only way past the wagon, it was unlikely that Verity would have any chance of escaping, even if his attention could be momentarily diverted.

Since that first gasp of horror she had made no sound, but he could hear her quickened breathing close beside him, and feel the trembling of her hand as it rested on his arm. In fury and despair he looked about him, seeking in vain for some kind of weapon in the clutter of rubbish piled against the wall of the barn, and Red Nat chuckled evilly.

"There's no sword to hand this time," he gibed, "and no meddlesome lackeys to come betwixt us, either. You chose the wrong man to cozen, my lad, when you cheated Nat Trumper."

"Give thanks that I am unarmed, you hulking coward," Fane retorted contemptuously, "for if I were not, you would not venture yourself so close. A swordsman? You?" He laughed shortly. "A butcher, more like!"

With a kind of animal snarl Trumper raised his sword, and Verity uttered a little cry and hid her face against Dominic's shoulder. He did not move, but looked with grim mockery into Nat's congested face.

"Aye, run me through!" he sneered. " 'Tis all you have the stomach for, to murder the defenceless, and to ravish helpless maids. God's death! is this the hero of Alsatia? A craven who dare not match his vaunted strength against a man still weakened by wounds?"

He spoke deliberately, forcing into look and tone all the jeering contempt of which he was capable, in the hope of taunting Nat into casting aside his sword and attacking him with bare hands. Against the giant's huge, unbroken strength he had no hope of prevailing, but it would at least provide the girl with an opportunity to escape, and if she were swift she might once more bring help in time to save his life. For a moment he thought he had succeeded, and then the blind fury in Trumper's face gave way to comprehension.

"Ye're a cunning devil, a'nt ye, Fane," he growled, "but not cunning enough! Ye'd have me match strength wi' you so that the wench can slip out and rouse the town against me, but I'm not to be caught twice by the same trick. Jeer as much as ye like! Reckon I'll have the last laugh."

He took a pace forward as he spoke, and then something flashed in the lantern-light, there was a soft thud, and Nat pulled up short, staring with startling eyes at the gleaming knife which was poised, quivering, in the side of the wagon between him and his intended victim.

For an instant he stood as though petrified, and then with a strangled exclamation he swung about. Framed in the open doorway, a gay figure in the garish finery of the stage, Barnabas Pike was standing, with a second knife balanced in his hand.

"That's for an earnest," he told Trumper with grim relish, "but the next one will find a lodging in your fat throat. Let fall that sword!"

A slight, suggestive movement of the hand holding the knife added force to the command, and in baffled rage Red Nat let the sword drop to the floor. He had seen, as he stood in the crowd about the market-house, Pike displaying his skill with those bright daggers, and the sight had inspired him with the liveliest respect.

Dominic caught up the fallen weapon, and a moment later its keen point was pressing painfully against its owner's stomach. Barnabas came forward, and slashed a length from a tangle of rope lying among the litter on the floor. As he secured Trumper's arms, he said cheerfully:

"Meg told me what was amiss, and I came seeking you. It seems 'twas as well that I did." He flashed an encouraging smile at Verity, who was leaning against the wagon, trembling in the reaction from the recent peril. "Keep a stout heart, lass, the worst is over! Go find the inn-keeper and bid him send the constable here, while we keep watch over this fine prisoner of ours."

She hesitated, glancing dubiously at Dominic. He was frowning, but after a moment he nodded. "Do as Barnabas says, Verity," he agreed. "It will be best to have this persistent rogue under lock and key."

So in due course, and after a good deal of tedious formality, Red Nat was haled away to the town lock-up, and it seemed that the adventure was at an end, though Dominic told Barnabas that he would have been easier in his mind had that unerringly-aimed knife buried itself in Trumper's heart rather than the side of the wagon. Pike regarded him quizzically.

"I've no wish to be facing a charge of murder, my friend," he said frankly. "I don't doubt that the rogue would be better dead, and had he chanced on us in some lonely spot I might have been less merciful, but here in the town I dared not harm him. A strolling player has troubles enough without provoking the law."

To this opinion he adhered until the following day, when, just as they were preparing to leave the town, word reached them that Red Nat had broken free during the night. The constable, it seemed, had underrated the strength of his prisoner or overestimated the solidity of the lock-up, and when he rose that morning had found the cage broken and the captive gone. Dominic cursed when he heard the news, and Barnabas inveighed bitterly against the constable's bungling, saying that had he known with what manner of fool he was dealing, he would have killed Trumper and risked hanging.

The harm, however, was done, and though Red Nat had seemingly disappeared, the whole troupe joined forces in keeping watch for him. From that time forward Verity was not left alone, and Dominic was never without a sword at his side, but their vigilance went unrewarded. The days lengthened into weeks, and as they roamed to and fro through the south of England, tending ever towards the west, it began to seem likely that Trumper had abandoned the chase.

To Verity it seemed sometimes that this was the only life she had ever known, the busy markets and fairs, the lonely camps between, and always the dusty road stretching interminably ahead. Her shabby clothes grew shabbier yet, the pale complexion which had been her pride gave place to the sunburn of a country girl, and a sprinkling of freckles appeared across her small, straight nose, until she wondered whether Sir Lawrence Templecombe would ever recognize his promised wife in the ragged vagabond she had become. Weariness and loneliness often seized upon her, bringing a desperate yearning for her home, and the safe, happy pattern of her childhood and girlhood, but she forced herself to keep her head high and a smile on her lips. No one, least of all Dominic Fane, should guess how tired and heart-sick she was.

He watched her more closely than she knew, marvelling at her spirit, yet dreading that the moment would come when it would break at last. He could guess something of what she must be suffering in body and in mind, now that for the first time in her life she was brought face to face with poverty and its ugly consequences, and he realized how her fastidious and sensitive nature must shrink from the coarseness of this roving life. He did what he could to ease the burden for her, and told himself that only thus could the pretence of brother and sister be maintained.

At such times, when admiration of her courage rose within him, he would remind himself fiercely of the wrongs he had suffered in the past, of how long he had waited to avenge them, and how skilful Sir Lawrence Templecombe had been in avoiding an open quarrel. Then the old hatred would spring up to conquer the impulse of compassion, and he would look at her with new eyes, seeing her only as the instrument of his vengeance, and be consumed with the impatience to reach the journey's end. He fretted against the slow pace the players set, yet dared not leave their company lest, after all, Nat Trumper should appear as suddenly as before to imperil his deadly purpose.

At last, when his patience was almost at an end, they crossed the boundary between Dorset and Somerset, and two days later he was able to tell Verity that on the morrow they would be close enough to Shere to part from the troupe. She received the news with an indifference that surprised him, until it occurred to him that weariness was probably the cause. Their march that day had been long and hard, starting at dawn and not ending until the sun had set, for they had earlier been delayed by a series of small mishaps, and Barnabas was anxious to reach Cloverton in good time for the fair.

The heat was unbearable, the sun blazing from a cloudless sky with no breath of wind to temper his fierceness. The countryside wore a parched and thirsty look, and the road was inches deep in dust which, stirred by plodding feet, rose in clouds that choked and blinded, until even the hardy, vagabond players lost their usual cheeriness, and tramped on their way in unaccustomed silence. Strangely enough, it was Dominic Fane who suffered least, for his wounds were healed now, and he had known forced marches before, under fiercer suns than that of England. Verity, watching him from one of the jolting carts, thought he seemed tireless as he tramped along, his dark face inscrutable in the shadow of the broad-brimmed hat, the strange eyes, unbetraying as the eyes of a cat, masking whatever thoughts were stirring behind them.

When at last evening brought a measure of relief, and they made camp beside a little river, Verity had no appetite for the food set before her. The meal over, the company sat or lay upon the grass, too tired even to rehearse their various parts, and watched a full moon rise above a ridge of hills. The dark youth plucked at the strings of his guitar, and sang now and then a snatch of song, but for the most part they were silent, some of them already asleep.

Dominic rose quietly and left them, his departure unobserved. He followed the course of the river upstream until he found a place where it ran deep and quiet, and there stripped and plunged into the water. When he had dressed himself again, he took his sword from its scabbard and watched the moonlight run in a blue-white glimmer along the bright blade, and thought of Lawrence Templecombe and the reckoning at hand at last. During these latter days he had fenced regularly with Barnabas Pike, and knew that strength and skill alike were fully restored to him; he had curbed impatience with a strong hand, and if the effort had cost him dear, it would bring its own reward.

It was as he approached the camp again, his footsteps soundless on the grass, that he came upon Verity. She crouched at the foot of a willow tree by the river's edge, her head resting against the grey trunk, and but for the sound of her quiet weeping he might have passed by without seeing her. Instead he paused, and after a moment's hesitation went slowly towards her. As his shadow fell across the grass beside her she looked up with a gasp of alarm, then, realizing who it was, sank back against the tree once more.

"What is it?" he asked abruptly. "Are you ill?"

She shook her head.

"No," she said wearily, "not ill, but oh! so tired." She looked piteously up at him. "Dominic, I do not think I can go on."

He frowned, realizing with dismay that this was the collapse he had feared, and that it could not have come at a worse time. He dropped to one knee beside her, forcing himself to speak in a tone of gentle reassurance.

"Another day will bring us to the journey's end," he said. "I told you so a while since. Had you forgotten?"

"No," she said again. "I had not forgotten. When you told me, I could have wept for very joy, and then afterwards I realized that I had good cause for tears." She looked up at him as he knelt beside her, an elbow on his bent knee. "Dominic, do you not yet see that our journey must prove vain?"

"In the name of God, what folly is this?" he demanded blankly. "We are within ten miles of Templecombe's house."

"Of his house, yes! but will he be there to greet us? Will he not have returned to London as soon as word of my disappearance reached him?" Fane's face was in shadow, but she sensed his sudden stillness, and gave a dreary little laugh that broke into a sob, " 'Tis so obvious, is it not? Yet neither of us had eyes to see it."

Dismay held him silent, as he realized the truth of her words. His original plan had been sound enough, for had they come straight and swift from London, no messenger could have been before them, but by this time Templecombe must have been in the capital for weeks, seeking his lost bride.

"And I cannot go to his house if he is absent," Verity went on hopelessly, "for none of his servants know me, and I have not the means to prove my identity. If I presented myself to them as the future Lady Templecombe, would they believe me? Would you, if you did not know the truth?"

He could find no reassurance to give her, for though a perceptive eye might still find evidence of gentle birth in her delicacy of feature and softness of voice, it was unlikely that, in the absence of their master, Templecombe's servants could be convinced. It was equally certain, however, that some of them at least would recognize him, and that, if Sir Lawrence were indeed from home, must be avoided at all costs. His thoughts hurried this way and that, seeking a way out of the impasse.

"The blame is mine," Verity said wretchedly after a while. "Misfortune after misfortune, brought about by my folly and carelessness. Oh, why was I so blind? When you recovered from your wounds, and we still had the money my trinkets fetched, we should have turned our steps towards Herefordshire, not Somerset. There is my home, my friends, my servants." Sobs threatened to choke her voice again, but she forced them back. "My home! Dear God! shall I ever see it again?"

"Have courage a little longer," he replied. "What you have said is true, but I think I see a way to achieve our goal. First, we must be certain whether or not Templecombe is at Shere, and there Barnabas can help us, for it will be known in the town. If he is in London, we must fine somewhere to await his return, which perchance may be hurried by news of your plight, if we can contrive to send it to him. Some remote cottage or lonely farm would serve our purpose best, for no one must yet know who you are."

"But we have no money," she said in a puzzled voice, "and who would give us shelter without?"

"I will find work. It will soon be harvest-time, when an extra pair of hands is welcome at many a farm."

She stared at him, trying to read his expression, uncertain whether or not he mocked.

"What do you know of such work?" she asked suspiciously.

He got up, pulling her to her feet with a hand about her wrist.

"More, I'll warrant me, than you knew of the duties of serving-maid," he replied with a short laugh. "I was a farmer before I was a soldier."

"A farmer? You?" Verity made no attempt to disguise her astonishment. "Oh, you are jesting! Never tell me you were bred to follow the plough?"

He stood for a moment, still grasping her wrist, his gaze on the moon-silvered ripples of the river. She could see his face now, for the pale light fell full upon it, and she was startled by the bitterness of its expression. Bitterness, too, invested the low voice in which he presently answered her. "No," he said, "I learned it perforce. Before that, my dear, I was a gentleman."

Some depth of unhappiness and conflict which she could scarcely comprehend rang through the simple words, and on a sudden impulse, stirred by she knew not what of sympathy or gratitude, she laid her free hand over the one which held her wrist.

"Farmer of soldier or what you will," she said quietly, "that you must always be, my friend, if to be truly chivalrous is to be a gentleman. I feared and mistrusted you at first, but I know now how much I wronged you in my thoughts. If ever man gave woman cause to trust him, you have done so during all these weary weeks."

She heard the sharp intake of breath with which he swung to face her, and wondered whether it was a trick of the moonlight which made him look so pale. For a moment he stared down into her eyes, and then he wrenched his hand away as though her touch had seared his flesh.

"Get you back to the camp," he said hoarsely, "and to the sleep you need, instead of prating here. Small wonder you are weary."

She went submissively, giving no sign of hurt or anger at the abrupt dismissal, but for a long time afterwards Dominic remained where she had left him, staring blindly at the placid stream, while shame and remorse struggled against the force of an old hatred.

Verity's avowal of her trust in him repeated itself again and again in his memory, but now the voice that spoke it was the voice of conscience itself. Deliberately and heartlessly he had set out to win that trust, to make her believe that he was her friend, but now the innocent victim who must be sacrificed to the cause of revenge was no longer the stranger she had been when the plan was formed. During the weeks which had passed since then, a bond he could not deny had been forged between them; hardships shared and danger faced together had fostered an odd comradeship, and though his hatred of Templecombe burned more fiercely than ever, it could not wholly consume his unwilling esteem for Templecombe's bride. He was still dedicated to vengeance, but he knew now that it could never bring him the peace he craved and had for so long sought in vain.

Next morning he drew Barnabas Pike aside and asked him to find out whether Sir Lawrence Templecombe of Shere Place was at present in Somerset. Barnabas looked at him rather hard, but refrained from comment, and when, at midday, they halted in a village to buy provisions, was lucky enough to overhear two men in the inn-yard talking of that same Sir Lawrence.

A question or two, put with apparent idleness, brought forth the information that the gentleman was at present to be found at his great house at Shere, having just come from London, whither he had gone in great haste some weeks earlier. Before his departure there had been talk of a bridal, but Sir Lawrence was now seen to be wearing mourning, and all preparations to welcome a new mistress to Shere Place had been abandoned, so it was to be supposed that the lady of his choice had since died.

Barnabas pondered this intelligence for a while, but could find in it no answer to the riddle of Dominic Fane's interest in the whereabouts of one of the richest and most powerful landowners in Somerset. He shrugged, and went in search of Fane.

He found him leaning against the cart in which his sister sat, busy with her interminable sewing. Pike spoke casually, but his dark eyes were watchful for their response to his news, nor was he wholly disappointed. The girl gasped and looked eagerly at Fane, as though she would have spoken, then, apparently recollecting herself, bent once more over her work, though her hands trembled so that she could scarcely set the stitches. The man's emotions were less easy to read; he merely thanked Pike for the information and began to talk of something else.

They went on their way again, following the road which would bring them, before the day was out, to Cloverton, and Dominic looked about him with mixed feelings. They were passing now through country he remembered well, where the name of Fane had been respected once, but where it was now forgotten, or remembered only with revulsion. There had been a day, fourteen years ago, when it had been upon everyone's lips, a name dishonoured, stained with blood; now the day approached when it would blaze through the countryside once more, before it passed into final extinction. Vengeance, and a vow fulfilled, and Templecombe brought to bay at last. Think only of that, keep that goal ever in mind, and forget the touch of a woman's hand and the trust so soon to be betrayed.

As they drew closer to the town he began to feel uneasy, for there were many in this neighbourhood who would know his face, even after a lapse of ten years, and he wished no word of his return to carry a warning to Templecombe. He frowned, and fingered the long scar seaming his cheek, and then went to speak with Barnabas.

Presently a fork in the road was reached, and Pike gave the signal to halt. While the rest of the troupe stared and wondered, Dominic went to the cart where Verity sat, and spoke abruptly.

"We leave our friends here. Make your farewells, and come."

She nodded with suppressed excitement, and caught up the bundle containing her few possessions. He took it from her and helped her to the ground, and watched the players crowd about her to bid her good-bye. After a moment he found Pike at his side.

"I am sorry that we must part so soon," Barnabas said frankly, then, lowering his voice, he added, "I ask no questions, Dominic, but I have been in these parts before, and heard the Templecombes spoken of as people more to be feared than loved. If you need a friend, we shall be at the fair as long as it lasts."

He put out his hand, and Fane gripped it with real regret.

"Our debt to you is already greater than I can ever repay," he replied, "and words are a poor guerdon at best. Nonetheless I thank you. Good-bye, my friend, and good fortune go with you."

There was no time for more, for the troupe was eager to reach Cloverton with the least possible delay. The carts jolted away, and Verity stood by the roadside and watched them out of sight, waving from time to time. When they had gone, she turned to Dominic with a smile and a sigh.

"They are good people," she said. "I must see that they are rewarded, though were I to give them every penny I possess it could not repay the kindness they have shown me."

He returned some non-committal reply and led the way along the other road. For some while they walked in silence, which Verity presently broke to ask how far they were from Shere Place.

"Some six or seven miles by this road," he answered briefly. "The other way is shorter, but 'tis best that we avoid the town."

She agreed, and lapsed into silence again, though not without a sigh at the thought of the distance to be covered on foot. Suddenly much of her eagerness seemed to have left her, and considerations which had appeared unimportant when viewed from a distance, loomed threateningly now that they

were close at hand. How would Sir Lawrence receive his betrothed when she presented herself at his door, ragged and
footsore and sunburned as a gipsy? Would he understand the
horror and despair which had gripped her that night in London when she had held an embroidered purse in her hands,
and realized whence came the gold which should have bought
her a passage into hell? Would he forgive the impulse of terror which had sent her flying through the night with Dominic
Fane, in search of the one person with whom she might account herself safe? Would he, in fact, place any credence at
all in her suspicions, now that the purse was lost?

She did not really know him very well, although they had
been contracted to each other for eight years. His visits to her
grandfather's house had been frequent, but the great difference in their ages was a barrier between them, while during
the time she had spent in London the greater formality of the
situation had precluded any closer understanding. Her sister-
in-law, Diana Halland, had always been present at their
meetings, and all that Verity knew of her future husband was
that he was wealthy and well-born, something of a fop, and
inclined, in her opinion, to set too great a value upon outward show. She could not, for instance, imagine him rubbing
shoulders with Barnabas Pike and his troupe, or treating Dominic with anything but haughty condescension.

She glanced sidelong at Fane as they trudged along, trying
to see him through Sir Lawrence's eyes. Certainly there was
little in his appearance to recommend him, and she could
only hope that she was sufficiently eloquent to make clear to
Templecombe the magnitude of the debt she owed him. That
it might be even more difficult to convince her betrothed of
the complete innocence of her association with Dominic Fane
was a possibility which she thrust resolutely from her mind.
He would not, could not, think ill of her, he who had known
her since childhood; and yet, how could she be certain of that?
He was more a stranger to her, this man she was to marry,
than Dominic himself.

They walked and rested, and walked again, speaking little,
both preoccupied with their own thoughts. The bright sunshine of morning had faded, and the windless air was sultry,
pressing upon them like a tangible thing. As the afternoon
wore on the sky darkened slowly, and the breathless silence
grew heavy and menacing with a brewing storm.

They had covered perhaps four miles, and were skirting
the edge of a dense and apparently extensive wood, when

Verity became aware that her companion's pace had slackened and that he was looking keenly about him. Before she could voice the question which rose in her mind, he gave an exclamation of satisfaction and turned aside from the road into the shadow of the trees.

"Does our way lie there?" Verity spoke with some dismay, for the wood was tangled and overgrown, as though no one had passed that way for many years. Dominic nodded. "It lies there," he answered, and pointed to the scarcely discernible track before them. "That path will lead us straight to your betrothed."

There was the faintest note of mockery in his voice, but she did not remark it. He set off along the path, and she followed him reluctantly, for it was so narrow that they were unable to walk abreast. Looking about her, she thought that never before had she seen a place so wild and desolate. Great branches and even whole trees lay rotting where they had fallen, half buried in dense undergrowth which had almost swallowed up the path; the silence was deep and oppressive, for no bird fluttered or rabbit stirred in those impenetrable thickets, and when a twig snapped underfoot, the sound struck the ear like a pistol-shot. Swarms of flies rose up from the shaken leaves to hover in tormenting clouds about them; brambles thrust out long tendrils to entangle their feet, or tore at them with thorny fingers; the very trees seemed hostile, rank upon rank of them crowding the green half-light, stretching interminably upon every side.

At last they came to a spot where the trees stood back a little around a stagnant pool. Thunder was muttering in the distance now, and the clouds were purple-black and low, seeming to rest upon the topmost branches. A weird, yellowish light suffused the scene, trapped between apprehensive earth and threatening sky. Verity halted and looked uneasily about her, pushing the damp hair back from her brow. "This wood seems endless," she said with an attempt at lightness. "Dominic, have we lost our way?"

"No," he replied in a low voice, "this is the road we must tread if we are ever to reach Sir Lawrence Templecombe. A tortuous road, but it will bring us to him in the end."

There seemed to be an odd significance in his voice, and she looked sharply at him. He was staring at her, and in that uncanny light the tawny eyes seemed more brilliant than ever in his dark face. For the first time the utter solitude of the place struck her. They might have been the sole inhabitants of a world bewitched, and suddenly the stillness, and the crowding trees, and the black pool at her feet seemed fraught with an unnamed menace. A wild sense of panic seized upon her, and she turned and hurried on along the path, tripping and stumbling in her haste. He followed her in silence, his long stride keeping him effortlessly at her heels.

Suddenly, to her unspeakable relief, the trees thinned a little and she glimpsed the pointed gables of a house. A minute or two later the track passed into the shadow of a high stone wall smothered in ivy, and brought them very soon to an entrance blocked by a gate of wrought iron. Verity halted, staring, her relief perishing in a flood of dismay. The gate hung drunkenly from a single hinge, its ironwork corroded with rust, its base lost in a tangle of weeds, while beyond, across a forsaken garden, the windows of the house showed shuttered and blind. A flicker of lightning pierced the black pall of cloud above the twisted chimneys, and a few large drops of rain fell pattering on the leaves.

Dominic laid his hand on the rusty iron, and stood looking in silence at the desolate scene beyond. Then he set his shoulder to the gate and forced a gap wide enough for them to pass through.

"There is shelter yonder," he said. "We will bide there until the storm is over."

"No!" Verity's voice was sharp with a fear which she herself scarcely understood. "Let us go on."

"Through the woods?" he queried sardonically. "It will be dangerous there when the storm breaks."

She cast a desperate glance to left and right, but he grasped her wrist and drew her with him into the overgrown garden. The path which had once lain beyond the gate was all but lost, but he followed it without hesitation, thrusting between bushes, stooping under low-hanging branches, not pausing until the house was reached. Here was the main door, set far back in an old-fashioned porch, and a weedgrown drive which curved sharply to the left and was lost to view behind a clump of trees, Dominic paused for a moment in the mouth of the porch, and then thrust the girl within.

"Wait you here," he said abruptly, and was gone before she could reply.

There was a stone bench along each side of the porch, and upon one of these she sank weakly down. Now was the time to make her escape, but a numb weariness seemed to have taken possession of body and of mind. A gust of hot wind

shook the trees, and the thunder rolled nearer. Verity pressed
a hand against her brow. Escape from what? From this house,
lost and forgotten in its bewitched wood, or from Dominic,
who seemed suddenly a stranger?

How long she sat there she did not know, but at last a
sound reached her from within the house, the protesting
screech of bolts long unused, and then the heavy door at the
end of the porch creaked open. Fane stood in the aperture,
holding aloft a candle in a pewter candlestick. "Come," he
said peremptorily, and stretched out his free hand towards
her.

Verity got slowly to her feet. It was almost dark in the
porch now, save when the lightning bathed everything for an
instant in a blue-white glare, and the light of the candle
seemed to dazzle her eyes. She put up her hand to shade
them, and then the ground seemed to give way beneath her
feet, and light and shadow alike were lost in an all-enveloping
darkness.

Dominic went swiftly forward and bent for a moment over
her huddled figure, and then he rose and re-entered the
house. The square, stone-flagged hall from which the stairs
rose steeply was bare of furniture, but there should be some
still in the room to the left. He flung open the door, stood for
an instant while his gaze passed over a familiar scene, and
then set the candle down on a table and went back to the
girl. He carried her into the room and laid her on the high-
backed settle by the empty hearth, and then stood upright
and looked again about the room he had not seen for more
than ten years.

Nothing had been touched. He had known that as soon as
he forced a way in at the rear of the house, and found all as
he had left it on that long-gone day, and the dust of years
undisturbed save by the small feet of rat and mouse. He was
not surprised, for he had expected no less. There was not a
man or woman within five miles who would willingly set foot
in this house of ill-omen.

It was raining fast now, and the thunder rolled deeply
overhead. Strange, he thought, that there should be a storm
today. So had the rain hissed and thunder rolled on that other
day, when a storm of emotion as violent as that of the ele-
ments had been loosed within these walls, and he had first set
his feet on the long and weary road which had brought him
back at last to this house where he had been born, and to
within reach of the vengeance denied him for fourteen years.

His vengeance! Slowly his glance came back to the girl, where she lay so still and quiet on the dusty settle. Templecombe's bride! The weapon with which he would force a treacherous coward to face at last the challenge of his sword. Let him die for it, he would pay his debt, and pay it in full.

Suddenly, through the dark chaos of his thoughts, there flashed unbidden the memory of a garden behind a country inn, and a girl who faced him proudly and answered mockery with fierce defiance. 'I pay my debts, Mr. Fane!' As clearly as though they had just been spoken, the words echoed in his ears. Yes, she had paid that debt in full, yet how did he mean to requite her? By linking her name irrevocably with his, and depriving her of her only hope of safety from the Black Mask? He stared down at her, and now in memory he stood again by a moonlit river, and heard the avowal of her trust in him.

With an abrupt movement he turned away, and stood with bent head, his hands clenched on the edge of the table and his tormented gaze fixed on the steady candle-flame. Was he then to turn coward in his turn, to renounce the vengeance for which he had lived for so many years? Renounce it, and for what? Neither hope nor ambition remained, and here in this ruined and forsaken house no illusions were possible. Only one thing could redeem his life from utter futility and failure, yet now, when his every thought should be of vengeance, the persistent voice of conscience mocked at his resolve.

He picked up the candle again and went out into the hall. There was one way, perhaps, to silence conscience and restore the grim purpose with which he had set out from London. From a corner of the huge fireplace he prised up a stone, and took a key from the hollow beneath. With this in one hand, and the candle in the other, he went past the stairs to another door, and fitted the key into the lock. Both were rusty from long disuse, and he was obliged to set down the candle and exert all his strength before the key would turn, but turn it did at last with a rasping sound.

He took up the candle and stood for a full minute, staring at that door which he himself had locked on a long-past, tragic night, for even now he was half minded to turn back and fight his battle out elsewhere, rather than pass through it again. Too many hideous memories lay behind it, too many ghosts out of the past were waiting for him there. He started to turn away, and then with sudden impatience at his own reluctance swung round again and flung wide the door. Another instant of hesitation, and then, drawing a deep breath, he stepped resolutely forward into the room which no mortal foot had trodden for fourteen years.

VII

A Debt of Dishonour

THE storm which had been threatening all day was now muttering darkly among the hills, and from the tavern window young Dominic Fane watched the lowering skies with eyes as stormy as they. The ominous weather exactly suited his mood, which was a curious blend of pain and humiliation and burning resentment, the latter centered wholly upon Harriet, his step-mother. He would like to take Harriet's smooth, white throat between his hands and choke the life out of her.

Dominic was eighteen, and he was in love. The lady in question was Alice Barlow, who had been the madcap playfellow of his childhood, but who was now, at seventeen, a plump and lovely creature with the fairest of curls, the bluest of eyes, and the sweetest smile in the whole West Country. So Dominic extravagantly declared, disregarding the fact that as he had never travelled farther than Taunton he was scarcely in a position to speak with authority.

Alice, however, was quite ready to believe it. She liked to receive fulsome compliments from Dominic, just as she liked to receive them from that other playfellow, John Mannering, while their open rivalry for her favours afforded her unalloyed pleasure. She had no doubt that she would marry one of them in the end, though which she preferred she could not be sure, quiet, imperturbable John, or dark, unpredictable Dominic, with his sardonic smile, and the gold-brown eyes that were so strangely compelling beneath his black brows. So she divided her favours impartially between them, and waited placidly for her father to make the choice for her.

Mr. Barlow regarded his daughter's suitors from a more practical point of view, and his choice had finally fallen upon

John. The news of Alice's betrothal had reached Dominic earlier on this sultry summer day, and his first reaction was disbelief, followed almost at once by blazing anger. Heedless of the enormity of his conduct, aware only that Alice was lost to him, he had ridden straight to her home, and, barely curbing his temper, demanded of her father the reason for his decision.

It was an unheard-of thing to do, in an age when young people were expected to accord their elders unquestioning obedience, but Mr. Barlow was a kindly man, and restrained his natural indignation in order to explain. He must, he said, consider his daughter's future. The Mannerings were careful folk; they husbanded their gold, and John would have a snug inheritance when his father died; there was no senseless extravagance in the Mannering household, no foolish aping of London ways. Finally, said Mr. Barlow, John's father had sought the marriage; Dominic's had not.

Dominic had listened with growing bitterness, and then thanked his host and bidden him farewell. He did not blame Mr. Barlow, for he knew only too well where the real mischief lay. Those shafts about extravagance and John's inheritance had gone home. It was Harriet, of course; Harriet who was squandering the Fane fortune on every costly whim that entered her head. Harriet who had dissuaded her husband from seeking Alice Barlow's hand for his son.

He had not returned immediately to his home, for out of the hell of anger and misery within him was growing the conviction that today a vital decision had been thrust upon him. Matters could not go on as they were; before he encountered Harriet again he must resolve upon a course of action.

A mile or so from the gates of Mr. Barlow's house there stood this small hedge-tavern, a rough place which Dominic had never before entered, though he knew it well enough by sight. Today, instead of riding past, he had dismounted at its door and stepped into the low-pitched, dirty tap-room. Flinging himself down on a bench by the window, he called for brandy, and when it had been set before him, sat brooding darkly upon the troubles which had beset him since his mother's death three years before.

For her sake he could not regret her passing, for it had been a release from years of ill-health and months of actual suffering, but it had left him solitary indeed. They had been everything to each other, those two, for life had not dealt kindly with Isobel Fane. Married against her will at the age

of fifteen to a childless widower already approaching middle-
age, she had never succeeded in conquering her fear of her
husband, and the only happiness she knew in her married life
came to her through her son. Dominic had never feared his
father—there was, perhaps, too much of the father's spirit in
him for that—but neither had he loved him. Geoffrey Fane
was a hard, selfish, obstinate man, with a temper which made
him the terror of his household, and more enemies than
friends in the surrounding countryside. He neither sought af-
fection, nor, save in one instance, did he give it.

When Isobel died, and was laid to rest in the little
graveyard by Shere church, her husband accorded her
memory all the outward observances of mourning for just
one year. It was a year during which his visits to Taunton became more and more frequent, but Dominic, still grieving
bitterly for his mother, thought nothing of this until the day
when he returned from one such visit with a bride on his
arm.

The third Mrs. Fane was a dark young woman of opulent
beauty, in age nearer by far to her stepson than to her husband. Geoffrey Fane had made his first marriage to augment
his fortune, and the second to provide the heir he lacked, but
he had taken a third wife because he was infatuated with her,
and in his eyes she could do no wrong. Whatever Harriet
wanted she must have, whether it were silks and jewels to
deck her lovely body, fine new furniture for the house, or a
new coach in which to drive abroad, with a team of horses to
draw it, and showy liveries for the servants.

Dominic had watched with increasing bitterness this prodi-
gal spending of his patrimony. He would have resented any
woman who took his mother's place, but it was not long before resentment turned to hatred, for Harriet's rich beauty
concealed a spiteful and greedy nature and she returned her
stepson's dislike in full measure. At every opportunity she
stirred up trouble between him and his father, until a relationship which had never been cordial was strained to breaking point.

Dominic was in little doubt of the motive behind this constant trouble-making, for he was the heir, who must inevitably take precedence over any child that she might bear. It
must be galling for her, he thought with grim satisfaction, to
have sold herself in marriage to a man old enough to be her
father, and still to find such an obstacle as himself in the way
of her ambition. If she could provoke a quarrel so violent

that he was disinherited she would be well pleased. Therefore he went warily, and curbed the hot temper he had inherited from his sire, so that even now, after two years of discord, there was still no serious rift between them.

Until today, he thought furiously as he stared out at the gathering storm. Now, by God! there would be a rift indeed, and that of his own making. He would not spend another night under the roof which sheltered that treacherous vixen. It was months now since he had broached the subject of his marriage to his father, and tentatively suggested Alice Barlow as a likely bride. Mr. Fane had been willing enough at first, for the Barlows were prosperous and Alice would bring with her a comfortable dowry; but Harriet had intervened, raising first one objection and then another, until now Alice was promised to John Mannering, and she could rest easy once more. It would not suit Harriet Fane to see her stepson with a wife and family.

Well, if it were Harriet's wish to be rid of him, he would grant it, and much good might her triumph bring her. With or without his father's consent, he would leave his home this very day, and if to do so cost him his inheritance, as well it might, then he would make his own way in the world. He was young and strong; he had a good horse and a sword and a litle money of his own; best of all, he had a friend upon whose help and guidance he could rely, a friend who knew the great world and could introduce him to people whose influence would be of most use to a young man eager to rise by his own merits. With all his heart, on that dark day which was to grow darker yet, Dominic Fane gave thanks for the friendship of Lawrence Templecombe.

It was a friendship which had come as something of a surprise to him. The Templecombes of Shere were the great folk of the village, and Sir Lawrence, who was eight years older than Dominic and had succeeded to the baronetcy at the age of ten, had spent most of his adult life in London. Some five months earlier, however, he had returned to Somerset, and almost immediately had singled out Dominic Fane and honoured him with his friendship.

Dominic was naturally flattered. It was very pleasant to be the chosen intimate of a man so much older and more experienced than himself, to visit him at his great house, Shere Place, and to entertain him at his own more humble home. Sir Lawrence was often to be found at the house in the wood, nor was it unusual for his resplendent figure to be seen riding beside Mrs. Fane's coach when she drove abroad, though upon these latter occasions Dominic generally found some excuse to withdraw.

In spite of his stepmother's intrusions upon it, however, he had revelled in his friendship with Sir Lawrence, and had even boasted of it a little to the Barlows and the Mannerings, though now he wondered whether that had been altogether wise. To be accepted by the Templecombes was to be the envy of the entire neighbourhood, but Mr. Barlow might perhaps have supposed that Dominic had been infected with Harriet's grandiose ideas.

Now the time had come to put Sir Lawrence's friendship to the test, but Dominic had no fear that it would fail him. He tossed off the rest of the brandy in his glass, and despondency gave way for a few minutes to roseate visions of the future. He saw himself, five—ten years hence, returning triumphantly to Shere, rich and successful, a man accustomed to moving in the great world, upon equal terms with the high-born and the famous. Then, perhaps, Mr. Barlow might repent of his hastiness, and his daughter regretfully compare her life as it was with what it might have been—for in this pleasant fantasy Dominic had overlooked the fact that had his suit been successful he would not now be setting out to seek his fortune.

The comforting vision was still before his eyes as he left the tavern and set out for his home, but it evaporated swiftly and he relapsed into the dark mood which had preceded it, a mood made doubly dangerous now by the brandy he had taken. He was by no means drunk, but he had taken enough to make him reckless, and to loosen the hold he generally kept upon his temper.

He rode into the village of Shere under a sultry pall of cloud, entering the street by way of the lane skirting the churchyard. It was in his mind to seek Sir Lawrence at once, and he had actually turned in the direction of Shere Place before he remembered that Templecombe was expected at his own home that day, and was probably already there.

He turned his horse and rode back along the village street. In the doorway of the inn the landlord was standing, gazing reflectively up at the storm clouds which grew momentarily darker. He lowered his eyes at the sound of hoofbeats, and touched his forelock as the rider reached him. Dominic drew rein.

"Has Sir Lawrence passed this way?" he demanded.

"Aye, sir, that he has, more'n an hour agone," the inn-keeper responded. "Stopped here, he did, and took a glass of wine with Squire Mannering and Master John, who'd just rode in on their way to visit his honour, your father." He stopped, and glanced slyly up at Dominic, for the whole village knew of John Mannering's betrothal, just as it knew of the rivalry for Miss Barlow's hand. What he saw in the dark young face startled even his stolidity, and he changed his mind about referring to the matter. Instead he said hurriedly: "After they'd gone, one of the wenches found a letter on the parlour floor. Sir Lawrence must have let it fall, for it bears his name. Belike 'tis important, and I'd be grateful if you'd take charge of it, sir, and give it to Sir Lawrence when you see him."

"Give it to me, then." Dominic spoke absently, and stretched out his hand for the paper which the innkeeper had produced. He glanced idly at it as he took it, and a quick frown came. For an instant he stared at it, and then thrust it into his pocket, nodded curtly to the landlord, and rode on.

Once the village was left behind he rode more slowly, and his thoughts took a different direction, prompted by the letter he carried. Harriet had written that letter—he had recognized her sprawling, ill-formed hand at a glance—but why should she be writing to Lawrence Templecombe? Was this, perhaps, some further evidence of her spite, an attempt to cause a rift betwen him and the friend whose opinions, in spite of his youth, must always carry weight with her husband?

The Fanes' modest estate lay to the west of Shere, border-ing the Templecombe lands. In fact, it did more than border them; it cut like a wedge into the larger estate and was com-posed in part of some of the best and most fertile land in that part of the county. Gradually, through several generations, the Templecombes had extended their property, here by pur-chase, there by marriage, until theirs was the largest estate for some miles around, but though they had often cast covetous eyes upon that fertile tract of land, the Fanes had clung stubbornly to their ancestral acres, resisting all attempts to dislodge them. Geoffrey Fane had often been heard to say that had his only child been a daughter, Sir Henry Tem-plecombe, Lawrence's father, would have come seeking her hand for his son before she was out of her cradle, so anxious was he to round off his estate by the addition of those same acres.

That part of the property which Sir Henry had eyed so avidly lay to the south of the road Dominic was now following, and the rest, consisting of two or three indifferent fields and the large stretch of woodland in which the old house stood, to the north. No one knew what had prompted the builders of the house to hack their site out of the woods instead of choosing one amid the pleasant meadows further south, unless it were a desire for privacy. The house itself stood only a few hundred yards from the road, but so thick was the belt of woodland between that not even its chimneys were visible, and nothing but the stone-pillared gateway betrayed its presence, while around and beyond it stretched .the thick-growing trees and dense undergrowth, isolating it from all its neighbours.

By the time Dominic reached the gates he had reined in to a walking pace, heedless of the fact that the storm was now very close. A brilliant flash of lightning set his horses stamping and snorting in alarm, and he quietened it while his thoughts still centred upon the letter. When the thunder-clap had rolled overhead, and he had passed through the gateway into the green tunnel of the drive, he drew the paper from his pocket and turned it over in his hand.

The seal was broken, of course; would the innkeeper have looked within? Unlikely, that! He would not venture to read Sir Lawrence's letter, even if he had sufficient learning to do more than spell out a name. For a minute or two longer Dominic fought temptation, while the first drops of rain began to patter on the leaves about him, and then with sudden resolution he unfolded the paper and bent his head to decipher its scrawled contents.

Five minutes later he was still sitting there, the letter crushed in his hand and his spirit shaken to its very depths with fury and humiliation. So that was the truth at last! That the friendship of which he had been so proud, for which he had so recently given thanks. Not liking for him, not kindness even, but a mere cloak for a sordid intrigue with Harriet. How they must have laughed at him, those two, at the raw country boy who imagined that he could command the friendship of a courtier. He bowed his head and clenched his hand on the pommel of the saddle while his spirit writhed in an agony of shame, and the thunder rolled over head like the mockery of heaven itself.

Suddenly he lifted his head as a new thought came, and the hand which still held the letter moved until it touched the hilt of his sword. There was one thing in which the country lad could match the town gallant. Geoffrey Fane had been a noted swordsman until age and increasing girth robbed him of his skill, and all he knew of the art he had taught his son. It was perhaps the one thing they had in common, that pride and delight in the excellence of their swordsmanship.

Dominic thrust the letter into his pocket again and urged his nervous horse forward through the lashing rain. He had but one thought now—to avenge this double betrayal of his trust and his family's honour, and to disclose to his father the true worth of the fair young wife he idolized. He laughed mirthlessly, thinking of the reckoning Harriet would have to face with the husband she had betrayed, whose temper had never yet been unleashed against her, and of the dismay with which Sir Lawrence, who detested violence, would no doubt received the challenge which Dominic would presently fling at him.

He rode straight to the stables, left his horse in the care of a groom, and entered the house by a side door. When he reached the hall he met the housekeeper, Mary Parr, and asked her abruptly where the company was assembled.

Mary, who had been his mother's attendant and close friend, studied him with some misgiving. His face was very pale, the lips grimly set, the tawny eyes so brilliant with anger that it seemed as though a flame had been kindled behind them. She knew him well enough to read a warning of danger in his expression, and returned an evasive answer, but next moment his hand closed on her arm in a grip so violent that she winced. "Where are they?" he repeated tensely. "By God! will you trifle with me? Where, I say?"

"In the parlour yonder," she replied reluctantly, "but do not you go in while this mood is on you. No good ever came of making trouble."

Dominic let her go, and looked past her towards the parlour door. His lips twisted with a mirthless mockery which made him appear suddenly much older than his eighteen years.

"No good at all, Mary," he agreed on a sneering note, "but this trouble is not of my making. I go merely to set it to rights."

He strode away from her to open the door, and paused on the threshold to take stock of the scene beyond. Harriet, elaborately gowned, jewelled and painted as though for a ball, was sitting in a high-backed chair near the empty hearth; Sir Lawrence was standing beside her, while Geoffrey

Fane and the two Mannerings were grouped by the table on which wine and glasses were set out. A portrait of the lady, lately completed, was propped against the wall nearby, and a branch of candles burned beside it on the carved chest on which it stood, to illuminate it and to dispel the gloom which the storm had induced in that low-pitched chamber.

Apparently the portrait was the subject of their conversation, for as he opened the door, Dominic heard Squire Mannering remark upon the excellence of the likeness, and then came Sir Lawrence's voice, its precise accents in marked contrast to the previous speaker's jovial tones.

"I cannot agree with you, Mr. Mannering, stap me if I can! Oh, the features and colouring are adequately portrayed, I grant you, but where is that charm, that grace, which so delights us? How, in short, can mere paint and canvas compare with the living, breathing beauty which we are privileged to know?"

Dominic's sardonic laugh echoed the words, drawing their attention to him as he came farther into the room, tossing his whip and gloves on to the table. His gaze was upon Harriet and Sir Lawrence; the blaze of scorn and anger in his eyes belied the jeering smile lingering upon his lips.

"And you are more privileged than most in that respect, Templecombe, are you not?" he sneered. "But you are greatly daring so to praise your mistress's beauty in the presence of her husband."

There was a moment of horrified silence, and then a tremendous clap of thunder came simultaneously with the explosion of his father's wrath. With an inarticulate exclamation of rage, Geoffrey Fane snatched up the whip which Dominic had cast aside and struck savagely at his son. The whip was a heavy one, with the full force of a powerful arm behind it, and the lash laid open the boy's face from cheekbone to chin. As the thunder died away in long, rolling echoes, Fane spoke in a voice thick and choking with anger.

"Get out of my house, you foul-mouthed, drunken lout! Out, I say, or by God! I will flog you from the door myself."

Dominic had started back with a cry of pain, clapping a hand to his face. Now, with the blood running between his fingers, he dragged out the letter with his free hand and dropped it on to the table.

"Read that, sir, and then call me a liar if you dare," he said bitterly. "Sir Lawrence should have had more care of his love-notes if he wished to keep secret his amorous dealings with your wife."

Harriet uttered a little, whimpering sound of terror and dismay, and it was that which checked her husband's hand in the act of sweeping the paper aside. After a piercing glance in her direction, he took it up and began to read, while she sat wide-eyed and trembling, the very picture of guilt, and Sir Lawrence stood frozen and pallid beside her.

Fane came to the end of the letter and let it fall fluttering to the floor as he raised his eyes. His face was dark and congested with anger, his head sunk a little between his powerful shoulders like that of an animal about to charge, and his mouth worked with uncontrollable fury.

"So!" he said between his teeth, in a voice of ominous quietness. "You have been false to me, have you, with that coxcomb there? You shall both learn that I am not lightly betrayed." His hand closed on the hilt of his sword, and wrenched it from its sheath; his eyes turned towards Templecombe. "Draw, you puppy! Draw, I say!"

Mr. Mannering tried to intervene, and was brushed aside. Fane bore relentlessly down upon Sir Lawrence, who was forced to draw his own weapon to protect his life, and next moment a mortal combat was taking place under conditions which could scarcely have been worse. The room was cumbered with heavy furniture, the single branch of candles barely dispelled the darkness of the storm, and both men were booted and fully clad. John Mannering dragged Harriet from her chair and thrust her into a corner where she would be sheltered from the flashing blades; his father had drawn his own sword and was waiting for a chance to separate the fighters; Dominic, aghast at the fury he had unleashed, leaned against the wall with a reddened handkerchief pressed to his bruised and bleeding cheek. This turn of events he had neither expected nor intended, but, dazed and half blinded by the pain of his injury, he could only wait helplessly for whatever might befall.

Anger, it seemed, had restored to Geoffrey Fane all his former skill, and only youth and agility had saved Templecombe so far. He was hopelessly outmatched, and even though Fane was gasping for breath, and the sweat was rolling in great drops down his face, it was clear that the duel could have but one ending. Even Harriet must have realized this, for suddenly, crying Templecombe's name, she started forward before John could restrain her and flung herself between them. What followed happened so swiftly that in the uncertain light not one of the three watchers could be sure just how it befell, for there was a flurry of movement, a sudden piercing scream, and Harriet sank to her knees and so to the floor, while her husband started back with a reddened sword in his hand.

For a few moments the five men stood petrified with horror, and then Mr. Mannering snatched up the candles and dropped to his knees beside her. She had rolled over on to her back, but now lay still, with a red stain on her silken bodice and her wide eyes seeming to hold still a look of incredulous terror. The candles shook in Mannering's grasp, and some drops of molten wax dropped down upon the white breast where life had been so hideously stilled, as he stretched out a trembling hand to close those dreadful eyes.

Geoffrey Fane's sword clattered to the floor, and a choking sound that was hardly human issued from his throat. One hand lifted to clutch at his cravat, the other clawed impotently at the air as he stood swaying, staring down at the body of his wife. Dominic and John between them were just in time to catch him as he fell.

Later, much later, Dominic stood alone in that room from which, hours earlier, had been carried the body of Harriet Fane, and the living corpse which was her husband. The horror of what had happened brooded over the whole house, and was concentrated here where the tragedy had been enacted. No attempt had as yet been made to set the room in order; the stained sword lay where it had fallen; the letter which had betrayed her had drifted under Harriet's chair. The wine still stood upon the table, and on the floor a shattered glass lay in the midst of a sticky pool. The painted eyes of the portrait stared blandly across the room where so recently the eyes of the woman it portrayed had glazed in death.

Dominic shuddered, and covered his own eyes with his hand. What exactly had happened in those brief seconds when Harriet flung herself between her husband and her lover? That thrust, so swift and sure to the heart, had it been meant for Templecombe, or had they seen deliberate murder done? Both John Mannering and his father declared Harriet's death to be accidental, but he had seen doubt in their eyes, doubt which was echoed horribly in his own mind, and which he knew would never be resolved.

Geoffrey Fane had lain for a long time unconscious, and when he eventually came to his senses they realized that this had been no ordinary swoon. He lay helpless, the whole right side of his body powerless and inert, and his face twisted awry, yet when at last he spoke, the first word to issue indistinctly from his distorted mouth was "Vengeance," followed by the name of the man who had wronged him.

For Lawrence Templecombe had made good his escape. In the confusion following Harriet's death and the collapse of her husband he had slipped quietly out of the house, fetched his horse from the stables and ridden away. By the time that Fane was mumbling his demand for vengeance, Templecombe must have been safe at Shere Place.

Safe, but for the present only. Dominic raised his head and straightened his shoulders at the thought. He, too, had something to avenge, and this time there would be no hysterical woman to shield Sir Lawrence with her own body and give her life for his. He looked again about the disordered room, and in a passion of fury and despair swore that the debt of dishonour should one day be paid in full. Today, between them, Harriet and Sir Lawrence had destroyed both his hope and his ambition, and henceforth he would live for vengeance alone. Come it soon or late, the day of reckoning would dawn at last.

On a sudden impulse he crossed to the window and closed and barred the heavy shutters. This room could never be aught but a chamber of death, and so it should remain until his vow had been fulfilled, its locked door and shuttered windows the symbol of a debt unpaid.

But that was for the future. He was too weary now, too sick at heart, to find more than a momentary consolation in the prospect of revenge. The tale of this day's happenings would spread through the countryside like fire in stubble, and lose nothing in the telling, for there were enemies in plenty to say outright what the Mannerings had out of pity left unsaid. So much would have to be faced, and faced alone.

He took up the candle and went out, locking the door behind him. Withdrawing the key, he stood with it in his hand, looking wearily about him in search of a safe hiding place for it. The great, square fireplace caught his eye. He went to it, and from its furthermost corner prised up a stone, and laid the key beneath, and covered it again. There let it lie, hidden and forgotten, leaving the room it kept to darkness and to silence.

VIII

"Remember Me!"

Now, at last, the darkness was dispelled, and the silence of years broken by a footfall on the dusty floor. Dominic stood in the middle of the room, holding his candle aloft in a steady hand, while his gaze passed over the desolate scene and his thoughts went back to the night when he had last looked upon it.

The tale of disaster had not ended with the locking of a door, for at that time the final, bitter blow was yet to fall. With his father stricken and helpless, the management of affairs passed into Dominic's hands, and only then did he realize the magnitude of the havoc Harriet had wrought. Geoffrey Fane was in debt on every hand, and when the news of his collapse became known, his creditors came flocking like ghouls about a corpse, demanding payment. The rest followed as inevitably as Time itself, and those broad, fertile acres south of the winding road passed at last from the keeping of the Fanes.

There was, of course, only one possible purchaser. Sir Lawrence was away—he had departed from Somerset on the day after Harriet's death, and no one, it seemed, knew whither he had gone—but through his grandmother, that autocratic old lady who had ruled Shere Place for as long as most people could remember, he had seized the opportunity so long desired. The Templecombes acquired the land they had coveted for so many years, and Dominic Fane was left to make what he could of his diminished patrimony.

He had since tried to forget the four heartbreaking years that followed, years in which he toiled like a labourer to wrest a living from the few wretched acres left to him. Had he been free to choose, he would have sold the whole estate and set out in pursuit of Templecombe and vengeance, but somehow a roof had to be kept over his father's head. There was no money to hire servants, nor would any have stayed now in that ill-omened house, but Mary Parr remained with

Dominic for his mother's sake. She tended the old man and contrived what comfort she could for his son, and watched with helpless pity as the latter changed from resentful boy to embittered man.

Geoffrey Fane's thoughts ran constantly upon the vengeance that was still to seek, but if his son's did likewise he kept them secret, knowing that he must bide his time. What chance had he while his father lived of calling Templecombe to book?

That the man feared him he knew, and found grim pleasure in the knowledge. For many months after the tragedy, Sir Lawrence had stayed away from Shere, and when at length he plucked up courage to return, he asserted often and with great emphasis that he had no quarrel with Dominic Fane. When news of these frequent protestations reached him, Dominic laughed with bitter comprehension, and looked forward impatiently to the day when Templecombe should learn that words alone could not protect him.

Though he had deliberately cut himself off from all contact with the few people who would have stood by him in this extremity, he knew that the sympathy of most was with Sir Lawrence. There were few bold enough to oppose the Templecombes, and, moreover, Harriet Fane had known how to make herself popular in a way which her husband and stepson had never learned. Now she figured in the minds of most as a victim of jealous persecution, for who, knowing Geoffrey Fane, could blame her for seeking happiness elsewhere? To be sure, she had sinned, but had not his sin been the greater when he struck her dead? Though the law had made no move in the matter, very few people believed that her death had been accidental, many offering as proof of Fane's guilt the fact that the power of movement had instantly been taken from the arm which struck the fatal blow. It was a judgment, they said, from a higher Power than man.

As death approached, Geoffrey Fane's lust for vengeance became an obsession. Rebellion against his own helplessness, and the desire to know that the dishonour put upon him had been avenged, inspired him to a kind of frenzy, and he alternately implored his son to demand of Templecombe the satisfaction which he himself had been denied, and cursed him because the man still lived. To the very last there was room in his mind for no other thought, and he raved like a madman until Mary Parr fled in horror from so dreadful a deathbed, and Dominic, stony-faced and implacable, knelt beside the dying man and swore again the oath of vengeance now four years old.

When at last the hideous vigil was over he went to his room and took his sword from the chest where it had lain for years. It was a fine weapon, with a blade of Toledo steel and a silver hilt, and as he balanced it in his hand something of the old exultation stirred in him, but his face was very grim as he sheathed it again and fastened it at his side. Sir Lawrence was at Shere Place, he knew, and now, with his father's passing, the moment so patiently awaited had come at last.

He came down to the kitchen where Mary crouched beside the fire, and one look at his face told her the errand upon which he was bound. She started up and caught him by the arms and tried to detain him, but he put her aside and went past her, out to the stables which were empty now, save for the stout old cob he used for his farming.

Stares and whispers marked his progress through the village, for he was rarely seen abroad, but though children tittered to see his threadbare clothes and the slow old horse he rode, their elders exchanged dubious, questioning glances as they observed the grimness of his dark, scarred face, and the sword at his side.

He came up to the door of Shere Place in the clear light of a fine spring evening, and told the disdainful lackeys that he had business with their master. They would not admit him, but one of them withdrew, the others remaining like statues at their posts, only their eyes moving to follow this shabby, sinister caller as he paced impatiently to and fro.

At last the sound of footsteps within the house brought him to a halt, but it was not Sir Lawrence who appeared at the head of the steps leading to the great door. Instead there came into the doorway the small but formidable figure of the old Lady Templecombe, his grandmother, a bent and witch-like figure in the heavy black widow's weeds she had worn for forty years. She stood leaning on her stick, looking down haughtily at the shabby young man confronting her.

Dominic returned the look, frowning. Then he uncovered and bowed abruptly. "I am seeking Sir Lawrence, my lady," he said curtly.

"He is not here."

"No?" Words, look and tone expressed his disbelief. "Then with your ladyship's permission, I will await his return."

The Dowager's faded eyes surveyed him coldly.

"I can guess the nature of your business with my grandson, Mr. Fane," she replied, "but he has no quarrel with you. If, however, you come here again with your impertinent demands, you will meet with the punishment such effrontery deserves." She paused, and looked meaningly at the stalwart lackeys. "Now go, while you may. My servants know their duty."

Dominic stiffened; a dark flush stained his lean face, and his eyes blazed under their black brows. At that moment his hatred was so intense that he would willingly have slain Sir Lawrence in cold blood and burned Shere Place about this old harridan's ears, but he knew that her ladyship did not threaten idly. He choked back his rage and humiliation, and with an effort steadied his voice sufficiently to reply.

"Your years and your sex protect you, my lady, and since your grandson chooses to cower behind your skirts, I will go now, but tell him this. For four years duty has bound my hands, but now that duty is done, and I am free to settle my score with him. For settle it I will, madam, no matter how long I have to wait, or how far I have to travel to do it."

The mortification of that defeat had been yet one more count added to the score against Templecombe, and even now the memory of it still had the power to anger him. He could feel anger stirring within him now as he came back to the present, and saw the lightning flicker beyond the cracks of the shutters, and heard somewhere in the woods outside the crash of a stricken tree. The defiance he had flung at the old woman had been a prophecy amply fulfilled, for the pursuit of vengeance had taken him far indeed.

He had learned next day that Sir Lawrence had in fact been in the house at the time of his visit, but he had departed in the first light of the following dawn—for London, so it was said. Thither Dominic had pursued him, as soon as his father was buried and Mary Parr installed in a cottage on the outskirts of the village.

He took with him his sword and very little else, for his hopes of selling the rest of the estate had not been fulfilled. The fields had gone, for less than their real, poor price, but the house and its surrounding woods no one would buy. Odd stories had grown up around that house during the past four years. It was said that whenever there was a storm, the clash of swords and the sound of a woman's scream could be heard behind the locked door of the room where Harriet

Fane had died; that her unquiet spirit walked the woods, crying out for justice upon her murderer; these and a host of other eerie tales born of superstition and fear made gentle and simple alike avoid it like a place accursed, and so Dominic Fane had barred its doors and gone his way, leaving the house in the wood to rot in solitude.

He did not find Templecombe in London. Sir Lawrence, warned of his coming, had crossed to France, and when Dominic trailed him as far as Paris, hurried on into the Low Countries. With the great resources at his command it was easy for him to evade the enemy clinging doggedly to his trail, but Dominic had no such resources, and at length sheer necessity forced him to abandon the quest. Close upon ten years had passed before he was able to take it up again.

Now he stood once more in the chill silence of this room which he had dedicated as a shrine to vengeance, and thought of the decision which must be made tonight. To take that vengeance, which was now within his reach, and in taking it to ruin irretrievably the woman who trusted him, or to renounce it for her sake.

He set down the candle, and went to the portrait which still leaned against the wall, and brushed away the dust that coated it. Harriet's dark beauty stared back at him, the heavy-lidded eyes which had so often turned their bright malice upon him, the full, curved lips which had whispered honeyed spite against him in his father's ear. He looked on it without emotion. She was dead, and whatever hatred he had felt against her was dead likewise, long since.

It was Templecombe alone whom he hated now, now as never before, with a savage intensity of emotion which must soon be satisfied if he were to retain his sanity. What ailed him, then, that he hesitated within reach of the goal sought for so many years, letting sentiment and conscience turn him from his purpose? Here in this ruined house which symbolized the ruin of his life, what place had thoughts of mercy or of honour?

He turned, and then stood petrified as a woman's scream rang out piercingly above the clamour of the storm. For one unreasoning instant he recalled the ghostly tales of this house, and felt the sweat start on his brow. Then he realized that it had come from beyond the room in which he stood, and that it was his name which had been cried, but even so the shock of it held him silent and motionless as stumbling footsteps sounded in the hall, and Verity appeared in the open doorway.

For a moment she paused there, pale as death, her wide eyes dark with lingering terror, and then there came a clap of thunder louder than all the rest, a tremendous sound which seemed to shake the old house to its very foundations. The candle-flame flickered wildly in some errant draught, and with a broken cry she flung herself forward, clinging to him in wild, unreasoning panic, hiding her face against his breast.

Instinctively, without conscious thought, he gathered her into his arms, and knew, in an instant of merciless revelation, the truth that could no longer be denied. The past was as dead as his desire to avenge it; it was for the future that he hated Lawrence Templecombe so fiercely, the future in which Verity Halland would be his wife. As the appalling implications of that discovery burst upon him, a stifled groan broke from his lips, and he buried his face against the girl's tumbled hair.

The last echoes of the thunder faded overhead, leaving a silence broken only by the hiss and trickle of the rain. Verity drew a deep, shuddering breath and lifted her head.

"I was so frightened," she whispered. "When I came to myself all was dark, and the air about me was like that of a tomb. I thought . . ." the words faltered and died, and she stood looking up into his face, faint colour rising delicately in her own, as though she, too, had made some discovery in which she could not yet quite believe.

A rapt stillness enfolded the room, a stillness which, holding wonder and anguish, yet held danger also. He felt it, and forced himself to let her go, and turned away from her. His tortured glance fell upon the portrait, and it seemed that the pictured face smiled on him now with a deeper mockery, taunting him with the thought of a vow forsworn.

Verity stood motionless, her hands clasped at her breast, and watched him with troubled, bewildered eyes. After a moment her gaze followed his to the painting, and then she looked slowly about her, observing for the first time the sinister disorder of this long-forsaken room, the scattered glasses, the fragments of one of them upon the floor, and almost at her feet, a naked sword, its blade brownish-red with rust—or was it rust alone?

She shivered, conscious once more of the dank chill of this shuttered house after the sultry heat of the woods; its very atmosphere seemed redolent of death and decay. Almost reluctantly her gaze came back to the portrait, and she wondered with sudden urgency who this woman could be whose likeness stared across an empty room, abandoned how long since? There was a small panel set in the picture's heavy frame; she bent quickly forward and brushed away the dust which coated it, revealing its inscription beneath: 'Mrs. Harriet Fane, 1684.'

For an instant she stared incredulously at it, and then swung round to face the silent man beside her. He had made no move to prevent her action, and she saw that his face was set and brooding, his eyes still staring at the portrait, but blindly now, as though he saw something other than the pictured face.

Verity clasped her hands together again, locking the fingers tightly to still their trembling. Some compulsion seemed to be driving her, so that for good or ill she had to know the secret this room held. She said in a stifled voice: "Dominic, what house is this?"

His gaze shifted from the portrait to her face, and his eyes were the eyes of a man in torment.

"It is the house where I was born," he replied with bitter mockery. "My home, Verity. I bid you welcome to it."

His tone stirred a chord of compassion within her which longed to comfort him but could find no expression in words. His home! A crumbling and forsaken house in a silent wood, a house that smelt of death. "And she?" she asked timidly after a pause, and waited with strange anxiety for his answer.

"She was my stepmother," Dominic said slowly. "She died—violently—in this room, fourteen years ago."

Violently? Verity's glance turned involuntarily to the rusty sword at her feet, and horror rushed upon her. Was this his secret, this the ghost that haunted him? "By whose hand?" she asked faintly. "Not by yours, Dominic? Oh, dear God! not that?"

He shook his head, his face still shadowed by the memories this place evoked.

"No," he said sombrely, "by my father's. She had taken a lover, a man we thought our friend. I discovered it, and because I hated her I betrayed them, in their presence, to my father. He forced the man to fight, and would have killed him had not Harriet flung herself between." He paused, passing a hand across his eyes. "I locked this room that same night, and until today no one has entered it since."

Verity shuddered and drew closer to him, wondering why

he had chosen to enter it now. Better, surely, to leave this chamber of death to its grim memories, barred and shuttered from the sight of man. She recalled the solitude of the woods through which they had come, and had the uneasy fancy that they had left the world behind them and entered some ghostly realm peopled only by the dead. When she spoke again it was in a hushed whisper, scarcely above her breath. "What of the man—her lover?"

For a moment she thought that he was not going to reply, and then he said briefly: "He escaped. When my father died, four years later, I sought to avenge the dishonour put upon us, but he evaded me, then, and now————" He broke off, and then added more slowly, "Now I know that he is beyond my reach."

The words fell clearly into the cold silence, and he heard them as though they were uttered by some other voice than his own. With a curious detachment he reflected that it was fitting they should be spoken here, the vow of vengeance renounced in the place where it had first been made, for though his hatred of Templecombe burned with undiminished fire, the man must go scatheless since to harm him would be to harm Verity herself.

She asked in a puzzled voice: "Do you mean that he is dead?"

As though he had not heard the question he turned away, picking up the candle and crossing to the door, and she had no choice but to follow him out of the room. He shut the door behind them, but when he sought to lock it again, the key refused to turn. After one or two attempts he let it be, and led the girl back to the room to which he had first taken her.

The storm was passing now; the thunder sounded more distantly and the hiss of the rain had ceased, but within the house the dank and mouldering air still hung cold as death. Verity shivered again, and Dominic picked up her cloak from the floor and put it about her shoulders. "The storm is almost over," he said gently. "Soon we shall be able to go on our way."

"Yes!" Her voice was scarcely more than a whisper. "But our journey is almost done, is it not? How far, Dominic? How much further shall we travel together?"

"Shere Place is only a mile or two from here, on the other side of the village," he answered slowly, but he knew that their ways must part before ever they reached Sir Lawrence

Templecombe's house. Yet how to convince her of that, without disclosing the whole truth?

He led her to the settle by the hearth and made her sit down there, standing beside her with one hand resting upon the seat's high back.

"Verity," he said quietly, "last night you told me that you had learned to trust me. Is that trust great enough for you to obey me, without argument and without question, even though what I ask may seem strange to you?"

Her grave, grey eyes were intent upon his face; she said softly:

"What would you have me do?"

"Let Barnabas Pike take you to Shere Place in my stead," he replied in a low voice. "Tell Templecombe that you were abducted by Nat Trumper, but escaped from him and found shelter with the players, who, learning your story, brought you safely to Shere. Forget my part in this. Forget that you ever knew of my existence." He paused, but she made no answer, only watched him with those wide, questioning eyes. He sat down beside her, and laid a hand over hers. "I told you just now what once happened in this house. Since that time my family has not been looked upon with kindness, and there are people in Shere who would recognize me, even after an absence of ten years. For her own sake, the future lady Templecombe must know nothing of Dominic Fane."

She flung up her head at that, her cheeks flushed, her eyes hurt, now, and angry. "Do you think I care for what people may say? That I am afraid to acknowledge the debt I owe you?"

"There is no debt," he said quietly, "but if there were, then this is the payment I should ask, that you should obey me in this. Think of it in that way if you choose, but promise me that you will do as I ask."

"If only I could see my way!" Verity's voice broke. She bowed her head, and covered her eyes with her free hand. "I am so tired, and my thoughts grow unruly. I do not know what to do."

"Trust me a little longer," he urged her gently. "I know what I do, believe me. Give me the promise I ask, and abide by it, and all will be well."

There was a pause, and then slowly she raised her head and looked at him with tear-filled eyes. He forced himself to meet that searching regard with no trace of emotion, though the piteous entreaty in her face tore at his heart.

"I promise then," she whispered at last, "and may God forgive me, for I shall never forgive myself."

She leaned her head against the back of the settle and closed her eyes. The candlelight showed him her delicate profile clear against the shadows beyond, the wistful curve of the lips, the darkness of the lashes against her pale cheeks, and he watched her with tenderness and longing. Sudden misgivings seized him, and an anxiety which had in it no thought of self. She was so gallant, so true of heart, so very young. What happiness could she ever find with a man such as Templecombe? She would be bound in a loveless union to a man with whom she had not a single thought or feeling in common, and she would suffer, as he had seen his mother suffer in a similar bondage.

Unable to be still under the goad of such thoughts as these, he got up and went out into the porch. The air was cooler now, freshened by the storm, and the scent of the rain-soaked earth was like incense after the chill darkness within the house. He stood staring across the ruined garden, and tried to fasten his mind on the problem of the immediate future, but he could think only of Verity, see nothing but her face.

His whole being rebelled at the thought of abandoning her to the doubtful protection of Sir Lawrence Templecombe, with the sinister shadow of the Black Mask still falling mysteriously across her life, yet he dared not take the risk of some chance word or encounter linking her name with his own. No, he must depart from Shere as secretly as he had come; it was the only way left to him in which he might serve her. Some day, perhaps, she would learn the whole truth, and realize how much he had renounced for her sake. Some day, when she was Templecombe's wife.

His wife! Dominic bowed his head and clenched his hands as he fought the storm of anger and jealousy that thought evoked. Verity, with her high courage, her fresh and lovely innocence, the wife of a man who had been a rake and a profligate while she was still in her cradle; a man who had not the courage to face the consequences of his own sins, but cowered for protection behind an old woman's skirts. She should be matched with some boy of her own generation, as brave and true as herself, and not with an ageing libertine, or even with a ruined, penniless soldier who loved her.

He realized the futile trend of his thoughts, and recalled them with an effort. Raising his head, he saw that the clouds were breaking, and sunlight striking through them to set every leaf and twig a-sparkle, but it was the rich, golden light that heralded the evening. Time was passing while he stood dreaming here, and Verity could not pass the night in this forsaken ruin. Shelter and a woman's care were needed if her strength was not to fail her at the last; but where, in safety, could he seek it? He thought of Mary Parr. Ten years was a long time, and she might well be dead by now, or have left the village, but if he could find her he knew that he might trust her implicitly.

He went back to Verity and told her what he planned, but she raised a wan, white face towards him and shook her head.

"I fear I must rest a little before I go further, Dominic," she said. "Go you and seek Mrs. Parr, and if you find her, come back for me. If not"—she shrugged—"at least there is shelter here."

He was reluctant to leave her alone in that unfriendly place, but she was plainly exhausted, and it would be wanton cruelty to drag her with him on what might well prove to be a fool's errand. So, with a promise to return as soon as might be, he left her, and went out and along the overgrown drive towards the road.

Some twenty minutes later he crouched in the shelter of a clump of bushes and looked across a neat, small garden to the cottage which ten years earlier had sheltered Mary Parr. The door was shut, but while he was debating the risks of approaching more closely, a woman came from the other side of the building which faced the lane, and went into the house.

Dominic watched her, and a faint smile touched his lips. No mistaking that erect, angular figure in its neat, sober gown. It was Mary Parr beyond all doubt. He went swiftly and silently across the garden and rapped softly on the door. It was opened at once, but she recoiled a pace at sight of the tall, shabby figure silhouetted against the sunset and the fading storm-rack, its face in shadow. He said quietly: "Ten years may change a man, Mary Parr, but you knew me well enough once," and turned his head so that the light fell upon his face.

She uttered a faint cry and started forward, grasping his sleeve and peering into his face. He could feel her hand shaking against his arm.

"Dominic Fane!" she whispered at last. "Merciful God! Is it you in very truth?"

"In very truth, Mary," he replied with a ghost of a laugh, "but let me come in, my dear, for I wish no one to know of my return."

She drew him into the house at once and closed the door, and shuttered the window also before kindling a light. She had changed very little, he saw. Her face was more deeply lined, and hair which he remembered as iron-grey was white now, but she was the same Mary—shrewd, practical and unflurried. As swiftly as could be, he outlined the reason for his presence there and the need for secrecy, and ended by warning her that Verity must be told nothing of the past beyond what she already knew. Mary listened and, typically, showed neither surprise nor the desire to question him, saying merely when he had done: "Go fetch her here, the poor young lady. Time enough for us to talk when she is safe abed."

Dusk had fallen by the time he once more reached the house in the wood, and beneath the trees it was almost dark. Verity was sitting where he had left her, and at first he thought she was asleep, but then he saw that her eyes were open, staring into the shadows which the light of the now guttering candle could not pierce. She seemed not to have heard him approach, for she did not move, but just sat gazing into the darkness, her head resting against the back of the settle, her hands lying on the dark wood on either side of her, like a wan, quiet ghost in this house of ghosts.

She received indifferently the news of his success, went with him obediently, and waited while he once more barred the doors of the desolate house. She scarcely spoke as, avoiding the road, he led her by way of wood and meadow towards the cottage, but her feet stumbled more and more frequently, until, disregarding her protests, he picked her up and carried her the rest of the way. So the future Lady Templecombe came at last to Shere, ragged and weary, borne in the arms of the man who for years had accounted himself the bitterest enemy that Templecombe possessed.

Mary Parr was watching for them, and admitted them at once to the cottage. There in the candlelit kitchen Dominic set Verity on her feet, and she leaned against the support of his encircling arm and looked about the homely room, and at the neat figure of their hostess, now occupied in locking and barring the door. Finally her eyes were lifted to meet his, with an expression in them he could not read, and she said, too softly for Mary to overhear:

"We tread a tortuous road indeed, as you have said. You are a strange man, Dominic Fane."

Mary had turned to speak to them before he could reply, but long after Verity had followed the elder woman up the steep, dark stairs to a little bedchamber under the eaves, he sat pondering the meaning of those odd words, and the unfathomable look which had accompanied them. Some deep significance he felt certain that they held, but try as he would, he could not read the riddle.

He did not linger at the cottage, but as soon as he had eaten the food which Mary insisted on setting before him, was off again to Cloverton in search of the player troupe. He did not return until the next morning was well advanced, but he brought with him the news that Barnabas was ready and willing to play his part. He would meet them later at a prearranged place on the road between the town and Shere Place, so that anyone who saw them approaching Templecombe's house would not suspect that Miss Halland had come from the village.

Verity was up by then and sitting in the little kitchen while Mary prepared a meal. She was still pale and quiet, and had he been less preoccupied he might have sensed a certain constraint in her greeting, but all his thoughts were centred now upon the parting which was drawing so close.

They made a silent meal of it, for Mary seemed infected by the taciturnity of her guests, and it was not until they had taken leave of her and were on their way to the meeting place that Verity uttered more than the most commonplace remarks. They had walked in silence for some time, and were traversing the grass-grown track winding between high banks that he had chosen for the rendezvous with Barnabas, when she said in a low voice: "What do you mean to do now, Dominic? Where will you go?"

He shrugged, not knowing the answer to her questions. He had not as yet looked beyond their coming to Shere, for until the previous day he had expected nothing to lie beyond it save death in one guise or another. "Does that matter, so that it is away from here?" he countered at length.

"It matters to me," she replied with gentle reproach, and again fell silent for a space. Then she asked quietly, and with no change of tone, "Dominic, what is the name of the man who escaped your vengeance so long ago?"

The question took him unawares, so that he checked his steps and stood staring down at her, for the moment at a loss.

She returned his look gravely, with something of challenge in her eyes.

"That belongs to the past, and should be forgotten," he said at last. "His identity does not matter now."

"I think it does," she replied, "but there is no need for you to tell me. His name is Lawrence Templecombe."

It was not a question, but a statement, and one which he knew it would be useless to deny. He said sharply:

"Who told you so? Did Mary————"

Verity shook her head.

"She would not speak of it at all until I told her that I knew the truth. I think I began to suspect it as soon as you told me what had happened in that house fourteen years ago. Then you were so strangely insistent that no one should know of the service you had done me. When you left me alone I went back to that room, for I remembered seeing a paper—a letter, it seemed to be—lying beneath a chair. It was faded and mouldering, and mice had nibbled at its edges, but enough remained to tell me what you had withheld."

"That accursed letter!" he exclaimed bitterly. "I had forgotten it." He regarded her with troubled eyes. "I did not mean you to know."

"When I told Mrs. Parr what I had discovered," Verity went on," she realized that in mercy she could do no less than tell me the whole story. Then, at last, I understood everything."

Fear clutched at his heart, and he could find nothing to say. Verity, with that clear gaze still intent upon his face, continued quietly:

"When Sir Lawrence fled from Shere ten years ago to avoid your challenge, he excused his cowardice by insisting that he had no quarrel with you. That pretext would not have served him now, had you flaunted his promised wife before him as your paramour."

A heavy silence fell between them, during which he dared no longer meet her eyes, but stared instead upon the white plumes of meadowsweet crowning the high bank behind her. Spoken at last, the dark purpose with which he had set out from London, and cherished through all the weary weeks of the journey, loomed monstrously, a thing of shame and evil. This, then, was the retribution which repentance had come too late to avert, this bitter knowledge that, in discovering the truth, she had discovered also how unworthy he was of her trust and gratitude.

"Yes," he said in a low voice at last, "that, God forgive me, was my intention, from the moment you told me the name of your betrothed. It seemed then that Fate had placed in my hands the weapon I had sought for years." His gaze was still fast upon the creamy meadowsweet against the blue sky, and his lean, scarred face was very pale. "That was why I rescued you from Red Nat and brought you here, why I took you yesterday to my old home. I sought only to serve my own ends."

"Yet you are sending me with Barnabas to Shere Place, and have made me promise to forget that we ever met," Verity said softly, "Why, Dominic?"

He shrugged, still avoiding her eyes.

"Let us say that I have been granted a little wisdom at last," he replied. "What use is vengeance, after all? Can it restore my lands or my fortune, or give me back the wasted years? If it could——" He broke off, choking back the words he had no right to say. With a sudden movement he went down on his knee before her and caught her hands in his and bowed his head upon them. "Forgive me," he murmured. "Forgive me—if you can."

"Forgive you?" she repeated, with a catch in her voice. "What need have you to ask forgiveness, when you have given up the vengeance you sought for so long?" Very gently she freed one hand, and laid it on his thick, black hair. "Dominic, what if I were to say, 'Come with me to Shere Place, tell Sir Lawrence what you will, and take your vengeance. I will do nothing to hinder you.' What answer would you make?"

His head lifted quickly, and the golden eyes sought hers at last, amazed and incredulous, to read in her face the assurance that these were no idle words. For one wild moment temptation clutched at him, and then, while he hesitated, from along the lane there sounded a whistle, clear as a blackbird's call, which piped a merry tune. Distant as yet, it drew steadily nearer, with a pause every now and then as though awaiting an answer.

Dominic let go her hand and rose slowly to his feet. "Barnabas," he said in explanation. " 'Tis the signal we agreed upon."

He whistled a few bars of the same melody, and after a second or two came the tuneful reply. Dominic looked again at Verity.

"You have your answer, my dear," he said quietly. "He

will take you to Shere Place, not I. My quarrel was with Templecombe alone, and it shall never be permitted to harm you. Our ways must part here." He paused, listening to the merry whistle drawing closer, and then went on, more quickly but none the less earnestly: "You are promised to Sir Lawrence, and in marriage with him I think you will find safety from the enemy who plotted against you. Remember that, and remember, too, that whatever wrong Templecombe has done me was long ago. You have nothing to avenge."

"Remember these things, but forget Dominic Fane," she murmured. "Is that indeed what you would have me do?"

He tried to say that it was, but his courage failed him at the last. Must he renounce, with all the rest, even a place in her memory?

"No, by God!" he said in a shaken voice. "Remember me!" And, catching her in his arms, crushed her lips beneath his own.

"So shall I be avenged indeed," he added with an attempt at lightness, and let her go as Barnabas came round the bend of the lane.

IX

Templecombe of Shere

SHERE PLACE was a solid, brick-built mansion, imposing rather than beautiful, set upon a slight rise in the midst of a timbered park. From this eminence its many windows stared blandly across formal gardens, as though the house were smugly aware of its own importance and the consequence of those who dwelt within it. Verity's first thought when she saw it was that here was the perfect setting for Sir Lawrence Templecombe. He, too, was in no doubt of his own superiority.

She realized with dismay that this was no proper frame of mind in which to approach her betrothed, particularly since she came in such strange guise and with so singular a tale to tell, but the sight of her future home had roused in her a feeling of panic rather than relief. Her steps faltered, and she felt an almost overmastering impulse to turn back, yet where, if not here, could she seek a haven?

With a sense of aching desolation she lived again those last moments with Dominic, when, as plainly as a woman might, she had shown him that she was willing to tread any road with him. No impulse of the moment had prompted her words, nor any notion of gratitude or duty, but only the simple knowledge that she loved him, and that to part from him would be a kind of death. That he returned her love she was certain, but he had renounced that love when he renounced his vengeance, and neither the one nor the other would he ever seek to claim.

They reached the point where the avenue they were traversing ended at the edge of the gardens, and Barnabas paused and laid a hand on her arm. There was sympathy and comprehension in his eyes. "Do we go on, or turn back?" he asked softly. "There is still time for you to choose."

Verity sighed, and shook her head. "The choice has already been made for me, Barnabas," she said wistfully. "We go forward."

"So be it, then!" He moved his hands in an expressively helpless gesture. "Are you sure of the story we have to tell?"

She nodded, and after another moment of hesitation he led the way once more towards the house. It was no easy task to penetrate the defences of Shere Place, to win past lackeys whose reaction to shabby strangers ranged from the merely offensive through outrage to magnificent disdain, but Barnabas carried off the situation superbly. Had she been less wretched, less ravaged by emotion, Verity must have laughed at the mixture of impudence and sheer artistry by means of which he at length prevailed.

His air would have done credit to a duke; his assurance transformed their shabbiness to splendour, and seemed to conjure up a prince's retinue out of the empty air. Never in their lives had Sir Lawrence's servants been called upon to deal with his like, and at length, without quite knowing how it came about, the bewildered steward found himself apologetically ushering this odd couple into his master's presence.

Templecombe, amazed and affronted, stared uncomprehendingly, but before he could speak, Barnabas took Verity by the hand and led her forward, saying with complete composure, and to the accompaniment of a deep bow: "Sir Lawrence, permit me to restore to you Miss Halland, whose disappearance has without doubt occasioned you no small degree of anxiety and grief."

The words he had been about to utter withered on Templecombe's lips, and his slightly prominent eyes seemed in danger of starting from his head as he stared at the ragged, sunburned girl before him, and recognized her as his promised wife. A sickly pallor overspread his face, and he groped blindly for a chair and clung to it for support.

"Verity?" he said in a strangled voice. "Verity Halland?"

There was astonishment in the words, and incredulity, but, more pronounced than either, a note of acute dismay. Too acute, thought Barnabas, to be occasioned merely by Miss Halland's present state. He glanced quickly at her to see whether she, too, had remarked it, but she was looking at Sir Lawrence with a kind of frozen stillness in her face that told him nothing.

Verity was, in fact, scarcely capable for the moment of coherent thought. Her first impression on setting eyes upon her betrothed was that he had changed immeasurably during the weeks since their last meeting, but almost at once she realized that the change was not in him but in herself. It was as though she were seeing him now for the first time, and she wondered with growing panic how she could ever have been content in her betrothal, and even a little impressed, as she undoubtedly had been, by the outward magnificence of her future husband.

As a young man, Templecombe had possessed a degree of good looks, but now, although his face retained its boyish roundness, there was a flabbiness about the jaw, and pouches beneath eyes which were at once petulant and cynical. Petulance, too, could be read in the set of his lips, and was allied to an air of self-consequence which was in itself offensive. Sir Lawrence Templecombe looked what he was—a vain, weak, egotistical man who cared little for anything besides his own pleasure and his own importance.

He was still staring at her with those prominent, blue-grey eyes, and with a supreme effort she controlled her voice sufficiently to say: "Yes, Sir Lawrence, 'tis I in very truth. I do not wonder that you are amazed."

"Amazed?" Templecombe let go the chair and caught both her hands in his, pressing his lips fervently to each in turn. "My dear, dear child, I am overcome! To have sought you in vain for so many weeks, to have mourned you as dead, and now to find you safely returned to me. I—I am bereft of words!" In proof of this he released her hands, and, apparently forgetful of his audience, clasped her in his arms and kissed her cheek.

Barnabas, regarding these transports with a shrewd, dispassionate eye, found himself unmoved by them, for after Templecombe's first, unmistakable dismay, this effusive welcome struck a note of insincerity. He had taken an instant dislike to Sir Lawrence, and felt that he would have done so even if he had known nothing to his discredit. In view of the story which Dominic Fane had told him the previous night, he had come prepared to dislike the man, and so far had seen nothing to cause him to alter his mind.

Verity had endured Templecombe's embrace rather than responded to it, and freed herself as soon as possible, saying as she did so: "Sir Lawrence, I must make known to you Barnabas Pike, without whose aid I should not be here today."

Barnabas bowed; Sir Lawrence regarded him with distaste and a hint of suspicion, and inclined his head slightly in response. At first he had been too much overcome by the fact of Miss Halland's arrival to pay much heed to her companion, but now he studied him with increasing disfavour.

"I am completely at a loss!" he announced pompously. "This whole affair is fantastic. Weeks ago I was summoned hurriedly to London by your sister-in-law, Mrs. Halland, who informed me that you had been set upon in the street, your attendants overcome, and yourself, apparently, carried off by your assailants. We had the town ransacked in search of you, but to no avail, and at last we were forced reluctantly to the conclusion that you were no longer alive." A movement of one plump, white hand indicated the deep mourning in which he was attired. "Now you come to me here, in Somerset, in this preposterous guise. Will you be good enough to explain?"

"That, sir, is my intention." Verity's voice was calm, and if her hands were clasped so tightly before her that the knuckles gleamed white, Sir Lawrence did not observe it. "I was abducted, as you supposed, but I contrived to escape from my captors."

She described her capture exactly as it had taken place, save that she made no mention of Dominic Fane. When Sir Lawrence protested that the servants had sworn to being attacked by three men at least, she hesitated only a moment before dismissing the matter with a shrug, and the comment that in the circumstances they were bound to exaggerate the danger in order to justify themselves.

Barnabas listened to the fluent recital and breathed a sigh of relief. He had feared some faltering here, for though he had coached her as best he could during their walk, it had been painfully obvious that her thoughts were elsewhere. It was clear, however, that at present she needed no help from him, and he was able to turn his attention to Templecombe, and endeavour to judge his reaction to the tale.

Verity was explaining now how her captors had taken her to a house in an unfamiliar part of the town, and there left her, first taking from her her troth-ring. This, she discovered from their talk, was to serve as proof of her capture to the man who had hired them.

"No doubt they thought me safely prisoned," she continued, "but it chanced that there was in that house a woman who bore the man Trumper a grudge, and so was open to bribery. I gave her my trinkets and my fine clothes, and in return she furnished me with this disguise, and let me out of the house, and told me how to reach that part of the town I knew. As ill-fortune would have it, Trumper and his accomplice, returning, saw me in the street, and gave chase. As I fled from them I had no chance to follow the directions I had been given, but at last, when I was near spent, I sought refuge in a courtyard, and so stumbled into the arms of Mr. Pike. He bade me hide myself nearby, while he sent my pursuers on a false trail. When they had gone he took me to his mother, and to them both I confided my story."

She paused, but before Sir Lawrence could utter either comment or question, an interruption occurred. The door opened to admit a shrivelled and ancient dame, clad in widow's weeds in the style of an earlier generation, who advanced into the room, leaning upon a stick. Faded yet piercing eyes in a white, wrinkled face surveyed first Barnabas and then the girl, but it was to Templecombe that she spoke, in the tone of one long accustomed to command. "What is going on here? Who are these people?"

Sir Lawrence looked uneasy, but he took Verity's hand and drew her forward, saying with an ingratiating smile: "Madam, it is a miracle, no less! My betrothed, Miss Halland, is safely returned to me. Child, this is my grandmother, Lady Templecombe."

Verity curtsied, but the Dowager made no response. Her eyes passed over the girl from head to foot until Verity felt herself flushing with mingled anger and embarrassment, and then went beyond her to Barnabas. After a similar study of him, the old lady looked once more at her grandson.

"So your betrothed is returned to you," she said sarcastically. "Unheralded and on foot, clad like a begger-maid, and after weeks of silence. Miraculous, indeed!" She indicated Pike with a flourish of her stick. "Who is this fellow?"

Barnabas took it upon himself to answer the question. He executed another of his graceful bows, and said glibly:

"My name, may it please your ladyship, is Barnabas Pike, and I am the leader of the troupe of players at present in Cloverton. It has been our privilege to render Miss Halland some slight assistance, the nature of which, and the manner of our meeting, she has just related to Sir Lawrence."

"Then she can relate it again to me!" Her ladyship went to a chair and sat down, motioning Verity to stand before her. "Now, mistress, your story, and we will have the truth, if you please."

Quietly, though with heightened colour, Verity repeated the story of her capture and escape. When she reached the point of her meeting with the players, the Dowager checked her with uplifted hand and looked again at Barnabas. "And you, young man, believed this fantastic tale?" she said dryly.

"I have heard many stranger, my lady," Barnabas replied coolly. "Moreover, despite her rags, Miss Halland's quality was plain enough. When she told me that she was betrothed to Sir Lawrence Templecombe of Shere Place, I suggested that she should travel hither in our company. We come each year to Goosefeather Fair, and Sir Lawrence's name was well known to me."

Templecombe, who had been gnawing fretfully at a fingernail, looked up, scowling.

"You suggested?" he exclaimed pettishly. "Upon my soul, you do not lack impudence! A fine thing, indeed, for my promised wife to go tramping the roads with a pack of vagabonds."

There came a flash of anger into Verity's expressive eyes, and she said indignantly:

"I would remind you, Sir Lawrence, of the magnitude of the debt I owe to Barnabas Pike and his friends. A show of gratitude would become you better than these unwarranted reproaches."

"It would become you better, my girl, to show humility, and a proper deference," snapped the old lady. "Why did you not ask your rescuers to take you back to your sister-in-law's house? Did it not occur to you that she, and all of us, must feel the greatest alarm at your disappearance?"

"I dared not!" Verity turned imploringly to her betrothed. "Sir Lawrence, the men who captured me did so at the bidding of some other person—that much I learned from talk I overheard between them—and since I had escaped from the trap, that person might well have set another, more successfully. You were far away, and I had no other protector. What else could I do but come seeking you?"

"My child, there is no need for such distress!" Sir Lawrence took the hand she had stretched out towards him and patted it reassuringly, forestalling any remark which his grandmother might have made. "I am concerned only lest this tale become widely known, and you find yourself the subject of gossip and impertinent conjecture."

The possibility appeared to horrify him, and though Barnabas felt certain that his concern was more for his own dignity than Miss Halland's, he did what he could to reassure him.

"Be certain, sir, that it will not become known through my people," he said quickly. "Only my mother and myself know the truth. To the rest of the troupe, Miss Halland is simply a maid whom we befriended and brought to Somerset to join her kinsfolk."

Mollified by the deferential tone of this remark, and never suspecting that it was assumed for Verity's sake rather than out of respect for the Templecombes, Sir Lawrence permitted himself to become a trifle more gracious. He was, he said, fully sensible of the great service the players had rendered him in aiding and protecting his betrothed, and restoring her safely to him. He had no wish to appear ungrateful.

"It is a wish I share, sir," Verity put in quickly, "but at present I lack the means to express my gratitude in anything but words. May I ask you to provide, on my behalf, some more tangible mark of thanks for those who befriended me in my need?"

"Of course, of course! That was my intention," Sir Lawrence agreed, with more promptness than truth. "I will see to it at once."

He went out, and silence descended upon the room. Lady Templecombe sat drumming her claw-like fingers on the arm of her chair and watching Miss Halland with a searching and malevolent eye. Barnabas, standing with mock humility a little apart from the two women, had no doubt that she was deliberating the means by which Verity was to be brought to a proper submission, and looked with some concern at the girl.

She appeared to be unaware both of her ladyship's baleful regard and his own sympathetic glance. She stood motionless, her hands lightly clasped before her and her face turned towards the window, where, beyond garden and park, the gentle countryside stretched in billows of greenery to the horizon. There was a great sadness in her face, as though she were bidding a silent farewell to some hope or dream that was infinitely dear; Barnabas, watching her with angry, impotent pity, could guess only too easily what that dream must be.

Sir Lawrence returned and bestowed upon him a heavy purse. His manner indicated that with this reward the whole matter ended, that his duty was done and any obligation wholly wiped out, so that Barnabas wished that he could afford the luxury of refusing it. Since this was impossible, he accepted it as though he, and not Templecombe, was bestowing the favour, and put it into his pocket. Verity laid her hand on his arm and spoke very earnestly.

"It is not a payment, my friend, for my debt can never be repaid in gold. It is the only way—and a poor one, at best—in which I can hope to aid one who has so aided me."

For a moment Pike's dark eyes met hers in a look of understanding and reassurance, and then he lifted her hand from his arm and brushed it lightly with his lips. A deep bow to my lady, another to Sir Lawrence, and he was gone, his swift, firm tread fading rapidly through the great house. With a sinking heart, and a feeling that her last friend was now lost to her, Verity found herself alone with her future.

"An impudent rogue," Sir Lawrence remarked distastefully, "though I suppose he has served his turn. It was a happy thought to bestow money upon him, my dear. I trust I gave him enough to buy his silence."

She looked at him with amazement and awakening contempt, for he had spoken quite seriously, with no intent to jest. "No gold was necessary," she said scornfully. "He has given his word."

"My dear child!" Templecombe's tone was indulgent. "The word of a wandering mountebank! Would you put your trust in that?"

"Honour is not the prerogative of the gently-born, Sir Lawrence," she retorted. "That, at least, I have learned during these past weeks."

The Dowager rapped her stick sharply on the floor.

" 'Tis not the only thing you learned, mistress, I'll warrant me," she snapped, "but more of that presently! Lawrence, have them send Kate to me. She will find the girl something more fitting to wear, for those rags would disgrace a beggar."

In accordance with this command there came presently a sourfaced waiting-woman, into whose charge Miss Halland was given. Lady Templecombe issued a brief explanation and sundry orders, and the maid bore Verity off to a handsome bedchamber, and left her there while she went in search of such suitable raiment as the house could provide.

In the room they left there was silence for a while after their departure. Sir Lawrence stood frowning upon space and plucking uneasily at his lower lip, and his grandmother watched him with bright, malicious eyes. At last she said: "Now that we are alone, perhaps you will be good enough to tell me what you intend?"

"Intend?" He started, and spoke with a vagueness which suggested that his thoughts were still elsewhere. "I do not understand."

"Towards the girl, you zany!" she informed him with some asperity. "Surely you are not credulous enough to believe the pack of lies she told us about a mysterious enemy who hires ruffians to make away with her? A likely tale, indeed!"

"But there is no doubt, madam, that she was abducted," Sir Lawrence protested. "I questioned the servants myself, as soon as I reached London. They had been most roughly handled, that is quite certain."

"Maybe, but it would not be the first time that an abduction had been feigned to cover a willing flight." The old woman's voice was cynical. "To my mind, you would do well to question that player fellow more closely. A plausible rogue, and told his tale too glibly for my taste—yes, and my fine madam yonder laughing in her sleeve the while, I'll be bound!"

"Good God, madam! you do not suggest———" Sir Lawrence broke off abruptly, and began to pace about the room as though endeavouring to subdue his agitation. After a minute or two he said with pompous dignity: "I will not permit myself to entertain so unworthy a suspicion. You must remember that I have known Verity Halland since her childhood. I do not believe that she is capable of such deceit."

"Then you are a fool," said her ladyship caustically, "and your folly may well cost you dear unless you heed what I say. Remember, Lawrence, you entered into this betrothal against my advice, and the whole matter has been grossly mismanaged from start to finish. I never liked the girl's grandfather, for one thing, although he was my son's close friend. Then instead of taking her when she was fourteen or fifteen, and might have been taught obedience, you must needs wait until she is twenty and more, because, forsooth, her grandfather was ailing and she wished to stay with him. She wished, mark you! 'Tis your wishes which should have been considered, not hers. Now, to crown all, she has been roving the roads with a band of strolling players—or so she says! It is my belief that the true explanation of her absence is vastly different. Hired assassins, indeed!" She gave a cackle of scornful laughter. "I suppose you believe that, along with all the rest?"

"Not in the least," Sir Lawrence replied stiffly. "It is my opinion that she was carried off by ruffians who intended holding her to ransom, and that she misunderstood some talk which she overheard between them. After so appalling an experience it is not to be wondered at that she succumbed to panic."

"And her troth-ring?" Lady Templecombe queried sarcastically. "They took that, remember, to show as proof of her capture."

"It was a jewel of great value, but of a singular design which must have rendered it dangerous to a thief. Naturally these rogues would desire to be rid of it as swiftly as possible. The fact that they took it from her merely lent colour to her delusion that someone was conspiring against her."

Her ladyship listened ill-humouredly to this ingenious explanation, and then said with sardonic comprehension: "To be sure, the girl brings with her a fortune not to be despised, and a fair face besides. 'Tis a combination rare enough to bemuse a wiser man than you, I make no doubt. Well, well, if you choose to be deceived by bright eyes and a sly tongue, you must bear the consequences, but do not be in too much haste to wed her! It would be an ill thing indeed if some beggar's brat were to inherit Shere."

Sir Lawrence uttered an explosive sound, and stared at her for a moment with indignantly bulging eyes before flinging petulantly out of the room. His grandmother's barbed tongue was the bane of his life, just as it had been the bane of his father's, but on this occasion he wasted little time in futile resentment. Other and more important issues occupied his mind.

The dismay which Barnabas Pike had detected in his reception of Miss Halland had been real enough, and though hastily dissembled, was still making itself felt. He had quite honestly believed her to be dead, and had even regretted that untimely demise, but her return from the grave was more untimely still. It placed him upon the horns of a dilemma, and, cudgel his brain as he might, he could see no way of escape from that uncomfortable and humiliating position.

Since he had his own reasons for believing Verity's story to be true in all its essentials, he did not share the Dowager's scandalous suspicions, which he knew to be prompted more by spite than anything else. She, with the future of the Templecombe estates in mind, had been pestering him to marry for close upon fifteen years, selecting one eligible young female after another as his bride. Eight years earlier, her machinations had gone so far that only flight had saved him from a most unwelcome match; he had sought refuge, as on a previous and more dangerous occasion, with his father's old friend in Herefordshire, and during his visit a brilliant scheme had occurred to him. Before he returned to Somerset he was formally contracted to his host's twelve-year-old grand-daughter, and could congratulate himself upon acquiring a notable heiress for his bride, as well as defeating his grandmother's persistent match-making.

He was in no haste to wed, and had agreed without protest to Verity's plea for delay. When her grandfather died, and the time for the marriage drew near, he made his preparations for it with the same indifference with which he had greeted the postponement. His plans were clear-cut and characteristically selfish. His wife was to remain at Shere, under the watchful eye of the Dowager, while he divided his time between Somerset and London, as he had done in the past.

His amusements were typically those of a man of fashion, but since the death of Harriet Fane and his own narrow escape from the avenging swords of her husband and stepson, he had never sought opportunities for gallantry among the country gentry. That, he had found, could be a dangerous pastime, and so he confined his amorous adventures to London, where the game was more clearly understood. That there were hazards to be faced there also he was only just beginning to realize.

Lady Templecombe, meanwhile, after brooding for a time

over the situation, rose to her feet and made her way slowly
out of the room and up the stairs. She was still active, despite
her eighty-odd years, and leaned but lightly on the stick she
carried. At the head of the staircase she paused for a moment
to catch her breath, and then went on to the bedchamber al-
lotted to Miss Halland, and entered.

Verity was standing in the middle of the room, wearing a
gown which Kate Meadows had unearthed from some forgotten chest in the attics. It had belonged to Sir Lawrence's
mother, dead these twenty years, and hung loosely upon Verity's slight figure, but neither this fact, nor the knowledge that
fashions had changed a good deal in the intervening period,
had weighed for a moment with a waiting-woman who was
almost as domineering as her mistress. The future Lady Templecombe was clad once more as befitted her station, in silk
and fine linen, and it was a small matter if the fit was poor
and the style antiquated.

Verity turned quickly as the door opened, and was conscious of a pang of dismay at sight of the small, bent figure
in its trailing black draperies and heavy veil. She realized that
she feared this ancient dame as she would never fear Sir
Lawrence, and knew, too, that she found no favour in my
lady's eyes.

The Dowager looked at Kate, who was gathering together
Miss Halland's discarded garments, and gestured towards the
clothes with her stick.

"Take those rags away and burn them," she commanded,
"and do what you can to check any gossiping among the servants, though I'll warrant that by now every impertinent
tongue below-stairs is wagging over this business."

She moved to a chair and seated herself, crossing her
hands on the knob of her stick and studying Miss Halland in
silence until the waiting-woman had left the room. Then she
said abruptly:

"Now, my fine mistress, we will have the truth concerning
this long absence of yours, but first I will give you fair warning. I have lived a deal too long in the world to be easily deceived, so let me hear no more tales of secret enemies and
hired desperadoes. I wish to know where you have spent
these past weeks, and with whom!"

Verity had neither moved nor spoken since the Dowager
entered the room, but now she turned slowly to face the old
woman. She was pale, and her breathing was a trifle hurried,

but these might have been signs of anger at the manner in which she had been addressed rather than indications of guilt.

"I have already told your ladyship that," she replied steadily. "I was abducted and I escaped; the player befriended me and brought me here. If Sir Lawrence disbelieves that, let him tell me so himself, and I will endeavour to set his doubts at rest."

Her ladyship paid no heed to this, but embarked without more delay upon the inquisition she thought was needful; question followed merciless question, their import leaving the girl in no doubt whatsoever of the suspicions which her ladyship entertained concerning her. Scarlet-cheeked now with anger and humiliation, she clung stubbornly to the story she had told earlier, and no amount of bullying could force her to alter it.

At last, baffled but still unconvinced, Lady Templecombe left her alone, and with a choking sob Verity sank down into the chair and buried her face in her hands. She could see now, all too clearly, the pattern of her future life. It was plain that Shere Place and all its occupants, Sir Lawrence included, were wholly under the sway of that terrible old woman, and that, while his grandmother lived, Sir Lawrence's wife would never be mistress of the house. This, then, was the manner of haven which she had striven so hard to reach.

She looked about the handsome, alien room, and wild thoughts of flight passed through her mind, thoughts which she could not conquer although she knew them to be futile. The choice, as she had told Barnabas, had been made for her; there was no turning back. Despair flooded over her, and she wept, with agony and vain regret, for the love that she had found only to lose again, and for the future which might have been. With her tears came remembrance of another occasion, such a little time ago, when she had wept beside a moonlit stream, and Dominic had found her there and comforted her. Weep as she would, there was no one to bring her comfort now.

X

Beginning—and End—of a Quest

WHEN he left Shere Place, Barnabas returned at once to the spot where he had parted from Dominic, for he knew that the other man would be waiting anxiously to know what had transpired. He was by no means easy in his mind. On the surface, Miss Halland's welcome to her new home had been as cordial as could be expected in the circumstances, but he could not rid himself of the feeling that Templecombe was less delighted than he pretended. Something had struck a false note, and after some deliberation Barnabas realized what it was. In that first instant of recognition, when relief at Verity's safety should have transcended every other emotion, Templecombe had betrayed dismay; but later, when some suspicion might have been forgiven, he had accepted her story without question, almost, it seemed, with eagerness.

To Pike's shrewd mind this suggested that Sir Lawrence knew, or at least suspected, rather more than he disclosed, and yet by no stretch of the imagination could he be thought to derive any profit from Miss Halland's disappearance. He wondered whether he ought to confide his suspicions to his friend, but eventually decided that to do so would do more harm than good. Verity must surely be safe in Sir Lawrence's charge, and Dominic Fane, under the double spur of love and hate, was in no mood to receive such a confidence calmly.

He found Dominic sitting on the bank bordering the lane, a shabby and somewhat sinister figure in that placid rural setting, his scarred face grim in the shadow of his broad-brimmed hat. He looked up as Barnabas came whistling round the bend, and for a moment there was a kind of tense expectancy in the very stillness of his lean figure. Then, almost imperceptibly, he relaxed, and went on breaking into small pieces the fragment of stick between his hands. Pike could guess the unspoken thought behind that searching glance. If their plan had gone awry, if Templecombe had refused to accept their story, Verity Halland might possibly have returned with him.

"Well, all goes merrily," he announced, dropping down on to the bank beside Fane and pushing his hat to the back of his head. "There was some small difficulty in winning past the lackeys—this Templecombe keeps princely state—but we accomplished it in the end."

"Did he accept her without question?" Dominic was still intent upon his handful of broken twig; his voice was level."

"With astonishment, of course, but with no small degree of delight," Barnabas assured him. "It seems that all hope of ever finding her alive had been abandoned, which accounts, I suppose, for Templecombe's return from London. As for accepting her story, his chief concern seemed to keep secret the fact that she has spent so long a time in such disreputable company. That appeared to trouble him more than all the rest."

"The years had not changed him, then," Dominic said contemptuously. "His dignity must be preserved at all costs, no matter what befall. It was ever so, and I'll warrant he showed you little enough gratitude for restoring Verity to him."

"He could have been more cordial," Barnabas admitted with a grin. "He did not seem to doubt the tale I told, but 'twas clear he found it offensive that a pack of vagabonds—I quote his own words—should have reached terms of familiarity with his promised wife." A chuckle escaped him. " 'Tis no submissive bride he has chosen, at all events. She told him roundly that a show of gratitude would better become him."

Dominic's eyes gleamed appreciatively, but at the same time he sighed faintly, and when he spoke there was trouble in his voice.

"She will have need of all her spirit! Templecombe is a craven, but he has never hesitated to bully those weaker than himself." With a sudden, impatient movement he flung aside the scraps of twig and rose abruptly to his feet. "By God, Barnabas! I am half minded, even now, to settle the score twixt him and me, if it can be done without involving Verity in our quarrel. You say he did not doubt your story, and no one knows of my return to Shere save you and Mary Parr."

"And the rest of my troupe," Barnabas reminded him. "They know your name, if they do not know your story."

"I could stay close until the fair is over and you go on your way. At that house of mine I could lie hid for months without anyone suspecting it. If I let some time elapse before disclosing my presence, and then made believe that I had but just returned, who would be likely to guess at any link between Verity and me?"

Pike shook his head. "You would betray yourselves," he said quietly, "and when tongues began to wag, as wag they would, the link would be forged soon enough. Do not deceive yourself on that score, my friend. Templecombe may desire to probe no further into the mystery, but there are others who would be more inquisitive. The old lady, his grandmother, for one."

"What! Does that old beldame yet live?" Dominic asked sharply. "I had thought her in her grave long since. How did she receive the tale you told?"

"Less readily than her grandson, so be warned!" Barnabas replied. "Unless my judgment is at fault, if once she had wind of it, she would not rest until the whole truth was in her hands."

"Well I know it!" Dominic agreed bitterly. "She is as keen to nose out a secret as a dog after a rat, and if she thought to put a stop to Templecombe's marriage, she would be more eager still. The prospect of another woman in that house must irk her beyond endurance. It used to be said that she drove her son's wife to the grave with her interference and ill-humours, and since then all has gone as she desires."

"More reason, then, for you to be prudent," Barnabas pointed out. "Templecombe is a man of straw, but her ancient ladyship could be a dangerous enemy, I'll wager, and she is already ill-disposed towards Verity. Let her hear but a whisper that you have had a hand in this, and all hell will be let loose."

There was a pause, while Dominic stared unseeingly before him, and Barnabas watched him anxiously and gave thanks that he had had the sense to keep to himself the disquiet he had brought with him from Shere Place. At length Dominic gave a sigh of mingled bitterness and exasperation, and the hand which had been clenched hard on the silver sword-hilt slowly relaxed its grip.

"Oh, you are right, confound you!" he agreed reluctantly. "A sword-thrust is no answer to this problem, much as it would please me to deal it. It would imperil everything if I were to linger here."

"Now you find wisdom," Barnabas said with relief. "You must go, and that with all speed. Only tell me whither you are bound, and belike we may meet again."

Whither, indeed? Dominic stood silent while the question echoed with cruel irony in his mind, and he faced for the first time the desolation of his future. What could lie ahead but an aimless drifting, an empty, endless wandering barren of hope or purpose? Nothing remained, not even the hope of vengeance which had been his beacon for so many years, and his courage faltered at the thought of the loneliness stretching before him into infinity. A passionate and hopeless longing surged up within him, and fierce rebellion against his own poverty and degradation. He turned away lest Pike should guess the storm of emotion that choked and blinded him, and so for a space there was silence in the lane, save for the sleepy fluting of a distant bird.

Barnabas, seated still upon the bank, pulled Sir Lawrence's fat purse from his pocket and balanced it thoughtfully on his palm. Its weight, and the pleasant chinking of the coins within, gave promise of a good round sum, but though he only held it in trust he did not grudge a penny of it to the man to whom it was truly given. He had entered readily into Miss Halland's scheme, propounded during their walk to Shere Place, to obtain the money, but the difficulty, he reflected now with a dubious glance at Fane, was to persuade Dominic to accept it.

It was a difficulty which Verity herself had foreseen, and warned him against, begging him to use any means he could think of to persuade Dominic to take the money which she intended to wrest from Templecombe on his behalf.

"Tell him," she had said wistfully, "to take it for my sake, if he will not for his own. It may help him to keep our secret safe."

A potent argument, thought Barnabas, and one which he could not surpass, but would it be potent enough? He rose, and touched Fane lightly on the arm, still holding the purse in his other hand.

"I had this of Templecombe," he remarked, and Dominic's brows lifted.

"Payment for services rendered?" he said with a sneer. "How like him to suppose that such a debt could be settled with gold."

"He supposed nothing of the kind, until Verity put him in mind of it," Barnabas replied mildly, "but in any event, the gold is rightly yours, not mine."

The tall figure stiffened, and there came a flash of anger through the heartbreak in the golden eyes.

"I want none of his vile gold," Dominic said harshly. "Keep it, or fling it away, whichever you choose, but do not offer it to me."

"The gold, I admit, was his," Pike agreed patiently, "but the thought was Verity's, and I know that she regards the money itself as a loan from him, to be repaid as soon as she has access again to her own. She told me so on our way to Shere Place, and asked me to bear it as a gift to you."

"Still less could I take it from her," Dominic replied with suppressed violence. "My God! can you not understand? Cannot she? Am I no more to her than a servant, to be paid and dismissed when my task is done?"

"A trifle of understanding on your part would not come amiss," Barnabas retorted with some heat. "You chose to send her back to that self-satisfied buffoon and his hell-hag grandmother, and now you would also fling back in her face the only token left in her power to give. If this is a salve to your damned stiff-necked pride, praise God I was not born a gentleman!"

There was a strained, uncomfortable pause, and then Dominic said wearily: "I sought no payment. She knew that."

"And you know that she never intended it as such. She bade me tell you to take it for her sake, if you would not for your own."

For her sake! Dominic's lips twisted wryly as he stared at the bulging purse. Was there anything he would not do for her, any wish he would not grant, if it lay within his power? Yet how little he could do, in spite of all, save take the gold and go his way. Templecombe could never be worthy of her, but at least he had the means to protect her from her unknown enemy.

The Black Mask! His gaze quickened, and he drew a sharp, audible breath, as with sudden inspiration he saw how he might continue to serve her, and at the same time find a purpose to guide his steps in the immediate future. Under Pike's gratified but wondering eyes he stretched out his hand and took the purse, feeling the weight of it with satisfaction.

"Sir Lawrence has been generous," he remarked. "There is more than enough here for my needs."

Barnabas pushed his hat even further towards the back of his head, and stared at him open-mouthed. "Plague take me if ever I saw your like," he declared. "What prompted that change of tune?"

"The remembrance of a task left undone," Dominic answered grimly. "Somewhere, my friend, is the dainty, evil-minded young buck who hired Nat Trumper to abduct Verity, and so pitchforked us all into this imbroglio. Now she is safe at Shere Place and I may go in search of him."

"Will you so?" Barnabas said softly. "And if you find him, what then?"

"When I find him," Dominic corrected quietly, "for be sure, my friend, that I shall not rest until I do, I know a certain way to keep him for further mischief." He drew his sword a few inches from the scabbard as he spoke, and slid it back again. The gesture left his meaning in no doubt at all.

"Well enough," Barnabas agreed, "but how can you hope to find a man of whom you know nothing, whose face you have never seen?"

Dominic shook his head.

"Two things I do know," he said. "He desires to be rid of Verity Halland, and he has the means to inform himself of details of her daily life. If I can learn nothing at the tavern where I saw him, I shall turn instead to the house of that Mrs. Halland with whom Verity was living, and see what I may discover there. Moreover, although I have never seen my quarry's face, his voice I could not forget. Let me but hear him speak, and I shall know him, never fear."

"He will recognize you even more easily. Do not forget that."

Fane smiled without mirth. "He may do so with my good will, if so be he betrays himself in doing it."

Barnabas was silent for a space, thoughtfully regarding him. It was clear that no considerations of personal safety were to hamper Dominic Fane in his search for the Black Mask, and though Pike had little hope of being attended to, he was moved to point out another danger which his friend had perhaps overlooked.

"If you are bound for London, best keep a keen watch for Trumper. We have seen naught of him since he broke prison, and belike he has returned to his old haunts."

"That will I do," Dominic assured him. "He would like to settle the score between us, no doubt, but perchance the tale will have a different ending next time." He held out his hand. "Farewell to you, Barnabas. You know how deep is my gratitude for all your aid."

"Little enough I have done," Barnabas grumbled, gripping his hand hard, "and I would I might go with you on your mad quest. This toy of mine can be as swift as your sword, and as deadly." With his free hand he twitched aside his coat and patted the hilt of the knife hidden beneath it.

"Swifter by far, as well I know," Dominic agreed ruefully. "I would I had your skill."

"Come back to us when your task is done, and I will teach you the trick of it," Pike replied with a grin. "You know whither we go when the fair is over, and there will always be a welcome awaiting you."

"Perhaps I will, and my thanks for the offer. Good-bye, Barnabas Pike."

"Good fortune go with you," Barnabas replied, and stood to watch Fane's tall figure out of sight. A moment longer he remained in frowning thought, and then with a sigh and a shrug turned to make his way back to Cloverton.

Dominic wasted no time, but turned his steps without delay towards London, tempering his haste with caution and keeping ever to lanes and byways. The sun was already sinking, and he was able to cover only a comparatively short distance before darkness fell. He slept that night amid the hay in a lonely barn, and was on his way again betimes next morning.

Save to buy food at an isolated cottage, he once more avoided the haunts of men, and followed still the devious paths he had chosen the previous day, for with Goosefeather Fair commencing on the morrow the whole neighbourhood would be astir, and he had no mind to ruin all at this late day by an encounter with some old acquaintance. The years had changed him, he knew, but not so much that his scarred face and curiously coloured eyes were likely to escape recognition should he chance upon one who had known him in other days.

With the coming of another dusk, however, he fancied himself sufficiently far away from his old home to be safe from discovery, and ventured to approach a village. Deliberately choosing the larger and busier of its two inns, he mingled unobtrusively with the humble travellers in the big kitchen, and bespoke food and a bed. One or two of his fellow guests tried to engage him in conversation, but receiving no encouragement, soon desisted, and he was left undisturbed to pursue his thoughts.

That these should centre around Verity Halland was inevitable. Her image was with him constantly, now stirring him with the memory of some moment of comradeship during their journey, now plaguing him with fears for her present and future welfare. Barnabas had said enough to disturb him, to revive recollections of Shere Place, which once he had known so well. He recalled the oppressive ceremony of life in the great house, the handsome, inhospitable rooms, the soft-footed, watchful servants, and the sharp-eyed old woman with malice in her heart and venom in her tongue, who presided over all. How could Verity endure such an existence? How long would it be before the Templecombes, between them, broke her brave heart and gallant spirit?

At that thought all his futile anger surged up anew, and, silently but none the less bitterly, he cursed his own helplessness. He could seek out and slay the mysterious enemy who had tried to destroy her, but because of his own poverty he could not save her from Templecombe, from the slow, intangible process of destruction which he was certain, from his knowledge of her and of the man she was to wed, must be the inevitable outcome of her marriage. He thought of his mother, doomed to a loveless union, fading gradually and painfully out of life after years of unhappiness and fear, and dread drove the anger from his heart. Verity would not be afraid—she was of a more courageous spirit than poor, browbeaten Isobel—but she could not be happy with Sir Lawrence, whom she could neither like nor respect.

He bowed his head upon his hands, his whole being shaken by the force of his hopeless, helpless love, the wordless agony of his desire. Of their parting he did not dare to think, that moment of rapture and of heartbreak when he had held her, yielding, in his arms, and felt her lips quiver responsively beneath his. For her sake even that memory must be renounced, forgotten save perhaps in dreams, for the ruined, wandering soldier could only love and serve her. He must ask nothing in return.

So now, having already forsworn his vengeance for old wrongs, Dominic Fane made, by his own choice, a surrender infinitely greater than the first. With all the force of his considerable will he directed his thoughts toward the object of his present journey, and took what comfort he could from the knowledge that it was to serve and protect Verity that he travelled now, even though they would never meet again, and she might never know of his efforts on her behalf. Beyond that he would not look; his quest was all-important.

On the following morning, finding that he had provoked no surprised recognition from anyone at the inn, he resolved to hire a horse and push on with greater speed. As soon as he had broken his fast, therefore, he stepped out into the courtyard on his way to the stables to seek out a likely mount, but, finding the attention of grooms and ostlers wholly occupied with a coach which was apparently on the point of departure, paused just outside the door to wait for the bustle to abate.

The vehicle, to which four powerful horses had just been harnessed, was obviously the property of a guest of some importance, to whom all humbler folk must give way, and Dominic watched with cynical amusement the haughty way in which its liveried attendants were issuing their commands to the inn-servants. It was, he reflected, the way of lackeys the world over.

Then, abruptly, his idle interest was banished, and he stiffened to incredulous attention. Behind him, and a little to the right, a casement stood open, and in the room it served a voice had spoken, a soft, husky voice, a voice he knew.

"Are those fools not ready yet?" it said impatiently. "Do they think I wish to tarry here all day?"

Dominic stood rigid, the breath checked in his throat, and saw not the animated scene in the courtyard, but a dimly lighted room in a squalid London tavern, and a slight, youthful figure with masked face, and Verity's stolen diamond flashing on one white hand. By a stroke of incredible good luck, or some odd quirk of destiny, the man he had set out to kill was within his reach, and his quest had ended before it had begun.

Spurred to action by that realization, he took a step towards the window, and then, on second thoughts, turned instead to the door again. Within the house he paused, and had just decided that the first door on the left of the passage must give access to the room he sought, when it was flung open and two women emerged. Dominic drew back quickly into the shadow cast by the open door behind him, and since the sunlight flooding in from the yard was full in their eyes they did not observe him, while he, on the other hand, had an excellent view of them as they passed by him and out of the inn. One of them was obviously a servant, and he bestowed but a fleeting glance upon her, but her mistress caught and held his attention.

She was perhaps five-and-twenty years old, tall for a woman and possessed of a dark, insolent beauty which struck him with a curious sense of familiarity in the brief instant that he beheld it, and then with a rustle of rich silks she had swept past him, and only a heavy, lingering perfume remembered her presence. For a second or two he did not move as

he groped after the elusive memory her face evoked, and
then he realized with a faint shock that she reminded him of
his dead stepmother. She, too, had possessed a rich, dark
beauty, but this unknown woman's face held a suggestion of
force which Harriet's had lacked, a force which, to Dominic,
was somehow repellent.

Only for a moment did the incident distract him from his
purpose, and then his thoughts fastened again upon the fact
that his quarry was still in the room from which the dark
beauty had emerged. The maidservant had closed the door
behind her, and, with his hand upon the latch, Dominic
paused for an instant to loosen his sword in its scabbard and
to smile grimly at the thought of the consternation into which
his arrival would throw the callous young villain who would
have sent Verity to so unthinkable a fate. Then he flung the
door wide and stepped forward to meet the Black Mask face
to face, only to stop dead on the threshold, staring in blank
disbelief. The room was empty.

XI

Goosefeather Fair

FOR perhaps half a minute Dominic stood rigid and unmoving, wondering if he had been the victim of some inexplicable
delusion, yet knowing, even as the question posed itself, that
the voice he had heard was no figment of his imagination. He
was roused from his stupor by a rattle and clatter and the
stamping of iron-shod hoofs beyond the window, as the great
gilded coach lumbered out of the yard, and he reached the
open casement in time to see it sweep through the arched
gateway and turn along the road by which he had come into
the village the night before.

A moment longer he stood there, frowning in deepening
perplexity, and then he turned once more to inspect the
room. There was no other door than that by which he had
entered, and it was impossible for the Black Mask to have
left the room without encountering him, unless, which was

absurd, he had gone by way of the window. There seemed to be no answer to the riddle.

A step sounded, and a maidservant came briskly into the room, a tray beneath her arm. At sight of him she stopped short, staring, and then demanded sharply what he was doing there. The kitchen, she said, and not a private parlour, was the place for the likes of him. Dominic ignored the question, and asked one of his own.

"Who has used this room today?"

The girl tossed her head.

"Your betters, Master Curiosity," she retorted pertly. "Now get you hence, and be thankful 'twas me that found you here, and not mistress. It's short shrift you'd get from her!"

"I asked who had used this room today," Dominic repeated impatiently. "Do not trifle with me, my girl! This is a matter of importance."

The servant, who had begun to clear the remains of breakfast from the table, looked up to make a tart reply, encountered the glance of tawny eyes beneath black brows, and thought better of it. In spite of his down-at-heel appearance, the swarthy stranger had an oddly compelling way with him.

"The lady who just drove off in the coach," she replied sulkily. "She spent the night here."

Dominic frowned. "Alone? Was there no gentleman with her?"

"Have done with your impudence!" the maid admonished him severely. "Indeed there was not. There was her maid, and four or five lackeys, that's all."

Dominic continued to stare at her, the frown lingering in his eyes. There was no reason to suppose that the girl was lying, and in any event her words were borne out by the fact that only one person had used the breakfast-table. Yet he would have staked his life that the voice he had heard speaking in this room not five minutes since was the voice of the Black Mask. The thing had begun to savour of the supernatural.

Then a sudden, incredible suspicion brought his thoughts up with a jerk, staggering him with its implications. It could not be, it was absurd, fantastic, and yet . . . "Tell me," he said urgently to the girl, "did this lady have occasion to speak to you?"

She stared, blankly at first and then with growing suspicion.

"Aye, that she did," she replied. "A queer sort of voice she had, deep and husky like, more like a boy's voice than a woman's, to my mind. Why should you want to know?"

Dominic turned away, not answering, scarcely even hearing the question. So it was that dark, beautiful face that the black silk mask had hidden, and Verity's enemy was no youth, but a woman. Her disguise had been excellent; he had had not the smallest suspicion, but now, in the light of his discovery, he began to remember some few insignificant details which served to convince him that he was not mistaken. The dainty whiteness of the hand on which Verity's troth-ring had been placed; the shrinking from bloodshed which he had deemed hypocrisy, and the spite in her voice when she believed Verity to be at the mercy of Red Nat; her curiosity concerning himself and his association with Trumper. There was no room for doubt. The Black Mask was a young woman, whose sex placed her beyond the vengeance of his sword. A ruthless and vindictive woman who was even now journeying in the direction of the place where Verity had found refuge.

But why? Was it pure chance which had brought her into Somerset, or had some whisper of the truth reached her ears? If Nat Trumper had returned to London, it was just possible that some contact had been established between them, and to anyone familiar with Verity's circumstances, a flight towards the West Country would suggest only one possible destination. If that were so, and the purpose of the woman's journey was another attempt against her, then Verity, all unsuspecting at Shere Place, was in the deadliest danger. But who, in the devil's name, was the Black Mask, and what the source of her enmity towards Miss Halland?

He questioned the servant further, but she could tell him neither the lady's name nor her destination. By this time she was eyeing him very much askance, and he realized the indiscretion into which the shock of his discovery had betrayed him. He had no doubt that in a very short space of time every person in the inn would be acquainted with his extraordinary interest in the strange lady, and from there to suspicion of his motives would be a short step indeed. He went abruptly out of the room, and, wasting no time about the business, paid his shot, hired a mount and set off in pursuit of the coach.

It was easy enough to find, and easier still to keep in sight without drawing attention to himself, for there was a fair amount of traffic on the road, amid which a single horseman attracted no notice at all. In coaches and carts, on horseback and afoot, the entire population of the district appeared to be bound for Goosefeather Fair.

Throughout the bright summer morning, Dominic held patiently to the trail of the Black Mask. The progress of the coach was slow, and more than once he deemed it prudent to dismount and lead his horse, lest it should be remarked that he was deliberately checking his own pace to that of the vehicle ahead. It was obvious that unless she turned off along some by-road before Cloverton was reached, the Black Mask would be obliged to pass through the fair itself, since this was held in the market-place and along the principal street of the town, and there, he knew, he stood in real danger of recognition.

Even if this occurred, however, his earlier precautions would not have been wasted, for, galling to his pride though such recognition must be, he could say with truth that he had only just arrived in the town. Only the strolling players could connect him with Verity Halland, and them he must do his best to avoid. The identity and destination of the Black Mask must be discovered, whatever the risk involved.

Presently he was given an indication that both his quarry and her servants were strangers to the district, for though the coach was driven straight into the town, it was no sooner fairly within the streets than it halted, and Dominic saw the lackeys looking about them in dismay. All around them surged an eager crowd in holiday mood, while from the market-place ahead, out of sight but within earshot, came the cheerful uproar of the fair itself. It was impossible, however, to turn the great, clumsy vehicle in that thronged and narrow street, and after a hurried consultation, in which, from the deferential turning of their heads towards the coach's window, it seemed that the lady herself joined, the journey was resumed.

Dominic, preparing to follow, caught sight of an old acquaintance of his father's emerging from a house a short way ahead; he dismounted hurriedly, and pretended to be busy with the girths, keeping his head bent so that his hat concealed his face. By the time the danger was past, the coach had turned a corner and was out of sight, but since he knew that the street led only to the market-place, he was not much perturbed. He mounted again and proceeded in the same direction, but before he had covered twenty yards a crowd of children burst from a narrow alley on his right and streamed across the roadway in front of him. Laughing and shouting, they linked hands in some improvised game, effectively blocking the street and obliging him to draw rein to avoid riding them down. He waited, chafing at the delay but unwilling to draw attention to himself by retreating, and then his worst fears were realized. Another horse was edged alongside his own, there was a light tap on his arm, and a woman's voice said merrily: "Well met, Mr. Fane? It seems that all the world comes to Goosefeather Fair."

He turned sharply in the saddle, but the speaker was a stranger to him, a slim, golden-haired girl, scarcely more than a child, richly habited in dark blue velvet laced with silver. Large blue eyes regarded his perplexity with an expression of sparkling mischief, and an enchanting smile mocked at his bewilderment. At her heels rode an elderly serving-man in green-and-gold livery, who met Dominic's blank stare with a nod and a friendly grin.

The lady gave an irrepressible gurgle of laughter.

"You are not likely to remember me, sir, so it is no use searching your memory for my name. I am Sarah Deverell. Are you fully recovered from your injuries?"

It was her last words, rather than the name itself, which gave him the clue to her identity. This, then was the sister of that Lord Urmiston to whose intervention at the time of Trumper's first attack he owed his life, but was meeting with a benefactress ever more inopportune? It meant not merely delay in his pursuit of the Black Mask, but also that the risk of betrayal was transformed from a possibility so remote as to be disregarded into a very real and pressing danger.

With these thoughts jostling each other in his mind it was not remarkable that he should answer his fair questioner somewhat at random. Lady Sarah eyed him speculatively. Even though her only previous meeting with him had been so brief, she had recognized him without difficulty, as easily, in fact, as she now perceived the discomfiture into which she had thrown him. She said lightly: "My acquaintance, sir, was with your sister rather than yourself. Is she with you today?"

Now how to answer that? The situation was one which demanded the most delicate handling, and yet he could not give it his full attention while the merrymaking crowds and this friendly child were, between them, allowing the Black Mask to slip through his fingers.

"No, my lady, she is at our kinsman's house, and I am bound thither to join her," he replied, and added recklessly:

"She will be grieved that she has not had the pleasure of meeting your ladyship again. She has spoken often of your kindness on that unlucky day."

"You must bring her to visit me, Mr. Fane." My lady's voice was guileless, but the blue eyes watched him closely as she spoke. "My brother and I are paying a visit to our sister, Lady Corville, at Manton Lacey. You know the village perhaps?"

Yes, he knew it, for it lay only a few miles from Shere. The great house, Corville Court, had been built some thirty years earlier by the first baron of that name, but if Lady Sarah's sister was the present baroness, the old man must have died, and his son, George, succeeded to his honours; and George Corville, Dominic remembered with growing dismay, had been one of Templecombe's intimates in the old days.

"Your ladyship is kindness itself!" How the devil was he to escape from this predicament, continue his pursuit, and at the same time prevent the tale of that earlier meeting with the Deverells from reaching Templecombe's ears? "I should be glad of an opportunity of expressing my gratitude to my lord your brother for his most timely aid."

"That, sir, you may have at once, if you will ride with me to the Seven Stars Inn. He is to meet me there. Your thanks, though, should go rather to Thomas here, for it was he who tended your wounds."

Another witness to the bond between Verity Halland and himself! Certainly he was having good and evil fortune in equal measure today. He made some civil reply, and then the crowd before them parted and they were able to move on along the street. Sarah Deverell's horse remained beside his, the serving-man fell in behind them. People stared to see this richly-clad young lady conversing upon such friendly terms with a shabby fellow in threadbare coat and rusty hat with draggled plume, and at every moment Dominic expected to hear his name spoken in astonished recognition, to see heads bent together and pointing hands, and to know that his return had been observed and remarked upon. Then they reached the spot where the street entered the market-place, and all other emotions perished in a bitter fury of chagrin and dismay. Look where he might, the gilded coach and its attendants were nowhere to be seen.

Almost without thought he drew rein again, while his keen glance swept the crowded space before him. No less than five other streets converged upon the market-place, and along any one of them the Black Mask might have passed. He could question the bystanders, of course, but though such inquiry might yield fruit, it would make his own recognition practically certain.

"Is something wrong, Mr. Fane?" Lady Sarah's clear voice beside him served as a reminder that the Black Mask, though the greatest peril to Verity, was by no means the only one. "The inn is yonder, sir." She pointed across the market-place with her riding-whip.

"Aye, my lady, I know it well," he replied, and allowed his horse to move forward again. The trail of the Black Mask might be picked up later, even if it meant proving each street in turn, but his present duty was obviously to discover how likely a meeting between Miss Halland and Lady Sarah might be.

"Do you know the village of Shere, my lady?" he asked abruptly as they skirted the square towards the inn. Her ladyship looked surprised.

"I was there not a week since, for Lord Corville is a friend of Sir Lawrence Templecombe of Shere Place. Why do you ask?" She broke off, a glimmer of mischievous comprehension in her eyes. "Has rumour spread so far so soon?"

"Rumour?" His hand tightened on the bridle, and he spoke more harshly than he knew. "Rumour of what?"

"Why, you must know, sir, that Sir Lawrence was to have been wed this month, but while he was at Shere a while since, preparing his house for his bride, the lady mysteriously disappeared. She was in London, you understand, and her servants swear to an attack in the street one night. When the news reached him, Sir Lawrence made all speed to London, but though he sought her for weeks, no trace of her could be found. When he returned to Shere Place, Lord Corville went to visit him, and my brother and I accompanied him."

"And is that the rumour of which your ladyship spoke?"

"No, indeed, sir, that is a matter of plain fact, culled from Sir Lawrence himself. The rumour comes later." She paused to edge her mount past the crowd surrounding one of the booths, and then resumed gaily: "Yesterday a tale reached us that the lost lady had been found. That she had, in fact, arrived at Shere Place, alone and on foot, having travelled thither with a band of gipsies, or something such. All manner of curious tales are abroad, and my sister begged us to visit Shere Place on our way home from the fair to discover, if

possible, what the real truth is. She is agog to know," Lady
Sarah added confidingly, "and so, to tell truth, am I, but she
is in delicate health, and does not venture from home at
present."

He was spared the necessity of a reply, for by this time
they had reached the inn, but he felt the sweat start on his
brow as he thought how nearly his elaborate edifice of false-
hood had been brought crashing down. Even now he could
see no way to avert the disaster, but avert it he must if Verity
were to be saved.

The big courtyard was busy with comings and goings, for
the Seven Stars was the town's principal inn, and this its
busiest time of the whole year, but almost at once Dominic
caught sight of the Deverell livery. The lackey who wore it
was standing by the main door of the house, apparently receiving orders of some kind from a young man in all the
glory of laced coat and monstrous periwig, who had paused
in the act of mounting the steps before the door and was effectively, but quite unconcernedly, blocking the path of any
who might desire to pass in or out.

"There is my brother," said Lady Sarah with satisfaction,
and thrust her horse forward to the foot of the steps.
"Robert!" she cried, as Thomas hurried to lift her from the
saddle. "I have found an old acquaintance in the town, one
whom we little thought to meet again."

My lord turned, and Dominic found himself looking into
the frank young face, with classically perfect features, and
blue eyes very like Lady Sarah's. For a moment these were
blank and questioning, and then recognition came, and a
swift smile.

"Mr. Fane, as I live!" the Marquis exclaimed. "This is an
extraordinary stroke of good fortune! What brings you to
Goosefeather Fair?"

"A matter of business, my lord!" Out of the corner of his
eye Dominic could see that the landlord of the inn, who had
been waiting to usher his distinguished guest within, was
looking at him very hard. The man was a stranger to him,
but it was clear that his curiosity had been aroused.

"And your—sister?" The pause was infinitesimal, but its
significance was not lost upon Fane, and the frown deepened
in his eyes. "She is well, I trust?"

Dominic came to a swift decision. Events had moved too
swiftly for him to weigh the matter carefully, but some instinct told him that this handsome boy could be trusted, and

in any case, matters could scarcely be more desperate than they were. He advanced a pace, and lowered his voice so that only the Marquis and Lady Sarah could hear his words.

"I think your lordship has guessed that the lady who was with me that day is not my sister," he said. "If you will give me five minutes in private, sir, you shall have the truth."

For a moment longer the blue eyes met the tawny gold in a direct and questioning glance, and then Urmiston nodded.

"Very well, Mr. Fane," he said quietly, and turned to the waiting host. "A private room, landlord, if you please, and I wish to be disturbed by no one."

Mine host, who had strained his ears to no purpose, made haste to obey, and within a very few minutes Dominic was alone with Urmiston and her ladyship in a pleasant parlour with windows looking out upon a garden. The Marquis handed his sister to a chair, waved Dominic graciously to another, and sat himself down on the broad window-seat.

"Now, Mr. Fane," he said pleasantly, "you may be sure of our attention. I will not deny that we scented a mystery from the first, and you have said enough to whet our curiosity to no small degree."

Dominic had not taken the chair indicated, but stood instead behind it, his lean, brown hands gripping its back. He looked from the brother to the sister, and back again. "The secret which I am about to divulge, my lord, is not mine alone," he said slowly. "For that reason only, I must beg you to share it with no one."

"You may rest easy on that score," Urmiston assured him, and Sarah nodded eager agreement. "We shall respect your confidence."

Dominic inclined his head in acknowledgment of the assurance, and his lordship reflected fleetingly that, for all his shabbiness, the mysterious Mr. Fane bore himself with some dignity. At first sight he had dismissed him as a mere seedy desperado, remarkable only for his association with the delicate and gentle girl who called herself his sister, but now he revised that opinion. This was a man of birth and education, however indigent his present circumstances might be.

"I thank you, my lord," Dominic said quietly. "You will appreciate, I think, the need for discretion when I tell you that the lady who was with me at our first meeting is Miss Verity Halland, Sir Lawrence Templecombe's promised wife."

Lady Sarah gasped aloud, and thereafter sat staring at him

with wide eyes, and a hand to her mouth. Her brother, after one moment of equal astonishment, said in a carefully expressionless voice: "No doubt she had some good reason for assuming such a disguise?"

"The best, my lord!" Dominic replied curtly. "She was fleeing for her life."

There was another and longer pause, and when Urmiston spoke again his tone was reflective.

"By my reckoning, our encounter took place at much the same time as Miss Halland's disappearance in London. Was that supposed abduction merely a cloak for her flight?"

"The abduction was real enough, my lord," Dominic said grimly. "I was one of the three who carried it out. The others were those who attacked us upon the road."

Briefly he described the nature of Nat Trumper's bargain with the Black Mask, the capture of Miss Halland, and his own subsequent meeting with the mysterious stranger. From that he passed on to the prisoner's warning of the treachery planned by his confederates, and her promise of rich reward if he would restore her to her friends.

"But she had friends in London, surely?" Sarah broke in at this point. "Why travel all the way to Somerset?"

"She had been in mourning, my lady, and so had made few acquaintances in London, but the real fault was mine. I convinced her that only here could she be certain of safety." He hesitated, and she saw his hands tighten on the back of the chair before him, though his voice was still level when he spoke again. "I was born and bred at Shere, and there is an old quarrel between Templecombe and myself. I saw in Miss Halland a weapon with which to avenge a certain wrong my family had suffered at his hands."

He paused again, but neither of his listeners made any answer to this, and after a moment or two he went on with his story. This time they heard him in silence, save only when he told how Verity, finding their money gone, had worked as a serving-maid in the inn until he recovered from his wounds. Then the Marquis said with strong feeling:

"If we had but known! I have since blamed myself bitterly that I did not insist more strongly upon her accepting our help, but how much greater would my regret have been had I guessed the truth!'

The whole story Dominic told them, up to the moment of his meeting with Lady Sarah, omitting only the fact of his visit with Verity to the house in the wood. When he had done, there was silence for a while in the sunlit parlour, a silence which Urmiston was the first to break.

"What is your purpose, Mr. Fane, in telling us this story? Do you seek our aid in bringing this woman to justice?"

Dominic made a fatalistic gesture.

"My lord, I had no choice but to tell you the truth. You will find Miss Halland at Shere Place. One word of your previous meeting, one whisper of my name in connection with hers, is sufficient to ruin her. Whether or not that word is spoken must rest with you, and with her ladyship."

"It never will be spoken!" His lordship sprang to his feet, and began to pace the room in some perturbation. "God's light, man! What monsters do you suppose us? Has she endured so little that we should bring all your careful schemes to naught through malice or heedlessness? We shall see her, but it will be rather to warn her that her enemy is at hand, to assure her of any help that is within our power to give, than to betray her to Sir Lawrence."

Lady Sarah, with an elbow on the arm of her chair and her chin on her hand, listened patiently to her brother's impassioned outburst. When he paused, she transferred her thoughtful gaze to Dominic.

"What of your vengeance, Mr. Fane?" she asked softly.

He looked at her in swift suspicion, but her expression was innocently inquiring, her eyes guileless and disarming. After a perceptible pause he said evenly:

"I could not take it, my lady, without involving Miss Halland in a quarrel which in no way concerned her. During our long and difficult journey I had come to respect her deeply, as I think anyone must who knows her, and I could not be guilty of the infamy of bringing further troubles upon her."

"Such sentiments do you credit, sir," Urmiston said warmly, "but since you cannot now appear in the affair without endangering Miss Halland, permit me to be your deputy. My sword shall be at her command."

"If it were a matter of swords alone, my lord, I should stand in no need of assistance," Dominic answered dryly. " 'Tis a woman with whom we have to deal, and so we must seek weapons of another kind."

My lord looked crestfallen.

"That is true, confound it! Who can this woman be, Mr. Fane? What is the source of her enmity towards Miss Halland?"

Dominic shook his head. "My lord, I cannot tell. Greed is

the motive which springs most readily to mind, but the heir to Miss Halland's fortune is her nephew, a child not yet breeched."

"Jealousy!" Sarah said suddenly, and nodded wisely. "Between women that is as likely a motive as any I can think of, but why cudgel our brains, when Miss Halland herself may well supply the answer? They must be acquainted. Describe the woman to her, and mayhap she will be able to supply the name, and from that the rest will follow, without a doubt."

The two men exchanged glances, and Urmiston laughed.

"You give good counsel, my dear," he said, and turned again to Dominic. "We will go to Shere Place, as we had planned, and endeavour to speak privately with Miss Halland. She is the person most closely concerned, after all, and it ill becomes us to take any action without consulting her."

Dominic was obliged to agree, though he would have had not the smallest hesitation in taking, out of hand, any measures he thought necessary for Verity's safety. Until they knew the identity of the Black Mask, however, they could do no more than grope blindly in the dark, and since he could not carry a warning to her himself, it was best to let the young Marquis have his way.

"You will wish to know the outcome of our visit, of course," his lordship continued. "Tell me where you may be found, and a message shall be sent to you before nightfall."

Dominic thought for a moment or two.

"There is a mill a mile or so to the north of Manton Lacey," he said at length, "and cross-roads a short way beyond it where a great oak tree grows. I will be there at sunset, my lord." Another thought occurred to him. "You have servants, sir, who saw Miss Halland at the time of Trumper's attack on us. It will not do for them to recognize her now."

"No, egad! That is a danger I had overlooked," the Marquis agreed, and was silent for a space. "Only Thomas shall go with us to Shere Place," he announced presently. "He is to be trusted in all things, and if I tell him to forget any previous meeting, you may be sure that he will forget. He shall bring you the message tonight, also, for the fewer concerned in this matter, the better."

"Your lordship speaks truly, and now, by your leave, I will go on my way. It is ten years since I left these parts, but if I am recognized, the news will not take long to reach Shere Place." He bowed deeply to Sarah. "Your servant, my lady! I am more grateful to you than I can tell. My lord!"

He bowed again, and withdrew from the room. The passage in which he found himself was empty, but as he went down the steps to the courtyard, a thick-set, fair-haired man who was standing nearby with two other gentlemen glanced casually at him, stared in round-eyed amazement, and then started forward.

"Dominic Fane, by the living God!" His voice was full-throated and hearty, a jovial roar which stopped Dominic dead in his tracks and brought round every head within a dozen feet of the speaker. "What in the devil's name brings you back to Cloverton after so many years?"

Fane stood rigid, his swarthy face a trifle pale and decidedly grim about the mouth, as John Mannering seized his hand in a crushing grip. The honest pleasure of his greeting, the beam of welcome wreathing his ruddy countenance, should have warmed the heart of any returning exile, but Dominic was conscious only of the fact that his precarious anonymity was at an end. People were staring; the two men with whom Mannering had been talking exchanged glances and walked quietly away; there was little hope that anyone besides bluff John would welcome his return, though everyone would be eager to gossip about it.

"Have you been to Shere? Have you seen Mrs. Parr yet?" John was asking eagerly. "Od rot it, man, we'd supposed you dead long since!"

Somehow Dominic forced a smile.

"I am not so easily killed, my friend," he said ironically, "and after ten years of roving I had a fancy to come home again. No, I have not yet been to Shere. I rode into the town not an hour since."

"Well, well! You'll not be in such great haste that you will refuse to drink with an old friend," Mannering declared genially. "No, I'll brook no refusal," he added, as Dominic made a gesture of dissent. "Alice is within, and she would not forgive me if I let you go without seeing her."

Dominic protested, unavailingly, and so, much against his will, was haled into the inn again. He had no desire to renew his acquaintance with Alice Mannering, or indeed, with any of his old friends, and though he could not but be grateful for John's welcome, he would have been better pleased to have avoided the encounter altogether. Setting aside all other considerations, he was acutely conscious of the contrast between his own poverty-stricken appearance and Mannering's unmistakable prosperity, and humiliated beyond measure that the utter failure of his life should be so apparent.

They found Mrs. Mannering awaiting her husband in the private room where they were to dine, and with her the two sons and the daughter who were old enough to be permitted a visit to Goosefeather Fair. Dominic, bowing over her hand, could find, in this plump, motherly woman with her children about her, no trace of the girl who had been his first love, nor was he troubled by the faintest pang of regret for what might have been.

Alice, for her part, when once she had recovered from her astonishment, could have wept for the change she beheld in him. She had always been completely happy in her marriage, and had not thought of Dominic Fane more than a dozen times since his departure from Shere, but now, at sight of him, she was overwhelmed by a flood of memories which reached back into the childhood they had shared. This gaunt, saturnine man, so like, and yet so tragically unlike, the boy she had known, had clearly seen more of suffering and sorrow than she could even imagine, and, being more perceptive than her husband, she realized at once how little pleasure he derived from the present reunion. When he declined John's invitation to dine with them, she neither pressed him to change his mind nor permitted her husband to do so, but as she bade him farewell she assured him, with a sincerity he could not mistake, that he might be sure of a welcome at their home whenever he might choose to come there.

He thanked her with more enthusiasm than he had yet shown, but would make no promise of a visit, and left them with no more idea of his future plans than of the reason for his return to Shere. He was profoundly disturbed by his encounter with the Mannerings, startled to receive a welcome where at best he had expected indifference, and aware of a feeling of guilt at his own lack of response.

By sunset, however, when he came to the rendezvous with Lord Urmiston's messenger, these heart-searchings were forgotten in more important issues. He tethered his horse in a convenient spinney, and walked the few remaining yards to the great oak tree. Leaning against its massive trunk, he watched the sun dip behind the rim of the hills, the afterglow fade from crimson to rose, and the blue dusk deepen over the countryside.

At last the sound of hoofbeats reached his straining ears, and a horseman came in sight and rode towards him through the gathering shadows. Something in the poise of the straight figure and the cock of the gay laced hat seemed familiar, and an instant later he realized that the young Marquis himself had come to meet him.

Spurred by a sense of impending trouble, Dominic started forward and caught the spirited horse by the bridle as it was reined in beside him. Urmiston leaned from the saddle, his face grave and yet excited in the shadow of the broad hat-brim, and answered the unspoken question in a low voice.

"The mystery is solved, Mr. Fane, but whether for good or ill, I know not. We have found the Black Mask." He heard Dominic's swift, indrawn breath and nodded grimly. "She is already established at Shere Place. Her name is Diana Halland."

XII

Diana

VERITY sat in the Long Gallery at Shere Place, and watched Lady Templecombe order the conduct of the estate. There was no doubt that the reins of government rested firmly in those withered hands, and equally certain that only death itself would persuade them to relax their grip. Verity wondered why Sir Lawrence had ever deemed it necessary to come to Shere to make it ready for his bride. His grandmother, she was sure, would have permitted not the smallest change to be made.

Forty-eight hours had passed since her own arrival at Shere Place, but she had not yet confided to Sir Lawrence her suspicions concerning the identity of the Black Mask. The opportunity had not arisen, for she would not speak of it before Lady Templecombe, and she had not once been left alone with her betrothed, but though it would have been simple enough to say that she wished to speak privately with him, she had made no move to do so.

What proof, after all, had she to offer? She had certainly recognized the purse given to Dominic Fane by the masked man as one belonging to her sister-in-law, but the purse had been lost, and without it, Sir Lawrence could scarcely be expected to believe so wild a charge, and other proof there was none. Diana had never liked her, and Diana's child was the heir to her fortune, but these were not matters great enough to prompt a woman to embroil herself in a capital crime. The unknown youths who had acted as envoy to Red Nat would be almost impossible to trace, for Diana had more admirers than Verity had ever met, and if she had persuaded one of them into aiding and abetting her crimes there was no way of identifying him. Dominic might have done so, but he had departed from Shere and gone she knew not whither.

Dominic! Always her thoughts came back to him, no matter in what direction she sought to turn them, or how resolutely she reminded herself that all had ended when he sent her from him. She could understand, if she could not share, his reasons for that renunciation, and in her desperate unhappiness found herself hating the fortune of which she was mistress, and the broad, fertile acres that she had inherited from her grandfather. Wealth, it seemed, could bring her no happiness. It had placed her in the deadliest danger—for what but greed could have prompted the plot against her?—and it had sundered her for ever from the man she loved, for Dominic Fane was too proud to come empty-handed to seek a wealthy bride.

She must not think of him! He had gone, and there was an end to it. Henceforth her loyalty and her duty must be to Sir Lawrence, even though her heart was given elsewhere, and she shrank from the thought of her coming marriage with a horror she could not overcome. In vain she reminded herself that the match had been the wish of her beloved grandfather, for she knew that he had desired nothing so much as her happiness, and that had he known the truth concerning Templecombe he would never have consented to his suit.

Sir Lawrence came into the gallery and was immediately buttonholed by his grandmother and consulted upon various unimportant domestic matters. Beyond a slight bow and a word of greeting to his betrothed he took no heed of her, but devoted his entire attention to the old lady, while Verity, seated somewhat apart from them, regarded him searchingly and tried, without much success, to believe that he had many admirable qualities.

He was fidgeting with the beribboned hilt of his sword. She wondered whether he had ever used the weapon in earnest, and had a swift, mental picture of Dominic fencing with Barnabas Pike while the players looked on and applauded. Even she, knowing nothing of the art, had realized then that Dominic Fane was a superb swordsman. What chance of survival would Sir Lawrence have had if Dominic had not renounced his vengeance? If he, and not Barnabas, had come with her to Shere Place two days ago, that bright, deadly blade which she had seen unsheathed in sport would by now have freed her from the prison she felt closing about her. Honour would have been a small price to pay for freedom, and perhaps for happiness. . . .

She rose abruptly from her chair and walked across to the nearest window, where she stood staring blindly into the garden beyond, remembering that moment of parting, the hard strength of his arms about her, the passion and tenderness of his kiss. Her eyes filled with slow, painful tears. Had it come already to this, that she was wishing Templecombe dead, and herself in the arms of a man who would have killed him? A fine augury, i'faith, for a happy marriage! She rested her forehead against the windowpane and closed her eyes, but could not shut out the dreary vision of the future.

At the far end of the gallery a door was opened, and the butler's sonorous voice shattered that nightmare with a new and greater horror, as he announced the visitor who had just arrived.

"Mrs. Halland, my lady," he said disinterestedly.

Verity turned incredulously, and saw her sister-in-law coming with insolent grace down the long room, completely mistress of herself and of the situation. Old Lady Templecombe was watching her with bright, inscrutable eyes, but Sir Lawrence had started up out of his chair and was gaping like a landed fish. Perhaps it was the wild glance he cast towards Verity which drew Diana's attention in the same direction, but whatever the cause, the effect was prompt and overwhelming. She halted in her advance, stared for one unbelieving instant at the girl by the window, while every trace of colour drained out of her face, and then she flung up a hand as though to ward off a blow, and dropped in a dead faint where she stood.

With an exclamation of dismay Templecombe hurried towards her, and the Dowager hoisted herself to her feet and hobbled after him, but Verity stood unmoving by the window, one hand still grasping the heavy curtain, and stared with frozen calm at the prostrate figure. Any doubts which had been in her mind were banished now; Diana herself had supplied evidence of her guilt.

Dimly she was aware of her ladyship issuing commands, of servants hurrying to and fro, of Sir Lawrence, helpless and distraught, in the background, and all the while a question was hammering insistently in her mind. Why had Diana come to Shere Place? Cold fear fastened a merciless grip upon her; she had never felt so defenceless or so alone. In vain she reminded herself that this was not London, that there was no masked envoys or hired cut-throats in this sleepy Somersetshire village. She had been shown all too clearly that she was of no account in this proud, hostile house, and who would believe her if she accused Diana of instigating the plot against her?

At length the old lady summoned her in a sharp, querulous voice and she forced herself to go forward, though her limbs felt leaden and she was conscious of the dryness of fear in her throat. Diana, pale but composed, was sitting in the Dowager's great chair, her head resting against a crimson cushion which threw her dark, compelling beauty into sharp relief, and as the younger woman approached she put out both hands toward her and smiled tremulously.

"Verity, my dear!" The deep, husky voice was rendered deeper yet by emotion; the white hands closed firmly upon Verity's, and drew her down to a kiss she could not bring herself to return. "What can I say? You are safe, and all the anxiety of these past weeks counts for nothing beside that." Her dark eyes searched Miss Halland's face and she gave a shaken laugh. "Child, how well you look! Brown as a gipsy, by my faith!"

Verity made what answer she knew not, and tried to withdraw her hands, but this Diana would not allow. It seemed that, having found her safe and sound, she must keep her within reach. Nothing would satisfy her but for Verity to sit down on a stool beside her and recount the story of her adventures, while she clasped one of her hands fondly between her own. Verity shrank from the touch as from some contamination, but forced herself to endure it lest Diana suspect she knew the truth.

She had no choice but to repeat the tale which she and Barnabas Pike had told two days before, though her heart misgave her as she did so. If Diana's were indeed the hand behind the plot, then she would know of Dominic's part in it, and must surely wonder why her sister-in-law so carefully refrained from mentioning him. Her suspicions would be aroused, and she might well begin to speculate upon how much more was being withheld.

Mrs. Halland, however, showed no outward sign of incredulity. She listened with well-simulated horror to the tale of Verity's capture and escape, and professed deep concern at the hardships she must have endured while travelling with the strolling players. When Verity had told her story, and Diana's exclamations and questions were at an end, Miss Halland ventured to ask what errand had brought the other woman to Somerset.

Diana cast a deprecating look at Sir Lawrence and the old lady.

"The lawyers beset me constantly with questions and legal matters," she said plaintively, "and I have not the least head for such business. Then I bethought me of Sir Lawrence, who by virtue of his betrothal to you and his long-standing friendship with your grandfather, was more nearly concerned than I, and I resolved to seek his aid. To escape the importunities of the lawyers I came myself instead of sending a messenger." She paused, and looked again at the Dowager. " 'Tis an unwarrantable intrusion, which I can only hope your ladyship will pardon. The strain of these past weeks has been such that I am nigh distracted with worry."

"You are very welcome, my dear Mrs. Halland," Lady Templecombe replied graciously. It was clear that Diana found more favour in my lady's eyes than Verity had done. "My grandson will be happy for you to leave everything in his hands."

"Of course, of course!" Sir Lawrence agreed hurriedly, with a warmth which to Verity seemed somewhat forced. "Now that my betrothed is restored to us, however . . . ! But you may leave all to me, madam. It is a confusing affair, damnably confusing!"

To Verity, the warmth of his agreement seemed false, but she had no chance to pursue the thought. Even as Sir Lawrence spoke, the butler once more threw open the door at the end of the gallery, this time to announce the Marquis of Urmiston and Lady Sarah Deverell.

In the brief silence which followed the announcement Verity sat paralyzed with horror, unable to move, to speak, scarcely even to think. Then, as Urmiston and his sister advanced, the calm of despair settled upon her mind and with it a feeling of relief that the game of cat-and-mouse was nearly at an end.

Sir Lawrence had gone forward to greet the visitors, almost as though he welcomed the interruption. Numerous compliments were exchanged, and then Lady Templecombe presented Mrs. Halland. As Diana made some conventional reply in her deep, husky voice to Lady Sarah's greeting, the young girl's eyes widened in surprise, and she exchanged a startled glance with her brother, a glance which Verity was too overwrought to observe. With some reluctance the Dowager then made Miss Halland known to her new guests, and Verity braced herself to meet the inevitable exposure, wondering as she did so what would follow.

But Lady Sarah made no reference to their earlier meeting, merely saying, with a good deal of vivacity: "Then it is true! We had heard rumours that Sir Lawrence's lost bride was found again. My dear Miss Halland, I am so happy to make your acquaintance."

Verity murmured an incoherent reply. She felt dazed, incredulous. Was it possible that Lady Sarah had failed to recognize her? She found the Marquis bowing before her, and mechanically curtsied in response. As she rose, she looked up timidly into his face, and encountered a glance from those fine blue eyes which puzzled her more than ever. He recognized her, without a doubt, but it was plain that he did not intend to betray her. Remembering his vexation when she had refused his proffered help, she was at a loss to understand this magnanimity, and, though reassured, could not feel entirely at ease.

Lady Sarah was all eager, innocent inquiry, and Sir Lawrence had no choice but to explain the circumstances of his betrothed's return to him. He did so reluctantly, in the manner of one whose thoughts were elsewhere, while Miss Halland vainly racked her brain for some excuse to draw Lady Sarah aside and beg for an explanation. It seemed, however, that the young lady herself had already considered this matter, for when the story had been exclaimed and wondered at, she turned to Verity, and with a disarming smile begged to be allowed to lend her some clothes to wear until her own could be brought to her.

"For I see that Mrs. Halland is too tall to supply your needs, while you and I are much of a size," she concluded. "Let us be private for a few minutes, and you shall tell me precisely what you require."

Scarcely waiting for Verity's reply, she drew her apart from the rest of the company, and as soon as they were out of earshot said quickly: "I am so sorry you were alarmed by our arrival, Miss Halland, but there was no way to spare you. We met Mr. Fane at the fair, and he told us the whole story. We come, in fact, to bring you a warning from him. By chance or design, your enemy is here in Somerset." She cast a fleeting glance over her shoulder at the group they had left, and drew the other girl into the embrasure formed by the nearest window. "My dear, ill news is best told quickly. It can be none other than your sister-in-law, Mrs. Halland."

She paused, but Verity neither moved nor spoke, and Sarah hurried into a description of Dominic's encounter with the Black Mask, and her own subsequent meeting with him in Cloverton. She had expected the story to be received with dismay, or even downright disbelief, and was astonished to learn that the news she brought merely confirmed Miss Halland's own suspicions.

"But have you told no one the identity of your enemy?" she said blankly. "Not even Sir Lawrence?"

Verity shook her head.

"How could I, when I have no proof? Even now, though I am certain of her guilt, I dare not accuse her, for Dominic must not appear in this matter. To do so would be to admit his own part in the plot, and Sir Lawrence would be swift to turn such a weapon against him. He hates and fears him, for reasons in which I have no part at all."

"Then what is to be done?" Sarah's voice was troubled. "You may depend upon my brother and upon me for any help that it is in our power to give, but there is so little that we can do, and who can tell what danger may threaten you now that Mrs. Halland has found you here?"

"You are very kind, my lady," Verity said quietly, "and I am grateful, but do not fear for me. I know Diana now for what she is, and I shall not fall again into a trap of her devising."

"Perhaps you are right," Sarah agreed thoughtfully. "While you are in this house it is unlikely that she will risk any fresh attempt against you, and once you are married, her child will no longer be your heir and so her motive will be gone. Then you will be safe."

Verity's glance turned involuntarily to where Sir Lawrence sat with his guests. For an instant her mask of calm composure was torn aside, and she said faintly, as though the words could be held back no longer: "Sometimes safety can be too dearly bought!"

Sarah was startled, but thought it best to make no reply to this, and instead began to explain the scheme she had evolved to communicate with Verity again upon the following day. Thomas should bring the promised clothes to Shere Place in the morning, and with them a letter to which Miss Halland would naturally reply, so that if any fresh development had occurred she could send word of it to her friends and well-wishers. From the ranks of these it was now tacitly agreed that Sir Lawrence must be excluded.

Verity agreed to the scheme, and they rejoined the rest of the company, the Marquis and his sister taking their leave a few minutes later. When they had gone, Miss Halland made an excuse to withdraw to her bedchamber, for she felt in need of a period of quiet reflection before facing her sister-in-law again. She knew that she would need to be constantly on her guard if she were not to betray herself to Diana, and she wished, for a few precious moments, to be free to revel in the bitter-sweet knowledge that Dominic was still close at hand, still watching over her. For that assurance, more than for all their promises of aid, her gratitude to the Marquis and his sister was boundless.

Sir Lawrence also having taken himself off, Diana was left alone with the old lady. For a while she was silent, apparently absorbed in troubled thought, and then she said abruptly:

"This player fellow who brought Verity here! Will your ladyship be so kind as to describe him to me?"

The bright, sharp eyes in that amazingly wrinkled face met hers shrewdly; her ladyship gave a cackle of triumphant laughter.

"So you do not believe her story either!" she remarked with profound satisfaction, and launched at once into a description of Verity's protector. The portrait she painted was embellished with a wealth of unflattering detail, but it left Diana more puzzled than before. She had naturally assumed that the self-styled player was Dominic Fane, but, even allowing for exaggeration and distortion on the old lady's part, this description could never have been inspired by the man whom Mrs. Halland had seen at the tavern in Fleet Street. Was it possible, then, that Verity's story was true? Yet, if it were, why had she described Nat Trumper in detail, and so carefully avoided all mention of his confederate?

These were questions to which Diana could find no immediate answer, and after listening for a little while longer to the Dowager's criticisms of Miss Halland, and adding a few sweetly-poisonous ones of her own, she pleaded fatigue and withdrew to the apartment which had meanwhile been prepared for her. The plea of weariness was borne out by the pallor which still lingered in her face, and was by no means wholly assumed. A journey which had taken many days to accomplish, culminating in a shock so great that she had not yet fully recovered from it, had tried her to the limits of endurance.

She had travelled into Somerset on an errand which, as she had known from the first, was likely to be attended by many difficulties, but one obstacle which she had never foreseen, even in her most pessimistic moments, was the presence at Shere Place of Verity Halland. All her careful plotting had gone for naught, and now, when it was a hundred times more imperative to be rid of the girl, she found herself faced with the prospect of being obliged to begin again, with none of the advantages which had been hers in London.

The key to the whole problem, she decided as she paced her room, too agitated to take the rest she needed, was Dominic Fane. Her thoughts went back to the night when she had seen him, and the memory of his bold, dark face, and of the contempt which he had not troubled to conceal, stirred uneasily in her mind. She had judged him then—and Diana Halland was no mean judge of men—to be a man of considerable forcefulness and intelligence, and had even been glad that her plot against Miss Halland was to rest in such capable hands. Now it seemed unpleasantly probable that her judgment had done him less than justice, and that he had not been slow to bend the situation to his own advantage, though what mysterious purpose he sought to serve she could not even imagine. That he had obtained some sort of hold over Verity seemed certain, since even in his absence she would speak no word against him, but where was he, and why was he holding aloof in this odd fashion?

The questions which only Verity or Fane himself could answer beat with merciless insistence in her brain and, finding herself menaced, as it seemed, by an enemy unseen and unknown, she began to realize in a small measure something of the mental anguish which Verity herself must have endured for so many weeks. The reflection did nothing to soothe or to reassure her.

XIII

A Lesson in Courtesy

DIANA might have felt some degree of satisfaction had she known that her own unexpected arrival on the scene was occasioning Dominic Fane almost as much uneasiness as he was causing her. The disclosure of the Black Mask's identity had not, it was true, stirred him to such depths of astonishment and dismay as Verity's presence at Shere Place had provoked in Mrs. Halland, but he was profoundly uneasy none the less.

When Lord Urmiston had finished telling him all that Lady Sarah had learned from Verity he was silent for a while. They had left their exposed position at the cross-roads and walked back to the spinney where Dominic had left his horse, and now, while Urmiston tethered his own mount beside it, Fane stood lost in frowning thought, absently fingering the hilt of his sword.

"I would be easier in my mind if we knew what purpose brought Mrs. Halland to Shere," he said at length. "It must be some more pressing reason than she had disclosed, to bring her so far upon so slight a pretext."

"You may be right," Urmiston agreed slowly, "and yet, to my mind, her original purpose is of less importance than what may follow, now that she knows Miss Halland escaped the fate she planned for her. Yet, in Templecombe's house and under his eye, it does not seem likely that she will dare to make any fresh attack upon her. How can she, without drawing suspicion upon herself?"

"As to that, my lord," Dominic said grimly, "she may not need to seek far for the means of mischief. We have been at great pains to keep secret my part in the affair, but Diana Halland knows of it, and she must be wondering already why Verity says nothing concerning me. Add to that fact that when I left you earlier today I walked straight into the arms of an old acquaintance, and you may perceive the danger I apprehend. It needs only some busy gossip to carry word to Templecombe that Dominic Fane has returned to Shere, and Mrs.

Halland will have a safe and potent weapon to use against Verity. A hint to the Dowager, a discreet question here and there—you take my meaning, my lord?"

"Only too well," Urmiston agreed gloomily. "Upon my soul, Mr. Fane, it is a damnable situation!"

"And the most damnable part of all, my lord, is the fact that from the time of her disappearance until two days ago, Verity was with me," Dominic added bitterly. "Let that once be known, and my old quarrel with Templecombe remembered, and who will believe any protests of innocence?"

"You think it will become known?"

"I am sure of it! The secret is shared by too many to remain a secret for long."

The Marquis frowned and slashed with his whip at a nearby clump of nettles.

"It is a thousand pities," he remarked, "that you did not think to assume a false name when you joined with the players."

Fane said nothing, and his face was a scarred and swarthy mask which betrayed nothing of the hell of anger and futile regret raging in his soul. Urmiston's words struck shrewdly. He had known from the first that to tell the players his real name was to court discovery once Cloverton was reached, but his purpose then had been such that he had revelled in the thought. He had wanted the whole countryside to know that Sir Lawrence Templecombe's promised wife had travelled across England with Sir Lawrence's bitterest enemy; that the future lady of Shere Place had become the vagabond light-o'-love of the despised and ruined Dominic Fane. Now, when he would have given his life to spare her a moment's pain, the evil he had sown then was yielding a fatal harvest. Repentance and renunciation alike were but empty words, and he had ruined her as irretrievably as though that storm-racked hour at the house in the wood had never been.

Urmiston was speaking again, and with an effort Dominic dragged his thoughts from the havoc wrought by his own blind desire for vengeance. The Marquis said in a troubled voice:

"Is there no way of averting a scandal?"

"One way, perhaps!" Dominic spoke slowly as a new idea occurred to him. "There is a factor, my lord, which we have overlooked, and that is Templecombe himself. If he refuses to believe anything against Verity, any gossip will die a natural death."

Urmiston frowned. "If my reading of his nature is correct, he will be only too ready to believe in any affront to his dignity or his honour. His self-conceit is monstrous."

"Not so monstrous as his cowardice!" Contempt rang in Fane's voice, and his smile was saturnine. "If he gives credence to the tale he must meet me, or be for ever branded a craven; and if he meets me I will kill him. That he knows and has known for fourteen years. For his life's sake, and whatever he may believe, he dare not show doubt of Verity's innocence."

"God's light! What a vile fellow he is!" Urmiston exclaimed impulsively. "How came such as he to be betrothed to Miss Verity? That will be an ill mating!"

There was a moment's silence before Dominic spoke again. It was almost dark now beneath the trees, so that subtleties of expression were lost in the dimness, and his voice betrayed nothing as he said:

"An ill mating indeed, my lord. He will break her heart and her spirit, for his is not a nature to appreciate the quality of hers."

"Blind, thankless fool!" His lordship fiercely apostrophised Sir Lawrence. "I tell you, Mr. Fane, if I could but win such a bride as his, I would count myself the luckiest of men!"

There was another and longer pause, while Dominic fought an inward battle as bitter as it was brief. Why not? he asked himself. His own love could have no hope of fulfilment, and it would be better, surely, to give her up to Urmiston than to Templecombe; to know that she had at least a chance of happiness, with a husband who could give her the place in the world of which she was worthy, yet cherish her as Sir Lawrence never would. In a tone which gave no hint of what it cost him to utter the words, he said deliberately:

"I believe that Verity herself has no liking for the match, but what can she do? She has no other protector, and as long as she remains unwed she stands in danger of further plots."

The Marquis looked sharply at him, as though trying to see his face. Failing this, he said slowly: "It is true that she said something to my sister which supports that belief, and it is unthinkable that she should be forced into taking a course repugnant to her merely for fear of her sister-in-law's scheming. From that I fancy I might contrive to protect her, if she would grant me the privilege, and my sisters would be more than happy to take her into their care."

"Then tell her so, my lord," Dominic replied harshly, "and

tell her also, for what it is worth, that I counsel her to accept your offer. I know Templecombe too well to suppose that he can ever bring her anything but sorrow." He did not wait for an answer, but continued before Urmiston could speak again. "Now I must ride back to Cloverton. All things considered, it will be best if I return quite openly to my old home, but I must make some few purchases if the place is to be made habitable, even for a short time. It will be as well, also, for me to see Barnabas Pike and tell him something of what has happened."

The Marquis appeared to give only part of his attention to these latter words, but when Dominic turned towards the horses, he came out of his reverie with a start.

"Do so, Mr. Fane," he assented, "for if the harm is not yet done, he may be able to impose silence upon his people, though in truth I have little hope of it." He put out his hand, and after an instant's hesitation Dominic gripped it in his own. "Meanwhile, have no fears for Miss Verity. As I told you, my sister has found a means of communicating with her tomorrow, and the least hint of danger to her will take me to Shere Place without delay. Between us, we shall bring this affair to a happy conclusion, depend on it!"

Dominic agreed somewhat curtly, and, bidding the Marquis farewell, turned his horse's head once more towards the town. His part, it seemed, was all but played, and soon Verity would have need of him no longer. Scandal or no, there was now little doubt that the Marquis would find some pretext to remove her from Shere Place to Corville Court, and the rest would follow naturally enough. Urmiston was just such a lover as maids must dream of, with his striking good looks, his youth and wealth and high rank, and if Verity lent a ready ear to his wooing, who had the right to blame her? Certainly not a man whose life and hopes had been laid in ruins while she was still in the nursery, who had sold his honour for a handful of gold, and whose only redeeming feature was the love which had taught him to put her happiness before his own.

So, riding through the scented summer dusk, Dominic Fane subdued, if he could not conquer, his demon of jealousy, though the struggle left its mark upon him in a dark and dangerous mood which, with little provocation, would flare into violent action. Such provocation he was presently to have. He came back to the little town to find it still noisy with merrymakers, though the crowds were somewhat less dense than they had been earlier in the day. He stabled his horse and made his way on foot to the place where the players had set up their stage, but, finding a performance in progress, went instead to procure food and drink and a few other necessities to take back with him to Shere.

This occupied him for longer than he had expected, and when he returned, audience and players alike had dispersed. He was about to go in search of the latter when a voice called his name, and he turned to find Maria, the dancer, coming towards him.

"If 'tis Barnabas you seek, he is yonder, at the Hand and Flower," she informed him, but when he thanked her and would have turned away, she caught his sleeve to detain him. In the flickering light of a nearby lantern he could see that her face was alive with curiosity.

"Is it true what they are saying?" she questioned eagerly. "That Verity is not your sister, but the bride of some great gentleman who wronged you years ago? Barnabas will tell me nothing, but the whole town hums with gossip."

"It does, does it?" Dominic's voice was grim. "Then whose tongue has been wagging, girl? Yours, perhaps?"

"No!" Maria tossed her head. "Blame Meg, if you must blame anyone."

Dominic sighed and cursed in one. He and Pike between them should have foreseen this danger and sought to avert it, for Meg was an indefatigable gossip and as silly as she was kind. He turned away, paying no further heed to Maria's impatient questions, and went in search of Barnabas.

The tap-room of the Hand and Flower was crowded, heavy with tobacco smoke and the fumes of ale and wine, and insufferably hot. Dominic thrust his way impatiently through the throng, provoking more than one indignant glance and muttered comment, and so found Barnabas Pike sitting on a bench against the wall, in morose and solitary meditation. He looked up with a start as Fane slid into the empty seat beside him.

"Maria told me where to find you," Dominic said by way of explanation and greeting, and Pike nodded, with no lightening of the gloom of his expression.

"Did she tell you also of the mischief made by that loose-tongued slut, Meg?" he asked in a low voice. "Fiend seize the wench! The whole town has the tale by now."

He went on to elaborate this statement, and Dominic's frown deepened as he listened. The fair, of course, was largely to blame for the speed with which the story had spread, for it had brought together large numbers of the people who, in the ordinary course of events, did not meet above two or three times a year, and brought them, moreover, in a mood and atmosphere which encouraged gossip. One came to the fair to enjoy oneself, and what was more enjoyable than a choice morsel of scandal, particularly when it concerned, as this one did, one of the most important and unpopular men in the country? So tongues chattered joyously, and everyone had some fresh incident to relate or theory to air, and the names of Templecombe and Fane and Verity Halland were upon everybody's lips.

Dominic called for ale, and when Barnabas had done, gave him, in a cautiously lowered voice, a brief account of all that had happened since their parting two days earlier. Before he had finished, however, an interruption occurred. On entering the inn he had been recognized by someone present, the word had quickly spread, and the crowd grown thicker than before, but no one ventured to address him until a young man, proclaimed a gentleman by his dress if not by his manners, thrust his way noisily in front of the street. Another lad and a man-servant trailed at his heels, and all three were in varying stages of drunkenness.

"I say 'tis all a hoax," the first youth proclaimed loudly. "Some wag has started the tale to set the town by the ears, and set all tongues a-clacking. Damme, Charles! I'll wager that Templecombe is in a sweat of fear already, and all for naught."

"But Tim says he saw the fellow here, Harry," the other insisted plaintively. "And with the player-rogue, what's more! Tim! Devil take it, man, where are you? Tim!"

"Here, sir!" The servant lurched forward past a group which had been impeding his progress and thrust aside two hapless farm lads who were gaping at these rowdy intruders. "I saw him right enough, not ten minutes since—ah! and yonder he is, sir, as I told you."

He flung out a wavering but triumphant hand towards the bench where Fane was sitting. The youth addressed as Charles peered with owlish solemnity through the smoky murk, while his companion reeled forward to rest his hands on the edge of the table and lean across it to peer into Dominic's impassive face. A sudden, uneasy hush settled over the crowded room.

"By all the devils in hell! The fellow speaks truly," Harry

announced at length, and stood upright again. "Dominic Fane it is! That damned, hang-dog face could belong to no one else."

He looked round, as though expecting applause for his perspicacity, but none came. Dominic turned his head, and addressed the man who stood nearest to him.

"Who is this cockerel who crows so lustily?" he asked mildly.

The man looked startled, but replied after only the barest hesitation.

" 'Tis Mr. Harry Duncan, Mrs. Mannering's cousin," he replied in a low voice, "and the other is Charles Dellaby." He hesitated again, and then lowered his voice yet further. "Best have a care! Mr. Duncan is reckoned a great swordsman, young as he is."

"Is he indeed?" The mockery about Fane's mouth deepened perceptibly. "It is a reputation I enjoyed myself at one time."

He remembered Harry Duncan now. When Dominic Fane and John Mannering were vying for Alice Barlow's favours, Harry had been a mischievous, dare-devil little boy who plagued them both impartially whenever his visits to the Barlow home coincided with theirs. John had taken it all in good part, but Dominic, less easy-going than his rival, had more than once retaliated in a manner as prompt as it was painful for his victim.

Harry, meanwhile, had been studying Dominic with all the silent concentration of the slightly inebriated, observing every detail of his appearance. Perhaps similar memories of his childhood were stirring in his own mind, for his next remark was charged with a quite unnecessary venom.

"Why, what a damned, out-at-elbows ruffian it is! Never tell me the rest of the tale is true, and Templecombe set aside for such a scarecrow, unless the girl be mad or blind!"

Dominic's eyes narrowed, and a small golden flame seemed to leap within them, but he gave no other sign of the sudden wicked fury the words provoked. Without shifting his gaze from Duncan's face, he said with fatal clarity:

"You were a graceless, ill-conditioned whelp when last I saw you, Harry Duncan, and I had not thought it possible for you to grow worse. I see now that I was mistaken."

For one incredulous instant Duncan gaped at him, and then a stifled chuckle from somewhere in the crowd behind him roused him from his stupor of astonishment. A tankard with perhaps half an inch of liquid remaining in it stood close by his hand, and with an incoherent exclamation of rage he snatched it up and flung its contents in Dominic's face.

The hush became a silence, the silence of bated breath and half-anxious, half-eager expectancy. Very deliberately Dominic wiped the trickles of ale from his face, and then, with a violence the more startling for the restraint which had preceded it, he heaved the table aside and was on his feet, the Toledo blade gleaming in his hand.

There was an inarticulate mutter of alarm and a hasty drawing back from his immediate vicinity. Barnabas came to his feet as swiftly as his friend and gripped his arm. "The young fool's drunk!" he said urgently. "Let be, Dominic, in pity's name!"

"Not so drunk that I cannot deal with this roisterer as he deserves," Duncan retorted in a voice thick with fury, and dragged his own sword from the scabbard. "Stand aside, Master Mountebank, if you value your own skin!"

He came at Dominic with no further warning, and Barnabas sprang hastily back against the wall. He was probably the only man in the room, with the exception of Fane himself, who was not astounded by what followed. The two blades rang together, and after one swift engagement Duncan's sword went flying from his hand, and he staggered back with a spreading stain of blood on his right sleeve, to fetch up in the supporting arms of one of the bystanders.

Dominic wiped his blade on the skirt of his coat and sheathed it again. He looked at Harry, and the mockery in his dark, scarred face was very apparent.

"You have taken no hurt beyond the letting of some of your hot blood," he said contemptuously, "and for that you may thank your kinship with John Mannering and his wife. I've no wish to cause them any distress, so strive to profit by the lesson, and let others do the same. I have a swift, sure answer for any who meddle in my affairs." He laid his hand on the hilt of his sword, his glance flickering with sardonic meaning over the staring crowd, so that more than one man glanced uneasily away from the challenge in those tawny eyes. "Remember it!" he said, and, turning, stalked towards the door, the onlookers falling back hurriedly to let him pass.

So, with Barnabas at his side, he stepped out of the Hand and Flower into the dark street, and in silence bent his steps towards the stable where he had left his horse. They had

crossed the market-place before either spoke, but at last Barnabas said in a puzzled voice:

"The sword-play I admire, and the need for it I perceive,
but what in the fiend's name was the purpose of that gascon-
ade which followed it? I might say such upon the stage, but
'tis not a style that comes naturally to you."

They had walked a few yards further before Dominic replied. It was too dark for Barnabas to see his face, but his
voice was fraught with an almost savage mockery.

"I was not concerned merely to teach that puppy a lesson
in courtesy. Be sure that the story of what happened yonder
will be carried to Templecombe with all the rest, to serve as a
spur to his efforts to disprove this scandal. Harry Duncan is
reckoned a great swordsman, we are told, but I have proved
myself a better. Templecombe will never send me his challenge now, not though the devil himself demand it."

XIV

The Bride

THE following morning was to prove Dominic a true prophet,
for the day was yet young when Charles Dellaby presented
himself at Shere Place and demanded to see Sir Lawrence.
Word of his arrival was carried to Templecombe, reaching
him at a moment when Mrs. Halland, whom he had been
zealously avoiding ever since her arrival, had just succeeded
in running him to earth. Therefore he welcomed the interruption with relief, and Dellaby himself, when he came into the
room, with a cordiality which the latter found almost embar-
rassing.

When greetings had been exchanged, and he had been
presented to Diana, at whom he stared in patent admiration,
Dellaby found himself in something of a quandary. The lady
obviously had no intention of withdrawing, and one or two
pointed hints that his business with Sir Lawrence was private
were ignored by his companions, deliberately by Diana, and
through obtuseness on the part of Templecombe.

So half an hour dragged by in polite and stilted conversation, until Dellaby perceived that the warning he brought must be given in Mrs. Halland's presence or not at all. Hoping that the mere mention of his business would show Templecombe the need for privacy, and unaware that nothing could be more surely calculated to keep Diana where she was, he said with desperate casualness:

"I expect you have already heard, Sir Lawrence, that Dominic Fane has come back to Shere?"

Diana started, and turned a wide, astonished gaze upon the speaker, but an instant later her attention was claimed by Templecombe. A strangled sound between a gasp and a groan had burst from his lips, and now he was leaning forward in his chair, his face curiously mottled and his eyes more prominent than ever.

"Fane?" he repeated hoarsely. "Dominic Fane?" Then, with a disbelief born of the desire to disbelieve: "Bah! 'tis impossible! Where heard you that tale?"

"It is no tale, Sir Lawrence, but the evidence of my own eyes," Dellaby replied wtih some indignation. "I saw Fane last night in Cloverton, and this morning the gates of his house stand wide."

Templecombe made a tremendous effort to control himself. His hands gripped hard on the arms of his chair and he swallowed once or twice before he spoke, but even so there was a perceptible quaver in his voice.

"You cannot be certain. Did you ever see him in the old days?"

"Once only, but his is a face one does not forget. Those strange, golden eyes and the scar across his cheek—but you need not depend upon my word alone! All the town is talking of it. Mannering was the first to recognize him, but I could name you a dozen others."

Sir Lawrence appeared to be giving him only a part of his attention. He gnawed furiously at his fingernails and stared at Dellaby with blank, unseeing eyes. At length he said apprehensively:

"It is ten years since he left these parts. What can have brought him back after so long?"

Mr. Dellaby scratched his chin and considered how to reply, glancing sidelong at Mrs. Halland the while. He had a very shrewd notion of the purpose which had brought Dominic Fane back to his birthplace, but it was difficult to word the warning he wished to convey in terms which would not give offence. He decided to temporize.

"Whatever the reason, he has not prospered meanwhile, for a more ragged, beggarly figure I have yet to see. There's none dare mock him, though, since he has proved himself so ready with his sword." He paused, and saw that now he had Sir Lawrence's undivided attention. "He drew on Harry Duncan last night, because Harry made some jest at his expense, and ran him through the arm before a man could take breath. Then he issued a veiled challenge to all those standing by, and a warning that anyone else who crossed him would go the same road.

"But—but Duncan is the finest swordsman in these parts," Templecombe stammered, aghast.

Mr. Dellaby shrugged apologetically. He could sympathize with Sir Lawrence's dismay.

"Nevertheless, he was no match for Fane. The man could have killed him as easily as you or I would kill a hare. He told Harry frankly that he spared him merely for the sake of his kinship with Mannering."

Diana had all this while been sitting motionless in her chair, her heavy-lidded dark eyes glancing from one man to the other. So Dominic Fane was a native of Shere, and a link existed between him and Sir Lawrence Templecombe other than that of her forging! She stirred, and said in her deep, husky voice:

"This man Fane, whoever he may be, would seem to be a very dangerous and hardy fellow, but surely it is unlikely that so turbulent a spirit will find any welcome here?"

"It appears, madam," Dellaby replied, with an anxious glance at Templecombe, "that he brings his own friends with him. When I saw him last night he was in close company with a certain strolling player, the leader of a troupe drawn hither by the fair."

Sir Lawrence started, and looked up with swift apprehension, but it was Diana who spoke first.

"You must be aware, Mr. Dellaby," she said with a hint of coldness, "that my sister-in-law, Miss Halland, who is betrothed to Sir Lawrence, was recently brought to Shere by a troupe of players. If you are hinting at some connection between that fact and the return of this Dominic Fane, I must ask you to be more explicit. You have said at once too little, and too much."

Mr. Dellaby hesitated, casting an imploring glance towards Sir Lawrence, but Templecombe was past caring for his guest's feelings. A horrifying premonition of what he was about to hear had him in its grip, and he could only stare at Dellaby with dropped jaw and starting eyes. The younger man made a helpless gesture.

"My reticence, madam, was prompted by the desire to spare you embarrassment," he said with dignity, "but, since you will have it so, I will tell you what is already common gossip in the town."

He did so, and because they had forced him into this uncomfortable situation, he revenged himself by withholding no detail of the scandal. As the tale progressed, Diana bowed her head and covered her eyes with her hand, but Templecombe sat as though turned to stone. His face was ashen now, and the sweat stood upon his brow; a ghost had risen up out of the past to confront him, and the threat of a vengeance he had forgotten, as he had forgotten the wrong which inspired it, hovered before his eyes like the angel of death itself.

When Dellaby paused, a heavy silence filled the room, but at last Diana raised her head. She was pale and obviously labouring under some strong emotion which she was endeavouring to dissemble. When she spoke there was a note of fierceness in her low voice. "So that is the shameful truth behind her so-called abduction! Upon my soul, we have been most grossly deceived!"

Neither of her companions made any reply. Dellaby could think of nothing to say, and Templecombe seemed not to have heard, for he still sat like a man stunned. For a moment or two Diana regarded him with a frown, and then she turned again to the younger man.

"We are grateful to you for bringing us this news, Mr. Dellaby," she said gravely, "for it is never pleasant to be the bearer of ill tidings. Will you leave us now? Sir Lawrence is quite overcome, as you can see, and I will confess myself to be profoundly disturbed and shocked by what you tell me."

"Of course, madam! I will go at once." Dellaby took the hand extended to him, and bore it reverently to his lips. "May I hope that you will be able to forgive me for causing you this distress?"

"The cause, sir, was no fault of yours, and your kindness in coming here I shall remember with gratitude," she assured him. "I trust that we may renew our acquaintance upon some happier occasion."

The glance and the slow smile which accompanied these words so dazzled young Dellaby that he bowed himself out of her presence without remembering to take leave of Sir Lawrence. When the door had closed behind him, Diana gave a little scornful laugh and then went quickly, with a rustle of stiff silks, to where Templecombe sat slumped in his chair, and bent over him and gripped him by the shoulder. "Now," she said, and there was a note of sharpness invading the husky tones of her voice, "who is Dominic Fane?"

"Who is he?" Slowly Templecombe lifted his bowed head, and showed her a face from which the last semblance of youth had departed. "I will tell you, madam! He is the bitterest enemy I have in this world. For fourteen years he has desired my death, and sought to force a challenge upon me in a quarrel which was not rightly his. Now he and that vixen between them have brought me to a pass where I must meet him, or be for ever dishonoured; and he is a master swordsman." He beat his hand on the arm of his chair and his voice rose to a note of panic which was almost hysteria. Now that the need to preserve appearances was gone, abject fear had him in its grip. "You heard what Dellaby said! Even Harry Duncan was no match for him. He fights like the devil incarnate, and if I meet him he will kill me! Oh, God help me! What am I to do?"

He buried his face in his hands, his fingers writhing amid the curls of his periwig, and Diana released her grip on his shoulder and stood slowly upright. Her lips were compressed, her eyes bright and dangerous, and for all its beauty her face was suddenly evil to look upon. Her thoughts had gone back to the night when she had spoken with Dominic Fane in London, and he had counselled her to order Verity's death. 'Fate plays strange tricks,' he had said, but the trickery here had been his, and not Destiny's. He had, in fact, amused himself at her expense, and that she would never forgive.

She looked down again at Templecombe's huddled figure, and an expression of impatience and contempt crossed her face. For a moment she stood undecided, and then turned and went quickly out of the room. Sir Lawrence was a broken reed, and no help was to be had from him, but she must act quickly if she were to attain the goal she desired; yet to act she must know more of this enmity between Templecombe and Fane, and there was only one person to hand who might supply it. As she hastened through the stately, comfortless rooms of Shere Place, Diana Halland gave thanks for the foresight which had prompted her to ingratiate herself with its mistress.

She found the Dowager in her favourite seat in the Long Gallery, and drawing a chair close to the old lady's, she sat down and in a low voice recounted the story told by Charles Dellaby. As she had expected, it provoked an outburst of fury, but behind all her ladyship's harsh words and angry condemnations of Miss Halland, Diana thought to detect a note of fear. Very little questioning was needed to draw out the old story, and when the tale was told she sat for a while in deep thought, an abstraction from which she was roused by the Dowager suddenly hoisting herself to her feet.

"That trollop!" said her ladyship, in fierce reply to Diana's look of startled inquiry. "That shameless doxy! Not another instant will I have her under my roof! Let her go back to the lover who brought her here, and may the devil take them both!"

"No!" Diana started up and caught the old lady's arm in urgent fingers. "I beg you to consider! As long as Verity remains in this house Sir Lawrence is safe, for who will give credence to scandal while you accept her presence here? If you turn her out of doors—which, I admit, is what she deserves—everyone will know it for the truth, and he will have no choice but to demand satisfaction of Fane."

For a moment Lady Templecombe stared at her, and then her face crumpled and she sank down again in her chair, her withered fingers plucking restlessly at her heavy black skirts. A sob shook her frail body, and, probably for the first time in half a century, she sought guidance of another.

"What would you have me do? I will not stand by and let him wed her."

"No, no, he shall not!" Diana dropped gracefully to her knees by the old lady's chair and took one wrinkled hand in both her own. "But we must do nothing without first considering it well. What if Fane himself could be prevailed upon to marry her? Would not that serve your purpose?"

Her ladyship dabbed her eyes and gave a scornful sniff. Her surrender to weakness had been but momentary and was already passing.

"Why should he marry her? Talk sense, my girl!"

"Why should he not? We know that he is very poor and Verity is mistress of a comfortable fortune. Would not that be a greater lure to him than mere vengeance? Any man— yes, and any woman, too—can be bought, if the right price can be found."

The Dowager's sharp glance approved this cynical utterance, but she merely said sarcastically:

"Who will undertake the task of buying Dominic Fane? It is not a matter to be entrusted to a servant."

"I will," Diana said steadily. "I am in part to blame for this, for had I kept a closer watch on Verity she could not have fled from London. Let me be the one to set matters to rights, for that I will do, believe me!"

For a second or two Lady Templecombe looked narrowly at her, and then she sighed and nodded.

"So be it, and the girl shall remain here meanwhile. I pray God you may succeed, for if you do not, the name of Templecombe will surely die." She paused, and her gaze softened; with her free hand she patted the younger woman's arm. "You are a good girl, my dear! Would that Lawrence had chosen a bride such as you."

Diana bowed her head in simulated confusion, but a little ironic smile was tugging at her lips the while. When she looked up, however, her expression was grave enough, and the mockery which lurked far down in her dark eyes was not apparent to the old woman confronting her. "I will go at once," she said quietly, "but let no one know of my errand."

A little more than an hour later, Mrs. Halland was riding alone along the overgrown drive towards Dominic Fane's house. One of her own servants had come with her from Shere Place, but she had left him to wait for her just out of sight of the road. She had no wish to advertise her visit, just as she had no desire for a witness of her meeting with Fane.

She had little fear that he would recognize her, for she had complete faith in the disguise she had worn at their previous meeting, and even if her voice struck a chord in his memory, he had no way of proving any suspicion it might arouse. So, for the second time, she made the mistake of underestimating the man who once already had made havoc of all her scheming, and she rode through the tangled woods confident of success.

When at length the house came in sight she drew rein and sat for a few moments to study it. In the bright light of noonday it presented a doleful picture, its walls rising from a wilderness of neglected garden upon which the woodland was already encroaching. Forsaken and silent, it might have been tenanted only by ghosts, but even as she watched the front door opened, and a man stepped out of the deep shadows of the porch into the sunlight and stood staring towards her.

His appearance matched the house from which he had emerged. His coat, so worn and faded that its original colour was hard to determine, bore more than one patch, his linen was coarse and plain, and his long leather boots dull and cracked. He was hatless, but the black hair which fell to his shoulders framed a face scrupulously shaven, a lean, dark, dangerous face which she had once seen by candlelight in a London tavern.

She let her horse move forward again, and picked her way daintily over the weed-grown space before the house until she halted again close beside him.

"You, I think, are Dominic Fane?" she said quietly.

He nodded briefly, his tawny eyes intent upon her face, revealing nothing. Diana slipped out of the saddle and looped the reins over her arm.

"I am Diana Halland," she informed him. "You may perhaps have heard of me from my sister-in-law."

There was no change in his expression; he said curtly:

"Perhaps."

She laughed, softly and maliciously.

"You are being needlessly discreet, Mr. Fane. Half the county knows by now of your association with Verity Halland, and is waiting with breathless interest to learn what follows."

"Does that half include Sir Lawrence Templecombe?"

"It does indeed! The tale was brought to Shere Place this morning by one Charles Dellaby, with whom you had an encounter last night. It seems, sir, that you can be very violent and headstrong upon occasion."

"As Harry Duncan learned to his cost," Dominic agreed sardonically. "I can guess Templecombe's present state of mind. Did he send you here to plead with me, madam, or merely to discover my intentions?"

"I come and go at no man's bidding, Mr. Fane. I am here to please myself."

She let fall the reins and stepped past him into the cool of the porch, and sat down on one of the stone benches there. Dominic made no reply, but, impassive though he seemed, he was very much on his guard. He had been surprised, even startled, to see Diana Halland riding up to his door, but now, waiting for her to disclose the object of her visit, he intended to betray nothing.

"I will be frank with you," Diana resumed at length. "I have heard your story, and I can understand your desire for vengeance, but I wonder whether you have considered what must follow. The Templecombes wield great influence in these parts, the old lady even more than Sir Lawrence, and she would never permit you to escape. What satisfaction can you possibly find in killing him—always supposing that he can be brought to fight—if your own certain imprisonment and probable death must be the sequel?"

Dominic continued to watch her with no change of expression, but behind that imperturbable mask a grim satisfaction was stirring. Consternation in no small degree must reign at Shere Place to provoke this visit, though he was still at a loss to understand why Diana Halland should have been chosen to voice it. He said cautiously:

"I swore long ago to avenge the wrong Templecombe had done my family, and that my oath is still unfulfilled after so many years is no fault of mine. His resources for flight were greater than mine for pursuit."

The bitter contempt in his voice held little promise of escape for Sir Lawrence, and convinced Diana that the Templecombes had good reason for their alarm. To a man who had nothing else, the hope of vengeance must surely outweigh all fear of the consequences; therefore some alternative must be offered.

"So you carried off his promised wife, kept her until she wearied you, and then flung her back into his arms, which, all unsuspecting, received her readily. Then you saw to it that the story became common knowledge. In heaven's name, sir! is that not vengeance enough?"

"Betrayal for betrayal, madam," he said grimly. "What follows now must rest with him. If he thinks he has grounds for it, let him call me to account."

"If he thinks it!" For a moment her scorn and impatience were too great for her to conceal. "As matters stand now, he has no choice but to challenge you!"

Dominic propped himself in the mouth of the porch, one hand against the wall, the other resting lightly on the hilt of his sword, and looked down at her with that expression of saturnine mockery which she was beginning to hate. Studying the lean, sinewy strength of him, seeing the expression in his tawny eyes, Diana felt certain that only her wits and boldness stood between Lawrence Templecombe and death. His next words confirmed it.

"Then let him challenge me," Dominic said deliberately. "He will find me more than willing to take up the gauntlet."

"I said, sir, 'as matters stand now'," Diana pointed out more calmly.

His brows lifted. "I can envisage nothing, madam, which would relieve him of the obligation."

"Can you not? Are you indeed so blinded by the desire to finish your father's murderous work? You are still young, Mr. Fane! What purpose is there in imperilling your future, perhaps your very life?"

"My future?" He straightened himself suddenly, and his eyes blazed with an anger as swift. "Do you mock me, madam? In this place, seeing me as I am, do you dare to speak to me of the future?"

She leaned her head against the wall behind her and regarded him with a faint smile, spitefully pleased to have pierced at last his armour of reserve.

"You are bitter," she said, "and yet the future might hold a great deal for you. A fortune was within your grasp, and you did not see it. Yet 'tis not gone so far that you may not recover it."

"Speak plainly, I beg of you," he said impatiently. "What fortune do you mean? Does Templecombe imagine that his money can buy a way out of this trap as it can buy all else?"

"It is Verity Halland's fortune I mean, Mr. Fane," Diana answered softly. "Would it not be more profitable to marry her, and so make yourself master of all that is hers, than to cast everything away for the sake of running your sword through a man so little able to defend himself? Wealth and a fair estate, and a bride who, it would seem, is not altogether repulsive to you. That is what your future could hold."

He stood staring down at her, trying to conceal the astonishment her words provoked. If she could offer Verity's fortune as a bribe to save Templecombe's life, then it could not be the desire to possess herself of it which had prompted the plot against Miss Halland. Unless some trickery was intended, the mystery was even greater than he had supposed.

"May I ask," he said sarcastically after a moment, "for whose sake you make this suggestion? For mine, or for hers, or for Sir Lawrence Templecombe's?"

She gave her rich, throaty chuckle.

"Not for yours, sir, and certainly not for hers, even though I can find it in me to pity the little fool in her present plight. For Sir Lawrence's a little, since it is my purpose to save his life, but chiefly for my own." She paused, regarding him with some amusement, and then added softly: "To be frank, Mr.

Fane, I intend to be the next Lady Templecombe, and nothing is going to prevent it."

This time his surprise was too great to be concealed, nor did he attempt it, but stood frowning at her with an amazement which was half disbelief. Diana chuckled again.

"It would seem that I astonish you, sir."

"You do, madam," he replied curtly. "I had not supposed it possible that any woman should covet that rôle, least of all a woman such as yourself."

"Oh, we are unpredictable creatures," she replied with airy mockery, "but my reasons need concern you not at all. You will understand, however, that Verity's return has sadly inconvenienced me. You have the power to relieve me of that embarrassment at no small profit to yourself, at the same time making what is, you must admit, the only possible reparation for the harm you have done her. Sir Lawrence will never marry her now, you know. Even if I did not exist, the Dowager would find a means to prevent it."

That, at least, was the truth, as Dominic well knew, and he did not need Diana Halland to point it out to him, but now he wasted barely a moment's thought upon it. He was dazed and blinded by the temptation which this smiling, scheming woman had laid before him, the vision of a future which Verity might share, a life which would repay him in full for the hardships and disappointments of the past.

He turned from her to look out across the garden so that she could no longer see his face, while his thoughts raced ahead into the paradise she offered him, and he tried to turn a deaf ear to the voice of conscience. In this he might have succeeded had Diana not spoken again, but in her anxiety to persuade him, and thinking that it was the prospect of vengeance which he found so hard to relinquish, speak she did.

"As for your vengeance, sir," she said softly, "that, too, may be yours, a vengeance more subtle and enduring than the mere thrust of a sword. I know Lawrence Templecombe better than he knows himself, and I assure you that the thing he fears most, next to death, is ridicule. In some measure you have already brought that upon him, but though everyone has heard the tale of your intrigue with Verity, as yet only a few of them believe it. Let her marry you, however, let her of her own free will leave Shere Place and all its dreary grandeur, to come to you, who have nothing but yourself to offer, and such a gale of laughter at his expense will sweep through

Somerset that I'll warrant 'twill blow him back to London, and keep him there for many a day."

She was watching him narrowly, and though his face was hidden from her she noted with satisfaction the sudden clenching of the hands which still rested on the hilt of his sword, and she congratulated herself upon her own shrewdness. 'Any man can be brought,' she had told the Dowager, 'but it needed quick wits and a perception of human weakness to know what price to offer.

"Vengeance, and a fortune into the bargain," she prompted slyly. "Come, sir! admit that my proposition offers the greater profit."

The words jarred unpleasantly on his ear, for there was an ugly ring to them. The greater profit! Yes, for him, but what of Verity herself? He did not doubt that Diana spoke truly when she said that the scandal was not as yet generally believed, but to agree to her suggestion would be to admit the truth of it to all the world. He had no more right now to ask Verity to marry him than he had had when they parted three days ago; less right, in fact, since now the powerful protection of Lord Urmiston was hers if she chose to accept it. Instinct protested rebelliously that there was no question of right, that Verity loved him as he loved her, but he stifled the insistent voice lest it sap his stern resolve. Without turning her head he said, in an ironic tone assumed to conceal his true feelings: "Why should you suppose, madam, that Miss Halland would ever consent to be my wife?"

Again that rich chuckle with its undertone of malice.

"My dear sir, she is in no position to pick and choose. A husband she must have, but who will marry her now that the truth is known? Her plight is desperate, believe me! Only my intercessions prevented Lady Templecombe from immediately turning her out of the house, and once that shelter is withdrawn, to whom can she turn if not to you?"

"You convince me, Mrs. Halland," Dominic turned to face her, and if the mocking twist of his lips was more pronounced than usual, she did not know him well enough to remark it, "but what do you suggest I should do? Ride up to the door of Shere Place and offer her my heart and hand?"

"Why not?" she retorted lightly, and fell silent for a space before adding more slowly, "Why not, indeed? You could wish for no greater triumph."

He laughed shortly. "Oh, a triumph indeed if Verity refuse me!"

"Trust me to see that she does not! Do you suppose that she is not all eagerness to be gone? You who knew that house and its mistress in the past? Believe me, neither the one nor the other has made her welcome, and now that her ladyship knows the truth her position will be intolerable. By tomorrow she will welcome escape at any price."

"You seem very certain," he said harshly, "but if she has suffered at my hands as you suppose, why should she return to me?"

Diana stood up, smoothing the skirt of her riding-dress.

"Let us not fence with each other, Mr. Fane. If you had carried Verity off against her will, she would have fled from you when you lay wounded at the inn where the players found you. She would not have demeaned herself to do the work of a servant that you might be cared for." She stepped past him into the sunlight and turned to look up at him, her dark eyes mocking in the shadow of her broad-brimmed hat. "I always supposed her a cold, prudish piece, not to be won by any man, but it would seem that you have mastered the trick of it. I confess it surprises me."

His lips tightened, but he refused to rise to the bait, and merely said: "There is much which surprises me, Mrs. Halland. You desire to marry Sir Lawrence, yet you show me a way to cover him with ridicule. You have no kindness for your sister-in-law or for me, yet you seek to provide her with a means of escape from her present plight, and to furnish me with a fortune. You will admit that your conduct is contradictory."

She moved away to where her horse was cropping the grass and laid hold of the reins, and Dominic followed her. She gestured imperiously to him to help her into the saddle, and not until she was mounted did she reply. Then she looked down at him with a sneer on her red lips.

"I aid you, and her, because it suits me to do so. If it served my purpose better to destroy you both, I should do it without the smallest compunction. As for Sir Lawrence, you may take what vengeance you like upon him, so that you spare his life. Are you answered?"

"Completely, madam!" He gave her back look for look, the contempt in his eyes like a blow in the face. "As for Templecombe, I can think of no worse revenge than to aid you to your goal. You are just such a wife as he deserves."

She smiled, but not pleasantly, and drew the lash of her

riding-whip lightly across his cheek. Her eyes glittered with a fury barely controlled.

"Take care, my friend, or your insolence will earn you yet another scar," she said between her teeth. "I am no country-bred innocent to be impressed by these roistering manners." She turned her horse's head towards the drive, but paused to add, in the tone she would have used to a lackey: "Come to Shere Place at noon tomorrow, and you shall have the prize I have promised."

"Tomorrow?" he repeated quickly. "Why not today?"

"Because I must have time to find some pretext to send Sir Lawrence out of the way, to gain the support of the Dowager, and to warn your light-o'-love of your coming. At noon. Do not forget."

She set spur to her mount and rode off without another glance in his direction, and Dominic stood looking after her until she vanished among the trees. He had agreed to her proposal lest, failing in this, she should concoct some other plot, but it must be the Marquis of Urmiston, and not Dominic Fane, who rode up at noon next day to the door of Shere Place. The hours until then would seem like centuries, for until Verity was safely out of Diana Halland's reach he would not know a moment's peace of mind. The forcefulness he had sensed in Diana the first time he saw her was no trick of the imagination, and he knew now that it was a force of evil, which would stop at nothing to attain its own incredibly selfish ends.

XV

Desperate Measures

Sir Lawrence Templecombe, after Mrs. Halland had left him, remained for some time in a mood of acute despondency. Despairingly he racked his brain for some loophole, some way of escape from the impasse in which he found himself, and, finding none, vented his panic in blasphemy and cursed aloud the enemy who had so tricked and trapped him.

Sir Lawrence had only once used his sword in earnest, and

of late years he had neglected even to practise, until the
weapon he always wore had become as much an ornament as
his jewels, or the lacing on his coat. To wear a sword was the
mark of a gentleman, and Sir Lawrence would no more have
appeared in public without one than without his periwig, but
the mere thought of using it to defend his life gave him a
sick feeling of fear. In memory he lived once again those moments, so brief in time and yet seeming an eternity, when he
had faced the furious onslaught of the man he had wronged,
and again felt the cold sweat of terror prickle his skin; and
Geoffrey Fane had been a man already ageing. Now it was
he who was at a disadvantage in the matter of age as in all
else. Where young Harry Duncan had been so easily defeated, what hope of survival had he?

He thought of Dominic Fane as he had known him fourteen years ago, and drew no reassurance from the memory.
Even at eighteen there had been an unyielding quality in
Fane's nature which was not likely to have lessened with the
years, and a temper as hot as his father's, which made him
reckless of its consequences. To Templecombe there was
something infinitely horrible in an implacability which could
cherish a hatred for so many years, and then place a man in
a position where he must choose between forfeiting his life or
his honour. For although the actual challenge must come
from him, it was Dominic Fane who had flung down the
gauntlet and was now waiting, like some beast of prey, for
his victim to take it up.

And take it up he must. There was no chance this time to
make a dignified retreat, under the plea that his quarrel was
not with Dominic at all. He had acknowledged Verity Halland as his future wife, had introduced her as such to the
Marquis of Urmiston and Lady Sarah, and allowed his servants to spread the news about the countryside, and all the
while it was Fane's mistress whom he had made free of his
house and his name. Any denial of the story would at once
be taken as a confession of cowardice, for there was no proof
which he could offer in support of such a denial.

At this point in his agonized reflections Sir Lawrence
reached the conclusion foreseen by Dominic the night before.
There was a way of escape, after all, a manner in which he
might cheat his enemy and save his own life, and that was by
marrying Verity in spite of everything. It was a bitter pill for
a man of his vanity to swallow, but as an alternative to death
it was welcome enough, even with the additional disad-

vantage of the trouble he would bring down upon himself from the Dowager and—an even more alarming prospect—from Diana. There was no help for it, and with innate vindictiveness, he consoled himself with the promise of venting upon Verity all the hatred and fury which he dare not, for his life's sake, betray to her lover. Having decided upon this desperate course, he gave his enthusiasm no chance to cool, but went at once in search of Miss Halland.

He found her, after some difficulty, in a distant corner of the gardens. There were traces of tears on her cheeks, for after Diana's departure the Dowager had wasted no time in informing Verity of the scandal which had broken about her head, and of her own belief in every word of it. She had stormed at her for close upon half-an-hour, venting upon the unfortunate girl the malevolent fury born of her fears for Sir Lawrence, and lashing her with every ugly epithet which a long life and a retentive memory could lay at her command. At length the violence of her rage had brought about a kind of collapse, and Verity, white-faced and trembling, had summoned Kate Meadows and then fled in search of a refuge from further reproaches.

Shamed beyond endurance by the old woman's wicked tongue, she at first had room in her mind for little else, but presently, when tears had brought a measure of relief, a tentative glimmer of hope awoke within her. This, surely, would be the end of her betrothal. Soon she could return to the home she had left more than a year ago, to the house which was now hers and to the friends among whom she had grown up. She would beg Dominic to take her there, and perhaps, if fortune were kind, they need not be parted again. So for a while she sat lost in dreams, until Sir Lawrence came to end dreaming for ever.

When she saw him approaching, Verity supposed that he had come to accuse her in his turn, and braced herself for a fresh volley of insults and reproaches, but she was soon undeceived. Sir Lawrence, it seemed, was filled with noble chivalry, and faith in the pure and stainless innocence of his bride—for so great was his fear of Dominic Fane that not even to her would he betray the truth, and took pains to conceal the impotent fury which possessed him. Her punishment must wait until the knot between them was safely tied, and all danger to himself at an end.

Verity listened with growing wonderment, and, believing him sincere, was filled with remorse for the wrong she had

done him in her thoughts. Fop and libertine he might be, and
even lacking in physical courage, but in all else she had mis-
judged him. It took courage of another sort to stand by her in
this extremity, and perceiving this, she perceived also where
her duty lay. She was his promised wife; a betrothal could
not be lightly broken, and though if Sir Lawrence had shared
the common belief in her shame she would have had no hesitation in following the dictates of her heart, this she could no
longer do.

So she agreed with outward docility to his plans for their
immediate marriage, and contrived somehow to dissemble the
shrinking which the prospect inspired in her, and the heart-
ache which was the sharper now for the transient hope which
had preceded it. To her relief he did not linger, but went instead to break the news of his decision to the Dowager.

This task he faced with the deepest misgivings, for he knew
how violent a storm of anger it would provoke. Had it been
possible to do so, he would have left his grandmother in ignorance of his intentions, but if his plan were to succeed, the
family must appear united in support of Miss Halland, no
matter what dissensions might rage behind the scenes.

Braving her fury, he pointed this out to her, and when at
length, finding that abuse and pleading alike left him shattered but unmoved, she besought him at least to delay the actual wedding for a time, he shook his head.

"As well admit the truth of the tale at the outset," he replied. "To hasten the marriage with every means at my command is a gesture which will convince everyone that it is
false. To delay is to imply doubt."

"Doubt?" screeched the Dowager. "Doubt, d'you say? The
only doubt in my mind is doubt of your sanity! You fool,
what if the slut is already with child? Do you want a brat of
Dominic Fane's getting to inherit all that is yours?"

"Madam, you go too far!" Furious at hearing her voice a
thought which had already risen hideously in his own mind,
Sir Lawrence took refuge in bluster. "My decision is made,
and unless you can bring yourself to support it, I must request you to deny yourself to any visitors, and to say no
more on this subject to anyone."

Stunned into momentary silence by such unwonted defiance, her ladyship stared at him in the most complete astonishment. Then, before anger could master her again, she
recalled Diana Halland's present errand, and realized that it

was pointless to exhaust herself to no purpose until she knew what had been the outcome of that.

"No need to browbeat me in that fashion," she grumbled. "If you want to hold yourself up as an object of ridicule before all the world, on your own head be it. Praise God my life is drawing to its close! If the next generation of our family is to be born of a fool and a wanton, I have no wish to see it!"

On that note she dismissed him, and he went thankfully. After some deliberation he summoned his coach and had himself driven to Cloverton, for, much as he disliked the thought of mingling with the crowds of common people who would be thronging the streets on this, the second day of the fair, he did not wish it to be supposed that he was skulking at home for fear of encountering Dominic Fane. That fear was, in fact, very lively in his mind, but it proved to be groundless, and he was able, without any risk of immediate retaliation by his enemy, to denounce the whole story as false, and to make known as widely as possible his complete faith in Miss Halland and his intention to marry her at once in proof of it.

He stayed to dine with several other gentlemen at the Seven Stars, and after the meal someone suggested cards. Thus the greater part of the evening was whiled away, and it was quite late when Sir Lawrence set off on the journey back to Shere Place. He was the poorer by a considerable sum, but well satisfied with the day's achievements and disposed to view everything through a rosy haze due to the wine he had drunk. Since it was one of his grandmother's most stringent rules that the entire household should have retired by ten o'clock, he had no fear of encountering any of the ladies that night. Diana would have to be faced eventually, and the meeting was bound to be unpleasant, but in his present optimistic frame of mind Sir Lawrence even felt capable of dealing with her.

He would have felt less confident had he been able to see the lady at that moment, for she was pacing up and down her bedchamber much in the manner of a tigress baulked of her prey—the prey, in this instance, being the hapless Sir Lawrence. She had returned to Shere Place well satisfied with the result of her meeting with Fane, but the Dowager had met her with news which rudely shattered her complacency. Dismayed at first, Diana had passed rapidly to anger and contempt, but she had dissembled these turbulent emotions, and eventually succeeded in persuading her ladyship, if not herself, that all would be well.

Having soothed the old lady with this assurance, Diana waited impatiently for Sir Lawrence to return. There were many things she desired to say to him, some of which she had travelled all the way from London to impart, and the longer she waited, the worse her temper became. By ten o'clock she was in a state of simmering fury, which was aggravated by the need to dissemble it. One small satisfaction she had permitted herself, for although one glance at Verity's wan face and haunted eyes had convinced her that Miss Halland found Sir Lawrence's reaction to the scandal as unwelcome as it was unexpected, Diana had maliciously refrained from telling her of her own schemes. Let the little fool spend a night of anxiety and uncertainty, and she would be the more ready to go with Fane when he came for her next day.

Lady Templecombe, meanwhile, had spent the afternoon brooding over Mrs. Halland's plans to remedy the disaster, and the longer she considered, the less she liked them. Unlike Diana, she was concerned for Sir Lawrence's dignity as well as his life, and blinded by her dislike of both Verity Halland and Dominic Fane. To see them escape while Sir Lawrence was made a laughing-stock was not at all to her taste, and at last she hit upon an alternative plan. Having recognized in Diana a woman with as little liking as herself for being set aside, she said nothing to her, but sent Kate Meadows, whom she knew she could trust, to summon the village Constable privily to her presence.

He came promptly, a stout, red-faced, bucolic individual, very much in awe of her ladyship and anxious to obey any command she might give him. When she told him what she required, however, he gaped at her with ludicrous dismay. "Arrest him, my lady?" he stammered. "Me arrest Dominic Fane?"

"Yes, arrest him!" snapped the Dowager. "What ails you, man? It is your duty to arrest wrongdoers, is it not?"

"Aye, but what has he done, my lady? I can't arrest a man without he's done wrong."

"God save us, you bumpkin! Where are your wits? The man is a rogue, a dangerous criminal! He abducted my grandson's promised wife in London, and brought her here with the intention of forcing a quarrel upon Sir Lawrence. Do I need to tell you, a native of Shere, of the grudge he bears our family, or the threats against Sir Lawrence's life he made ten years ago?"

Acutely uncomfortable, the Constable twisted his hat between his hands and shifted his weight from one foot to the other. He could recall all the circumstances of the original quarrel between the Fanes and Lawrence Templecombe, including some which her ladyship had chosen to forget, and although not a particularly quick-witted man, he realized that he had now been chosen as a scapegoat for Sir Lawrence. It was not a rôle which appealed to him, but on the other hand he did not dare to defy the family which, in Shere, was all-powerful.

"Is it Sir Lawrence's wish that I should arrest him, my lady?" he asked doubtfully.

"It is my wish," her ladyship replied shortly. "Is not that enough?"

"Aye, my lady, indeed it is," the unfortunate man assured her, terrified by the gathering wrath in her voice and eyes. "But abduction, now! 'Tis a matter I know nothing of, never having had to deal with it afore. Be your ladyship certain o' Fane's guilt?"

"Of course I am certain, you simpleton! Have you not heard the vile stories the rogue has spread about?"

"I've heard 'em, my lady, but—saving your ladyship's presence—there's a deal o' nonsense flies about at fair time, when folks have got naught better to do than gossip at other folks' expense. Now Fane was never in Shere till last night, but the young lady's been here three days and more. There's none as ever saw 'em together, not as I've heard of." He hesitated, and then added with what he imagined to be great cunning: "If I could have a word with the young lady herself, now, maybe we'd find out more about it."

He did not expect the request to be granted, since, from what he had heard, Miss Halland could scarcely be depended upon to incriminate Fane, but he was unprepared for the storm it caused to burst about his unsuspecting head. The Dowager drew herself even more upright in the great chair, and raked him from head to foot with an affronted and fulminating glance.

"A word with her?" she repeated awfully. "Upon my soul, Job Daggett, your effrontery passes all bounds! Do you dare to suppose that she, a young girl of gentle birth, could bring herself to speak to you of such a matter? She has suffered violence and outrage at the hands of this man, and you expect her to describe her ordeal to you! Why, you insolent upstart, not even Sir Lawrence himself has yet heard the full sum of that rogue's infamy! It is only by degrees that I, and Mrs. Halland, her sister-in-law, have coaxed the story from her, but, now that I know the truth, I have wasted no time in sending for you. The man Fane must be arrested, and that at once! So be about it, and let me hear no more excuses, or, by heaven! I will make you rue the day you were born."

Daggett had recoiled a pace before this exhibition of a temper which was legendary in Shere, but of which this was his first personal experience. He was shaken, but he retained a sufficient grasp on his wits to protest, albeit feebly, that if Fane were arrested and brought to trial, Miss Halland would be obliged to give evidence against him.

"And so she shall, numskull, but not to you! Not to a presumptuous village Constable whose only thought is to evade the duties of his office. I tell you that Dominic Fane is guilty of these crimes. Is my word enough, or must I send to my kinsman, the Lord Lieutenant, to tell him that the Constable of Shere has wantonly neglected his duty, and permitted a known and dangerous criminal to come and go as he pleases?"

The luckless Constable realized that he was in a position from which there was no escape. By birth or marriage the ancient fury confronting him was connected with half the influential men in Somerset, and against such an opponent a humble fellow like himself had no defence at all. If, on the other hand, he agreed to her demands and sought to arrest Dominic Fane, he might well get a foot or so of cold steel through his vitals, for there was a wild streak in all the Fanes. The tale of Harry Duncan's humiliation had travelled as far as Shere, and lost nothing in the telling, and the Constable had not the smallest desire to arrest an armed and desperate man who knew so well how to use his weapons.

"Well, which is it to be?" The Dowager queried impatiently. "Make up your mind!"

The menace of Dominic Fane faded into insignificance before the more immediate danger. Job Daggett swallowed convulsively, and miserably gave her ladyship to understand that he would endeavour to carry out her commands. He was going on to ask for some advice on the manner of executing so formidable a task, but her ladyship cut him short without ceremony and signed to Kate Meadows to take him away. He went despondently, convinced that his life was in mortal danger, and vainly seeking a way of escape.

Left alone, the Dowager relaxed at last and drew a deep breath of satisfaction. She anticipated no trouble from Miss Halland. With her lover under arrest, the girl could soon be brought to see the wisdom of supporting her ladyship's charge against Fane, giving the evidence required of her—it took more than a trifing matter like perjury to dismay the autocratic Lady Templecombe—and relinquishing all claim upon Sir Lawrence. No doubt she would be thankful to escape so lightly.

So, in their several ways, Sir Lawrence, his grandmother and Diana Halland each sought to remedy the ills the day had brought forth, while in Cloverton, amid the gaiety and bustle of the fair, the tide of gossip rose ever higher. It reached soon enough to the ears of a stranger who came slouching into the town as the shadows began to lengthen, a travel-stained and dusty stranger who seemed to belong neither to the throngs of country revellers nor to the motley crowd of vagabonds who had come to entertain them.

In the yard of one of the smaller and meaner inns the stranger halted at the pump to quench a thirst which, from the beggarly look of him, it would seem that he lacked the means to satisfy within, and it was as he stood there that a scrap of conversation between an ostler and a groom caught his ear.

". . . not known for certain," the groom was saying, "for there's none as will go to see. Small blame to 'em, says I! You'd not get me into that wood, by night or day, not for a sackful o' gold."

"They say as Dominic Fane fears neither man nor devil," remarked the ostler, spitting thoughtfully and with great accuracy at a nearby wisp of straw. "If there was bloody murder done in that house years ago, he'll lose no sleep over it, from what I hear."

He broke off with a strangled yelp of alarm, for the stranger's hand had shot out and descended heavily on his shoulder. Looking round indignantly, the ostler found himself confronting a veritable giant, a huge, lumbering ox of a man whose features were all but hidden by a tangled beard as red as the unkempt hair which fell to mingle with it. From beneath a low, animal brow a pair of fierce blue eyes were narrowly regarding him. "Did ye say 'Fane,' cully?" the apparition demanded. " 'Dominic Fane'?"

"Aye!" The ostler jerked his shoulder from the stranger's grasp and rubbed it tenderly; his tone was resentful. "What if I did? 'Tis a name you'll hear often enough in Cloverton to-day."

"Will I so?" The giant's tone was genial enough, but there was that in his eyes which made the ostler retreat a cautious pace or two. "And be this Dominic Fane a tall man, wi' black hair, and a scar across his cheek?"

"Aye, that he is!" The ostler hesitated, but then curiosity overcame caution. "D'ye know him, then?"

"Know him?" Broken and blackened teeth were displayed in a sudden grin. "Him and me's old comrades, friend, and there's a debt I owes him as must be paid. Aye, a debt! I've tramped many a mile to settle it." He seemed to brood for a moment or two, and then shot the other a quick glance under lowering brows. "There's a wench with him, belike?" he added sharply. "A small, neat doxy as says she's his sister?"

The ostler made haste to correct him on this point, and went on to recount, with relish, the tale which was abroad concerning that same young woman. No aspect of the story did he leave untouched, from Harriet Fane's violent death fourteen years before, to the rumour which had just begun to circulate regarding Sir Lawrence Templecombe's condemnation of the scandal as a pack of malicious lies, and he was flattered to find his formidable new acquaintance an avid listener. When he sought in return, however, some information about the curious comradeship referred to by the red-bearded stranger, he received an answer which discouraged further probing.

Red Nat, in fact, had no wish to draw any attention upon himself, for it had begun to dawn upon him that in Cloverton he stood in some danger of recognition. For the first time in his life he wished that his size and colouring were less distinctive, for if Verity Halland had described him to this Sir Lawrence Templecombe who seemed to be such a power in these parts, and Templecombe had passed on the information to the authorities, then it would not be long before he was recognized.

Yet relinquish his hope of vengeance on Dominic Fane he would not. Fortune had not dealt kindly with Nat Trumper during the last few weeks, for although after his escape from prison he had resumed his pursuit of the strolling players, he had soon found that neither Fane nor the girl ever ventured far from the safety of the little band. Nor did he fancy the risk of following too closely upon their heels, for he recalled uneasily Barnabas Pike's uncanny skill with a knife. Against such weapons he had no defence, and after living for a few days in constant dread of a silent, keen-edged messenger of death from some unsuspected ambush, he fell back a safe distance and thereafter followed the troupe by hearsay.

The route they followed, however, governed as it was by the need to choose halting places most likely to profit them, taxed his limited resources to the uttermost, for Red Nat had never learned to husband such money as came his way. Of the fifty guineas he had had of the Black Mask, drink and the dice had taken their toll before ever he left London, and his subsequent journeying had depleted his purse yet further.

The day came when his pockets were empty, and to fill them he resorted to the only trade he knew, but it was one thing to cut purses in the dark streets of London, with the sure sanctuary of Alsatia at his back, and quite another to do the same thing in open country. Born and bred in the backwaters of a great city, Nat Trumper found himself now in an alien world, and though he had succeeded in laying hands on a meagre sum of money, such a hue and cry was raised after him that he barely escaped with his life. Flight from that danger had taken him in a different direction to the player-troupe, and thereafter he wandered aimlessly, until word reached him of a fair to be held at Cloverton, and he had come thither in the hope of picking up his quarry's trail again.

Luck had favoured him for the first time for weeks; now he had the whole truth, and the seemingly pointless flight of Fane and the girl was explained. With a surge of baffled, savage fury he realized that Verity Halland was beyond his reach, for not even his thwarted desires, aggravated by the long pursuit to an almost unbearable pitch, could blind him to the impossibility of laying hands on her now that she was safe in a great country house. There would be servants about her, both indoors and without, and one word from her would bring them down upon him like a pack of hounds. From that it would be a short step to prison, and an even shorter one to the gallows, a gibbet at some lonely cross-roads. No, it was impossible, and the delicate beauty which had tantalized him for the brief time it lay within his reach in London was lost to him for ever.

With a redoubled violence of hatred his thoughts returned to Dominic Fane, who had cheated him of possession of it.

Fane was a false-hearted traitor, a renegade who had played
his comrade false and robbed him not only of the girl, but
also of close upon a hundred pounds in gold, and all for the
sake of avenging some wrong done him years before. Well,
more than one man could deal in vengeance, Trumper reflected savagely; Fane had had his fill of pleasure during these
past weeks, and now he should pay for it. He recalled what
the ostler had told him of an old house hidden in a wood,
shunned by everyone in the village, and the prospect of what
might be done there, with none to see, brought a grin of evil
satisfaction to his lips.

The obliging ostler was willing enough to describe direction
and distance, and a short while later, his weariness forgotten,
Red Nat had left the crowded, noisy town behind him, and
was striding, beneath the torn crimson and purple banners of
a stormy sunset, along the road which led to Shere.

XVI

Conversation at Midnight

THAT same wild sunset had blazed and smouldered into early
darkness when Verity Halland put out the candles in her
handsome bedchamber at Shere Place, and, feeling her way
to the window, flung back the heavy curtains. Beyond, the
gardens lay lost in gloom, for a pall of cloud was shutting out
the stars, and a rising wind sighed fitfully among the leaves.
She opened the window and sank to her knees beside it,
resting her arms on the low sill.

For a long time she remained there, a prey to unhappiness
which came very close to despair. The conviction of duty
which had seemed so clear to her that morning had since
been assailed by doubts which must be regarded with deep
suspicion because they accorded so well with her real desires.
Was it fair to Sir Lawrence, she wondered, to take advantage
of his belief in her innocence, and marry him knowing that in
thought if not in deed she must be false to him every day of
her life? Was the sin any less because only the opportunity to
commit it was lacking?

She recalled with a shiver the intolerable evening which had just ended, with the Dowager missing no opportunity to hurt and humiliate her, until even the impassive, perfectly-trained servants exchanged meaning looks and covert smiles at her expense, and she knew that this was but a pattern of countless other evenings stretching into an infinite future. Another doubt, this time of her own fortitude, fastened itself upon her mind, and she wondered whether, in the end, sheer desperation would drive her to betray both her husband, and the memory of the love she had renounced.

For renounce it she had only that afternoon, when she sent Dominic his final dismissal in the supposed note of thanks to Lady Sarah. The servant, Thomas, had brought the raiment her ladyship had promised, and Verity was wearing one of the gowns now, a soft, golden-yellow silk heavy with lace and embroidery. In the beautiful and elaborate garments she felt a stranger to herself, and when Diana's maid had dressed her hair in curls and flowing ringlets, and crowned it with an ornate cap of lace and ribbon, Verity, studying her own reflection in the mirror, could almost believe that the ragged girl who had tramped the roads with Dominic Fane, and fetched and carried for the guests at a country inn, had never existed save in her own troubled dreams.

In the letter which came with the clothes, Lady Sarah had begged her to leave Shere Place and take refuge at Corville Court, assuring her, in Urmiston's name as well as her own, of protection and hospitality for as long as she desired it. There was a good deal more in the same strain, but though Verity's gratitude was profound, she had written to inform Lady Sarah that all was well between herself and Sir Lawrence. He steadfastly refused to believe anything to her discredit, and they were to be married almost immediately. Would her ladyship add to her many kindnesses by sending to Dominic Fane the letter which Thomas would bring with him to Manton Lacey?

This second letter had been harder by far to write, but she had accomplished it in the end, telling Dominic what had occurred, and begging him to stay no longer in a neighbourhood where so many wished him ill. She had watched the words flow from her pen as though they came at the bidding of another mind and hand, for a sense of frozen desolation had closed about her heart like a sheath of ice.

Kneeling at her window in the darkness, she had lost all count of time. Once, in the distance, there sounded the noise of hoofs and wheels, and the murmur of voices which heralded Sir Lawrence's return, but after that brief subdued commotion, silence settled again over the house. The wind grew stronger, so that the heavy curtains shifted and stirred on either side of her, and at intervals the light of a waning moon peered through gaps in the drifting cloud and the shape of trees and walls and shrubberies became visible for a minute or two as shadows upon a lesser darkness.

Verity shifted her position, easing her cramped limbs, and at the same moment heard a door close sharply in the corridor outside her room, as though an unexpected draught had twitched it from cautious fingers. She turned her head towards her own door, and then got slowly to her feet as she remembered with vague disquiet that only one other bedchamber nearby was in use, and that one her sister-in-law's. With her back to the window now, she stared at a gleam of light marking the crack below the door, and watched it grow and fade again as though someone bearing a candle had passed along the corridor.

On an impulse of curiosity she crept across the room and opened the door an inch or two, and so saw Diana, clad in a loose robe of some light-coloured stuff and with her dark hair flowing about her shoulders, moving away from her along the wide corridor, her tall figure mysteriously revealed by the light of the single candle she carried. As Verity stared after her with astonishment and perplexity, a clock somewhere in the house chimed the hour of midnight.

Almost without conscious thought, Verity stepped out into the corridor, closing the door behind her with infinite care, and stole in pursuit. She had forgotten for a time that it was Diana, in the guise of the Black Mask, who had first sought to prevent her marriage, but now her suspicions were fully roused once more. Some new plot must be hatching in that scheming and unscrupulous brain to send Diana creeping about the corridors of Shere Place at this hour of the night, and it would be well to learn, if possible, in what guise the danger might come.

With the other woman's light to guide her it was not difficult to follow unsuspected until they reached the broad landing at the head of the great staircase. Diana crossed it swiftly, shielding the candle-flame with her hand, and entered another corridor upon the opposite side, but Verity hesitated, for a dim light was burning in the hall below and throwing a faint, reflected glimmer across the landing, and if Diana chanced to

look back she could not fail to detect her pursuer. Not until
the gleam of the candle had completely disappeared from
view did she venture out of her place of concealment, and
when she reached the beginning of the corridor along which
Diana had passed, she found it wrapped in darkness and
silence.

Cautiously, inch by inch, she felt her way along it, until it
turned at a sharp angle, and the tips of her outstretched fingers touched the surface of a door which gave a fraction
beneath the pressure. She halted, the breath checked in her
throat, and stood staring at the slit of dim illumination, a
mere inch or so in breadth, which the slight opening of the
door had disclosed. What lay beyond she could not see, for a
tall screen of some kind was blocking the view, but Diana's
voice, muted to a whisper yet charged with angry mockery,
was speaking within the room.

"Prudence! Caution! Such counsel comes somewhat tardily,
my friend! It was not thus you spoke in London."

"We are not in London now!" That was Sir Lawrence's
voice, fretful and apprehensive. "My God! What if you were
discovered here?"

"My God! What then?" she mocked him fiercely. "Who is
likely to discover me, you fool, when everyone was driven off
to bed two hours ago? And if I were, no one would be to
blame but yourself for so persistently avoiding me ever since
I arrived at this house. I did not come all the way from London without good reason, believe me!"

"You do not seem to realize the need for circumspection,"
Sir Lawrence retorted petulantly. "'Od rot it! Have I not
troubles enough at present that you must needs come
plaguing me also?"

There was an ominous pause, and then Diana spoke again,
her husky voice dangerously sweet.

"So now I plague you, do I? By my faith, here's a change
of tune! Let me remind you of a certain promise you made
me on the day before you left London to return to Shere, a
promise to which I mean to hold you, Lawrence, make no
doubt of that."

"But when I made it I believed Verity to be dead. I cannot
set aside a betrothal of eight years standing. Be reasonable,
my love, I implore you!"

This time the tone was conciliatory, but it had no effect
upon the lady, as her next words showed.

"Are you reasonable in saying that you cannot set aside

your betrothal?" She gave a scornful little laugh. "Cannot! Say 'will not,' rather! You are in such a sweat of fear of Dominic Fane that you will go to any lengths to avoid sending him your challenge, even to the extent of taking to wife his cast-off mistress." He tried to speak, but she swept on, unheeding. "Delude yourself, if you must, but do not think that you can delude me. You have no more belief in her innocence than the rest of us, but you feign it because to admit the truth would mean a meeting with Fane, and that you dare not face. God save us, and you call yourself a man!"

"What proof of manhood would it be to let myself be butchered by that devil?" Sir Lawrence demanded indignantly. "As for the girl, I will admit the truth of what you say, but what right have you to cry shame upon her? At least she was carried off against her will."

"And within a matter of days was working as a servant that Fane might be healed of his wounds. Mark you that, Lawrence! Would she do as much for you?"

There was a pause, and in the darkness outside the door Verity stood trembling with shame and anger. This was the man for whose sake she had renounced all that was dearest to her, whose pose of noble chivalry had deceived her into setting duty and gratitude above all else, this shameless coward who would go to any lengths rather than imperil his worthless life.

"But it was not to talk of Verity or of Fane that I came," Diana resumed at last, "but of other matters that concern you and me more nearly. That promise of which I spoke, for instance. Do you mean to keep faith, or must I make public the tale of all that has happened during this past year?"

Templecombe's gasp of alarm and dismay came clearly to Verity's ears, but for some seconds he seemed to have difficulty in framing any words. At last he stammered: "You would not dare!"

"There is very little I would not dare, my friend, so be warned. Do you imagine 'twas mere chance that Verity so conveniently disappeared, or must I show you this to prove to you how much I am in earnest?"

There was another pause, and then Sir Lawrence said in a strangled whisper: "The ring! The troth-ring I gave to Verity! My God, then what I suspected is true! You did have a hand in that damnable business!"

"Yes, Lawrence, I did, and but for a cursed twist of fate she would have troubled us no more. I had long since resolved that you should not marry her. While you were concerned only with dalliance, I had already determined to become your wife. I was weary to death of being constantly in debt, of never having sufficient money for my needs." The husky voice was bitter now; it was clear that Diana considered herself extremely ill-used. "My husband was rich, but he left me only a beggarly pittance out of all his wealth. The rest is in trust for our son, and so hedged about with legal barriers that there is no coming at it. As with that, so with Verity's fortune. If she died unwed, 'twould go to Jamie, and I not benefit at all, though I was expected to house the silly chit, and bear with her false modesty and simpering manners. Lord! how I came to hate her during that year she lived with me!"

The venom investing these latter words left no doubt of their sincerity, and Verity shuddered as she heard them. The thought that she had lived for weeks and months in the shadow of such jealous hatred chilled her with a renewed sense of fear.

"So I resolved to find me another rich husband," Diana resumed after a moment, "but for a woman with no fortune, marriage is none so easy to contrive. Oh, there were many—like yourself, Lawrence—who came wooing me, but not one who was willing to make me his wife. So I was obliged to contrive a little, and once I was sure of you, I set about the task of ridding myself of Verity. Shall I tell you how I accomplished that part of my scheme, and of the trick fortune played upon me to bring it all to naught?"

"No, no! I do not want to hear it!" It was plain that Sir Lawrence was fearful of being implicated. "How could you be mad enough to go to such lengths? I thought——"

"You thought that you might have the best of two worlds, a wife at Shere and a mistress in London, but you were wrong, Lawrence, you were wrong! You could not afford to keep us both!"

"Afford?" He sounded affronted. "Confound it, Diana, does nothing matter to you save in terms of money?"

"Nothing!" Her voice was like a knife, pricking the bubble of his vanity. "I would sooner be dead than live in poverty! Did you cherish the delusion that I took you for my lover because I was enamoured of you? Dismiss it, my dear, dismiss it! It was your fortune charmed me then, as it charms me now, and I intend to have first claim upon it."

He laughed, a sneering, unpleasant sound.

"Do you think you can force me to marry you?"

"I think you would be unwise to refuse." Diana's voice was silky, almost caressing, and yet with an undertone that sent a little shiver of dread through Verity as she heard it. "Discretion is not one of your virtues, Lawrence. I have letters, notes writ me in the early days of our acquaintance, in which, safe, as you supposed, in your betrothal, you rail against it, and wish yourself free of it that you might offer me marriage. With those, and with this ring, I could so easily shift the blame for Verity's abduction on to your shoulders. I could bestow the ring somewhere in this great house of ours, so that you might search for a week and not find it—no, do not seek to take it from me! I might be obliged to cry out, and if the house were roused, and I found here, it would serve my purpose almost as well as the other."

There was another pause, a silence broken only by the man's heavy, baffled breathing. It was clear that the threat was working powerfully upon him, for when at last he spoke there was none of the earlier confidence in his voice.

"Vixen! It was an evil day when you first crossed my path!"

A soft laugh answered him.

"Upbraid me as you please, my dear, if 'twill relieve your spleen, but marry me you will, and that at once."

"At once?" His voice was more startled now than angry. "But it was agreed that we should wait a decent interval, that there should be no unseemly haste which might provoke gossip."

"It is delay which would be unseemly now," she interrupted. "That is what I travelled from London to tell you, what I have been seeking an opportunity to tell you these two days past. Our marriage has become a matter of some urgency, if our child is to have a right to the name of Templecombe."

The silence which succeeded this disclosure seemed interminable, and then Sir Lawrence said: "Oh, my God!" in a kind of muffled groan which suggested that he had buried his face in his hands.

"So you see, Lawrence." Diana went on after a moment, "I am no longer to be fobbed off with promises and delays. The hurried wedding to which you so rashly committed yourself this morning will indeed take place, but 'tis I, and not Verity, who will be the bride."

"Devil take it, how can I marry you?" The words seemed to be torn by force from Templecombe's lips. "Have you forgot that scoundrel, Fane? If I set Verity aside I must send him my challenge, or be for ever dishonoured. How will it profit you, or the child, if I am slain?"

"I will rid you of Dominic Fane," Diana said softly, and in the darkness beyond the door the unsuspected listener caught her breath in swift dismay. "Do I order things so ill that you think I have overlooked that danger?"

"You will do so?" Templecombe's voice was more suspicious than grateful. "What can you do?"

" 'Tis already done, in part," she replied calmly, "and tomorrow will see you rid of both your embarrassments. You may trust me, Lawrence. I do not make empty promises—no, nor empty threats neither."

The last remark was clearly intended as a reminder of the consequences of refusal, nor did it fail of its purpose. Sir Lawrence said hurriedly: "God knows I have no wish to marry that rogue's light-o'-love! If you know how I may avoid a meeting with him without dishonour to myself, in the devil's name tell me of it!"

"I shall tell you nothing, Lawrence, nor need you be by when it is done. Get you to Cloverton in the morning, and keep yourself in company all day, and by the time you return to Shere all danger to you at Fane's hands will be past. I will do all that is necessary, and you need have no hand in the business, so no aspersions can be cast upon your courage."

Verity waited to hear no more. If Diana had resolved to keep her own counsel, then it was very sure that nothing Sir Lawrence could say would turn her from that purpose. Slowly, and with infinite caution, she retreated along the corridor, guided after the first few steps by that faint glimmer of light from the staircase. Her passage through the silent house seemed endless, but at last she was safe in her own room and fumbling with hands that trembled to kindle a light.

Sickened with disgust though she was by what she had overheard, by this heartless betrayal of her trust by the two people to whom, out of all the world, she had looked for kindness and protection after her grandfather's death, yet her own wrongs were by no means uppermost in her mind. Still in her ears echoed those ominous words in Diana's deep, husky voice, 'I will rid you of Dominic Fane,' and the calm confidence which had invested them, and her subsequent remarks, filled Verity with apprehension. Whatever infamous plot had been formed for Dominic's undoing, it was plain that events had already been set in motion, and he, all unsuspecting, was alone in that desolate house amid the woods, a house which none would approach by night or day unless they were bent upon some nefarious business.

There was only one thing to be done. She had realized that from the moment she had started to retreat from the door of Sir Lawrence's room, nor did she waste time in setting about it. A search among the clothes so generously provided by Lady Sarah yielded a cloak to cover her yellow gown. She slung it about her shoulders, and, discarding the elaborate cap, covered her hair with a dark silk hood, knowing as she did so a pang of regret for the ragged gown and stout shoes in which she had come to Shere. They would have served her well in this extremity.

Shielding the candle-flame as best she might, Verity opened the door an inch or two and looked out into the corridor. No sound reached her ears but the gusty sigh of the wind, and no light heralded Diana's return. She stepped out and closed the door, and, with one hand bearing the candle and the other holding up her trailing skirts, flitted along the corridor and down the wide staircase to the hall.

The huge, double-leaved front door she did not dare attempt, but she knew that at the end of a passage to the left a smaller door gave on to the garden. Hastening thither, she drew the bolts which kept it and slipped out into the darkness, pulling the door shut behind her. At first she could see nothing, but as her eyes became accustomed to the gloom, she was able to discern the outline of paths and flower-beds, for though the moon was still hidden by clouds the darkness was not impenetrable. She thrust her candle-stick into the midst of a clump of flowers beside the door and moved cautiously forward along the dim-seen pathway. At the edge of the gardens she paused and looked back, but the great bulk of the house loomed silent and unlighted against the faintly luminous sky. Her escape was complete.

Out of the gardens and along the avenue which cut through the park; a struggle with the great iron gates, closed but by good fortune not locked; and then the road, dimly discernible as it curved to skirt the wall bounding the park. Its dusty, rutted surface was rough to light-shod feet, and there was a weary way to go, but a new-found sense of freedom lifted her above fatigue. The night was her friend, covering her escape from the oppressive gloom of Shere Place, hiding her from curious eyes as she flitted through the sleeping village, past the square tower of the church and the creaking sign-board of the inn, and so at last to the spot where the first fringe of the woodland reached out to touch the roadside.

The trees which had stood so still and silent under a stormy sky when first she saw them were full now of the voice of the wind, and at those moments when the moonlight pierced the drifting clouds the shadows of their branches danced wildly on the white road. Verity hurried on until she reached the rusty gates which stood defiantly wide, to let all Shere know that Dominic Fane had come home at last, and with no hesitation, but only a glad, eager lifting of her heart, passed between them and hastened along the rough, overgrown tunnel of the drive.

It was very dark there in the midst of the woods, and against her will she remembered what Mary Parr had told her of the tales surrounding the old house. She did not really expect to encounter the wraith of Harriet Fane, and yet the demented creaking of two boughs far above brought her heart into her mouth, and the sudden, silent swoop of an owl over her head made her gasp with fright. She quickened her pace, and though she stumbled often, and once a fallen branch tripped her and brought her to her knees, she held doggedly on her way until the trees thinned and she saw the pointed gables and twisted chimneys of the house against the sky, and, low down to the left of the porch, a light which burned steadily behind an unshuttered window.

She gave a sob of thankfulness and paused for a moment to regain her breath, and then moved forward again towards the lighted window. She had covered perhaps half the distance when a twig snapped sharply a few yards away, and something moved in the shadows beneath a tree, to halt her in her tracks with a swift return of fear. The light was increasing slowly, for only the thinning edges of a cloud now veiled the moon, and after a moment she could make out the tall figure of a man, who seemed to be standing there and looking fixedly towards her. With a relief which carried her too far towards confidence she moved towards him, never pausing to question his identity.

"Dominic," she said eagerly. " 'tis I, Verity."

She had almost reached him when a sudden misgiving brought her to a standstill again. He had made no response, and now that she could see him more clearly it seemed that he was too massively built to be the man she sought. She said again, uncertain this time: "Dominic?"

This time he did move, stepping out from under the tree,

and at the same instant the moon broke free of the last veil of cloud. Its cold light swept over his advancing figure, and with an overwhelming rush of horror she recognized the great bulk and the coarse, bearded face of Nat Trumper.

A scream broke from her lips and she turned to fly, but now her fringed, silken flounces betrayed her. She had taken barely half a dozen paces when the thorned branches of a neglected rosebush laid hold of her flowing skirts, and before she could free herself Red Nat was upon her, and her second cry stifled by a great paw clapped across her mouth. Helpless in that terrific grip, her senses reeling, she heard the chuckle of evil satisfaction with which he signalized the capture.

XVII

The Tempting of Dominic Fane

RED NAT had reached Shere just after dark, and by that time, although his lust for vengeance was as hot as ever, he had had time to recall some of the things which the ostler had told him concerning Dominic Fane. Among these had been all the more lurid tales connected with the house in the wood, and since Trumper was superstitious to a degree remarkable even in that age of superstition, these had caused him a good deal of uneasiness. So apprehensive had he become by the time the village was reached that he found it necessary to halt at the inn to revive his failing courage and to fortify himself against the ordeal ahead, for though he had not the smallest fear of Fane himself, it would need every ounce of resolution he could summon to approach a house which was the source of such eerie legends.

In the tap-room he soon found himself an object of curiosity, for even at fair-time strangers were rare in Shere. For a while he drank in silence, but then, the liquor having loosened his tongue and overcome his caution, he engaged the landlord in a conversation which he presently led, with what he fondly imagined to be great cunning, to the subject of Dominic Fane.

The host and the other customers were willing enough to

talk, and to question in their turn, and presently Trumper was repeating the story he had told in Cloverton, of old comradeship with Fane and a debt he had come to pay. They warned him then of the terrors surrounding the house in the wood, but though his heart quailed within him, Red Nat's conceit would not let him reveal his fears. So he boasted of his intention to seek out his old comrade that very night, and in admiration they supplied him with more to drink, and he accepted it readily and with it bolstered up a bravado which was no more than a cloak for a monstrous uneasiness. He was decidedly fuddled by the time he reeled out of the inn again and set off, watched by an admiring group of villagers, along the road leading westwards out of Shere.

The bravado lasted only until the last houses were left behind and he found himself alone in the windswept darkness, with the white road stretching inexorably ahead of him and only the strange, small sounds of the country night for company. Then uneasiness returned in full force, his steps lagged, and finally he sat down in the long, dry grass of the roadside. The pause was fatal; in a very short while the liquor had done its work, and Nat Trumper was flat on his back and snoring prodigiously.

When he awoke it was still dark, but the sky had cleared a little and the moon now shone intermittently through gaps in the clouds. He was stiff and cold and irritable, and the realization, which came all too soon, that he had spent his last penny at the inn served to exacerbate his feelings yet further. He remembered the errand which had brought him to Shere, and now anger revived to an extent which overcame even his dread of the supernatural. He heaved himself to his feet, loosened his sword in the scabbard, made sure that his pistol was ready to hand, and set off again on his interrupted journey.

He came presently to the ruined gateway his well-wishers had described to him, and after only the barest hesitation plunged into the woods beyond. Without any accident other than those caused by the darkness and the roughness of the path, he came in sight of the house, and, his courage fully revived by the reassuring sight of a lighted window, made his way cautiously across the overgrown garden towards it.

He had reached the shelter of a tree within twenty yards of the house, and had halted there to consider how best to achieve his purpose of taking Fane unawares, when out of the corner of his eye he detected a movement a short way off.

He turned his head, and then involuntarily recoiled, sick and cold with a fresh wave of horror, for, faintly discernible in the gloom, a cloaked female figure was gliding silently across the open space before the house.

A twig had snapped beneath his foot as he moved; the ghostly figure halted, and then came slowly towards him. He stood paralyzed, incapable of further movement, until a soft greeting came to tell him that this was no wraith, but the prey which had escaped him in London. As she halted again he stepped out into a sudden flood of moonlight, and then plunged in pursuit as she fled, her scream ripping through the silence even as the treacherous thorns of the rose-bush ripped the silken folds of her gown.

Dominic, when that first, terrified cry reached his ears, was sitting, as he had sat for a long time, on the settle by the empty fireplace, his head bowed on his hands. A crumpled letter lay on the floor at his feet, a letter from Verity which Urmiston's man, the shrewd old soldier named Thomas, had brought secretly to him during the evening, but it was not this alone which had destroyed in him any desire to sleep. It was another letter, that which he had sent back to the Marquis by the same messenger, which had conspired with the first to induce in him his present mood of hopelessness.

It had not been easy to write, destroying as it did his last faint hope of happiness, closing for ever the door which Diana Halland had that morning set open before his tempted and dazzled eyes, for in it he had told Urmiston of Diana's visit and begged him to go in his stead to Shere Place at noon on the following day. Mrs. Halland would be satisfied, he explained, if Verity would withdraw and make no further claim upon Sir Lawrence, while Templecombe would no longer press the matter of marriage if he, Dominic, left the district again, which he intended to do as soon as he knew that Verity was safe.

He had written it and given it to Thomas, and watched him disappear into the woods again, without permitting himself to contemplate the consequences of what he had done, but once the letter had gone beyond recall he had been plunged into an abyss of despair from which he was only roused by that shrill cry from the waste of garden beyond his window.

It was Verity's voice, he knew that beyond any shadow of a doubt, and started to his feet wondering whether, after all, he had fallen asleep and that frightened cry been uttered merely in his dreams. Then it came again, unmistakably real and this time cut off abruptly as though stifled by force. In a moment he was at the window, the casement flung wide, and the cold, indifferent moonlight was revealing a scene which roused in him a blind and reckless fury. He snatched up his sword from the chair where it lay, tossed the scabbard aside, and with the slim, deadly blade in his hand vaulted over the low sill and raced towards Red Nat and his struggling captive.

Trumper saw him coming, and with a curse let the girl go and dragged out his own sword. This was not as he had planned it, but, remembering his earlier victory and not realizing how completely it had been due to the fact that Fane was then already wounded, he was not troubled by any doubt of the outcome. Relying, as was his custom, upon brute strength and tremendous length of reach, he leapt confidently to meet his enemy, and so met death instead. His first clumsy thrust was parried without difficulty and he had no chance to make a second, for the bright Toledo blade leapt on to take him in the throat, and at the same instant another cloud swept across the face of the moon and darkness descended upon the garden.

To Verity, that sudden withdrawal of light set the seal of horror upon the night's adventures. She had seen the two men come together, heard the vicious scrape of steel upon steel, but now with darkness had come silence, save for the long-drawn sobbing of the wind among the trees. For what seemed an eternity she stood there, too terrified to move, vainly straining eyes and ears to discover what the darkness was hiding, and then Dominic's voice urgently spoke her name, and his tall figure materialized out of the gloom beside her. With a sob of relief she stumbled against him, clutching with both hands at his threadbare coat.

"Is he—is he dead?" she faltered.

"Yes," he said curtly. "Too fine a death for such scum, but it was best to make an end swiftly." He realized how violently she was trembling, and put an arm about her shoulders, adding more gently: "Quiet you, my dear, the danger is past. He will trouble you no more."

She was too spent to reply, and he led her towards the house. Coming to the window, he set aside his sword and lifted her into the room, climbing in after her and drawing the casement shut once more. Verity dropped into the nearest chair, leaning her head against its high back while he studied her white face with some anxiety. After a little a tinge of colour crept back into her cheeks and she contrived to smile faintly at him. Dominic leaned against the table and looked down at her with a frown.

"What in the name of heaven brings you here at this hour?" he demanded. "Did you come on foot?"

She nodded, and told him of the discovery she had made. Comprehension deepened in his eyes as he listened, and by the time she had finished he was smiling, not pleasantly, but with that mocking twist of the lips which lent his dark face so saturnine an expression.

"So that is the full sum of it, and Templecombe is caught fast in the snare of his own sins," he said musingly. "There is some justice in that, I think. Madam Diana is more than a match for him."

Verity's eyes were puzzled.

"Is that all you have to say? She is plotting against you, Dominic, and she will shrink from nothing, I am sure, however infamous it may be. If you could have heard her speak of it—I was so desperately afraid for you!"

His expression softened and he started to speak, but then, as though thinking better of it, moved away to snuff the candle which was guttering and smoking at the other end of the table. After a moment he said:

"So you came to warn me, to this place, at dead of night. God knows I have never doubted your courage, but I never knew the extent of it until now."

It was not, she felt sure, what he had first intended to say, and the strangeness of his manner served to increase her bewilderment. It was as though a barrier had grown up between them since their last meeting, invisible and intangible, but a barrier none the less.

"I am not as brave as you suppose," she said slowly. "Coming through the wood I was mortally afraid, but if you were in danger——"

"You pay your debts, as you once told me," he broke in harshly. "Oh, I am grateful, my dear, but the only danger was from that rogue, Nat Trumper, and your sister-in-law had no hand in that. She planned to be rid of both you and me at one stroke, but no violence was intended."

Briefly he recounted the story of Diana's visit the previous day, and of the proposal she had made. Listening, Verity thought that she knew now the source of the constraint in his manner, and relief flooded her whole being. She rose to her

feet, her breathing a little hurried, and faced him with the
length of the table between them.

"And you agreed?" she asked breathlessly. "You were coming to Shere Place at noon, as she suggested?"

He misunderstood the source of her agitation, and made
haste to soothe it. His reply struck her like a blow between
the eyes.

"I agreed simply to ensure that she would make no other
attempt against you. A letter has gone to Lord Urmiston, explaining the situation and asking him to go, with Lady Sarah,
to fetch you to Corville Court. Thus at one stroke you would
have been placed in safety, and this damned scandal crushed
for all time."

She could not believe the implications of his words. She
said desperately: "But you would have come to me there?
That is what you mean, is it not?"

He stared at her for a second or two without replying, and
then turned abruptly to pick up the letter from the floor.

"I do not understand," he said, and tossed it on to the
table in front of her. "In that you bid me tarry here no longer, since so many wish me ill."

"Yes, yes," she replied, "but that was when I believed Sir
Lawrence sincere in his trust in me. I thought it my duty then
to remain with him, since he was prepared to stand by me in
spite of everything. Even then, and despite all that I knew to
his discredit, I still did not realize how despicable were his
motives. Now I know the truth, and at last I am free, bound
by no ties of duty, or by promises made in my name, when I
was too young to understand them."

She paused, her eyes fixed in anxious pleading upon his
face, but for several moments he made no response. At last,
in a voice strangely unlike his own, he said slowly:

"They were promises which should never have been made,
and which could have brought you nothing but unhappiness.
I pray God that the freedom you have found may serve you
better."

"That is my hope," she replied in a low voice, then, finding
him still silent, she went on: "Dominic, I want to go home,
back to my grandfather's house that now is mine." Again she
paused, but he did not speak, and she added with a kind of
desperation: "Will you take me there?"

It seemed a very long time before he answered her. He was
not looking at her, but down at the candle on the table beside

him, and in its clear light his face seemed oddly pale, the lines upon it very apparent.

"I will take you to Manton Lacey," he said at length in a level voice. "No doubt Lord Urmiston will be happy to furnish you with the means for your journey, and to escort you to your home. Under his protection you will travel in greater safety and comfort than I have the means to provide."

There was hurt bewilderment in her eyes, but he did not see it, and with an effort she kept her voice as calm as his own when she replied.

"Lord Urmiston and his sister have been kindness itself, but I desire to trespass no further upon their good nature. For the rest, have you found me so delicate a traveller that you think I must have a coach and servants at my command before I venture upon a journey?"

He shook his head.

"I know that when necessity compels it you will face hardship and peril without complaint, but now the necessity is past. You have found friends who will care for you better than I. It is time I went my way."

"No one could care for me better than you have done," she retorted, and now there was a break in her voice, a tremor which could not be controlled. "Oh, why are you so blind? Why will you not help me?"

She paused, twisting her hands together in distress, and then her glance fell upon the letter which he had cast down between them. She drew a deep breath, and moved round the table to stand beside him.

"I will tell you something, Dominic," she said quietly. "When first I heard of the rumours which were linking my name with yours, I was glad of it, because I thought it would mean the end of my betrothal to Sir Lawrence, and I cared nothing for what might be said of me if only I could be free of that. Then he told me that the scandal made no difference, that he believed none of it, and because I deemed him sincere I resolved to abide by the promise I had given him, cost me what it might. So I sent you that letter, though it broke my heart to do it, and then spent the rest of the day regretting what I had done."

As the soft, hurried voice ceased, Dominic turned to look at her. A curious conflict of emotion had him in its grip, for even while his heart exulted at the confession implicit in her words, his mind spoke coldly of the immeasurable gulf which yawned between them. It was symbolized by the change in

her appearance since their last meeting, and the contrast between that and her present surroundings, a contrast as sharp
as that which had struck him when he first saw her in the
dingy garret in Whitefriars. No amount of rough usage could
disguise the richness of her attire, and to him the silks and
laces she now wore betokened the world of wealth and luxury
and idle frivolity to which she, and Templecombe, and the
rest of them belonged. It was a world which Dominic Fane
could never enter, save by the unworthy means which Diana
had suggested.

'The greater profit'! The ugly phrase she had used echoed
once more in his mind, bringing with it a distrust to poison
even further his first instinctive joy. What could he, the broken and ruined adventurer, offer to a woman such as Verity
Halland? He did not doubt her sincerity; at that moment, he
felt sure, she honestly believed that she cared for him, but at
present she was wrought to a pitch of emotion capable of
sweeping her headlong into a decision which a calmer and
more mature judgment would surely bring her to regret.

Betrothed since childhood, and leading a life which, until
his own tempestuous entry into it, had been extraordinarily
sheltered, it was not wonderful that she should mistake gratitude for love, and regard him in a heroic light which he in no
way deserved. He had protected her, he had risked his life
and renounced his vengeance, he had even killed to shield her
from harm, but to let these things weigh in the balance
against her lack of experience would be a deed as selfish and
treacherous as any of which Templecombe had been guilty.
She would recover from any hurt he might deal her now; the
letter she had sent him earlier proved that she spoke tonight
on the impulse of the moment; there would be the company
of the young Marquis to divert her thoughts. So he reasoned,
with a man's logic which took no need of womanly instinct
or the insight with which this girl was blessed.

"Diana need not have plotted so secretly to be rid of me,"
Verity was saying softly. "Had she told me what was in her
mind yesterday I would have done as she desired, and been
grateful to her for ever."

Dominic shook his head.

"No," he said in a low voice, "you might have been grateful to her now, but who can say with certainty what the future may bring? You are young, Verity, and you have lately
endured an ordeal which has so clouded your judgment that
you see all men as monstrous villains or paragons of virtue,

but it is not so. There is good and bad in all of us, and I am not the hero you seek to make me. Have you forgotten the purpose with which I set out from London, the manner in which I would have sacrificed you to my own blind and senseless desire for vengeance?"

"I have forgotten nothing." Her voice was gentle; her eyes, resting upon his face, compassionate and tender. "Why are you trying to belittle yourself to me? Surely you know that no words, your own or any other's, can weigh for a moment against the truth my own heart tells me?"

"The heart can be a false counsellor," he replied curtly. "Better to trust one's head. There is less risk of disillusion."

There was a pause. The wind sighed eerily, and the candle-flame flickered in the draught, so that their shadows leapt and quivered on the wall behind them. The letter drifted slowly across the table, poised for an instant on the edge, and then floated to the floor again, and Verity watched its fall unseeingly.

"What would you have me do then?" she asked wistfully.

"I would have you go back to the world where you belong," he said harshly. "Chance has tangled our lives together for a space, but this is all. I belong to the past, to this mouldering house with its ghosts and memories. In the present I am an intruder, and in the future I have no place at all. Look well at me, Verity! See me as the rest of the world sees me—a beggar, ragged and penniless, a man who has failed in everything! An outcast to be shunned and made the butt of covert sneers which would be uttered to my face if those who speak them did not fear my sword."

She looked as he bade her, her grey eyes wide and grave, the wistfulness which had invested her words echoed in them, and in the curve of her lips.

"That is not what I see," she said steadily. "I see the man I love, and who I think loves me a little, but who is so proud that he would break both our hearts rather than yield one jot of that pride."

"Proud?" he repeated blankly. "God's light! What cause have I to be proud?"

"Is it not so?" she countered quietly. "Can you tell me truly that it makes no difference that I have lands and gold and other worthless things, and you have none? That were our positions reversed, you would still be determined to send me from you?"

The challenge struck shrewdly, for there was truth enough

in what she said, but not so shrewdly that it turned him from his purpose.

"I cannot deny it," he said bitterly. "A man should have something to offer the woman he marries. He should not be her pensioner, living in her house and upon her money. If it be pride to wish to provide these things for myself, then I will admit that I am proud indeed, but it is an empty pride, as well you know. Therefore it is better that we should part."

"I will not believe it!" she cried passionately. "Why should a few acres of land, a few bags of gold, stand between us? These things are mine only by the chance of inheritance! I am neither to be praised nor blamed because I am rich! Without you I am lost! I have nothing, I am nothing!" She broke off, and stood with bowed head, struggling to control her emotion. After a little she continued more quietly: "If you deny me, do you know what those who now have charge of my fortune will do? They will say that I must marry, that an estate cannot be left masterless, in the hands of a mere girl, and they will choose me a husband, as my grandfather chose Sir Lawrence. Dominic, this is our only chance of happiness!"

He had moved away, as though by placing some distance between them he could make the parting easier to bear, and stood now by the fireplace with his back to her, and his hands gripping the great carved beam above the hearth. Every word she uttered, every note of pain and pleading in her voice, added to the monstrous force of temptation which he was striving with all his will to resist.

"Do you suppose these guardians you speak of would permit your marriage to such as I?" he said hoarsely when she paused. "They would demand someone more worthy of you, and they would be right to do so. You think you love me, but what can you know of love? The time would come when you realized that what you feel now is no more than an illusion, born of gratitude and perhaps of pity. Do you think I will let you forfeit your whole future for a passing whim?"

"Oh, you are blind, and worse than blind!" she exclaimed despairingly. "How can I convince you of what I know to be true? That what I feel for you is as strong and changeless as time itself?" She paused, but he neither moved nor spoke. Her shoulders drooped suddenly: a stifled sob escaped her. "I cannot make you believe me! If it is not enough that I have come to you, that I offer you my lands, my fortune, my very self, what other proof is it in my power to give?" She drew a deep, quivering breath, and pressed her hands against her cheeks. "I am shamed, I think! I was too certain that you loved me."

"Love you?" He swung abruptly to face her, and she saw that he was white to the lips, his tawny eyes strangely brilliant. He took a step towards her, and then halted, as though restraining himself by a tremendous effort. "For God's sake, tempt me no more!" he said huskily, and strode past her and out of the room. The door slammed shut behind him, and a few moments later, like an echo, came the more ponderous crash of that which gave on to the porch, the sound of it booming through the empty house.

Verity sank down on to the settle and buried her face in her hands. She was alone in the house which legend had peopled with ghosts and troubled spirits, and in the garden a man lay stark in death, but neither the one fact nor the other found any place in her thoughts. She was beyond fear, and beyond hope, and nothing was real but a pain too deep and all-pervading to find relief in tears.

XVIII

The Constable of Shere

JOB DAGGETT, the Constable of Shere, woke very early on the morning after his momentous interview with Lady Templecombe. The worthy Constable, in fact, had slept very little, in spite of liberal potations indulged in at the village inn during the evening, for he was sorely troubled. Having neither wife nor family with whom to discuss his problems, he was obliged to bear his burden alone, and the night had brought forth no helpful counsel. Rather had it increased his dread of the task which was being forced upon him, for, lying awake through the slow, dark hours, he had had time to remember every horrible tale he had ever heard of the house in the wood, and to reflect, more prosaically, that by now Fane had presumably been reinforced by that self-styled comrade of his who had been in Shere the previous evening. Job Daggett would have shrunk from the prospect of tackling either Dominic Fane or the red giant alone, but the thought of facing both of them together, and traversing that awful wood to do it, bathed him in a sweat of sheer terror.

Finally, in the period of cold, grey light preceding the dawn, he came to a decision. This was not a matter to be dealt with on his own initiative; someone in authority must be consulted, someone who, if they agreed with Lady Templecombe, could provide Mr. Daggett with the necessary assistance. The obvious person to apply to was the nearest magistrate, who in this instance, happened to be Lord Corville. Comforted by this thought, the Constable rose, dressed himself with care, and then set off, an unwitting instrument of destiny, for Manton Lacey.

Since the household at Corville Court kept country hours, it was not long after his arrival there that Daggett was admitted to his lordship's presence. Corville had an easy way with him, and at first the Constable had little difficulty in explaining the object of his visit, but no sooner had his lordship grasped the gist of the story than he bade Daggett pause, and, summoning a lackey, sent him to request Lord Urmiston to join them.

A few minutes later the Marquis came into the room, very fine in a suit of dove-grey heavily laced with gold, his great periwig exquisitely curled. He looked at his brother-in-law, and then at the Constable, and his brows lifted in faint surprise.

"This man has come to me with a curious story, Urmiston," Corville informed him. "It concerns a matter in which you have shown some interest, and I desire you to hear what he has to say."

The Marquis strolled forward, seated himself on the edge of the table at which Corville was sitting, and swung one foot in its perfectly fashioned riding-boot idly to and fro.

"'Slife, Corville, this is vastly intriguing!" he murmured, and sent a humorous, inquiring glance at the perspiring Constable. "Who is this worthy fellow?"

"He is the Constable of Shere," Corville replied dryly, and in an instant all the bantering amusement had faded from Urmiston's face. The swinging foot was stilled, and the blue eyes narrowed beneath frowning brows. "The devil he is!" he said softly. "And what news does he bring from Shere?"

"Something that puzzles me a trifle," the elder man replied, and added with a touch of impatience, "Come Daggett, speak up!"

Thus adjured, Mr. Daggett repeated his story, but less fluently this time, for the presence of the fine gentleman from London flustered him. He observed with growing dismay that the frown had deepened in the blue eyes, and that one white hand in its wealth of lace was tapping, in impatience or annoyance, upon my lord's grey-clad knee. He wondered uneasily what possible interest this young nobleman could have in Dominic Fane, and whether his own decision to consult Lord Corville had been as happy an inspiration as it had seemed at the time.

When he had done, and several questions had been asked and answered, he was dismissed, to await their lordships' pleasure in another room. He went thankfully, and as the door closed behind him, Corville looked at the Marquis.

"Well, Robert?" he asked quizzically. "Since, for reasons best known to yourselves, you and your sisters have chosen to befriend this young woman, I thought it best to let you hear that tale. Do you still insist that Miss Halland knows nothing of Dominic Fane?"

Urniston thought rapidly. Acting upon the advice of Lady Anne, he and Sarah had told Corville nothing of their previous meeting with Verity, merely insisting on their belief in the utter falsity of the scandal now raging about her. Anne had added her voice to theirs, announcing her intention of extending hospitality and protection to Miss Halland should the need arise, and since Corville adored his young wife he had raised no objection. That he would be equally complaisant if he knew the full story, the Marquis did not for one moment believe. There was a strong streak of the Puritanical in his character, and he would never countenance anything in the nature of an intrigue, even one which existed only in the unkindly gossip of his neighbours. He said cautiously:

"Why not? All that this story proves to us is that Lady Templecombe herself believes the rumours to be true, and fears that if they are generally accepted, Sir Lawrence will be obliged to meet Fane. May I know what action, if any, you propose to take?"

The elder man shrugged.

"I cannot ignore it, that is certain! I suppose the only thing to do is to question Fane and discover what answer he makes to the charge. From what I remember of him, it is quite likely that he did abduct Miss Halland out of hatred against

Templecombe. More likely, at all events, than that he would seek to gratify that hatred by spreading unfounded slanders against her, as Sir Lawrence seems to believe."

"Or as he chooses to believe!" Urmiston's tone was scornful; he made a gesture of distaste. "I cannot stomach such cowardice. By God! were I in his place, I would not rest until I had crossed swords with a man who dared so to defame my promised wife."

"I doubt it not," Corville replied dryly. "You are too hotheaded by far, my dear Robert." He rose to his feet. "I suppose I must go to Shere without delay, and endeavour to sift some grains of truth from this harvest of gossip. Do you ride with me?"

"With all my heart!" The Marquis stood up; his voice was brisk. "Whither do we go? To Shere Place?"

Corville shook his head. "No, first to Fane's house, but if he cannot or will not answer the charge, it may be necessary to question Miss Halland, and that, believe me, is a task for which I have no taste at all. Oh, the devil take Job Daggett! Why must he embroil me in this infernal business?"

Urmiston made no reply. He felt extremely uneasy, for, knowing from Fane's own confession that he had indeed been guilty of abducting Miss Halland, he did not see how the charge could be proved false. He was concerned not so much for Fane himself as for Verity, for he could guess something of the dismay she would feel if the man to whom she owed so much were to be placed under arrest. There was no doubt that, but for his encounter with Diana and his subsequent return to Shere, the danger in which he now stood would never have arisen, but though Verity would undoubtedly make every conceivable effort to save him, all must surely prove futile.

Corville had gone to his desk and taken out paper and ink. As he picked up a pen, he remarked over his shoulder:

"Templecombe himself must bear some share in this investigation. I will send him word of what has happened, and bid him meet us at the inn at Shere."

The letter was soon written and despatched, and while Corville was thus engaged, the Marquis seized the opportunity to tell his sisters what had passed. Their dismay was profound, but neither had any helpful suggestion to offer, and after advising Sarah to set out betimes for Shere Place, in accordance with Fane's request, and adding that he would join her there, Urmiston left them and sent for Thomas. To this most

trusted of his servants he explained what had happened, and
ordered him to make ready to accompany him to Shere.

So, presently, their lordships got to horse, and with
Thomas and Job Daggett following, and further reinforced by
a couple of Corville's grooms, set off upon their errand. They
rode for the most part in silence, for Corville was considering, with growing irritation, all the more distasteful aspects of
the task which had been thrust upon him, and Urmiston
vainly cudgelling his brain for some means of averting disaster. He would have been even more uneasy had he known of
Nat Trumper's arrival in Shere, but Mr. Daggett, who had as
little liking as any other man for advertising his own lack of
courage, had refrained from mentioning this fact, and the
Marquis was spared this additional cause for disquiet.

The servant bearing the letter to Templecombe made great
haste, as he had been ordered to do, and reached Shere Place
while their lordships were still some way from the village.
The letter was carried to Sir Lawrence just as his valet was
putting the finishing touches to his toilet, for, mindful of Diana's instructions, Templecombe was on the point of remov-
ing himself to Cloverton.

He broke the seal, wondering idly why Corville should be
writing to him in such haste, and glanced over the contents of
the letter. The valet, still hovering attentively about him, saw
the colour fade from his face and his jaw sag perceptibly.
Then a hand crept to his mouth, and for several seconds he
stood fingering his lower lip and staring before him with an
expression of the most acute dismay. Then, with the letter
still crushed in his hand, he swung round and hurried out of
the room, the fact that he did not even glance in the mirror
denoting the measure of his consternation.

The Dowager was still in her own apartments when her
grandson burst in upon her, but she was fully dressed and
ready to commence the business of the day, for despite her
age she was no sluggard. Sir Lawrence waved away the attendant Kate, and thrust Corville's letter into her ladyship's
hands.

"Is it true?" he demanded. "Did you order the Constable to
arrest Dominic Fane?"

Her ladyship gave him one shrewd glance, and then, without replying, turned her attention to the letter. She read it
through and then handed it back to him.

"Yes, I told him," she snapped. "but I did not expect the
fool to go whining to Corville with the tale. Merciful heaven!

Is there no one with the courage to deal with that rogue as he deserves?" She looked Sir Lawrence over defiantly. "Stop glowering at me in that fashion! I tell you, there is no harm done."

"No harm?" he repeated furiously. "No harm, you say, when Corville demands that I go with him to confront Fane? What if that revengeful devil persuades him that the charge is false, that Verity went with him of her own free will? What then, madam? Yet I cannot refuse to go, without laying myself open to a charge of cowardice." He screwed the letter into a ball and flung it to the floor. The gesture was petulant, but there was more of fear than of anger in the high pitch of his voice. "This is the fruit of your poking and prying, your meddling in matters which do not concern you! Would to God you would permit me to manage my own affairs in my own way!"

On that he flung out of the room again, hesitated for a moment in an agony of indecision, and then went reluctantly out to his coach, which, summoned to carry him to Cloverton, was already at the door. Fear of Dominic Fane had brought a dryness to his throat and a sick emptiness to his stomach, but his fear of ridicule was stronger still. With the feeling that he was going to his execution, and only partially reassured by the recollection that Diana had already set in motion some plot against his enemy, he climbed into the coach and gave the word to drive to the inn at Shere.

At about the time that Sir Lawrence was fearfully setting out to meet Lord Corville, Diana was sitting before her mirror and staring impatiently at her giggling maid. She was pale, and there were dark shadows beneath her eyes; neither her health nor her temper were at their best, and she was certainly in no mood to be diverted by her woman's antics.

"Well, what was it that Sir Lawrence's valet gave to you?" she asked querulously. "Come, Agnes, tell me and have done, or keep silent and dress my hair, I care not which!"

Agnes smirked. She knew a good deal about her mistress's private concerns, and there was a spitefulness in her nature which revelled in her present small triumph.

"He gave me something he picked up just outside the door of Sir Lawrence's bedchamber this morning, madam," she replied with mock demureness, "and he said I'd best give it back to the person that dropped it there, and warn her that my lady wouldn't be best pleased if she found out."

She extended her hand, on the palm of which lay a small

knot of ribbons in a soft shade of yellow. Diana stiffened,
and her hand clenched hard on the comb she was holding.
She recognized those ribbons, just as the servants had done,
as belonging to the dress which Verity had worn the previous
evening, but she had her own reasons for knowing that the
conclusion to which they had both jumped was mistaken. Yet
if the ribbons had been found outside Lawrence's room . . . !

She remembered suddenly how last night a draught had
snatched the door of her own room from her grasp and
slammed it shut. The sound had not been loud enough to
awaken anyone, but if Verity had not been asleep she might
well have heard it and sought to find out the cause. Staring at
the ribbons, Diana had time to regret the malice which had
caused her to refrain from telling Verity last night of the bargain she had made with Dominic Fane. She might still be
able to persuade her to agree to it, but her own position was
far less strong now that she must bargain with the girl instead
of assuming the guise of impartial but well-intentioned friend.

"Where is Miss Verity?" she demanded, and Agnes
shrugged.

"Abed still, I suppose, madam," she replied. "She's not sent
for me yet."

Diana nodded, and rose to her feet.

"Give me those ribbons," she commanded, and added, as
the maid reluctantly obeyed, "Wait for me here, and Agnes,
let me hear of no more scandalmongering with Sir
Lawrence's servants. It does not please me."

She did not wait to see the effect of her warning, but went
out of the room and along the corridor to Verity's bedchamber. A light tap brought no response, and after a moment she
opened the door and went in. What she saw made her close it
behind her rather hurriedly. The bed was made and undisturbed, and the night attire which Agnes had laid ready for
Miss Halland to wear had not been touched: one window
stood wide, the curtains swaying in the wind; on the floor lay
crumpled the cap of lace and yellow ribbons which Verity
had been wearing the last time she saw her.

It was not difficult to guess why the girl had fled, or
whither she had gone. Diana stood thinking, still grasping the
handle of the door, and slowly her first dismay gave way to
satisfaction. There would be no need to bargain; Fane had
been brought to see the wisdom of securing Verity's fortune
rather than pursuing an empty vengeance, and that Verity

herself had needed no urging to return to him made certain the success of the scheme to save Sir Lawrence.

She went out into the corridor again, and discovered the Dowager hastening towards her. Something in the old lady's manner was vaguely disquieting, but without pausing to pursue that thought, Diana opened the door again and beckoned Lady Templecombe into the deserted room.

"We have troubled ourselves unduly, as your ladyship may see," she said by way of explanation. "Verity must have fled from the house during the night."

"Fled?" Lady Templecombe repeated sharply. "Fled whither?"

"To her lover, no doubt. Where else could she go, without resources of any kind?"

She broke off in alarm, for her ladyship had uttered a moan of dismay and was swaying perilously. Diana flung an arm about her frail, tottering figure and guided her to a chair, and then knelt beside her to chafe the wrinkled hands. The old woman's face had assumed an alarmingly livid hue and her eyes were half closed, but when Diana would have moved away to summon assistance, the claw-like fingers closed fiercely on her arm.

"Wait!" her ladyship gasped painfully. " 'Tis Lawrence! Oh, dear God! what are we to do?"

In gasping, broken sentences she explained the situation which had arisen out of her own plan to dispose of Fane. Sir Lawrence was already on his way to meet Corville and Urmiston. It could not be long before they all reached the house in the wood.

"And if they find the wench there with Fane, who will believe any talk of abduction?" she concluded frantically. "Lawrence will have to challenge him, and with Corville and the Marquis to act as witnesses, they may even fight then and there."

"God in heaven!" said Diana blankly, and sat back on her heels, staring in furious dismay at the Dowager. Lady Templecombe gazed back with stricken despair, for under this final blow her domineering spirit had broken at last.

"Think of something, my dear," she besought her piteously. "Some way of preventing it. Your wits are quick! Think, in God's name!"

"There must be a way!" Diana whispered fiercely, half to herself, and then, after a moment's pause, raised her eyes to the Dowager's face. "They are to meet in the village, you say? Is there any other way of reaching Fane's house, any shorter road?"

Lady Templecombe pressed a hand to her forehead.

"Yes," she said, after a few seconds' furious concentration. "Across the park to the Manton Lacey road, and then by way of a lane through the land which once was Fane's. It reaches the high road not a hundred yards from his gates."

Diana jumped up, and took the old lady's arm to help her to her feet. Her lips were compressed, her eyes hard and bright.

"Have two horses saddled, my lady, and choose some servant you can trust to show me the road," she said briefly. "If I can reach Fane's house ahead of Sir Lawrence, I may be able to save him."

Her ladyship permitted herself to be led to the door, but looked up doubtfully at the tall young woman beside her.

"But what can you do?" she asked. "What arguments can you use?"

"Play upon Fane's greed, and warn him again that if he harms Sir Lawrence he will not escape with his life." Diana turned the key in the lock, withdrew it, and put it into the Dowager's hand. "Your ladyship had best keep that, and tell anyone who is curious that Verity is unwell and must not be disturbed."

She hurried back to her own room and bullied the startled Agnes into activity. In astonishment the maid helped her to put on her riding-dress, and in greater astonishment still accepted her refusal to have her face painted or her hair properly dressed. Diana bundled the heavy black tresses up anyhow under her riding-hat, snatched gloves and whip from the maid's hands, and ran out of the room and down the stairs.

Lady Templecombe had wasted no time. The horses were at the door, in the charge of a middle-aged groom who had apparently already been given his orders, for without delay he assisted Mrs. Halland into the saddle, mounted his own horse, and led the way towards the main gates. After a short distance he bore to the left along a grassy ride which cut diagonally across the park. Here they were able to urge the horses to their greatest speed, and in the first few minutes of the journey Diana's hopes rose high.

All too soon, however, these ideal conditions ended, and the ride dwindled to a mere track as it entered a belt of woodland where they were obliged to slacken pace considerably. At last the track gave on to a road, along which her guide turned right-handed, volunteering as he did so the information that this was the most direct route from Shere to Manton Lacey.

With Lord Corville in mind, Diana was thankful when they left the road again for a narrow and apparently seldom used lane which wound its way between fertile meadows, but her relief was short-lived. The surface of the lane was in an appalling condition, criss-crossed with ruts many inches deep and baked to the hardness of rock after much dry weather. Here and there an attempt had been made to fill the worst potholes with stones, but the second state was worse than the first, and for yards at a time the riders were obliged to rein in to walking pace and pick their way over ground which might have been prepared with the deliberate object of delaying them.

Diana's nerves were strained to breaking point. It was not for Sir Lawrence's sake alone that she was making such frantic efforts to reach Fane's house ahead of him, for if Fane were accused of abduction he might, now that Verity knew the identity of the Black Mask, make accusations in his turn. Once it was shown that Diana Halland had urgent reasons to wish herself rid of her sister-in-law, the finger of suspicion would be hard to avoid, even though the only material proof of her guilt was the diamond ring at present concealed in her bosom. She would have known more ease of mind had she been able to dispose of that damning piece of evidence, but she knew that if she hid it or threw it away she would suffer agonies of fear lest it be found and used to incriminate her. The thought crossed her mind that it would be an excellent plan to conceal it somewhere in Fane's house, thus at one stroke ensuring her own safety and providing proof of his guilt, but to do that successfully she would need to be extraordinarily fortunate.

The hazard-ridden lane came to an end at last, and brought them out upon the high road, which for as far as they could see lay deserted under a cloudy sky. With a sigh of relief, Diana turned her horse in the direction indicated by the groom and urged it to a canter along the strip of turf bordering the road. Her hopes had soared again, and she turned in between the crumbling pillars and rusty gates of Fane's house without pausing to reflect that the road could as well be deserted after the passing of Templecombe and his companions as before it.

Thus it was with no premonition of what she was to find that she emerged from the woods into the forsaken garden which seemed more forlorn than ever on this grey and windy day. She was unprepared for the ponderous coach at rest in the drive ahead of her, for the group of men, some mounted and some on foot, clustered about something which lay upon the ground a short distance from the house. It was impossible to retreat, for they had already seen her, and so she went forward as slowly as she dared, seeking desperately for some convincing explanation of her presence there. She was acutely conscious of their faces turned towards her. Templecombe's apprehensive, and yet with a certain inexplicable triumph in its expression; Corville's grave and frowning; the young Marquis, fair and handsome, watching her with narrowed eyes which seemed to hold more than a hint of suspicion; the other men, pale and uneasy, keeping close together, looking now at her, now over their shoulders at the old house which loomed, silent and forbidding, behind them.

She had drawn level with them, had opened her lips to utter she knew not what of greeting or of question, when her gaze fell for the first time upon the thing which had been engaging their attention. It was a dead man, who lay on his back amid the stained and trampled grass, his red beard matted with blood and his sightless eyes staring horribly at the lowering sky. It was Nat Trumper.

A wave of nausea swept over her, and house and gardens and encircling trees whirled dizzily before her eyes, for despite her ruthlessness her horror of bloodshed was very real. She heard anxious exclamations, felt hands lifting her from the saddle, and presently came to herself to find that she was sitting on the step of the coach, with the gentlemen clustering rather helplessly about her.

"Thank you, I am better now," she assured them faintly. "Forgive me! I did not mean to trouble you." Shock had cleared her mind, and the lies came fluently. "Lady Templecombe told me where to find you, gentlemen. She is in some distress, fearful that this man, Fane, will provoke Sir Lawrence into quarrelling with him. I came, at her request, to beg him to remember his duty to his name, and to her. If, as we believe, the man is guilty of abduction, let the law deal with him as he deserves.'

"It is no longer a question of abduction alone, madam," It was Corville who spoke, his tone of a gravity to match his looks. "What we have found yonder makes it seem likely that

Fane will have to face a charge of murder—unless, as I suspect, he has already fled."

An exclamation from Job Daggett interrupted him. The Constable was staring towards the house, and there was that in his face which brought every glance round in the same direction. Framed in the mouth of the porch, lean and shabby, and seeming like the sinister spirit of this sinister place, Dominic Fane was sardonically regarding them.

XIX

The Accusation

DOMINIC, after his abrupt departure from the house, had crossed the garden and entered the wind-tossed woods beyond, where tormented trees sobbed and groaned in the darkness. A turmoil as fierce was raging within him, and his flight—for it was nothing less—had been prompted by desperation, was a final effort to resist a temptation rapidly becoming irresistible.

For, come what might, he must not yield to it, must somehow steel himself to deny the instinctive promptings of heart and mind and body. Verity was as far above him as the stars, and must remain for ever as inaccessible as they. He, who had the worldly knowledge which she lacked, must remember that they would not always be thus solitary, that there would be eyes to stare and voices to whisper, that their marriage would be taken as a confession that all now being said of them was true. The world, whether shocked or cynical, would have to be faced, and the insidious power of its censure might well poison and destroy their happiness.

In her presence he could not remember these things, but now, alone in the gusty dark, he forced himself to think of them, and to look back dispassionately upon the past ten years of his life. They were not years of which he could be proud. Seared and embittered by the disasters which had befallen him, and by his failure to inflict retribution upon his enemy, he had not cared greatly how he lived. He had sold his sword always where the price was highest, not troubling

to inquire whether or not the cause he served was just. At
best he had been one of a brutal and licentious soldiery, at
worst no better than a hired brigand, until he had become so
lost to all sense of decency that he could evolve a warped
and pitiless scheme of vengeance and see no wrong in it.
Though he had been saved from that ultimate crime, though
by the slow and difficult ways of renunciation he had been in
part redeemed, he was in no way worthy of the wondrous
guerdon offered to him. Better to be strong now, to endure
the anguish of parting and know that she would remember
him with kindness, than to watch her bright illusions fade as
she realized the cruel trick her emotions had played upon
her.

So for the rest of that night Dominic Fane tramped woods
which for him were haunted in very truth, by phantoms of
the inescapable past, and by tantalizing visions of all that the
future might have held. The conflict within him found a
measure of relief in physical exertion, and when he came at
last, in the grey light of a dismal morning, into the garden
once again, he was not conscious of any bodily fatigue,
though a sick weariness possessed his spirit.

He went into the house, to the room where he had left
Verity, and found her sleeping on the rough pallet in the corner, as though she had cast herself down there in the uttermost extreme of exhaustion or despair. She did not wake, and
after a moment he withdrew again, and went out to the
crumbling stables, where his hired mount moved restlessly in
a musty, echoing dimness which could have housed a dozen
horses without difficulty.

While he groomed and fed the animal, he forced his tired
mind to decide upon a course of action. Though he was still
determined to place Verity in the care of Lord Urmiston and
his sisters, it would not do to ride up with her to the door of
Corville Court, and finally he resolved to turn once more for
aid to Mary Parr. Leaving Verity at her cottage, he would go
alone to wait on the road to Manton Lacey until the Marquis
and Lady Sarah came by on their way to Shere, when he
would intercept them upon some pretext or other and tell
them where Miss Halland was to be found.

That, for him, would be the end of the adventure. Assured
that he left her in good hands, he would return to London,
though what he would do when he reached the city he neither
knew nor cared. The thought of London evoked a memory of
Nat Trumper and a thought in passing for the corpse now

lying amid the tangled grasses where they had fought. He wondered whether it would be prudent to conceal it, but then decided that so much was not necessary. No one would penetrate the eerie fastnesses of that forgotten garden, and Red Nat would lie undisturbed there as surely as though he were six feet underground.

Verity was awake when he returned to the house, and accepted without comment or protest his curt explanation of his plans. All the spirit seemed to have gone out of her; she listened to him in silence and with downcast eyes, and when he concluded by saying that the sooner they were away the better, and that if she would make herself ready he would fetch the horse to the door, got up without a word and fetched the cloak and hood she had cast aside.

Dominic turned away to take his sword from the stool where he had laid it the night before. The scabbard which he had cast down when he went to Verity's aid still lay upon the floor. He picked it up, slid the blade into it, and was fastening the weapon at his side when an unexpected sound caused him to raise his head. An ejaculation of astonishment broke from his lips, and he stood arrested, staring blankly through the window at the cavalcade which had just emerged from the shadow of the trees.

His exclamation brought Verity to his side, and for several seconds they both gazed dumbfounded at the lumbering coach and its attendant horsemen. Then one of the riders cried out and pointed, and after a moment's confusion the gentleman who rode at Urmiston's side spurred forward and reined in to look down at some object hidden in the grass. The Marquis followed, and then, with obvious reluctance, Sir Lawrence Templecombe alighted from the coach and went to join them. The other men clustered about the three, and there was some excited talk and waving of arms, and apprehensive glances towards the house.

Dominic took Verity by the arm and drew her further back into the room, so that, although the group in the garden was still visible to them, it was unlikely that they would be seen by those outside. He was frowning, in perplexity and a good deal of disquiet, at the three principal figures in the group, when Verity gave a gasp and clutched his arm. "Dominic, look!" she whispered. " 'Tis Diana! What does it mean?"

They watched Mrs. Halland ride slowly forward, and, as though the sight of her had roused him from a paralysis of amazement, Dominic woke to a sudden realization or urgency.

In a matter of minutes, without a doubt, those unlooked-for and unwelcome callers would be pounding at the door.

"God knows!" he said abruptly. "But whatever their business, it will not do for them to find you here. You must hide until they have gone."

She did not move, but looked up at him with questioning and rather frightened eyes.

"You think they will go, Dominic? Even though they have found Trumper's body?"

He did not think it, but strove to hide from her the conviction that when Templecombe and his companions returned to Shere they would take him with them, a prisoner. He shrugged the question aside.

"He sought my life and I killed him in fair fight. What have I to fear? Now haste you, before they come beating at the door."

"Diana may know, or guess, that I am here. Why else should she have followed them?"

He laughed shortly on a note of scorn. "If she knows, be sure she will say nothing. Is not Templecombe here also? Were he to find us together he must call me to account, as Madam Diana is well aware. Rest easy, she will not betray you!"

He had gripped her arm again and drawn her out into the hall as he spoke. There was one sure hiding-place for her, for even if the intruders took it upon themselves to search the house, into one ill-omened room they would not venture, of that he was certain.

"Dominic, are you sure that you are in no danger?" Verity had halted in the middle of the hall; her voice was anxious. "They must have some urgent reason for coming here, for Sir Lawrence would never venture himself within your reach unless it were in his power to harm you. I am sure their coming bodes you no good!"

"Whatever their errand, it will not help me or hinder them for your presence to be known," he replied. "If anything should take me hence—if they should desire to question me concerning Trumper's death, for instance—wait until all is quiet, and then make your way to Mary Parr's cottage. Tell her what has happened, and ask her to find some way of sending word to Urmiston. Remember, if any question you, tell them that when you fled from Shere Place you sought shelter with her. No one must know that you came to me."

"All this to save myself," she said impatiently, "but what

of you? It may be that by telling the whole truth of Trumper's death I could absolve you from any blame. I will not cower in hiding if it is in my power to help you."

"Nothing you can say would affect the issue," he lied, and tried to draw her onward, but she hung back, resisting him with all her strength.

"I do not believe it!" she said urgently. "Oh, my dear, let me stay with you! Whatever comes, let us meet it together."

In a sudden rush of impatience, and ignoring her words because to heed them was to try his hard-won fortitude too far, he swept her up off her feet and carried her past the staircase and into the dark, shuttered parlour. She said no more, but as he set her down again, put her arms about his neck and pressed her lips to his.

His clasp upon her tightened, and for one timeless moment they clung together, forgetful of everything in the world but each other. Then he let her go, and stepped back. He was very pale, with a curious mingling of grief and gladness in his eyes.

"Stay hidden, I beg of you," he said in a low voice, and without waiting for a reply drew back into the hall and closed the door, leaving her in darkness.

He took the useless key from the lock and dropped it into his pocket, and then went quickly across the hall to the door. Just for a moment he paused there, his hand on the latch, to look back towards the parlour, and then with a sigh flung open the door and went out to face his enemy at last.

In the few brief moments before they became aware of him, he studied the composition of the group and tried to find in it some clue to the purpose of this strange visitation. Then one of the men caught sight of him and gave the alarm, and so for a space they stared upon each other. Then the third gentleman rode slowly forward, and as he drew near Dominic recognized, through the changes the years had wrought, the face of George Corville.

Uneasiness, born of the adventurer's instinct for danger, deepened within him, but he hid it behind a mask of mockery, and looked up at the mounted man with a faintly derisive query in his tawny eyes.

"Good-day to you, my lord," he greeted him, his tone in itself a challenge. "That your visit takes me by surprise must excuse the meagreness of your welcome."

Corville's brows lifted, and the eyes below them were very stern.

"It is a visit not of my seeking, Mr. Fane," he replied coldly, "but, had you had warning of it, I can well believe that in one respect at least you would have set your house in order. You will admit, I think, that the presence of a dead man at your door demands some explanation."

There was no change of expression in the scarred, swarthy face confronting him. After a moment of silence, Fane said quietly:

"That would depend, my lord, upon who voiced the demand."

"I voice it, Mr. Fane, in my capacity as magistrate. Are you answered?"

Dominic inclined his head, but looked past his questioner at the silent, staring group beyond. The mockery about his mouth grew more marked.

"And these others, my lord? Not all magistrates, surely?"

Corville frowned.

"This levity is ill-timed, sir," he rebuked him. "Serious charges have been made against you, into which it is my duty to inquire, and so we will not, if you please, bandy more words here, but go within and deal with the matter with due decency, and without an audience of servants."

Dominic hesitated, sorely tempted to utter a curt refusal, yet aware at the same time of the utter futility of defiance. To refuse Corville admission to the house would at once arouse suspicion, and if his lordship resorted to force it was quite certain that Verity would disclose her presence. Hoping with all his heart that she would remain in hiding, he stepped aside and gestured with exaggerated civility towards the uninviting interior of the house.

"Pray enter, my lord," he said ironically. "Since my house has been shunned for so many years, it would be churlish in me to refuse you admittance now."

A glimmer of something which might have been sympathy softened Corville's glance for a fleeting moment, but he merely said: "I thank you, Mr. Fane. Allow me to give order here, and then we will despatch this disagreeable business as speedily as may be."

He rejoined his companions, and Dominic stood motionless, watching the oddly assorted group and considering Lord Corville's words—'Serious charges have been made against you.' That suggested a plot of some kind, but false accusations were of small account beside the damning fact of Nat Trumper's corpse.

He saw Corville offer his arm to Mrs. Halland and lead her forward. Urmiston delayed a moment to speak to Thomas, and Sir Lawrence wavered miserably between the two couples. Dominic sneered. He could appreciate Templecombe's reluctance to enter the house where Harriet Fane had died upon her husband's sword, and from which he had fled in craven terror to escape the consequences of the wrong he had done.

Urmiston moved briskly after Corville, with Thomas and a stout, red-faced man at his heels, and Sir Lawrence unwillingly fell in beside him. As he approached, Dominic studied the face which was like a caricature of the face he remembered, and felt a savage regret that vengeance had been denied him. This was the man, this pallid, over-dressed poltroon, whose selfishness and base desires had exposed Verity to the dangerous enmity of her strong-willed and ruthless rival; who came now to snare with lies and garbled half-truths a man whom he had wronged and robbed, and was afraid to meet in open fight.

Sir Lawrence had so far studiously avoided his eyes, but now, as he passed into the house, he glanced quickly, as though against his will, at this man whom he feared as he feared no other living being. The sight of the dark, bold face with its sneering lips, and eyes that blazed beneath straight, black brows, brought back with dreadful clarity the memory of the last time he had crossed this theshold, and so vividly real was the recollection that it was with a sense of shock that he looked round the empty, mouldering hall, and breathed the musty odour of decay which hung so heavily in this long-deserted dwelling. Involuntarily his glance strayed to the door of the room where he and Geoffrey Fane had fought, and Harriet had died. A strong shudder shook his whole body, for he seemed to hear again the piercing scream she had uttered as she fell and which, so legend declared, still sounded from time to time behind that ominous portal.

Fane led them into the one habitable room, and with an inscrutable expression watched them range themselves about it. Lord Corville led Diana to the settle, and Sir Lawrence took his place beside her, though whether to give or to seek protection Dominic was not sure; Urmiston took up his stand by the window, and Thomas leaned against the door-post. Dominic wished that they would close the door. Whatever was going to be said, it would be better if it did not reach the ears of the girl hidden in the room across the hall. Corville took a seat at the table's head, motioning the red-faced man to stand beside him, and for a moment or two his gaze roved about the dismal room, returning at last to the man who stood with his back to the gaping mouth of the fireplace, facing them all with a fierce and bitter pride.

"Mr. Fane," he said quietly, "if you have an explanation to offer concerning that which we found in the garden yonder, I will hear it now."

Dominic shrugged.

"The man was an old acquaintance who bore me a grudge," he said curtly. "He sought my life and I killed him—in fair fight, my lord! You will have perceived that his sword lies where it fell from his hand. Is that sufficient?"

The frown deepened in Corville's eyes.

"No, sir, it is not," he said sharply, "and permit me to warn you that you do yourself no good when you take that tone with me. Fair fight or not, if it took place without witnesses it must be accounted no better than murder, and must carry the same penalty." He turned his head slightly, addressing the man beside him. "You say, Constable, that you recognize the dead man as one who was drinking at the inn last night?"

"Aye, my lord, that I do. He asked where he could find Dominic Fane, and said as how they were old comrades, and he'd travelled a long way to pay a debt as he owed him."

"A debt of hatred!" Dominic interjected scornfully, and looked meaningly at Sir Lawrence. "Such debts are commonly paid more eagerly than any other."

Templecombe shifted uneasily beneath that menacing glance, and put up a hand to tug at a cravat which seemed suddenly to be choking him. His earlier fears, overcome by vindictive triumph at the discovery of Red Nat's body, were fast reviving, and with them came renewed doubts of his own immunity from harm. He looked imploringly at Diana, but she was watching Fane with narrowed eyes, and did not turn her head.

Job Daggett scratched his chin; he seemed puzzled.

"He never said what manner o' debt it was, my lord," he remarked, "but 'tis true he seemed mighty set on paying it. We warned him as this weren't a place any God-fearing man would come to by night, nor by day, neither, for that matter, but he said he weren't afeared o' ghosts and goblins. We watched him set off to come here, and that's the last anyone saw of him—till this morning! There's three or four others able to tell your lordship the same, if you'll trouble yourself to question 'em."

"If it seems necessary, I will do so presently," Corville replied, and turned once more to Dominic. "You say that this man—I believe his name was Trumper—bore you a grudge. Did it perhaps arise out of the abduction in London of Verity Halland?"

Quietly though it was voiced, the question seemed to explode into the silence. Dominic never moved a muscle, but all the implications of Corville's words struck him with staggering force. Here, at one stroke, was destroyed every hope of denying the link between Verity and himself, for he had forgotten that in her anxiety to protect him, she had given very particular descriptions of Red Nat and Giles. Trumper had made no secret of his search for Dominic Fane, and now he lay dead in Fane's garden, a mute but effective witness to the fact that some truth, at least, was at the source of the flood of gossip which had joined the name of Sir Lawrence Templecombe's intended bride with that of his bitterest enemy. Dismayed and furious, he remained silent, his dark face impassive while his mind sought vainly for some way of disproving something already proved beyond hope of denial.

"I should perhaps warn you," Corville resumed after a moment, "that an accusation of complicity in that crime has already been made against you. It is to inquire into it that I came here today."

Dominic looked again at Templecombe, and this time there was profound contempt in his eyes.

"By Sir Lawrence, of course!" he said in a tone which matched his glance for scorn. "He would feel a deal safer if I were in gaol."

"The accusation," Corville replied in an expressionless voice, "was made by Lady Templecombe on behalf of Miss Halland. I understand that Miss Halland has already named the man Trumper as one of her abductors, and his presence in Shere would appear to support the charge against you. Have you any answer to make to it?"

Dominic looked past him, through the open doorway and across the hall, but the parlour door was beyond his range of vision, and he prayed that Verity had not heard his lordship's words. By what means, he wondered, had Lady Templecombe expected to prevail upon her to support that accusation? How little they knew the steadfast spirit of her, to think that she could be forced into a betrayal; even now he feared at any moment to hear her come hastening to his defence, heedless of the consequences to herself.

'Stay close, my love,' he thought desperately, and knew, even as the words formed in his mind, that the silent prayer was vain. Verity would never stand aside while he was taken forth a prisoner.

He had been staring at Thomas, still lounging against the door-post, but without really seeing him. Then suddenly he realized that the man's keen grey eyes were fixed upon him in a strangely compelling way, and as he became aware of this, one of them was veiled in the briefest of winks, and Thomas's head jerked sideways in a gesture as slight as it was unmistakable.

In a flash Dominic realized that immediate escape offered the only hope, for Verity as well as himself. If he could win free of the house, she had wit enough to know that the disclosure of her presence would hinder rather than help him, and in the tangled woodlands he would have a good chance of complete escape. When Thomas, with or without Urmiston's knowledge, signified his willingness to connive at his flight, he rendered him a service greater than he knew.

"I am still awaiting your answer, Mr. Fane," Corville reminded him, and Dominic's mocking, tawny gaze returned once more to him.

"Answer, my lord?" he said, and though he looked at Corville, it was to the Marquis that he spoke. "Only this, which I will swear before God. No matter what Lady Templecombe or any other may say, Miss Halland has never suffered harm of any kind at my hands. For the rest, suspect and be damned to you!"

As the last word left his lips, he sprang towards the door, ready to make some show of striking Thomas from his path as he reached it. Whether or not the ruse would have succeeded was never known, for as he sprang, so, too, sprang the Constable of Shere. Inspired by some dazzling vision of glory or of reward, carried away by the prospect of preventing, single-handed, the escape of so dangerous a villain as Dominic Fane, Job Daggett launched his burly person across the younger man's path.

They collided with a force which brought them both to the ground, and since Daggett was uppermost as they fell, sheer weight made up for what he lacked in strength and agility. Dominic, shaken and breathless, had no chance to free himself from the Constable's crushing bulk before the point of

Corville's sword was pricking his throat, and resistance was out of the question.

Corville spoke sharply to Thomas, and the old soldier came forward and reluctantly assisted Daggett to heave the prisoner to his feet. When they had done so, and each was grasping one of Dominic's arms, his lordship sheathed his sword once more and spoke coldly.

"Your actions, Fane, damn you more surely than any words. I think we need waste no further time here. Urmiston, be good enough to summon my servants and bid them find something with which to bind the prisoner so that we may take him hence."

Before the Marquis could reply, or make any move to protest or obey, the sound which Dominic had been dreading to hear fell upon their ears, the creak of an opening door, and then a woman's footsteps, light and swift, on the flagstones flooring the hall. Job Daggett caught his breath in a gasp of horror, and Templecombe uttered a strangled exclamation and started to his feet, and then she appeared in the doorway, no dark and tragic ghost, but a slender girl in a yellow gown, with red-brown hair framing a delicate, child-like face and falling in confusion about her shoulders.

For a moment she paused there, confronting their astonished stares with steady eyes and head erect, looking from Sir Lawrence and Diana by the hearth to Urmiston at the window, and then at Dominic, haggard and dishevelled between his two captors. Last of all she looked at Corville.

"I am Verity Halland, my lord," she said simply, "and there is a deal more to be said before Dominic Fane leaves this house. The accusations made against him are wholly false!"

XX

The Defence

WITHOUT waiting for a reply she came forward to Dominic, who was watching her with agony in his eyes. As though they were alone in the room, she smiled tenderly at him, and laid one small hand against his breast.

"Do not look so, my dear," she said gently. "I could not stand aside and let them take you hence. You know that."

Corville, shocked to the depths of his being, made a determined effort to regain his composure. The situation was one which he would have given a good deal to avoid, but since he was committed to this unsavoury business he desired to end it as speedily as possible. He was not a man given to shirking unpleasant duties.

"Madam," he said sternly, "one of those accusations was made by you, and with that we will deal in a moment. The other, that of murdering the man Trumper, cannot be false, since the rogue's body lies at the door."

Verity turned to face him. She was pale, but very composed. "You said, my lord, that it must be accounted murder if they fought without witness. They did not. Dominic killed Nat Trumper to save me. He attacked me as I came through the garden last night."

His lordship swallowed hard, and glanced at Sir Lawrence, who had dropped down again on to the settle, his face moist and pallid with dismay. Beside him, Mrs. Halland sat staring straight before her, her beautiful countenance mask-like in its lack of expression.

"It was not the first time that Nat Trumper had sought Dominic's life," Verity continued quietly. "There was another occasion, on the road from London, when he and a man named Giles pursued and attacked us. Dominic was wounded then, and his life saved only by the intervention of a gentleman who was travelling that road with his servants." She looked towards the Marquis, not pleadingly, but with a calm certainty of his support. "Lord Urmiston will bear out what I say. He was that gentleman."

Corville stifled an exclamation, and Sir Lawrence looked up with dropped jaw and starting eyes. Even Diana's unnatural calm was ruffled by that unexpected disclosure.

"You, Robert?" Corville said incredulously. "You said nothing of it."

Urmiston shrugged slightly. "No mention of the incident had been made by Miss Halland, or by Fane," he replied with some reluctance, "and so Sarah and I decided to respect their obvious wishes and keep silent likewise. It is none the less true."

"No doubt, if you say so!" Corville still seemed a trifle puzzled. "Did you see Trumper on that occasion?"

"I did not. We heard shots coming from a wood through

which we had lately passed, and I rode back with Thomas and another servant. We met Miss Halland, who begged us to hasten to the aid of a man fighting for his life. The servants rode on while I paused to bid her seek safety with my sister. By the time I arrived on the scene, Fane lay senseless on the ground and his assailant had fled. The second rogue he had slain."

"I saw him clear enough," Thomas announced, "and so did William. It was that red-bearded devil right enough!"

There was a pause. Lord Corville paced the width of the room and back, his hands clasped behind him, his brow furrowed with mystification. Verity calmly awaited further questioning, and Dominic, released now, although the suspicious Daggett still hovered at his side, watched her wretchedly. His own fate troubled him not at all; he could think only of the irretrievable ruin she had brought upon herself by aiding him. After this, even supposing that Urmiston's offer of protection were not withdrawn, neither he nor his sister could save her.

"There remains the charge of abduction," Corville said suddenly. "Will you tell me, Miss Halland, why you made an accusation which you are now seeking to withdraw?"

"I made none," Verity replied firmly. "It was Red Nat and Giles who carried me off, as I told Sir Lawrence, and they were acting upon the orders of some other person. They imprisoned me in a house in Whitefriars, and there left me, taking with them my troth-ring to serve as proof of their success. I had pleaded with them to spare me, using Sir Lawrence's name in the hope that fear of his influence, or hope of rich reward, would prevail upon them, but in vain. Then, when they had gone, Dominic Fane came to me. He lodged in the same house and had overheard what passed between us. He told me that he was a native of Shere, and would take me to Sir Lawrence, whom he had known long ago. It was not until we had fled from London that I learned I was to be the instrument of his vengeance."

Dominic bowed his head, tortured by a burning sense of shame which could not have been deeper had he carried his pitiless scheme to its vile conclusion. Remorse, as bitter as it was futile, seized upon him once more, as he contemplated the sacrifice she was making to save him.

"It would seem, madam, that there is little to choose between your captors and your rescuer," Corville said dryly. "For his own unworthy purposes Fane did not scruple to force you to remain with him, and yet—"

"You mistake me, my lord," she interrupted tranquilly. "I stayed with Dominic Fane of my own free will. I, too, had something to avenge."

In the shocked silence which followed these words, Diana and Sir Lawrence exchanged an uneasy glance. Then Mrs. Halland said, in a voice which was a shade less placid than usual:

"How credulous you must think us, child! Because you desire to save your lover now, do not suppose that you can do so by telling this preposterous tale to conceal the violence he must have used towards you at the outset."

For a moment Verity regarded her in silence. Then she looked again at Corville.

"I must call upon Lord Urmiston for confirmation once more," she said. "The encounter I spoke of just now took place on the second day of our flight from London. Though I told him, and Lady Sarah, that Dominic was my brother, they guessed at least a part of the truth, and offered to furnish me with the means to complete my journey alone. I could have done so without difficulty. Dominic lay helpless of his wounds, and could not have prevented me." She turned to the Marquis. "Will you tell them, my lord, what answer I made to your offer?"

He was watching her with a strange expression, almost, it seemed, with admiration, and answered promptly, with none of his previous reluctance.

"You refused to leave Fane," he said quietly, "and no argument of mine or my sister's could turn you from that purpose. So we were obliged to go on our way, leaving you both at the inn to which we had carried him."

She thanked him, and then told briefly of their meeting with the players, Red Nat's second attack, and their wanderings with the troupe on the way to Goosefeather Fair. When she paused, Corville said, with the air of one discovering an inconsistency:

"I have heard that it was the player, Barnabas Pike, who went with you to Shere Place. If the story you have told us is true, why did not Fane take you there himself?"

If he thought to confuse or embarrass her, he was disappointed. She answered at once, in a completely steady voice.

"My lord, I was ragged and travel-weary, with no means of proving my identity. Do you think Sir Lawrence would have acknowledged me as his promised wife had I arrived at his door on the arm of Dominic Fane?" She shook her head, a faint, scornful smile about her lips. "There was only one thing that we did not foresee, and that was the infinite cowardice of Sir Lawrence, which prompted him to protest a belief in my innocence which he did not feel."

"Madam!" Corville's voice was very stern; his glance condemned her. "Have a care what you say! The admissions you have made do you no credit, and some decent show of shame would become you better than such brazen defiance."

A moment passed before Verity replied, a moment in which every eye in the room rested, with varying expressions, upon her. A curious dignity enfolded her. Her head was high, and though there was more than the normal colour in her cheeks, the grey eyes were shining. She did not look like a woman shamed, or even defiant; she looked glad and somehow triumphant.

"So you deem me shameless, my lord?" she said quietly at length. "Perhaps I am, but in justice to me you shall hear how I learned to be so." Templecombe made a convulsive movement, and her clear gaze turned contemptuously towards him. "Yes, Sir Lawrence, we will have the whole truth, if you please. Said I not that I, too, have something to avenge?"

She looked again at Corville, who, arrested by her tone and bearing, was watching her with a faint, puzzled frown. Sir Lawrence subsided in slack-lipped dismay, and beside him Diana sat rigid, one hand pressed to her bosom where, beneath lace and velvet, the diamond ring seemed to burn into her flesh.

"Before you condemn me as brazen and shameless, my lord," Verity went on, "consider this. When my grandfather died, a little more than a year since, I went to London to live with my brother's widow. I was a stranger in a strange city, without kindred, and sundered from my friends; I knew no one, save my sister-in-law yonder, and Sir Lawrence Templecombe, whom I was to marry. To them I looked for sympathy and consolation in my loss, them I trusted, implicitly and without question. Yet they betrayed me, as deliberately and mercilessly as I have since betrayed them. He is her lover, the father of the child she is to bear. Is it wonderful, then, that I should have joined Dominic Fane in his quest for vengeance?"

A silence which was almost palpable succeeded her words. Lord Corville was plainly shocked. The disgraceful disclosures which had followed so hard upon each other since he entered the room filled him with repugnance, and one swift glance at the couple on the settle had been enough to convince him that Miss Halland's accusation was just. A hangdog expression had added itself to the alarm in Sir Lawrence's countenance. A flame of colour had swept across his companion's dark, proud features, and the eyes which she had turned towards Verity blazed with fury and with hatred. She said, in a low, vicious tone:

"What profit do you look for in making that disclosure? It does not prove Fane's innocence in the matter of your abduction, any more than your refusal to leave him two days later proves it. If you sought vengeance for your paltry wrongs, of course you would not leave the man who might help you to it." She gave an angry, spiteful little laugh. "You have ruined yourself to no purpose, my girl! You will see your scarecrow lover hang, and may think yourself lucky if you escape unscathed."

Verity turned her head to look at her, and it was as though swords had met and crossed in the quiet room. For a moment the men were of no account; it was the two women, facing each other like duellists, who held the issue of the dispute in their hands.

"I think not," Verity said at last, and there was a wealth of meaning in her cool voice. "Had Dominic been involved in that, he would be able to identify the person who hired him. The person who was so eager to be rid of me, and who took possession of my diamond ring. It would be interesting to discover that person, would it not? I had no enemies in London, just as I had no friends."

Some of the high colour faded from Diana's cheeks, for the threat was unmistakable, and it scarcely needed Sir Lawrence's gasp, and his warning clutch upon her arm, to show her the danger in which she stood. She glanced at Corville and saw suspicion in his eyes. He was by no means dull-witted, and must have realized immediately who had the most urgent reasons for wishing Miss Halland out of the way, while a swift glance at Urmiston made her aware that his sympathy was entirely with Verity and Dominic Fane. To press the charge against Fane was to invite accusations against herself. She saw disaster looming before her, and choked back her fury and further allegations she had been about to make.

Lord Corville was relieved. A revelation of the truth had been granted to him, but he had no wish to embroil himself more deeply in this scandalous affair, and if only those con-

cerned would refrain from flinging accusations against each
other, he was more than willing to let the matter drop.

"No one," he said severely, into the pause which followed
Verity's words, "emerges creditably from this affair, which
would appear to be a matter concerning only those four
people immediately involved. Much as I deplore the circumstances which have led to the present situation, I cannot intervene in any official capacity. The charge of abduction,
which must rest solely upon Miss Halland's evidence, is apparently unfounded in the case of Fane, while Nat Trumper
is beyond the reach of justice." His stern glance rested briefly
upon Diana. "I see no reason to doubt Miss Halland's word
in this. She has been shamefully treated, and though one may
not condone her subsequent actions, it is possible to comprehend the feelings which prompted them."

"I thank you, my lord, but I seek neither condemnation
nor pity," Verity struck in calmly. "What I have done, I have
done, and I regret nothing. All I desire now is your lordship's
assurance that Dominic Fane's innocence is proved to your
satisfaction."

"You have it, madam," Corville assured her, but he spoke
without warmth, resenting the tone she had taken. "We have
been brought here, it seems, upon a fool's errand, in which I,
for one, would have preferred to have no part. It but remains
for us to take our leave and go."

A muffled groan of despair came from Sir Lawrence, for
to him these words signified the withdrawal of his last protector. Corville heard it, and replied with a glance of undis-
guised contempt. Urmiston heard it, and a smile, grimly
scornful, touched his handsome mouth. Dominic Fane heard
it, and out of the turbulent welter of emotion within him, the
hatred he thought he had conquered roused again to vengeful
life.

He looked at Templecombe, huddled, grey-faced and trembling, on the settle, and the memory of his own wrongs, and
Verity's more recent betrayal at the hands of this man, rose
up and clamoured for vengeance. It was as though destiny,
after making sport of him for so many years, had chosen at
last to grant him the reckoning so long desired. He had
renounced it once and gone his way, but the inscrutable ways
of fortune had brought him back again to Shere and de-
livered his enemy into his hands. All that remained was to
goad Templecombe into action.

"Accept my thanks, my lord," he said ironically to Corville, "and my apologies that I can offer you no better entertainment. No one can regret more deeply than myself the unwarranted demands which have today been made upon you. That you are in haste I perceive, but surely"—he paused, and his eyes, with wicked mockery gleaming in their golden depths, turned now towards Templecombe—"Sir Lawrence has something to say to me before he leaves this house?"

Sir Lawrence cast a hunted glance about him. Corville and Urmiston were waiting expectantly for his answer to that deliberate taunt, and beyond them he glimpsed Job Daggett's stare of open-mouthed wonder, and the derisive grin wreathing Thomas's weatherbeaten countenance. No smallest hope now that the matter could be kept secret; unless he gave proof of his courage he would be ruined, shunned by men of honour, and made the butt of coarse humour by the common people. He was caught fast in the trap he had evaded for so long, from which the only escape was death or sure disgrace.

He looked again at Fane, at the scarred and swarthy face, and the cold flame of hatred in the tawny eyes, and out of the despair that possessed him an answering hate was born. It was transient emotion, compound of fear and rage, but it gave him the moment's courage necessary to bring him up out of his seat to strike furiously at the dark face and sneering mouth.

He regretted the deed the instant it was done, and he saw triumph flare into Fane's eyes. Diana's gasp of anger and alarm he scarcely heeded as his enemy's low-voiced retort to that frantic blow fell like a warning of doom upon his ears.

"At last" Dominic said between his teeth. "So you have some spark of manhood in you, after all, though it has taken fourteen years to rouse it!" Suddenly brisk, he turned to their lordships. "Gentlemen, it will be best to settle this matter here and now. My lord Marquis, may I call upon you?"

"You may, Mr. Fane. I shall be happy to serve you." Urmiston moved at last from his position by the window, and strolled to the middle of the room. "May I suggest the hall yonder as a place apt for the business in hand? You agree, Corville?"

His brother-in-law, finding himself drawn willy-nilly into an affair which he could only regard as wholly deplorable, gave a short assent, but added, stepping close to Urmiston and speaking for his ear alone: "This is a damnably ill-managed business, and I would as lief have no part in it. Can it not be otherwise arranged?"

"I doubt it," Urmiston replied in the same tone, casting a disparaging glance at Templecombe. "Give your man time to dwell upon it, and you will never succeed in getting him to the ground. You will be hard put to it to do so as it is."

Sir Lawrence was indeed a pitiable sight, his face as livid as though death had already laid a cold touch upon it, his hands shaking amid the froth of lace which almost covered them. He stood as though petrified by his own temerity, plucking at his trembling under-lip and staring straight before him, oblivious of his surroundings until Corville, with a murmur of mingled scorn and exasperation, took him by the arm and led him out into the hall.

The other men followed. As Dominic passed her, Verity put out her hand as though to detain him, but when he made no response, let it fall to her side. Diana got up and went quickly after the men, but a moment later Fane's voice spoke sardonically just outside the door. "My lord Marquis, pray desire the ladies to remain within. One woman already has died in this house to shield Sir Lawrence Templecombe, and we will risk no repetition of so foolhardy a sacrifice."

Corville's voice was heard, adding a request more courteously framed but no less firm, and Diana came reluctantly into the room again, Thomas pulling the door shut behind her. She returned to her place on the settle and sat silent for a while, her face sullen with fury and fingers plucking restlessly at the folds of her skirt. At last she raised her head and looked at the younger girl.

"As God is my witness, I will have full payment for this day's work," she said in a low, tense voice. "Be it soon or late, you and that hell-born lover of yours shall pay, and not Urmiston, nor Corville—no, not the devil himself—shall prevent it!"

Verity seemed not to hear her. She had gone across to the door and was standing close to its heavy panels, her hands pressed against the dark wood, her whole attitude full of an urgent, wordless supplication. Her face was pale and still, her eyes closed; it was as though she sought, through that bodily quiescence, to reach in spirit to Dominic Fane, to convey to him some message of entreaty or of warning.

Outside, in the bare and dusty hall, Corville and Urmiston consulted together in low tones, while their two principals waited with the width of the room between them. Job Daggett had slipped out to join the servants clustered about the waiting coach, but Thomas leaned with folded arms against

the wall beside the door of the room where the two women
waited, and his experienced eye rested upon each of the duellists in turn. Sir Lawrence stood where Corville had left him,
his arms hanging limply at his sides, his face set in lines of
the uttermost despair. He seemed to shrink inside his fine
laced coat, and his brow was wet below the thick curls of his
periwig.

From him the old soldier's gaze passed to the tall, shabby
figure of his opponent. Gaunt as a wolf, tough and dangerous
as the supple blade now balanced between his hands, Dominic Fane stood in his ruined hall and waited with sinister patience for the reckoning which was at hand at last. Thomas
decided regretfully that the duel would offer poor sport; it
was as unequal as a battle between a pigeon and a hawk.

Their lordships parted, and returned to their respective
principals. Sir Lawrence permitted himself to be divested of
coat and shoes, and the ruffled sleeves of his shirt to be rolled
back from his plump white forearms, but though Dominic
had laid aside the scabbard of his sword, he replied to Urmiston's inquiring glance with a curt shake of the head.

"I think so much is not necessary, my lord," he said sardonically, and the Marquis smiled in grim appreciation of the
words.

So, at length, they confronted each other in the centre of
the hall—the man of action, whose sword had never long
been idle during the past ten years, and the man of pleasure,
called to pay for his philanderings at last. Templecombe, a
grotesque figure with his cropped head and stockinged feet,
held his weapon awkwardly as he tried to remember some of
the subtleties of swordplay, but could think only of the immi-
nence of death.

The word was given, the blades flashed in salute and came
softly together. It had been Dominic's intention to bait Templecombe a little, to make him pay, in terror and the certainty of doom, for the suffering he had inflicted upon others,
before dealing the thrust which would end their enmity for
ever, but their swords had scarcely crossed before he realized
that this was impossible. So poor a swordsman was Sir
Lawrence, and so feeble his defence, that Fane might have
run him through at once as though he were unarmed.

The three witnesses of that unequal combat awaited its end
in grim silence. but it did not come in quite the manner they
had expected. In a very few moments, Templecombe's sword
slipped from his slack grasp, and he, finding himself thus sud-

denly defenceless, uttered a rattling sound in his throat and dropped to his knees, covering his face with his hands.

For the space of seconds there was utter stillness in the hall while the three onlookers held their breath, and Dominic Fane stood with shortened sword above his cowering and defenceless enemy. At last, after what seemed an eternity, he spoke, the icy scorn of his voice echoing strangely through the mouldering house.

"You damned, craven wretch!" he said slowly. "God save us! there's naught but dishonour in killing such a thing as you!" He turned then to the staring Corville, adding, in a tone of savage, impatient mockery: "In the devil's name, my lord, take him out of my sight lest I am tempted to work some harm upon him after all!"

He swung abruptly away from Templecomb's huddled figure, and went, his sword still in his hand and his footsteps loud on the stone-flagged floor, to the room in which Verity had been hidden. Laying his weapon on the table, he went across to the window, and after a struggle with rusty bolts, flung the creaking shutters wide. Grey light filtered through the grimy panes, revealing the stark desolation within, but now for the first time he could look upon it unmoved.

He forced open the casement, and the summer wind, sweet with the scent of living, growing things, rushed into the room to set rotting draperies swaying and stir the dust of years, driving away the musty odour of corruption and decay. He stood by the window, feeling the wind upon his face, and it was as though, in some mysterious way, his spirit was cleansed of the burden of hatred it had borne for so long.

So he stood, not moving, scarcely even thinking, but savouring this new-found sense of peace and liberation, until Verity came slowly into the room. He turned then, and looked at her, for she had halted by the table and was gravely regarding him, her grey eyes large in her pale face.

"You spared him," she said in a low voice. "Oh, Dominic, I am so glad!" She paused, but when he made no reply, she went on: "I prayed with all my heart that it might be so. There was death in your face when you went out to fight him, and I was afraid, for it was I who had given you the chance to claim your vengeance. If you had killed him, that thought would have stood between us all our lives long."

"And does nothing else stand between us?" he asked in an anguished voice. "Oh, my love, why did you not stay hidden, as I begged you to do? My freedom, my life itself, are as nothing beside your well-being and the future you have cast away."

She shook her head, smiling a little.

"Nothing to you, perhaps, but all the world to me," she replied softly. "What, do you doubt me still?" He made a gesture of denial, but she went on, speaking now with the utmost earnestness. "Make no mistake, Dominic! It was not easy for me, publicly to brand myself a wanton, to place myself on a level with Diana and her kind, and to invite the condemnation of such men as the Marquis and Lord Corville. Gratitude alone could not have spurred me to it, nor pity neither, yet I did it, not just willingly, but gladly. Gladly, because here was the chance I had prayed for of proving my love for you."

He bowed his head, his hand clenched hard on the frame of the window by which he stood.

"I am not worthy!" he said in a stifled voice. "God in heaven! If I could but make all right, convince them of your innocence, that you told that tale only to save me—"

"You cannot!" she interrupted him gently. "They believed it, and they have gone. They will not return."

She was mistaken. Even as she spoke, hasty footsteps sounded in the hall and the Marquis appeared in the doorway. Just for an instant he checked there, to flash an astonished glance about the room, and then he came forward and bowed deeply before the girl.

"Miss Halland," he said quietly, "by now, my sister should have reached the village. Will you permit me to escort you thither, so that you may go with her to Corville Court?"

Amazement which was almost disbelief dawned in Verity's eyes, and at first she could find nothing to say. By the window Dominic stood still as death.

"You are generous, my lord," Verity said slowly at length, "but after what he has learned of me today, I do not think Lord Corville would welcome me to his house."

"He would do so, madam, if . . ." Urmiston hesitated, the colour rising in his face, and then added impetuously: "If you would do me the honour, the infinite honour, of coming there as my future wife."

In the silence which followed this declaration, Dominic drew a long, slow breath. After a moment or two, Verity said wonderingly: "You offer me marriage, my lord, knowing me for what I am?"

"I know nothing to your discredit," he retorted quickly. "You sacrificed yourself to save a brave and true friend, and for that I honour you more than I can say. I think you are the most gallant lady I have ever known!" He caught her unresisting hand in his and spoke eagerly, forgetful of Fane's presence or indifferent to it. "I have admired you from the first moment of our meeting, and everything I have since learned of you has increased that admiration. Say that you will marry me! The world will not dare speak ill of my wife, and if any venture it, be sure that they shall answer to me."

She had stood passively, her hand in his and her eyes fixed upon his face, while he so recklessly cast himself and all he had at her feet, but now her glance went beyond him to the shabby figure by the window, and he knew, even before she spoke, that in the eyes of this rare girl, his proud title and great estates, his youth and looks and personal charm, counted for less than nothing. He had wooed often and never unsuccessfully, but now, when for the first time so much more than a transient pleasure hung upon the outcome, he wooed in vain, because Verity Halland set no store by worldly things.

At last her gaze returned to his face, and there was kindness in her eyes, and tenderness. She looked at him, he thought, as she might have looked at a child.

"My lord, you honour me far beyond what I deserve," she said gently, "and I am truly grateful, but it cannot be. Continue to think kindly of me, if you can, but let us say farewell and part now. Our ways do not lie together."

He looked from her to Fane and fetched a sigh.

"I understand, I think," he said quietly. "I feared that it might be so." He raised her hand to his lips, and then released it, and stepped back; a faint, rueful smile touched his lips. "Good fortune go with you both!"

He sketched a bow and turned quickly away. They heard him cross the hall, and speak to his servant as he got to horse, and then the sound of retreating hoofbeats. When at last it had died away, and silence closed once more round the silent house, Verity went to Dominic and set her hands on his shoulders, and looked up into his face. He took her in his arms, but there was still trouble in his eyes. "He has so much to offer you, and I have nothing," he said in a low voice. "Heart of my heart, can you indeed be happy with me?"

"With you, and only with you," she whispered, and reached up to set her lips against his scarred cheek, and then, as his arms tightened about her, surrendered gladly to his kiss.

The grey clouds were parting, and now the first sunlight of that day broke through them, to transform the sombre woodlands and flood into the room which for so many years had been shuttered against it. It fell like a benediction about them where they stood by the open window, and reached past them to the table, to gleam on the silver-hilted sword which, bright and unstained, rested, forgotten, upon it.

The Scarlet Domino
by Sylvia Thorpe

P2600   **$1.25**

"You would have preferred to remain in Newgate Prison rather than take me for your wife!" Antonia said scornfully. "The thought of freedom would not have tempted you, nor the chance to squander my fortune as you have squandered your own. Do you expect me to believe that?"

"No, perhaps not, Geraint said in a wry tone. "I think I would have taken any way of escape. I did so, in fact, when I agreed with your grandfather's proposal that I should marry you."

Antonia was strikingly beautiful, full of brooding hatreds, and raised in a sheltered world. Geraint was exceptionally handsome, charming, and something of a rogue.
Within an hour of meeting they were married.

They were both surprised by what happened. They fell in love. And Antonia found the freedom she had always been denied. And Geraint discovered that his life was in danger. . . .

FAWCETT WORLD LIBRARY

Tarrington Chase
by Sylvia Thorpe

Q2843 $1.50

From the very beginning of her employment as the governess at Tarrington Chase, lovely, young Perdita Frayne was warned to have absolutely nothing to do with Jason Hawkesworth. To disobey this order would mean instant dismissal.

Mere mention of Jason's name evoked intense hatred among every member of the household. Perdita couldn't figure out why this was so, but she intended to keep out of his way.

It was impossible for her to avoid "accidental" meetings with the handsome and mysterious Mr. Hawkesworth. In fact, she began to look forward to seeing him.

Perdita could not deny the powerful attraction she felt for Jason. But she knew that she would have to overcome the strong feelings that stirred inside her everytime they met—or leave Tarrington Chase forever. . . .

FAWCETT WORLD LIBRARY